# QUEEN OF JUPITER

## INK AND LYRICS DUET
## BOOK TWO

# NACOLE STAYTON

Want to stay up to date with Nacole and her books, consider joining her newsletter here:
http://eepurl.com/ipH3Ho

*To all the book girlies who love rock music, sex, and fantasizing about fictional men—in no particular order, of course—this one's for you.*

"Night Prowler" AC/DC
"Take Me First" Bad Omen
"Would You Still Be There" Of Mice & Men
"Smoking Section" Jelly Roll
"Night Moves" Bob Seger & The Silver Bullet Band
"Kiss Kiss" Machine Gun Kelly
"Dancing with The Devil" EMO
"Shame On Me" Catch Your Breath
"Best I Ever Had" Drake
"Let it Bleed" The Used

Queen of Jupiter is the conclusion of the Ink and Lyrics Duet. This why-choose romance features spicy scenes between our female heroine and her three-love interest as well as detailed scenes between the male members of their *situationship*. While there is plenty of banter, there is also a lot of angst and heartache depicted in the following pages.

If you would like to read a list of potential triggers, I encourage you to visit my website before proceeding to the next page.

Rock on,

Nacole

# CAPTOR

SOPHIA

THE SKY BLEEDS pink through a small hopper window in the basement, where I'm currently being held against my will. Its shade has to be much lighter than the crimson drop I feel dribbling down my face, an unwelcome present from my assailant's Glock across my temple.

"How'd you find me?" My attempt to hide the quiver in my voice falters.

Julian Caddell's eyes are dark, impenetrable, and his reply is equally terse. "You and your sister were never lost."

If my hands weren't bound, I'd smack the smug bastard.

"Tell me, Sophia, how did your freedom taste? Did the thrill of the run excite you as much as the chase did me?"

The threat that loomed over me for a decade has finally caught up with me. Said threat is here to serve his retribution or take what he claims he's owed.

"I'm going to take your silence as a yes, seeing as you just kept running."

No wonder my father stole from him. He's a real jackass.

"Did the safety of being in another country help you sleep at night, or did you dream of me and wake, screaming my name?"

"I dreamed of your face on Freddy Krueger's body. Though your presence in real life is even more repulsive."

A thin smile forms on his lips. "You don't look so hot yourself unless you're into blood, bondage, and body odor."

I know I've been touring with a group of rock artists when the chorus of AC/DC's "Night Prowler" plays in my mind as Caddell's repulsive voice sounds around me.

*He is a night prowler.*

Cultivating a suggestive smile, I flash it at my abductor. "You pegged me all right. The three B's are my favorite."

Defiance is my middle name.

"What about the three D's? Despair, despondency, and death?"

Hope vanishes at the recognition of his question. My smart-ass mouth has saved me more times than I can count. This might actually be the one time that I can't bullshit my way out of a situation. This might be the day I'm forced to stop running. I'm keenly aware of the look he offers me when he comprehends what I just realized as well.

*I'm royally screwed.*

Though I don't answer his question, I'm sure my face speaks for itself. No one even knows I've been abducted, and the last person to see me was Mazen, who looked almost relieved by my sudden departure.

"I asked you a fucking question." Anger surges in his veins. The smile that displays on his taut, worn face is borderline satanic. Roughly, he grabs my face, fingers pressing into my jaw with force.

*That's going to leave a mark.*

"Screw you and your questions. I don't owe you anything."

A diabolical laugh bubbles from his mouth. "That's where you're wrong. Very wrong. Contrary to whatever notion is in that pretty head, you owe me. A lot. I'm guessing there isn't a checkbook in that bag you were carrying off the plane though, is there?"

My silence rings loud.

"I didn't think so. There are other ways to get what I want."

My stomach bottoms out. *Please, no,* I chant in my mind.

I've read enough dark romance and watched enough television shows to know that men love the fight, the chase. I decide to play my hand using a different angle—again, shout-out to the dark romance authors of the world.

"I haven't been properly fucked in a while. Go ahead. Untie me, and have at it," I lie through my teeth, using some bookish backbone and reverse psychology.

There's nothing more I want than to be untied. At least then, I might have a fighting chance.

His disapproving glare cuts me like a knife. "You foolish girl. I'm not going to rape you. What kind of monster do you think I am?"

"You're gauging pretty high on my psychopath index." Swiveling my head around the dim basement, I add, "I am tied to a chair in a basement, am I not?"

"I'm a businessman, not a rapist. I can assure you of that." His uncompromising voice is surprisingly tender.

I sigh in relief, accepting his words hold truth.

"I might have no choice but to kill you though. That verdict is still out."

As the real warning leaves his tight-lipped mouth, I know with certainty that this is the last time I'm fleeing my past. It's caught up to me, staring me in the face like a tiger about to eat its prey. I've never felt sorrier for a baby elephant in my entire life.

There's a sudden feeling of acceptance that registers deep in the marrow of my bones. This ends today. Even if the source of payment is my death.

I'm tired of running, looking over my shoulder, pretending that my world didn't tumble off its axis when *his* thugs came after me last time. I'm even more tired of being the protector. That duty has worn me thin over the years.

My eyes close, heavy from staring at the same wall all night. Maybe my body has caught up with my heart, and my subconscious is surrendering too. I can do this for her. I can protect her life one more time by offering up my own.

*Lacey will be free of this ugly curse once our father's debt is paid.*

Before I tap out, a lingering question slides off my tongue. "What is Knox's part in all this? The nephew tidbit was shocking—I'll give you that. But there's something else. What am I missing?"

Caddell's voice is strident, and a mixture of rasp and influence draws my eyes open again. "Loyalty means something to our family."

My tired, heavy lashes fly up. I'm instantly wide awake. The conversation with Knox when he surprised me at the airport flashes in my mind.

*"My uncle ... Julian. You remember him, don't you?"*

I have a hard time believing that he'd give up years of his own life just to follow me around like a shadow. He's a tattoo artist, for Christ's sake. I was his apprentice. He has a whole career outside of aiding his piece-of-shit uncle in his stalking endeavors.

"You might have thought you had a leg up on me, that you were off my radar. Sadly for you, you'd be profoundly mistaken. I'm appalled that you think so little of me. Of the power and pull that I have. Is it because you *think* your father outsmarted me? You figure if he could, then so could you."

"He obviously didn't outsmart you. He's in prison."

If I weren't watching his every movement like a hawk now, I would have missed the forceful swallow that slides past his Adam's apple.

"Indeed, he is."

"Why didn't you just kill him?" Every curve of my body flinches.

"We're getting off topic here. We can swing back to all those pesky little details later."

Biting the inside of my cheek, I inhale deeply, filling my lungs with courage. Even if I've accepted my fate, my sass won't allow me to go down easy. Words fly out of my mouth involuntarily. "I asked *how* you found me anyway, not why."

How did he know I was touring with the band Kings of Jupiter, and how did he know I'd be on their private plane last night?

Knox might have been keeping tabs on me, but no one is Jason Bourne good. Except maybe Jason Bourne.

"I already know the why. You made sure of it when you sent your last warning. The one that ended in me burying my son." My spine hardens at the memory. I steel my shoulders and push past the grief that collects in my chest like dust in an abandoned building. "If Knox is your nephew, why are you just now showing me your face? You've had ten years to demand payment. Something changed. It had to have. Is your empire crumbling? Is that it?" I don't cower or retreat. I must be on to something. "Did Daddy steal more than money? It was your pride, wasn't it? You can't sleep at night, knowing that someone broke that so-called loyalty you admire so much."

Cracking his fingers, he ignores my questions altogether, giving no hint that I've hit the nail on the head.

"I can't thank Knox enough really. He's been patient. Bided his time. I think he's earned his spot as my right hand. Don't you think, Sophia?"

"You both can go straight to hell," I say through gritted teeth before spitting on his designer shoes.

Saliva and blood splay on the toe of his shoe moments before his fingers tangle in my hair, yanking my head backward.

Using the large palm of his free hand, he skirts it across my cheek in a reverberating *smack*. My head can't move from the impact because he's holding me firmly in place. I refuse to show how badly it hurts, both physically and emotionally.

Fortifying myself like armor, I close my eyes, begging my tears not to fall. Even if I'm ready to die to protect Lacey, to end this cat-and-mouse game, I refuse to show him one ounce of weakness. On an inhale, I open my eyes, lift my chin as far as his hard grip on my head will allow, and boldly meet his stare once more.

Slicing me with precision, Caddell's hooded eyes bore into mine. "You want to know *how*, you little bitch? When you left Chicago, Knox followed your career all the way to Tampa. Your profession is a truly small circle. It wasn't hard to keep tabs on you. The how isn't the question you should be asking." His grip tightens on my scalp. "It's the *why now*. Go on, ask."

His command falls on deaf ears when I refuse his bait. He doesn't deserve my words, only my wrath. He's already stolen too much from me.

My trust in humanity. My heart. My child.

"I said, ask!" Spit sprays my face as he bellows. "You're going to regret not listening. Just like your father did. He couldn't leave well enough alone."

My heartbeat skyrockets at his jab. There's a piece of the puzzle I'm missing. There's got to be. It's like Caddell is obsessed with my father or something. The man who betrayed my sister and me, leading us to the lion he'd once claimed as a friend and delivering us on a silver platter. My father chose to get into metaphorical bed with an unhinged maniac, and now, we're paying the consequences for his actions.

The rawness of my situation overwhelms me as I sit, tied to a wooden chair in the center of this basement. My head is throbbing like it's been used as a human punching bag.

Oh, wait. It has.

Knox's pent-up resentment—most likely over my ending things with him years ago—was felt in his every punch. He was resourceful in the time between when he pulled me from the backseat of the vehicle and when he heaved me by my hair down the steps, not giving a flying fuck as I screamed in agony mere inches behind him. My eye is swollen shut—that much is certain. I block out the physical pain, choosing to focus on the emotional turmoil. My imminent death is a reminder that I can do this. I can be strong right now. I can face death with pride, knowing that Lacey will be free once our father's debt is paid.

I'm a far cry from weak. This battle just isn't worth fighting anymore. I no longer care about the how or why. If Julian Caddell wants to get his rocks off by beating me, killing me, so be it. I won't give him what he wants, longs for ... my fear. I refuse to run from him or cower to him any longer.

I'll welcome the pain he inflicts, becoming as unhinged as my captor.

I won't allow him to hunt us like prey any longer. Lacey is my only living relative, and I'll give my life if it means ending this war with him just to keep her safe. She has a means to survive as co-owner of our tattoo studio and apparently the adoration of Devon, our security guard, from what my groggy brain remembers from her frantic phone call what seems like days ago.

Musty air wafts around us, cloaking me in dread as I sit in the dingy basement that is imprisoning me like a jail cell. My mind is languid, absent of faith. The numbness helps camouflage my deep desire to claw Caddell's eyes out of their wrinkly sockets and feed them to him.

Said eyes peer at me triumphantly when he notices my defeat as my spine curves in my chair in a clear show of my forfeit.

"Your father's a fucking rat. Seems like he could have learned a thing or two from you. Maybe then he wouldn't have run his mouth like the little pussy that he is. You're not a pussy, are you, Sophia? I can see it in your eyes ... eye."

*What I'd do to see myself in a mirror right now.* As superficial as that sounds, I know my talent as a tattoo artist has only gotten me so far. The fact that I'm an attractive woman has aided me in more ways than one. I guess my looks no longer matter at this point.

His maniacal laughter drags me back. "They're darker than his were."

"Fucking kill me already. I'm as good as dead anyway, right? I can't pay his debt, but you already knew that. Just get it over with." Unbridled anger sets in my tone as I stare at him with a burning in my eyes that I hope he feels. Any lingering vulnerability vanishes, and my spine straightens once again.

I swallow hard, not even trying to hide my contempt for him. "Or are *you* the only pussy in this room?"

Caddell stands before me, tall and irritable. His face is a glowering mask of rage.

As if hearing his own voice pleases him, he opens his mouth, and a rush of words comes out on exhale. "My daughter's been a mess. Fucking hysterics."

*Why the hell is he telling me about his daughter?*

"Crying all the time about some singer who fell head over heels for his tattoo artist. The punk she idolized, Mazen Wilde, has apparently settled down. Imagine my surprise when she read an article from one of those tabloids she subscribes to online and saw your face on-screen, right next to her heartthrob. A heartthrob that I happen to know personally."

The strange surge of affection I feel when he speaks Mazen's name is both rousing and frightening. Alarm knots in the pit of my already-hollow stomach.

Disoriented thoughts scamper around Mazen's farewell. *"Where is your son?"*

A question floats to the surface of my tired mind, a small reprieve from the conversation with my captor.

*How did Mazen know about Roman?*

Sharp like a laser, Caddell's beady eyes look like they're ready to cut me in half, impaling me with hatred.

"Imagine my fucking surprise," Caddell says in a disgruntled voice, drawing me back to my harsh reality, as his large, demonic eyes sweep over me once more. "When she showed me a picture of you and the Tommy Lee wannabe of this generation. He always was a pain in his father's ass," he says the last part under his breath. "Instantly, my left palm started itching. You know what that means, right?"

A mixture of curses gallops through my mind. In my heart, I always knew him finding Lacey and me was a huge possibility. We haven't lived our lives in the shadows—a fact I now regret. No one with a popular, blooming business could accomplish all we have while in hiding. Rather, I gave myself a false illusion that the distance between Chicago and Tampa kept us safe. Like the miles were enough to keep my fears from invading my reality.

Keeping my eyes trained on the porous brick wall adjacent to me, I silently curse myself. The media and their damn need for pictures.

*I did this. I put a target on our backs.*

There's no one to blame but myself. And my piece-of-shit father. Incarcerated or not, he's the one at fault for this whole mess. Daddy dearest set this all in motion and left his daughters to sink or swim. We've been swimming against the current for so long ... too long.

What I can blame myself for is accepting Oliver's proposition. Agreeing to fake date Mazen and falling for three men that I vowed not to just a month earlier. It seems like I've known them for years instead of weeks. I guess that's what happens when you basically live with someone, spend every waking minute with them. My cheeks burn in remembrance of the Kings, my clients turned employers turned lovers.

"Money," he says amusedly, answering his own question. "The look in the eyes of that sorry waste of space appears genuine enough though. Even on-screen." Caddell draws back my attention. "Like the fool might actually be in love with you."

My pride keeps me from disagreeing. Sheer willpower forbids me from trembling at his assessment.

"One might even call it fate, seeing as he is the father of your child."

A myriad of emotions sweeps through my mind in a tailspin, like a tornado wrecking every single memory that once stood firm and certain in my life.

One second passes. Then another before his words really set in. My bottom jaw comes unhinged at about the same time my eyes widen as big as a football field in confusion. If my hands weren't tied behind the chair, rendering me immobile, I know they'd be covering my mouth. I wheeze in paralyzing disbelief. Stunned into silence.

He uses my unexpected submission to dig deeper, twisting the knife he just impaled in my stomach. "Surely, you're not naive enough to *not* have known or at least considered him as the possible sperm donor, right?"

I shrink in my chair, shriveling inward by his question. *There's no way.* Is there?

"A little footwork is all it took. Knox pieced the puzzle all together. Little shit will definitely be getting the promotion he's been after. The look on your face is priceless." His voice carries more than a hint of boastfulness. "You didn't even consider him? Damn. This is good. Almost better than collecting what I'm owed."

A raucous laugh echoes around us.

Caddell's amusement at my grief and confusion is almost as revolting as his little lap-dog nephew, Knox.

How could I have been so blind to not see that Knox—my friend, mentor, lover—had been planted in my life? Could the same be said for Mazen? The suggestion of Caddell's implication would rewrite ... everything.

*Stupid, stupid Sophia.*

I want to protest his accusation. I want to open my mouth with dismay, tell him to cram his idiotic story down his throat. To choke on it. I want to do all those things, but I can't. Because a sickening feeling stirs inside of me. A sliver of doubt.

*What if he's telling the truth?*

A possibility. A horrible possibility.

I was young and reckless, not blind. Surely, I'd remember him, *Mazen Wilde* ... if he fathered my child. No one with two eyes, a beating heart, and a clit could forget him.

"No." The pain etched into my strained voice is startling.

I huff in thin air, refusing to believe anything this vile man is spewing. *Lies.* Wave after wave of apprehension shocks me like another blow to my already-battered face.

If I wasn't already numb, void of tears and sentiment, I know a heavy stream would be visible.

"No, no, that's not true," I plead with the universe as my mind reels, trying to make sense of the giant bomb that was just tossed onto my lap.

*Now is not the time to ponder on his lies.*

I don't need a mirror to know that my pea green eyes widen in disbelief as I stare wordlessly at Julian Caddell, bemused by his allegation. As much as I want to throttle him for tormenting me with his hand and for his deceitful-as-sin nephew using his fists on me, it's this claim that has me shouting in his smug face.

"You're grasping at a narrative that doesn't exist. You want your payback for my father's wrongdoings. You want the money he owes you. You want retaliation ... you come after *me* and me alone. My sister... "

*What are the members of Kings of Jupiter to me? Hookups? Boyfriends? Bosses?*

I settle with the easiest choice—friends.

"My friends. That's where I draw a line. You can weave any lie you want. I refuse to believe it. Mazen has nothing to do with any of this. Leave him the fuck out of this mess, our mess. Better yet, just kill me already!"

# 2

# STREAK OF DOMINANCE

**SOPHIA**

**CADDELL'S VOICE** rings with a command when the word, "No," leaves his mouth with force.

I ignore the finality in his tone. "I'm still alive hours after Knox kidnapped me. Why? Does your little girl want me to snag her a T-shirt from the tour? Don't feed me any more bullshit or drag this out any longer than it has to be." My eyes burn with exhaustion. "Just do it. We both already know you're capable of an atrocious crime like murder."

"Unlike your father, I never lie or ... kill anyone." There's a heavy dose of sarcasm laced in his malicious words.

"It wasn't your hand that pushed me down those steps, but it was your men. You sent them. You killed my son." I bite out the words as bile rises in my esophagus like a swimming pool on the verge of spilling over after days of rain. "You're a monster hidden behind a cheap tie and an army of minions." Hate coats my words as pent-up venom toward the man responsible for my child's death spews from my mouth.

Caddell's cold glare meets my accusing wrath. If words were enough, I'd show him no mercy. There'd be no remorse for his death. Just like there wasn't when his pack of leather-clad bandits left me lying at the bottom of that staircase, clenching my swollen stomach in agony.

We're suspended in a battle of wills, both refusing to look away first. I refuse to give him one ounce of power over me despite how dirty I feel under his steady scrutiny. My throat is raw with unspoken protest. The misery of not knowing who Roman's father is haunts me to this day. It's a truth I've accepted I'll never have the privilege of knowing.

A painful knot forms in my stomach when Caddell finally breaks the silence. "You got pregnant after a one-night stand following a tattoo convention in Chicago."

Eyes no doubt ringed with black circles meet his as I thrash in my chair, muscles screaming from my strain.

Unmoved by my sobs and thrashing, Caddell continues his assault, slicing at an already-gaping wound. His words are salt burning my flesh. "Do you miss home—Chicago?"

Whirling with confusion, my head swirls with a flash-back of ten years ago. My life in Chicago feels like a dream, or a nightmare, a bleak blip on my life's radar. Momentarily rebuffing his deception, I straighten my spine. The story he's trying so desperately to weave can be read in any romance book available for purchase nationwide. *One-night stand.* He thinks he pieced an integral puzzle together, a glass mosaic. He doesn't know jack about me or my past.

I steady my erratic pulse. "Too many people in the Windy City, so, no, I don't miss it."

"Does that mean you don't visit his grave then—Roman's?"

My son's name rolls off Caddell's tongue, and a metallic taste dances in a tango over my tongue as I bite the inside of my cheek. My senses are drugged by his acid-dripped words causing my breathing to become labored.

"I did once." He has the gall to appear sincere. "I genuinely feel bad about what happened. You have every right to call me a monster. Losing someone you care deeply about changes a person."

My son's name ricochets like a ball, lost in the frenzy of my thoughts, it pounds against my skull against another name that jars my recollection. *Rosella.* The Italian word for little rose.

That name plagues my memory, threatening to choke the air from my lungs. Questions hammer from my subconscious. My stomach knots tighter as Caddell's imposing glare cuts me at the knees.

I cling to the memory of my sweet son's face like a life preserver in the capsized mess that has become my reality when hot tears slip down my cheeks. A choking cry yanks itself from my chest, tethered to a firm warning. "Don't you dare say his name!"

The last trace of resistance on Caddell's face vanishes. "There's no father listed on Ro—your son's birth certificate. Which leads me to believe that you really don't know who his father is ... *was.* You should be thanking me. I did the legwork for you."

"Hell will freeze over before I thank you for anything." I've never wanted to commit murder more so than I do in this instant. If I could just free one hand ...

"Not even for all of my detective work?" The slimy excuse for a man presses on, a smile etched on his worn, weathered mouth. "Around seven or eight months following the convention where you met Mazen, a baby was brought into the world. Unbeknownst to him, of course. By the look on your ghostly face, you still don't believe me, but you will. We'll get to that—the good part—in a minute."

Caddell's thin lips move, although I can't be certain I'm comprehending the words he's saying. "Sadly, my men roughed you up a little too hard when I sent them to give you a message. That was a tumble down the stairs. I am truly sorry for my part in his death... "

Both my mind and body are immobile in an emotion-charged stupor.

Have you ever had an out-of-body experience? That's what I fear is happening right now as my senses blur. My wrists burn from the rope, tight against my flesh. I pull in a fervent attempt to free myself, all the while clenching my jaw to quiet the sobs threatening to erupt from my throat. The thick rope bites into my flesh, finally drawing blood from my incessant pulling.

"I draw a line at hurting children."

All rational thoughts are pulverized by the influx of grief that tightens around my throat like a chokehold of epic proportions.

"You're sorry? For what part? For making the call to sic your unstable goons on me to collect a debt my fucking father owes you or for ruining my life? You have to live with being a murderer. So, no, I don't want you to ever say his name out loud again, but don't you ever fucking forget it. You killed him! You stole him from this world, from me ... and I swear on every star in the sky that you will wish he were earthside. Because now that he's gone, I don't have anything holding me back from hunting you and ending you."

His smile doesn't meet his eyes. "While I love intimidation tactics, you're the one tied to a chair." A long pause builds between us. It's thick and ireful like my rage. "My guilt is precisely why you're not dead already. Despite your constant pleading. Well, that and the fact that I want what's owed to me. Regardless, I couldn't give an order for Knox to kill you without offering my respects for your loss face-to-face. That's the real reason you're still breathing, Sophia."

Julian Caddell's personality switches—between donning his monster mask and seeming almost concerned—is giving me whiplash.

"Contrary to what you think of me, I didn't intend for death to be your child's fate or yours. I just want my money!"

I scoff, and all rational thought flies out the window and my mouth. "Go to hell, where you belong. You and your piece-of-shit nephew. Did you hire him to get into my pants too? Was that a part of his act? Screw me into oblivion and then coax me into signing over my business to you as payment or something?"

"Knox thinking with his dick was all on his own terms. Trust me. I told him you were bad news, tainted by your shithead father. That's why I'm so proud he was able to get the intel about your flight back to Tampa. I really thought he had formed a soft spot for you. He proved me wrong there, too, when he gave you that shiner."

I thrash against the chair again. Arms pulling against the rope that binds them, my feet kicking wildly, trying to break free in a fury like I've never known before.

"We're getting way off subject." He settles into a chair adjacent to mine, unbuttoning the bottom button of his suit jacket with an unhurried flick of his wrist. "Don't you want to know how I *know* Mazen is your son's father?"

*"Where is your son?"*

The question that Mazen asked me before I boarded the

flight to rush home has played on repeat in my mind for hours, like unending movie credits.

I was so distracted by Lacey's call that I refused to see what was right in front of me. My head is dizzy as I recall Mazen retreating to his room to open fan mail. When I saw him again, he held a manila envelope in his hand with a death grip. I missed the flared temper of Mazen's scowl and the scalding fury in his steel eyes because I was too preoccupied by my own angst to notice the waves of it rolling off his hard jawline. The faint flare of his nostrils when he saw me makes sense now.

He looked like he had been gutted and lived to tell the tale. Bearing the scars of a truth that wasn't his to know. A truth that I'm not sure is even a real possibility.

Someone tipped him off that I had a child, and that someone is sitting right in front of me with a devilish grin on his face.

"I'm listening," I spit out contemptuously. "Enlighten me as to why you think he's the father of my son." Bile rises in my throat as the words leave my mouth.

"It's a *wild* story, really. You see, his father, Lorenzo Wilde, and I go way back. He was my college roommate."

*Of. Fucking. Course.* Kismet can kiss my ass.

Caddell's earlier confession about Mazen always being a pain in his father's ass hits me like a brick to the face.

He admitted he knew Mazen personally, and through the pain and panic in the forefront of my mind, I foolishly didn't let that comment register.

Thoughts flash back to the night of Murphy and Vanna's wedding, when I met Mazen's father. He put off bad vibes like the toxic pollutants when some idiot burns a tire. I knew that night that Lorenzo Wilde was trouble. I know just how much now if he's friends with Julian Caddell.

The web of deceit could house a thousand spiders.

"He called me, claiming that his son had fallen in love. Then asked me to do some digging. This type of work was usually your father's forte. With him behind bars for some foolish mistake, like laundering money from the hand that kept him fed, Knox took on his role within my organization. Imagine my surprise when he stumbled upon credit card charges that both you and Mazen swiped at the same hotel in Chicago on the same evening."

Frustration claws at my mind, but I sit still, listening with conflicting emotion.

"The twist was the connection you had before the hotel bar camera caught all the flirting. Some more digging revealed there was a tattoo convention that same weekend. Don't you recall tattooing him?"

*Think, Sophia.*

"The footage we hacked from the convention showed you tattooing a young man with dark hair and no other ink visibly in sight. Later that night at the hotel, footage showed you and Mazen—the same guy you'd tattooed earlier in the day—both walking, stumbling rather, right into your hotel room."

Decade-old memories assault my already-throbbing head. I recall meeting a guy that night. He was a tattoo virgin. I tattooed a small rose above his left pectoral muscle. The guy had a quiet charm that intrigued me just enough that I remembered him when he later approached me at the bar in the hotel's lounge. We shared some laughs and drinks, and when his featherlight lips found the shell of my ear, he asked to walk me back to my room like a gentleman. I dived headfirst into the smoldering pit of his persuasion.

The illusion he had painted of himself—as the coy, misunderstood, aspiring musician—was a front. Because when the elevator doors closed and we were all alone, his true colors came out, along with a streak of dominance. I remember panting breathlessly and staring into his inky-silver eyes as he shifted to pick me up and pin me up against the wall. When our lips met, a savage harmony echoed in the small space. His kiss was as challenging as it was rewarding, and the handsome stranger made me work for him up until the very end.

When daylight came, he was gone. Like a bandit in the night. The only trace of him was a note sprawled on the hotel's napkin.

A throaty voice grabs my attention once more, steering my wayward thoughts back to reality. "The next thing of interest we uncovered were charges on your credit card for copayments at your OB/GYN's office."

My skin crawls, like a bucket of ants have been dropped over my body and I'm a contestant on *Fear Factor*. "Aren't medical records supposed to be confidential?"

"Is anything in this life really ever confidential?"

Apparently not. *How does he have this much pull to gather all this intel?*

"Don't discredit my resources again, or you'll have a matching pair of black eyes." He waits for a protest that doesn't come, so he continues. "The records indicated your date of conception was dangerously close, spot-on really, to the night you and young Mazen had met. Even though Lorenzo met up with Knox and provided a DNA sample, I can't confirm it. I'd need a sample of Roman's DNA to be certain. I can only speculate that Lorenzo would have been a grandfather. But he's willing to go to great lengths to end his son's music career, and as you know, I'm willing to go to great lengths to collect what is rightfully mine."

An undiluted laugh floats up from Caddell's throat. He's back in devil mode, waving farewell to the facade he keeps flaunting that leads me to believe he might have a heart in his malicious body. Pain swells in my chest, along with the distinct mockery of my captor.

Hysteria rings in my tone as I ask the most pressing question I've ever asked in my life. "Did you tell Lorenzo about Roman?" My mouth feels like I used mouthwash with acid. "If he provided a DNA sample, you must've told him why you needed it."

Did Lorenzo tell Mazen I had a child?

There was nothing but cold resentment in Mazen's eyes when he asked me about my son before I boarded my flight. Either Lorenzo told him or the envelope he had informed him I had a son.

"Why would you get involved in this?" I pry, not understanding. "Their feud doesn't concern you or my debt."

"I'm tired of fucking waiting! I want my money. If I have to stir the pot to kick your ass in gear, I will. What were the chances that Lorenzo asked me, out of all people, to dig up dirt on his son's new piece of ass?"

I know with certainty that there's no coming back from this. Not that I really thought I'd be able to casually fly home, save my sister, evade Caddell for the second time in my life, and then return to the men who had wormed their ways into my heart like nothing suspicious had ever happened anyway. Still, the far-fetched desire of being with them again—all three of them—sends a joyous glint of admiration to the deepest part of my soul.

Caddell's sharp eyes bore into me, and I glance at him quickly, questioning him with my own impassive coldness.

His thick voice holds a challenge when he admits, "Lorenzo wasn't told why we needed his DNA. I mailed Mazen an item, informing him that his current lover was keeping secrets. Big secrets. Secrets that might warrant his attention. That's all. For now. Consider your secret my leverage to keep you in line."

I've never been more relieved in my life.

Forcing my consuming emotions into order, I attempt to conceal them from the bastard who has just imploded my life for the second time in a fucking decade.

*Mad props to you, asshole.*

Julian Caddell has taken too much from me already. I refuse to let him bask in the delight that he's won simply because he thinks he's solved a mystery. Without Roman's DNA, he hasn't solved anything. He can't confirm his suspicion. That's not why he brought it up. No. He wanted to plant the seed, to watch me squirm.

Another question barrels into my mind. *Why would Lorenzo want Mazen to fail at being a musician?*

*One dilemma at a time.* I tell myself.

My head swirls with doubts that he'll see straight through if I'm not careful. There's a slight hesitation as I choose my words cautiously. "Even if I did believe you, we're not *really* together. He's not my lover. He's never been my lover. If this elaborate-as-hell story holds any truth to it at all, he *was* a one-night stand, nothing more. You and your daughter have sadly been mistaken if you believe what the media says about me and him. It's fabricated. All of it."

*His kiss in the hot tub didn't feel fabricated.* It felt like I was free-falling off the highest mountain top in the world and sprouted wings that carried me back to the top, just to jump off over and over again. Kissing Mazen was sinful, like

I was Eve and tasted a forbidden fruit and couldn't get my fill, no matter how wicked I knew it was.

"Don't you wonder why Knox is so distraught? Beside himself with anger. So much so that he'd willingly kidnap you without batting an eye."

I can't tell if it's his rambling, jumping from topic to topic, or if the dizzy feeling settling inside me is from the start of dehydration or delusion.

"He thought the baby was his. You spent so much time riding his dick while he was reporting back to me over the years." He laughs. "You thought he was just your mentor."

Anger beats like a drum in my chest, hammering against my breastbone. "Knox is a coward. A deceitful scumbag. Fuck him."

"That mouth of yours." His composure evaporates, welcoming a chilly edge to his voice. "Keep running it, you little bitch, and I'll end all their lives, not just your precious Mazen's. Sources say you're with all the members of Kings of Jupiter. Do they all rock your world?"

A battle of personal restraint ensues.

I'd rather be dead than listen to Caddell's nonsense for a second longer. Biting the inside of my cheek for the thousandth time, I permit my harsh thoughts to break through the wall of what-ifs I have refused to truly consider, to give light to. Allowing them to steal my attention from the vile man in front of me, I zone out, my mind drifting into a ruthless reality. Could Mazen actually be my son's biological father?

Knox has long been ruled out based on the date of conception given by my doctor. Much to his disappointment, apparently. Why didn't I consider the man who had slept with me and held me tight against him like he was afraid I was going to slink into his dreams after the convention? The same man who melted my hard exterior with his boyish charm and then left me alone and confused the next morning.

Embarrassment of my sexual prowess weighs heavy on my shoulders in a hefty coat of shame. I didn't think of *him* because I had meaningless sex all the time. I couldn't narrow down who the father might be, so I didn't even try.

*Sleazy Sophia is how I should start introducing myself if I live to see tomorrow.*

3

# GOOD LUCK

SOPHIA

I'M stunned into silence for a long moment. Blood pounds, and my face and ears grow warm with humiliation as realization of my idiocy clouds my senses. I'm startled by the thought that this could be true, not just some lewd fabrication that Caddell is spewing. Though the chance is small, it's possible. I refuse to believe him without obtaining a DNA test for good measure.

God, do I even want that? The truth. What would Mazen do with it? What would *I* do with it?

"So, she *can* heed orders."

At the sound of his animated voice, I lift my head to him, keenly aware that this night will go down as the longest night of my life. If I survive it, that is.

"Good. Like I was saying, for your sake, you'd better hope Mazen gives two shits about you. If he doesn't comply with the ransom request Knox issued, you'll be dead before their dog ... what's his name? Jupiter, is it? Yeah. Before he takes his morning shit. Frankly, I'd like to see how the media spins that one. People love that dog. He is a cutie, I will admit."

Taking a quick, sharp inhale, I breathe out another appeal as hopelessness settles in the pit of my empty stomach. "You might as well let Knox have at it then because Mazen won't comply. Especially after you planted the notion that I'm keeping secrets from him. He probably hates me now. Good luck getting a dime. They probably all hate me now and are glad you took out their trash."

"I want to send a picture of me covered in your blood to your piece-of-shit father rotting in jail."

This tangent is disorienting.

"Hell, I had planned to do just that." He motions to a large black bag and shovel resting against the brick wall behind him. "This revelation unfolding is too good to miss though. Knox will be upset. The poor fucker is still jaded. That whole *if I can't have her, no one will* mentality he has is rather childish if you ask me. I honest to God want to see how this all pans out now. Call it curiosity."

Setting my lips into a stubborn line, I stare wordlessly at him from my chair. Finally, I manage a reply. "Curiosity killed the cat, you idiot. He's not going to pay you. I told you he's not my real boyfriend. His publicist staged our relationship for the media. It's nothing more than a facade to trick listeners into thinking that their idolized singer has a heart, a good side."

"What kind of angle do you think the publicist will play when the world learns of your child ... *his* child? Maybe she'll plant it like there was a sordid affair between the band members, and you didn't know who the father was, so you went into hiding, only for them to find out the truth ten years later. It could be a soap opera or a romance novel. I love it." He grins wide, devouring the sound of his own ignorant voice.

Ignoring his taunt, I try to erect a wall of defense against him. "If Lorenzo is your friend, business associate, or whatever the hell you call two morally screwed-up men plotting the demise of his son, you would know that you can't ruin his son's life without some blowback. The news of Mazen fathering a child will surely impact his in-the-spotlight governor father. Who's to say that Lorenzo isn't trying to capitalize on you? You out his son, and he gets the glory, playing the *grandfather-in-mourning* card."

"Staged or not, you owe me. I'm collecting. Lorenzo won't be a problem. I can assure you. We both want the same thing."

"Which is?"

"What does everyone want? Power. He wants to ruin his son's career. Haven't you been paying attention, Sophia? Lorenzo never wanted his son to be a musician. You're the answer to that."

A thick chill forms between us.

"Mazen would have given up everything if he knew he had a child. He wouldn't be the rock star he is today. He'd be by his father's side, running their business and raising little Roman."

Bile rises in my throat at another mention of his name, but I welcome the burn. It takes a solid ten seconds before I swallow. The fiery tingle is a reminder that I'm still alive, even if only as Caddell's sole entertainment. My life is in shambles while he looks as chill as one can be.

"Evidently, the family business you're referring to runs deeper than politics."

"Beautiful and smart. It's a pity you didn't marry Knox.

I think you could do better than owning that little tattoo studio."

I toss my head back in laughter. "You don't have to smooth-talk me. You've already won. My father is behind bars. It's been ten years since his damn arraignment. What do you get out of all of this? If Lorenzo wants Mazen to stop making music, what's your reward for engineering that demise?"

"Your father can't pay me from behind bars, now can he? I don't care that his life is ruined. He still owes me. Which means you owe me the one hundred fifty thousand dollars he embezzled. Either your little lover comes calling and pays up or you're as dead as the man who was shot as a noble sacrifice to frame your good ole dad, which landed him in jail for his unfaithfulness to me."

A mixture between astonishment and anger clouds my vision. I knew my father couldn't have killed a man. Embezzling money from someone as slimy as Caddell? Sure. That's believable. Did he spiral after my mom's death? Absolutely. I never believed he could stoop so low as to commit murder. Suddenly, it all makes sense. He was caught skimming money from Caddell, so he set my father up, leaving the debt incurred from stealing from him onto the shoulders of me and my sister, Lacey.

"You framed him for murder because he stole from you?"

Caddell's lips flatten as he stiffens under my scrutiny for once. I hear his quick intake of breath, and for a minute, I feel like I'm the powerful one in the room. Sure, I'm still tied to a chair. My bladder feels like it's expanded big enough that it could house a grand piano in its large quarters, and I'm fairly certain that my face resembles that of an MMA fighter after a title upset. In this fleeting moment, he's speechless, which means I hold a sliver of control over him. Surprise is written across his face at my audacity to call him out.

"No one steals from me."

"And no one has that kind of money either, least of all me. I wouldn't have run from you in the first place if I could have just written you a check, called it a day, and been on my merry way. So, are you going to try to incriminate me for a crime I didn't commit, too, or are you going to have Knox do it so you don't have to stain your pretty hands? It's what you're good at, right? Calling the shots, but never enforcing them yourself."

His right hook comes out of nowhere. The impact jars my cheek, moving my head to the side, away from my perpetrator.

"Knox has been my informant for years, you foolish girl." He jumps up from his seat in front of me again, wrenching my throbbing face in his rough, callous hand once more before he tilts my chin up so I'm forced to look directly into his soulless eyes. "Have you not been listening? If you had a pot to piss in, it'd already be mine. I have every reason to believe that Mazen will call. He'll pay your debt, and then I'll end your miserable life, track down Roman's DNA. There's got to be something you saved of his. I'll solve my old friend Lorenzo's problem too. Mazen will be crippled by your loss and the loss of a child he didn't even know he had. It's a win-win."

I grit my teeth, biting back the words that are desperate to escape the cage my teeth are housing them behind. I'm desperate to throw it in his face again that he doesn't have the balls to do anything himself. The heavy sting of my throbbing cheek silences me enough to hold in my desire to fire off another question.

My willpower is short-lived when I ask only seconds later, "How will my death help Lorenzo gain Mazen's compliance?"

"He'll spiral. Hard. I have no doubt. When Bethany—I assume you know about his deceased sister—died, he went off the rails. He'll be shattered by the news of your death and about Roman. Lorenzo, the best father in this sunny state, will be there to pick up the pieces."

"I think you're underestimating how much Mazen hates his father," I sneer as the beginning of a smile tips up the corner of my mouth. Rebellion should have been my middle name, yet my parents settled on Rose. "You see, his sister, Bethany, would still be alive if their wack job of a sperm donor hadn't sealed her fate by putting her into a vehicle with her brother, knowing he had been drinking. Mazen despises his father."

*There's a plot hole the size of Texas in his plan.*

I watch as Caddell's face goes grim, his mouth dipping into a grimace of despair. His determination falters in the next heartbeat. I can see the realization settle in the deep lines of his face. He knows I'm not lying. No ransom will be paid tonight. My father's debt will only be paid with my bloodshed.

I straighten my shoulders, clear my throat, and raise my chin with an icy stare in his direction. If this is the end, I'm going to run my mouth until my heart stops beating. "He blames Lorenzo for taking his sister away from him. Just like I blame you for stealing my son from me and framing my father! You're nothing but a washed-out, small-sack, middle-aged man who's trying to keep his empire from crumbling. News flash: you've been chasing me for years, banking on a pipe dream that I'd ante up. Which means that empire you think you're sitting at the top of is already turning into rubble at your feet. Why else would you be so needy for a payday?"

"Don't for one fucking second insult me. You might have felt safe, running from Chicago and settling here, but you've been on my radar. You just haven't had jack shit that I could take from you. That heap of a building you rent wouldn't cover a fraction of the debt I'm owed. The only way I saw it happening was you winning the lottery or paying with your life, and I promise my balls are plenty big."

He cups his junk through his dress pants. I instantly want to hurl.

"Your boyfriend will pay the ransom by"—he looks at the gold watch on his wrist—"midnight. Or you'll be the perfect late-night snack for the sharks."

I struggle against the zip ties around my wrists. "Don't you listen, or is it only when you can hear yourself speaking that you actually pay attention? He isn't my real boyfriend," I repeat like a broken record. "He doesn't give two shits about me. I work for hi—"

*That's it.* An epiphany clamors against sensible rationality in my chest. I pray like hell that Caddell is as money hungry as he claims he is. Regrouping, I square my shoulders as my thoughts reel, assembling a plan to get out of this unfortunate situation. My lips part in surprise before a thoughtful smile curves them upward.

*I will* not *become shark food today.*

"I have a contract with Mazen's label, Near Death Records." A sudden feeling of optimism soars in my chest like a hot-air balloon whizzing into the big, open blue sky. "That's how you'll get paid. They're paying me to date him."

"Go on," he instructs.

"It's simple. All you have to do is ..." I pause. My determination to get my plan out falters when a lump in my throat stalls my breathing. I swallow down my nerves that are sharp as the point on a tack. "Let me go." Anticipation stirs in my chest as hope blossoms. A bloom flourishes in the space for the first time in hours. "I won't tell anyone about what happened. I'll ... I'll tell them I needed some space or something."

"And what, you ran into a brick wall as you were hell-bent on getting away from them?"

"Listen, I want you out of our lives just as much as you want your money. This is how we both walk away, alive and satisfied. Once the tour is over, I'll earn my check from their label. I'll pay you. You have my word, and then we'll end this delightful partnership like two colleagues who will never ever need to cross paths again."

"Your face, Sophia," he presses, stating the obvious for the second time as he ignores my plan entirely. "You can't just stroll around the city like that and not cause alarm. People will ask questions."

"Shit." *Think.* "I'll say I got mugged outside of my apartment. Like I told you, none of them care about me like you think they do." My body wants to revolt at the words as soon as they leave my dry, parted lips. "They won't even bat an eye at my appearance. I'm nothing more than their tattoo artist. I swear it."

I try convincing my tormenter, knowing, at least hoping, that I do mean *something* to them. Even if I've been harboring a giant secret about my past. Though I know damn well that as soon as any member of the band sees me, they're going to lose their shit and demand answers. Answers I'll fight like hell to protect. I don't need a mirror to know that my face is battered, like my heart. Because as I try to smile wickedly at Caddell, the pain that tugs as my cheeks pull wide is nothing compared to the lashes Knox unleashed, threatening those I loved before he dragged me down the steps and into the path of his awaiting uncle.

"When's payday?"

*Hook, meet fish.*

I spit on the floor, finding a perverse pleasure as it spews across the toe of his shoe when I reply, "Four weeks."

In a swift move, Caddell grabs a fistful of my hair in his iron-clad grip. I can feel the roots screaming as his blunt clasp rips them from my head. I'm truly fearful that I'm going to have a bald spot with how many times he's done this same move.

"Don't fuck this up, Lozier." His sharp eyes bore into mine. His threat is tangible as his fingers now hover at the base of my neck. "You'll get it far worse than your daddy ever thought possible."

On my next breath, the rope around my wrists loosens. I didn't even realize he was cutting me free. Greed is by far the most powerful sin.

"My trust is waning by the minute."

On shaky legs, I rise, chin held high. "I have more to lose than you," I say through gritted teeth as Caddell's brow arches in question. "My family"—I realize briefly that the band, their adorable dog, and everyone I've met while working for them are lumped in that declaration, along with my sister—"will not have a hair on their heads disturbed while you wait for this money. Do you hear me?"

He nods, listening to my every demand as if my words were coated in gold themselves. "You have my word."

I turn, holding myself together with mere pride, refusing to fall by the weight of his stare as he watches me walk up the wooden steps. It takes every ounce of control left in me not to turn around and tell him that his word means nothing to me.

One foot in front of the other, I climb, even though my body feels like crumbling. Because if getting beaten to shit has taught me anything ... it's that I'm more resilient than I ever thought possible.

When the basement door swings wide, revealing a freedom I prayed for ... hours ... a whole day—hell, I don't even know how much time has truly passed—nothing but rage fills my chest, and I know that I'll happily go through hell and back if it means protecting those I love.

*Lacey, Mazen, Oliver, and Cannon.*

# 4

## BAND OF MORONS

OLIVER

AS THE ENCORE ends and the lights dim, I exit the stage. Feeling an instant lump form in my throat at the thought of Sophia. It was easier to mask my sorrow during the show when my mind was occupied with our set list and the echoes of hundreds of screaming fans. Now that the gig is over, I'm back to facing a bleak, sorrow-filled night without her in my arms.

A thick curtain separating this side of the stage from being visible hides my frame from our fans, granting me a moment to look into the crowd without being noticed. My gut tells me she won't be there. She hardly attended our shows when she was working for us. Still, my eyes scan the sea of faceless fans. My heart aches to find the fiery, red-haired siren who owns me as the crowd parts and heads for one of the many exits in the venue.

A couple of times after a show, I found her in our green-room, reading, or on our tour bus, getting her tattoo station set up. Despite the knowing pull in the pit of my stomach, I search anyway, eyes darting from person to person in pursuit of the woman who sets my soul on fire.

The spark of hope I had is extinguished, and my heart feels heavy and weighed down, like the steel-toed boots covering my feet, as I thud down the steps behind the stage and round a corner into a dim hallway leading to our greenroom.

Like a dense fog dancing along the shore, Soph has vanished without so much as a goodbye. Don't ask me to explain why I'm so distraught because I won't be able to put my emotions into words. It's more of a feeling. A thick, sinking feeling that has taken up residence in both my heart and mind since we learned she had left. Between the miles and truths we shared, I thought I had forged a path into Sophia's heart. I trudged through the debris of past lovers that had left her heart cold and scorned. Wielded every weapon in my arsenal, and just when I thought I had demolished her walls, ready to claim her trust and companionship as my prize, she disappeared. I've lived a shitty life, and only one other time have I ever felt this utterly miserable.

*Everyone always leaves.*

Mazen greeted us this afternoon with some lame story that seemed a bit too fabricated and coincidental for my liking. Apparently, Soph was rushing around the suite in the middle of the night, seemingly frantic, spouting off about flying home to make sure her sister, Lacey, was safe.

As much as I love my bandmate, I wouldn't put it past Mazen to have paid her off, doubling what the label and I were already going to fork out. He's wanted her gone since the first day he laid eyes on her. Knowing him, the kiss they shared in the hot tub the day before was just another fabrication.

A means to an end.

There's no other explanation.

Especially not after the mind-blowing night she, Cannon, and I shared. Someone doesn't just walk away after sex as earth-shattering as we had. Least of all Soph.

She's the tether that binds us. The white flag in our ten-year war. Our ceasefire, clothed in jeans and a crop top. Without her, I'm afraid of what today will hold. Cannon and I will no doubt be back to ignoring the chemistry between us. Concealing our lust and feelings with insults and cold shoulders.

With my hands shoved into my front pockets and my shoulders hunched in defeat, I trek down the long, dark hallway, feet shuffling mindlessly as I go. My thoughts are too preoccupied, racing like an untamed wildfire burning through a forest the closer I get to our small oasis from the chaos of the venue.

Roadies croon my name as I saunter by. I offer a quick nod of my head, nothing more, which should be a giant red flag that I'm not in my normal state of mind, before pushing open the door and shutting out the noise behind me. I wish I could do it to the raging racket in my head as easily. I'm so overwhelmed by the torment of her absence that I can't recall how the show even went. I was half on autopilot, half numb.

Soph seemed to always be composed, methodical, even in her words and actions. And as much as Mazen tried to ruffle her feathers, she never cowered to his brashness, giving it back twice as hard. That was what attracted me to her first, that iron will of hers. She is both confident in her skin and who she is. Being a pushover isn't in her nature.

That's the only thing that doesn't add up. If he couldn't force her hand before, how did he accomplish it last night?

The alternative was that she willingly left, breaching her contract with both me and our label. I know how much the money meant to her—what she planned to do with it. I rack my brain over the last three and a half weeks spent with her. Nothing of importance stands out or leads me to believe that she would willingly forgo our deal and forfeit her payday. Hell, she's made it blatantly apparent that not even her distaste for Mazen—the dude who teased her endlessly and then had the audacity to drive her to the fucking airport himself—could get her to back out of this deal.

*She* needed *the money from this arrangement.*

My gaze lands on Mazen, who is slouched over in a chair, a bottle of amber liquid in his hand. His unruly black hair looks like he's run his fingers through it repeatedly. His chin is set in a hard line, and his silver eyes are glued on the bottle's label. Metal-covered knuckles tap on the glass lightly. It's an absentminded gesture—I know because that's how I felt during our entire show.

Thank fuck I can play every song while drunk, standing on the edge of a cliff, or getting a Brazilian wax.

*Wait. Is it still called a Brazilian if it's a dude getting stripped?*

No. It's a *Brozilian.* Don't ask me why that sliver of knowledge is lodged in the back of my brain. It's wedged somewhere between how to make a woman squirt and how far up a man's prostate is located.

I draw nearer to the frontman of our band, ready to demand to know what really transpired between the two of them last night while Cannon and I were sleeping soundly down the hall. Sizing him up, I notice that his thick brows are pulled into a deep crease. I watch him carefully, like a predator, as he takes a swig, abandoning a chaser, and when his eyes meet mine, realization throttles into me like I've hit a wall going ninety miles per hour.

The clear absence of his signature smug smile on his square jawline tells me all I need to know. I take in his dark expression and tight brows, knowing without a shadow of a doubt that he'd be gloating if he finally got his wish and ran Soph off. Mazen's innocence is confirmed by his quietness. It's not in his nature not to run his mouth. Right now, his demeanor is resigned. He's as quiet as a statue.

If it wasn't *someone* who pushed her to leave, it had to have been *something*.

Like a thief in the night, she fled. This irrational knee-jerk decision to catch a plane and fly back to the States can't be as black and white as it seems. Something is going on, something bigger than checking in on her grown-ass adult sister. Call it intuition or whatever the fuck you want. I've been abandoned enough in my life to know the signs, and all the ones she left, which are scattered around her room, point to the conclusion that she left in a hurry.

My adrenaline is waning, much like my patience, as I try her cell again for the millionth time. It's not a shocker when it goes straight to voicemail.

"Fuck." I toss my cell phone onto the coffee table that's littered with booze and ashtrays.

The stage's sweltering lights, paired with my concern for Soph's whereabouts, have me breaking out in a sweat.

I rip my drenched shirt up and over my head with one quick swoop before biting out, "Band meeting. Right. The fuck. Now." The usual softness of my voice has been replaced with that of a deranged banshee. All of these mixed-up feelings swirling in my mind are pushing me into dangerous territory.

"You guys can sort your shit out later," Nick, our band's

manager, mumbles under his breath, holding an iPad in one hand, walkie-talkie in the other. "You have a meet-and-greet in twenty. I suggest you focus on what's important—your careers—not some piece of ass."

As if on instinct, Cannon's wrought iron physique slides in front of me. A wall of anger and muscle blocks my view of Nick, so I don't see our manager when he adds gas to the already-engulfed fire that's a heap of our collective hearts.

"Who cares about the loose tattoo artist who couldn't make it on the road? The way I see it, she voided her contract. Saved the label a hundred grand. It's a win for the home team."

Nick's words, like the rolling sound of thunder, reverberate in my chest.

"I suggest you shut your fucking mouth unless you want it wired shut." Cannon's back is stone, a formidable force. "That would be a win for this team."

Cannon's a man of few words, so I sincerely hope for our manager's sake that he heeds Cannon's warning. Otherwise, I think Nick is flying right by Wired Jaw Avenue and headed straight into Full-Body Cast cul-de-sac.

"Enough." Lindsey, our band's publicist and childhood friend, comes out of nowhere like a ninja. Springing into action, she tosses herself into the trenches, shoving between them like a wedge of reason. "Nick, tell the fans that Mazen ate some bad sushi for lunch and isn't feeling well. Give them a couple of signed shirts, then send them on their way. I'll handle this from here."

When Nick doesn't budge, she squares up with him, chest to chest. "I said, I got it from here."

Rolling his eyes like a child being sent to his room, Nick shakes his head disapprovingly. "Go ahead and pacify them some more. It's what you're good at. Probably the only thing, if I'm being honest."

"Would you rather I let Cannon clobber you? Because right now, he looks like he could demolish a hotel, turning it to rubble with just his fists. If that's the route you want to go"—she waves a hand toward Cannon's expanded chest—"be my guest. It'll be your funeral."

"Fucking children," he says as he tucks his tail, slamming the door behind him.

"Sit down," Lindsey demands, her blonde ponytail hanging over her shoulder. "Now."

· The four of us—Mazen, Murphy, Cannon, and I—slide to any open surface in the room. I take a small navy-blue ottoman. Murphy's wife, Vanna, remains standing, sorrow etched on her face, mirroring my own.

"I have a bad feeling." Vanna sighs.

She's a newbie, and she hasn't yet learned what Lindsey's cut-the-bullshit face looks like.

"Join the club." I chew the inside of my cheek—a nervous tic—as my eyes dart around the crowded room. They land on Vanna once again and find her holding her hands tightly around her core in a protective gesture. I don't even think she realizes she's doing it.

Her mouth parts when she adds, "Everything was fine at the beach. Dinner felt a little off, rushed. But Mazen didn't irritate anyone enough to want to stab him with a butter knife. I call that a win. Everything fell apart in the span of one evening after we parted ways. So, what happened last night, guys?"

Vanna's nutmeg eyes, like a laser, land on Mazen. Her glare is unrelenting.

He hasn't said much since he told us that Soph left. I

can see straight through his aloofness. There's something he's not saying, and it's pissing me the fuck off.

"Sex happened." Mazen shrugs, breaking his vow of muteness.

"Is your dick so small that she decided to skip town because she couldn't bear to look you in the eyes again?"

"It wasn't my dick that scared her away."

Murphy pulls his bride onto his lap, whispering a faint, "Don't goad him, Van."

"Seriously?" She huffs from the safety of her husband's lap. "He's been provoking Soph since they met."

Lindsey fires off a message on her cell before pocketing it and turning her attention back to us. "We have no reason to believe anything bad has happened. Mazen watched her board the plane—the label's plane, your plane—which took her back to Tampa. Her phone could be dead, and she was probably too exhausted from the flight to charge it when she got to her apartment. Give her the benefit of the doubt, guys. You know it's not like me to give trust away easily. It's my job to call bullshit when I see it. I usually see the bad in everyone until they prove me wrong. That's pretty much my mantra. Sophia hasn't given us a reason *not* to trust her. Let's assume she's jet-lagged until we hear otherwise."

"Trust is earned." Mazen's raw voice cuts through the room, demanding to be heard. There's a rasp to his voice, and I don't for one second think it's from him performing onstage for two and a half hours. He's a master at manipulation. He's trying his damnedest to conceal something, or he chain-smoked ten packs of cigs between last night and today. Both are likely.

Another pang of doubt and apprehension stirs in my stomach.

"And what, she hasn't earned it? She's abided by all the

label's rules. Hasn't once posted on her social media accounts without Lindsey's approval of the content first. Who the hell are you to say she hasn't earned our trust?" My temper flares.

"You didn't care about trust when you were fucking her throat with your fingers yesterday. Did you, Maz?" Cannon's voice is cold, exact, and lethal.

Adding fuel to the already-blazing inferno engulfing us, Mazen diverts his eyes from our fuming drummer and directs his gaze toward me. "She hasn't even been on tour with us for more than a fucking month, and you're already planning your nuptials, aren't you? How will that work anyway? Will you legally marry her"—his chin nods toward me and then swivels to face our drummer once again—"and Cannon will be the one to consummate the marriage or will it be the other way around?"

I see red. My resolve breaks like a string on my axe. "Fuck you. You're the sorry bastard who's going to end up alone. Just like your miserable father. At least Cannon and I have each other."

As soon as the words leave my mouth, a deep crimson warms my cheeks. Heat ignites my entire body like a marshmallow to a flame. Did I really just casually admit to Cannon and I having a...thing?

"Stop! This is bullshit. You've been friends for too long to be acting like you don't give a damn about one another." Lindsey's rationale does little to calm the situation.

"Casting judgment like stones, are we now? How about we throw stones at your precious tattoo artist?" Mazen's eyes darken, his voice deepening when he says, "She's flighty as fuck and hightailed it home in the middle of night." He finishes the bottle of amber liquid and smashes it against the coffee table in front of him before his eyes cut around the room. "She's just another bitch the road can claim."

A frustrated growl comes from Cannon, who's sitting with his elbows on his knees at the edge of the couch. He flexes his jaw, and his lips part. "If you call her a degrading name again, Mazen, I'm going to forget that we've been best friends most of our lives. You'll wish that you never met me in seventh grade gym class. I promise you that."

Mazen stands, eyes gleaming with mischief. There's a smile hanging off his mouth. Shit. This isn't going to be good. Murphy must realize it, too, because he jumps to his feet at the same time that I do. I place a hand on Cannon's broad shoulder to keep him seated as Murphy pushes against Mazen's heaving chest.

Distance certainly hasn't made our hearts grow fonder.

"We're more than a band." Murphy's voice rises with dismay, though he tries to rein in his twisted irritation. "We're family ... brothers. Don't cross a line we can't come back from."

Mazen stares at Murphy, face paling with wrath. His steel-gray eyes darken like an angry thundercloud as his accusing voice stabs the air, "The line was crossed when Ollie hired her without consulting the rest of us."

"I agree," Murphy says, and I halt in shock.

# 5

# ANSWER ME

OLIVER

**THE RELATIVELY CIVIL** way our bassist, Murphy, disses Sophia sends my rebellious emotions into a frenzy. Rage radiates from my pores.

With his arm bent at the elbow, I feel Cannon's long-fingered hand hover over mine on his shoulder. The script is flipped when the comforting touch I extended is now held captive in his grasp. I glance from his hand to his face, only to find his blonde hair tumbling carelessly around his broad-carved face, worry for both me and Soph etched in the glimmer of his robin's-egg-blue eyes.

A flash from last night caresses my memory.

*Like a puppet master, I whispered into the thin air, coaching Soph and Cannon's movements with heated words of praise, "Just like that. Look how good her pussy is taking you."*

*My jaw ached as my teeth clenched so hard that I was fearful of breaking a molar while I watched Cannon's thick shaft inch deeper and deeper into Soph until he disappeared* into her sweet cunt, filling her to the hilt. The sounds they both expelled wreaked havoc on my willpower.

Tilting his head so that the back of it rested on my clavicle, I ran my fingers through his mixed strands of iced and honey-colored waves before splaying my palm on his scalp and pulling his strands taut in my grasp. I turned my head so that my lips danced across the shell of his ear, offering him an out, one that I prayed to the fucking stars he didn't take.

"I've thought about fucking you, owning the part of you that I claimed ten goddamn years ago. You've haunted my dreams. Do you feel how hard my dick is for you? Do you want this as bad as I do?"

A millisecond later, Cannon's hips thrust into Sophia with so much force that her body jutted forward on the bed as a moan tore from her lungs, the sound echoing in the confined tour bus bedroom. As he continued his domination of her pussy, I slid my palm down the back of his neck, watching as his throat bobbed under my iron grip. His muscles tensed with the change in pressure of my hold. When he inclined his head toward mine with compliance, I watched intently as a bead of sweat slid down his creased forehead while he steadily pounded into our girl. No doubt, his tempo increased from the thick-as-honey lust lingering between our bodies.

"Answer me."

He groaned an intoxicating, "Yes," before his bravado deepened, and then his voice slid into a low hum as he said, "I'd rather feel how hard it is sliding into me."

My senses fogged, as if his answer had somehow managed to short-circuit my brain.

I'd always prided myself on being sensible. I hid behind humor as a mask, and my true identity clung to order despite the chaos that loomed over my childhood. I thrived on being *in charge, giving fate the middle finger, and reclaiming something I had been denied in adolescence. I took life by the balls, demanding my stake in this world, creating my path. Denied control, safety, and stability as a youth, forced to waver to the whims of a world I was lost in. As an adult, I was powerless no more.*

*I vowed never to forbid myself anything that caused a sliver of happiness, no matter the cost. Cannon Rhodes was the only exception because he held all the power in the palm of his hand. The sincerity in his blue eyes shone bright enough to dismantle my resolve. The adoration for my best friend, my only true weakness in the hard armor I wear like a second skin.*

*Refusing him, turning his declaration of love into a wasteland of swirling emotions, was my last-ditch effort at grasping the control that I needed to survive, knowing full well that he held it all. I longed for control so much that I refused to see that it had withered in the wind the moment our eyes locked for the first time all those years ago.*

*Cannon's lips parted, curving into a smile that held a hint of eroticism before he said, "It's your turn to answer me."*

*My eyes widened, darting from his luscious lips to the rich outline of his broad shoulders to the sheen of sweat glimmering across his defined chest, which was now heaving. I knew that I'd willingly hand over control ... my heart ... my soul. Anything the brute drummer asked for was his, even my deepest, darkest truth.*

*I've loved him ever since he taught me the meaning of the word.*

*The sound of his balls slapping against Soph's body mocked me more than his words ever could, though I tried to* hold on to the fragments of power between us as I said, "You didn't ask me anything."

"It was a silent invitation. Let me rephrase it so you'll hear me this time." He looked into the depths of my eyes, and the rest of the world faded around us, including the moans of the red-haired siren bent on all fours in front of us.

Soph's trust in the two of us sent a shiver down my spine.

"Every man I've screwed has been a placeholder for you. You rejected me, but that doesn't mean every time I buried my dick in someone else's ass, my heart didn't ache, wishing it were you claiming me. My second-most-sensitive body part is all yours. It's always been yours, Ollie. Only yours."

"What's your first-most-sensitive part?"

"My heart. It's going to take a little more than a quick fuck to fix that though."

I couldn't breathe. Words escaped me.

Cannon rolled his hips before spreading himself wide with both of his large hands. The veins in my cock thickened, and a bead of pre-cum glistened at the tip of my cock.

"I want you to fuck me so thoroughly that you refuse to forget me ever again. Mark me as yours, Ollie. Tell me we don't have to hide from how we truly feel anymore, speak it into existence, and then, I'll see if you're worthy of my heart again."

I shattered into a million tiny shards at his request, all of them belonging to him. In one swift motion, I shoved Cannon forward like his physique was no match for the hunger coiling around my own wanton need, demanding to be released in a reign of ecstasy. With his chest now sealed to the velvety skin of Soph's naked back, I grabbed hold of his perfectly molded ass, rubbing my hands over his soft flesh before cupping his balls, pulling slightly.

"Fuck," he muttered.

*"Please ..." Soph's voice was muffled as she begged for release. "Fuck him into me, Ollie. You hold all the power."*

*Her foolish words landed flat at my feet. Because we all knew damn well that she owned the three of us.*

*"As you wish, baby," I told Sophia as my palm slapped Cannon's ass, the sound ringing louder than our harsh breaths. "You're both mine now." Dominance poured from my lips as my index finger met my best friend's puckered hole.*

*With an expert move, I squirted a dollop of lube onto my hard-as-steel dick and a small amount onto my finger. The liquid pooled around the inked tentacles of my jellyfish tattoo and dripped to the floor below my feet.*

*There was no warning as my finger entered his hole, just a bucking of his hips, and a grunt of pleasure tearing from his mouth. I worked him with precise movements of my fingers until his greedy desire tore through my restraint. I positioned myself behind him, and then I fully buried myself into him in one solid stroke with my jellyfish-tatted dick.*

*"F-fuck ... mmm," I called out as my force pushed Cannon into Soph, and the three of us chased euphoria.*

"OLLIE." Cannon's gruff voice pulls me out of my sex-crazed trance.

I glance down into his ocean-blue eyes as he tethers me back to reality. Though his profile is rigid and strong, his blue eyes remind me of a child's, kind with a sort of gracious beauty. He's always had a hold on me, even in the years I spent trying to smother my attraction toward him. One night was all it took for the wall of defense to crumble at our feet. With that barrier no longer between us, I get lost in his arresting good looks. My attention is captured for a moment of suspended time.

Until Cannon's hand squeezes mine, once again beckoning me back to reality.

The gesture speaks volumes after my previous blunder about me and him being together last night. I appreciate his public display of affection, at least until my mind replays the scene in front of me. Then, I forgo his loving touch and dive headfirst into the darkness of Murphy's betrayal.

"What the fuck? I thought you were on our side." I motion to myself and Cannon, staring wildly at Murphy, who appears to have woken up and decided to wedge himself in the middle of this fight.

*Fucking traitor.*

"Let me finish." He turns to face us, Mazen on his heels. "I was going to say, I agree that a line was crossed when Ollie hired her without asking anyone else. But," his pause adds a dramatic effect that I'm not sure he was aiming for, but it works. I feel like I'm being edged, hanging on his every word. "I'm glad he did. In the short amount of time we've known her, she became one of us."

The sound of Vanna sniffling isn't lost on me. I might have been greedy with Sophia the last couple of weeks, but it's clear that she made an impression on all of us. Even the ones *not* fucking her into oblivion.

Jupiter too. He's the biggest turncoat of us all. Our four-legged road dog has been lost without his belly-scratching pal.

Murphy turns back to face me. "If she's not answering, then it's simple. Call her sister. She rushed home to be with her—so Mazen claims. Let's just contact her and get to the bottom of this. It's not rocket science. I know none of us went to college—"

"Excuse me, I did," Lindsey interrupts.

"Thanks to us," Mazen adds tersely.

"We'll call Lacey right now. Okay?" Murphy asks, staring at us like we're a band of morons and not the fully capable men we are.

# 6

## FIND A CLUE

### CANNON

WE'RE SITTING around the large kitchen island, hearts hammering louder than my sticks on my snare, eager for answers, when Lindsey saunters into the kitchen thirty minutes later. It's not hard to miss the hard line of her lips. The frown on her normally jubilant face is a bad sign. Second is the crease in the center of her forehead. An indication that whatever she's about to say will be like pulling the detonator on the bomb in the pit of my stomach.

I turn off my music, effectively stopping the sound of Bad Omens' "Take Me First" with the press of my index finger.

"Lacey said that Sophia never showed up."

One simple statement sends me on a rampage of anger and confusion. I lose all sense of ... everything. Becoming a fatality to the darkness, I let it envelop me, dragging me into its murky depth. In one quick sweep of my hand, everything flies off the counter—our coffee cups, a glass bowl that was resting in the center of the island. As it hits the tiled floor, it shatters into a million pieces, just like my heart.

"Call her back," I growl. "Call her sister back. I want to talk to her."

"And say what exactly?" This comes from Murphy, the mediator. The most levelheaded person in our band, brotherhood, and lives. "Hound her about her sister's whereabouts? I'm sure she's as distraught as everyone else. We need to call the police, file a missing person report, and let the authorities do their jobs. Plus, we're thousands of miles away."

"Lindsey"—my voice is heavy, strained as it passes my lips, while I ignore the mediator's suggestion—"please call her back. We're missing something. I can feel it. Please."

The desperation displayed across my knit brows and in my tone must be dire because within a matter of seconds, Lindsey's phone is on speakerphone, ringing with an outgoing call from its place in the middle of the island. No one dares to move an inch, not even to clean up the mess I made on the floor. Six sets of eyes bore holes into the small device as we will Lacey to answer it.

"Lindsey?" Lacey's voice sounds hopeful. She thinks our publicist is calling back with good news. "Did you hear from her?"

"This is Cannon. I'm, uh, the drummer for Kings of Jupiter." I bite the inside of my cheek—a nervous tic.

"I know who you are." I imagine a sad smile pulling on her mouth. "I'm a little busy right now, so if you're just calling to chitchat, spare me."

I laugh internally. "Chitchat isn't my style."

"This I know as well."

"Busy doing what?" Mazen chimes in. His mock concern grates on my nerves.

He's the fucktard who drove her to the airstrip. I want to pummel him into next Tuesday, but now isn't the time.

A hefty exhale leaves Lacey's mouth. "Combing through my sister's office, trying to find a clue or something. Hell, I don't know. It's better than just sitting around, willing my damn phone to ring with her name flashing on the screen."

The six of us helplessly exchange glances over the tiled countertop.

"I want to help. I need her ... back," I say as I clutch my hands behind my neck, biting back the word I really want to say ... *home.* My home is on wheels and made of metal, but I need her in it, with me. *With us.* "Tell me what happened last night. All we know is that you called her, and then she left. Mazen said she was visibly shaken and rushing home to help you. What happened? What don't we know? What aren't you telling us?"

Mazen cuts me a look that says, *Sherlock Holmes has arrived.*

"To help me," she whispers. "She was coming home to help, to keep me safe. It's always because of me. She'd step in front of a flying bullet to save me. I should have waited to call her until I was in a better frame of mind. It just all happened so quickly. I freaked out."

Oliver leans down, speaking into the receiver, as if he can pull Lacey's truth from the phone, as if time and distance aren't hanging between us. "Lacey, what happened? We're all here, and we're all eager to make sure Sophia is safe. She's our priority just as much as she is yours. We care about her too. Why did you call her, upset? We can't pool our resources together and help if we don't have all the facts. Let us help."

"I played right into his game," she says hoarsely after a

beat of silence. "It's because of me that he was able to get to her." Her next words slice my chest open. "Her life is in jeopardy, and it's my fault."

"Whose game? Who has her?" This time, it's Lindsey's turn to lean toward the receiver.

We're all fishing for clues, on high alert and demanding answers, but I don't know if we're prepared to hear what she has to say.

"Julian. He's going to kill her this time, and she'll let him to protect me."

A collective gasp reverberates through my friends as the late lunch I had before the show lurches in my stomach. A drowsy warmth spreads across my body like a wildfire, consuming all rational thoughts before my entire body is set ablaze. It feels like a flame starting at the soles of my feet, and it engulfs me.

I'm lost, unaware of what is happening. Then, a wave of obsidian drags me under, and everything goes dark.

WINCING like I was struck on the head, I force myself to pry my eyes open when I wake up. "The fuck happened?"

"I expect you'll need this." I hear Vanna's voice before my senses align.

I realize we're on a plane, and she is sitting in the seat next to me, eyes wide with hesitation as they sweep over me. She holds a small bag of ice, dangling it like a sack of gems, a peace offering.

"I told him not to do it." She winces. "Though you honestly didn't leave us with another option."

*What's she droning on about?*

The ringing in my ears intensifies.

Reading my confusion, she answers, setting the record straight, "You went ballistic with a capital B. Blacked out or something. You're going to have a hefty damage claim on your credit card statement when the hotel—"

"Why does it feel like I was in a fight?" I run my hand through my hair that hits the collar of my leather jacket.

"Because you were." Vanna shrugs her shoulders. It's a dismissive gesture. "Look, you sort of lost it. Started breaking everything within arm's reach in the kitchen. We needed to get to the tarmac. You wouldn't calm down, so—"

"Spit. It. Out."

"So... " She sounds out a long O. "Oliver hit you with the heaviest thing within reach."

I arch my brow, demanding her answer.

"An air fryer. Like one of those big, fancy, industrial ones."

My voice breaks as I try to make sense of what she just said. "He did what?"

Oliver plops down in the seat adjacent to us. "Your skull became acquainted with the largest air fryer I've ever seen that wasn't in an industrial kitchen. Down you went, man. Like a sack of potatoes. You're heavier than you look too. Ashton's back is going to be fucked up from trying to carry your dead weight to the car. If he files a worker's compensation claim, you're footing that bill."

Memories resurface as I stare out the plane's window. Nothing but fluffy white clouds as far as the eye can see stare back at me. Ollie whistles softly, his innocence blowing out with the warm air from his mouth. My closest fucking friend—Lover? Boyfriend? Hell, I don't know what we are—assaulted me by throwing a kitchen appliance at my head. Things must have escalated pretty quickly for him to turn to KitchenAid for assistance in subduing me.

"Who's Julian?" I ask with a hedge of understanding that I'm not going to like the answer before it's even given. That name rings clearer in my mind than the ordeal he and Vanna are trying to explain with worried expressions.

It's Ollie's turn to rub his temples. His index fingers make small circular motions a couple of times before he settles back into the tan leather seat. I don't miss the pause before he clasps his slender hands together, answering me honestly. "Someone needs to make sure we have a countertop ice maker on standby." A trace of unease lingers in his reply, like he's scared his words are going to throw me into another fit of rage.

I'm irritated by his mocking tone, and a faint growl leaves my lips.

"Simmer down, or I'll take you to the back room and fuck some sense into you." The threat in both his tone and punishment is appealing.

*Apparently, we're* out, *out to everyone now.*

Though my skull is throbbing, I welcome the pain as I lean forward into his personal space and snarl once more, demanding an answer. "Tell me who he is before I take you to the back room, bend you over the bed, and fuck the answer out of you."

He already outed us, so I figure, *What the hell? It's my turn to send him a message loud and clear.* If my brain didn't feel like it had been pureed in a blender, I'd show him how serious I am. Instead, I say, "A lot has changed since we were boys fooling around after school, Ollie."

I cup his semi-hard junk through the front of his pants, not caring that Vanna is observing the whole scene. Her thin, dark eyebrows are pinched together, but there isn't an ounce of shock on her face. That fact alone should alert me that we weren't as stealthy as we thought since we decided to stop fighting our feelings and attraction.

"I don't just take orders or dick anymore. I give it just as much and as hard as you do. Keep running that pretty little mouth of yours, and I'll stuff it so full that your tonsils will hurt for weeks."

Flames of passion ignite like a forest fire in his eyes as his mouth spills for me. "He's some wanna-be-mobster that Soph's father owes a shit ton of money to. Apparently, that's why they fled Chicago. Only they didn't know that they were being followed all the way to Florida. The other night, someone threw a brick through the tattoo studio's window with a note. That's what started this whole fucking fiasco. Someone knows she's working for us too."

I bite back a *good boy* for his eager compliance because I can still feel Vanna's curious eyes honed in on us.

"The note. What'd it say?"

A troubled look passes between Oliver and Vanna. Their exchange is anything but reassuring. My suspicion is confirmed when his next words sting like battery acid dousing the already-burning inferno in my chest.

*"I've been counting your breaths like I've been counting my money. Both don't exist to me. Give me what I'm owed or prepare for your shop and your sister to catch fire."*

"She's been kidnapped," I seethe with a mounting rage that not even a refrigerator, Jeep, or the entire fucking Icon of the Seas cruise ship to the skull would be able to diminish. My blood soars the longer the threat resonates.

"No shit," Mazen calls out from the row behind us. "Jupiter could have figured that out before you."

Ignoring him, I speak to everyone on the plane, not giving two shits that they just heard Oliver and me talk about taking and tossing dick like a champ. Narrowly missing looking everyone in the eyes directly, I ask, "This Julian guy, do we know anything about him? Why does her dad owe him? How much does he owe? Where is her dad, and why haven't any of you nitwits gotten your checkbooks out yet?"

Lindsey, our publicist, holds a finger in the air from her seat in the row across from us. A silent motion to calm the hell down. It's not lost on me that I'm usually the quiet one of the group.

Sophia helped me find my voice. It's my turn to help her now.

"She's been on the phone since we left, trying to gather intel." It's Vanna's composed voice, layered with a new gentleness that gains my attention.

She nods to where Lindsey sits, looking fierce, businesslike. A lady on a mission to find our friend.

"So far, all we know is that he's a scumbag businessman who has connections all over the globe. We did find out that Sophia and Lacey's father is incarcerated for murder. Apparently, he owed this Caddell guy a lot of money for skimming off him for years, and with their father out of the picture, he's made it his mission to collect from Sophia and Lacey. Their mother passed away—"

"Ovarian cancer," I say, voice choked. "We think he took her hostage for what, ransom? Like I said, call up ... whoever our accountant is these days. Let's settle this debt, collect Sophia, and be on our way. It's a no-brainer."

Oliver crosses a leg over his kneecap, his voice stoic, "No one's reached out to us yet. Trust me, I've already texted Kenneth and had him pull some numbers. She's worth every penny I have and then some. I've been poor as dirt before. It's nothing new."

I know how hard it was for him, growing up. His statement speaks volumes. I feel the same though. I'd cash in everything I own, my entire bank account, to have her back safely in our arms. I don't care if I've only known her for a little over a month. I want to know her forever, until the end of time.

"He's had her for hours by now." My voice is edged in steel. "Statistics say—"

The shuffling of movement behind me has me moving the bag of ice from my head, just in time to look up to see Mazen sinking into the seat Vanna abandoned next to me.

"While you were both busy stuffing Sophia like she's a flipping toaster, I assume this Julian fella was busy getting this into my hands." Mazen holds out a worn manila envelope.

Oliver and I exchange a wary glance before I grab the envelope, roughly pulling out its contents. There's an audible gasp from Vanna, who appears in the walkway, when she recognizes what the document is mere seconds before the rest of us.

Women really are the superior gender.

"It's a birth certificate," he acknowledges for us in a rush of words. "For a son she's never mentioned having. She didn't mention owing some mobster either. Fuck. Are you both this stupid or just blinded by good pussy to see the truth in front of you?"

Murphy makes his presence known when the sound of his voice echoes down the aircraft. "Her past isn't any of our business," he says, ordering us with cool authority to get our shit together. "There's plenty of reasons why she never mentioned bearing a child. Was she supposed to sign her contract with the label and dish out every detail of her twenty-nine years before she climbed on the bus with us?

That's stupid, and you know it, Maz. I didn't see you airing out your dirty laundry to her. Forget that we've known you since before you had braces. There's a shit ton of dirty laundry in your basket, isn't there?"

Mazen's mouth opens, then closes before it parts again. "Mine's only one click away on Google, fucker."

"There's a perfectly good reason she kept this to herself. I wouldn't board a bus with five strangers and then air out my secrets either." Vanna's dark eyes dance between us, as if she's daring us to disagree. "She'll explain everything when she's ready. We just need to find her first and make sure she's okay. Tell her that she's a part of our family now. She has to know she can tell us about her secrets and trust us not to react like ... well, this. It's not like you've done much to earn her trust thus far, Mazen. Did you even stop and consider why her kidnapper would send *that* to you specifically?"

The thought shatters me, tearing at my insides. This was all premeditated.

*Yep, they're going to need a submarine to hit me over the head with this time.*

"Trust isn't given freely," Mazen retorts ruthlessly, rubbing his hand over the five-o'clock shadow on his sculpted jaw.

Crumpling up the document, I stuff it into my front pocket. "I can't speak for you guys. I just know that all I care about is finding her, forging a future with her. Earning her trust and her heart. If we're not working toward the same goal, Maz, I don't want to hear your fucking commentary."

"When did I become the enemy?" he grinds out.

I ignore his question. "The fact that this man, Caddell, knew to send this to you means he knows she works for us. This is a good thing." I nod, trying to check the crazy mixture of fear stirring in my chest. "This means he knows we're good for the money. We just need to wait for the ransom call."

There's a bitter edge of what seems like regret in Mazen's voice when he admits, "I broke my phone." He quickly follows up with, "Not that I think I'd be the one to get that call or anything," masking the brief slip of his mask. "Someone wanted to ensure I'd get a copy of that birth certificate though, and I'm here, aren't I? Despite feeling conned by her ... being here should earn me a little credit. Give me that before you write me off like she did."

"What's that supposed to mean?" Oliver's greenish toffee-colored eyes are wide with wild curiosity glinting in them.

"Nothing. Let's just find her. We'll figure the rest out later."

Everyone's voice fades into a hushed stillness as we collectively lose ourselves to the possibility of never seeing Sophia again.

# 7

## DUSTING OF MAUVE

SOPHIA

WITH WHAT I assume is a broken nose, merited by my defiance and smart mouth, I find my way home, stomach clenched tight with unease. I can't believe I managed to pierce Julian Caddell where it counts and convince him that the best route to ensure his payday was to free me, allowing me to go back on tour.

Money really does talk.

I'm one step closer to getting my freedom. I'll collect my check at the end of the tour, a check that will now go directly to him. Liberating Lacey and me from his wrath for good.

Triumph curls my lips despite how swollen and dry they are. It's not lost on me that people walking the busy streets with their sun-kissed shoulders and saltwater-waved hair are all gawking at me like I just climbed out of a gutter.

I hear several clicks from what I assume are cameras as I stroll by, unhurried.

Abandoning the need to sink into an alleyway and call

for help, I feel like I've won the right to walk down the street with my head held high despite my unruly appearance. I survived being kidnapped. I survived being beaten like a grown-ass man and not the one-hundred-thirty-pound female that I am. I close my mind as my feet guide me home on autopilot, knowing that somehow Lindsey, the band's PR lady, will spin this incident into a fable that the world will believe. There's no way in hell she'll allow the band's name to be tarnished by my almost-comatose walk of shame.

There's a giant rip at the sleeve of my shirt. Two of my fingernails are missing, and my nose feels like it was used as a human punching bag. I'm afraid that my eye socket is broken. If anyone should cower though, it's not me. It's Knox and Julian because if our encounter has taught them anything, it's that I'm not going down without a fight.

My feet ache as I climb the stairs to my apartment. Trying to hold on to some control is futile at this point. I can't barge through the door looking like death while crying my eyes out, so I sniffle back my tears, caging them once more.

Even when I begged for death, I did it out of spite. I did it to protect my sister. I vow to turn the tables on Caddell. The weak woman he thought I was gained a fiery pair of wings in that basement. Ridding him from our lives once and for all is all I care about.

I'm barely able to control my gasp of surprise when I fling open the door to my apartment, only to find every member of Kings of Jupiter in my living room, including Jupiter himself.

The shock of their presence hits me full force when the room goes quiet. Several pairs of eyes widen in a mixture of relief, mingled with what appears to be pure terror in their gazes, no doubt from my appearance. Their silent frowns convey a clear message—they care about me. The thought of that alone hurts worse than the back of Caddell's hand. Their looks of anguish only solidify what I already knew in my heart—I care about them too, and now, I have more people to protect with my life.

Like an old wound aching on a rainy day, I take one step inside my apartment, mind still colored with the memories of the days before ... before the world goes black.

A RAINBOW OF EYES, skin tones, and worried expressions stare at me wordlessly as I peel open my eyes. Correction: one eye. The one that isn't completely swollen shut. My vision is blurry. Fortunately for me, my other senses kick in. I'm relieved to be alive.

The sound of a sharp intake of breath rings louder than the sound of the loud machine beeping seconds before I feel a pair of arms around my neck.

"Easy," I muster, my warning broken off mid-sentence. An inexplicable feeling of happiness brushes over me.

A soft gulp escapes my hugger. "I'm sorry, sis. I'm just so glad you're okay. I'm so sorry."

*Lacey.*

I want to retort. Tell her that she has no reason to be sorry. I want to hug her back, tell her that everything is going to be fine. That I have a plan.

My heart thuds in my chest as tears stream down her face, little pieces of pink hair sticking to her cheeks. I'm already emotionally spent, seeing her come undone in front of me. I've only just awoken, and I already feel like both my mind and body ran a marathon. Settling my head, I nestle onto a soft pillow, breathing a sigh of relief as my eye meets hers.

She's alive and safe. That's all I've ever wanted.

I'm disappointed when a series of questions, rambled off by various unnamed voices, interrupts our exchange, leaving my head throbbing in an excruciating melody.

"What happened?" Oliver's timid voice registers through the onslaught. His voice sounds puny, scared.

I turn my head to meet his concerned glare and find his mouth twisted with worry.

There's no time to agonize over how to explain what happened without bringing more danger to their doorstep.

Another gravelly voice demands my attention. "You had me ... us ... worried."

I know without turning my head in the opposite direction to sneak a glance at the blond-haired drummer that it's Cannon speaking. I'm remarkably proud of his blunt admission. He's made strides in silencing his dark, brooding persona that he hides behind like his massive drum set. I can't fight the magnetic urge to turn toward him any longer. When I face the man staring back at me, he doesn't appear to be worried in the slightest about his reputation, his tortured identity, or his emotional admission. No. The man staring back at me is torn only by conflicting feelings that he's trying to harness, though he's failing miserably. I want to tell him that he can speak freely. That I want to hear his words more than I want this incessant machine to keep beeping so loudly. I need to be overcome by the intense smile that he fights but loses against more than I need my next breath.

"I missed you. So. Much. I thought ... I can't ... lose you, Sophia. You're the ..." He shakes his head, collecting his thoughts. "You mean a lot to me," the brute of a drummer says before looking around the room. "To all of us."

His declaration adds to my sudden bewilderment. Was he truly that scared to lose me? Has Mazen not told him about my son yet? Surely, if he knew I've been keeping secrets, he wouldn't be showering me with this deep emotion and blunt adoration, right?

I feel my hospital mattress dip before a dainty pair of hands grasp on to my arm. I'm painfully aware of the IV that is plunged into my vein by the way that Vanna's soft embrace nearly misses the tubing.

"What he means to say is, we're all relieved that you're okay. Safe. Alive. I'm going to drag them to the waiting room before I fetch Mazen. I think that's him I hear right now." She tilts her head slightly, like she's straining to listen to something. "For hours, he's been yelling at everyone who walks by in a pair of scrubs, demanding to know why you haven't woken up yet."

The dam on my eyes breaks, like my heart. The waterworks flow freely.

"I didn't mean to make you cry."

"Sorry." I struggle to get the words out. My throat dry. "Why would he care?"

"Don't you dare be sorry. We're sorry. We had no idea about your ... past."

There goes my secret. Though I don't know if she's referring to the monster in it or the ghost of my deceased child.

Forging on, Vanna continues, "Why wouldn't he care is the bigger question? It seems that you've checkmated the world's biggest bachelors with your charm. You and I both know it's that magic pussy though." Her smile is wide, her teeth strikingly white against her tan glow. "You're their queen, Sophia. Make them bow. It'd do them some good to be put in their place for once."

I want to say so many things, ask so many questions. What does she know about my past? Why does she think my kitty—using the P-word sometimes makes me cringe if it's not said between a sheet and a warm male body—is golden enough to tame almost an entire band?

The intensity in the room shifts from the relief seen in my friends'—family's—eyes to discomfort as my heart rate increases. Its increase is mimicked by the sound on the overhead machine. It chimes loudly, echoing in the private hospital room we're in.

Words die on my tongue when my brain decides it's had too much, and my extreme fatigue, paired with the cocktail of pain medication flowing freely in my IV, pulls me into its tight grasp again.

What must be hours later, I wake to a black sky and a nearly empty room. Covering my face with my hands, I'm careful not to touch my pounding nose. When I glance up, I'm surprised to see Mazen Wilde's intoxicating eyes watching me intently. Something along the lines of relief and a dash of indifference take up residence on his handsome face.

*Handsome?* These must be top-tier drugs running through my veins.

"I can smell myself." Breaking the silence, I gesture to my gown-covered body under the white hospital blanket that wouldn't keep a flea warm—it's so thin. "Help me get to the shower, please? I know if I can smell myself, we have an issue." I honest to God don't know what day it is or the last time I showered.

His straight-lined mouth gives nothing away as he rises from his chair. In one step that leaves me wondering if he's turned into a vampire—*Team Edward for life*—he's at my bedside.

I've been the victim of Mazen's harsh moods on many occasions. Far too many, it seems, for the time in which I've been working for them ... tattooing them. Though, if I'm being honest, thanks to Julian Caddell, I now remember that I know Mazen, or knew him in a previous era of our lives.

There's a heavy silence that lingers between us. Even in the dead of night, it's deafening. I fight through the cobwebs of trying to figure out Mazen, redirecting my thoughts to my life that has been turned upside down. It's utter chaos. The last thing I have time for is trying to piece together the man in front of me. Still, I can't swallow down the need to stop giving a crap about him and focus my mind on other very important matters.

Vanna's comment about him threatening the entire hospital staff sends a current of curiosity through me. For someone who knows without a shadow of a doubt that I kept a huge secret from him ... them ... he doesn't appear to hold the same distaste in his eyes as he did when he bid me farewell and watched me board his private plane.

I'm suddenly hyper-focused on him. Everything about him.

The way that his large hands—one covered in the jellyfish I tattooed on him—hold on to the side of my bed railing with more force than necessary. I'm fearful he's going to crack the hardened plastic in half. To the glint in his eyes that cuts through the dimly lit room, seemingly staring into my soul.

Hooded eyes, which once held hatred toward me when his friend hired me to follow their band on tour, have morphed into something akin to the color of a silvery fog..

It's as if a painter swiped away and erased the tarnished steel that once held my gaze. Those same eyes now hold a muddled stare. The both of us feel confused ... chaotic... cautious.

It's not until Mazen offers a wordless dip of his chin, a brief nod, that the spell is broken, and I'm slammed back into reality. I swallow down my foolishness. His heated glare has nothing to do with feelings of relief that I'm alive. Most likely, he's contemplating smothering me with my own pillow for lying and deceiving him.

He turns his back, gracing me with the sight of him in ... sweatpants? Why is he dressed so casually? Thoughts race as wildly as a stampede of horses through my drug-altered brain. My thoughts still aren't in order when he reappears a moment later and lowers the rail to my hospital bed.

Moving my IV rod out of the way so I don't trip over the long tubing that's connected to it, I breathe in a smidgen of relief. Thoughts of him strangling me with said clear tubing infiltrate my mind as we stand in place, rooted to the floor. Call it guilt or my subconscious screaming at me, demanding my mouth to move when I'm able to weave together a sentence, an answer to the question he left me with.

*"Where is your son?"*

Mazen has every right to put me out of my misery, using the only tools at his disposal. I probably wouldn't even put up much of a fight.

Any fight I had has vanished.

Caddell stole that too. The only shred of willpower floating through my veins is knowing that if I bow out of this life, Caddell will turn his attention to my sister. Demanding she pay his debt, just like I inherited it from my dad.

# 8

## ACT OF CHIVALRY

SOPHIA

"YOU HAVE TO WALK, unless you want me to get the aide to give you a sponge bath." The lack of animosity, of resentment in his tone tells me he doesn't want to strangle me to death. He sounds ... tender, earnest even.

My worry evaporates when Mazen reaches behind my back, grasping the sides of my hospital gown and holding them in place. The gap of material closes in his fist at my spine.

"Let me help you. It's a little drafty, or I can get you some of the clothes Vanna got for you from the Target down the street." Silently, he bends to help me slide on a pair of slippers I've never seen before and then offers me his arm.

There's a boyish charm to his demeanor. It calls out to the still somewhat foggy recollection of him in my mind. Mazen is assessing me like he knows he's struck a chord in my memory. Still, I bite back the truth and take a step toward the private bathroom in my room.

"I want to shower first."

He nods.

"Then, I'll take the clothes."

"Yeah. Yeah. Sure. That works."

We walk a few feet until we reach the door to the secluded bathroom. I want to make a quip about his sudden act of chivalry. Deciding against it, I hold on to this strange peace that has settled between us. We've always been hot and cold. Our rapport with one another is as confusing as constructing an origami swan out of newspaper. This change between us feels tangible, like we've turned a new leaf.

Mazen's nearness is as disturbing as it is exciting. I want to ask him where my sister and everyone else went. I want to ask him if he knows about my injuries and how long I'll feel like complete garbage. To inquire what day it is and how long I was asleep for. I want to know why he's wearing a cape of calmness, not bombarding me with questions I know are lingering in his mind.

Mustering up the energy to ask any of it is too big of a task as I push my way into the bathroom. Instead, I take a page from his book, swallow down my troubling questions and let him plant me in front of the foggy mirror before he shuts the door behind him, offering a solitude he doesn't know I don't want.

The bathroom is already filled with steam, its warmth enveloping me. A snide retort about him being overly gentlemanly is on the tip of my tongue. I swallow it down, concealing all emotion, even my favored armor—humor. Preparing myself for a heavy dose of reality, I take a long, deep inhale and wipe away the fog on the mirror. Horror stares back at me.

Complete devastation starts at the soles of my feet and travels up each leg until it finally engulfs my entire body in its cocoon. My once-ivory-tinged skin tone is now a deep purple with flakes of yellow in several areas surrounding my left eye socket. The opposite cheek has a dusting of mauve alongside my jawline. My nose is covered in white bandages.

*A sight to behold I am.*

On a sharp intake of breath, I gaze at the woman in my reflection. I look as battered and broken as I feel on the inside. Long gone is the resilience I once wore like a cape. A cloak of courage. The woman whose eyes I connect with looks ghostly, hollow even. She's a shell of the spunky soul I was just days ago.

I was assaulted on the inside just as clearly as I was on the outside.

There are no words to describe how utterly shattered I am. It's not just because of my appearance. I'm not that flipping vain. It's ... everything. The fight-or-flight stamina that rushed through my bloodstream is gone. I might have walked away from that basement, only to find myself in a new cage.

I feel completely defeated.

Trying to rein in my emotion, to keep it in check so that Mazen doesn't hear the wails that are fighting like hell to break free, steals the rest of my energy. It's a futile attempt because the next thing that happens in a slew of shitty things is that my legs give out. My body goes crashing to the cold tile floor in a thud that reverberates down to my core. The gown that he held shut is now puddled around me.

I'm left sitting on the ground, as confused and unclothed as when I entered this world.

Violent sobs break free from my lungs without prompt. Years of pent-up emotions spill out of me like a bucket overflowing in a rainstorm. My reflection is just the icing on the cake to everything that Julian Caddell stole from me. He took my heart, pulverized it, and placed it back into my gaping chest. Then patted me on the back like the good little payday that I am to him.

I yield to the compulsive sobs that leave hot lines running down my cheeks when the bathroom door creaks open. My mind and body, already on high alert, go rigid. My glistening pale face freezes when I go as still as a statue, immobilized by fear so irrational that I know I'll battle it alone for years to come.

"It's been a minute. Wanted to see that you're okay."

"No." My voice cracks. "Don't come in. I'm okay. Be out shortly." Lies. They're all I've ever fed him, apparently.

Reading through them, Mazen opens the door and steps inside. I wonder if he so easily cast aside my other lie as well. It's not lost on me that his eyes remain glued to the opposite wall, pinned just above my head.

"It's okay to *not* be okay."

That's all the permission I need for the dam to break once more. Tears cascade down my cheeks like a waterfall.

"What can I do?" His frame inches closer to my own.

Though I can tell by the pull in his shoulders that he's hesitant to embrace me. His stance is locked in place for a moment before he moves to kneel on the floor in front of me.

No words. Only sniffles are offered.

"I need you to tell me what to do. *Rosella*, please."

With the gap between us now closed, his large hands hold on to each of my exposed shoulders. His eyes lock on to mine. They don't waver once.

"I don't deserve your trust. I know I haven't earned it, but I can help. Let me help you even if you have no reason to grant me this."

How many blows can one woman take?

The next words from his mouth cut me like a thousand shards of glass. "Sophia." My name is a plea on his parted lips. "Let me be what *you* need right now. Let me shoulder this burden. I won't fail you. You *can* trust me."

All the years of meaningless, faceless sex catches up to me as I allow my eyes to meet his—Mazen Wilde, the alleged father of my child, the man who just pledged to pull me from the wreckage I'm drowning in. He's looking at me like I'm both his saving grace and the detonator of a bomb.

Reckless.

Trusting him will be my undoing.

My naked body crashes into his embrace with so much force that it causes him to stumble off his kneecaps, his ass landing on the floor beneath him. The moment our bodies collide, he scoots backward to prevent us from tumbling over. Forcefully, his back presses into the wall. Mazen's hand hits the light switch in his haste to keep our bodies upright, and the room goes dark. Mazen welcomes me into his arms, shielding me with a strong hold. I hug him back like I'll die if I don't. My very existence will cease, like the memory of us when we first met did. He squeezes me back just as tightly, as if saying, *I vow to go with you when the detonator is pulled.*

There's beauty in being naked in front of someone in the dark. A certain level of trust forms. Water sprays hot in the shower still. I imagine it will turn cold before long.

Mazen's mouth finds the shell of my ear. "Trust that I won't let you go again," he whispers.

His plea packs a punch so forceful that my thoughts flounder between the past and present.

*Tangled in sheets and his arms.*

*Flying down my apartment steps, unable to shield my stomach from each wooden ledge.*

*Raw agony as Roman's premature body was cut from mine, and he was rushed to the NICU.*

*The surgeon sewing me up, knowing that my uterus was lying in a metal basin somewhere next to him.*

*Knox's face, lined in hostility as he punched me in the face not once, but three times before he used my hair as a leash, dragging me down the basement steps toward his awaiting uncle.*

"Breathe, Rosella."

I feel the warmth of his palm when he covers the area over my left breast in the most platonic embrace I've ever felt.

It's as if he's grounding me by both his touch and his words.

Mazen's voice is pained. "I need you to take a deep breath, or I'm going to pull that red wire and call for a nurse."

He's drowning under the weight of my unspoken sorrow, and I'm suddenly the anchor he's seeking reprieve from.

I gasp for air. "Mazen."

Every single memory, suspended behind a door in my mind that wouldn't unlock, floods into the forefront of my mind all at once. I feel like my brain has been comatose for years, though a part of me knows that I'm just naive. I'm a stupid whore of a woman who uses men and sex to feel something ... anything ... other than alone. We shared more than our bodies the night we met. That hard reality wafts over me as my breathing grows more labored.

There was no accident that stole my memories.

Only shame.

Shame that is lodged in my throat.

I blocked it out, every detail about the stranger who had grown up to be Mazen Wilde, rock star extraordinaire. A subconscious decision to protect my heart at all costs from a world that had already taken too much. There's no one to blame but myself and my constant need to numb a heart that was broken, damaged beyond repair by my mother's death. I let my grief devour me as my body consumed as much insincere sex as I could. I was irresponsible.

Evidence of my recklessness is now standing before me, clad in black, like my battered, on-the-verge-of-death heart. The man has the power to undo the rest of me like a ball of yarn.

Memories race like they're on a high-speed chase through my mind, each one vying for my attention, begging for me to piece them all together. To make sense of their madness. To make sense of the connection I feel toward him. I've always felt toward him. Yet, as he calls out to me, not with my name Sophia, but *Rosella*, a tidal wave of memories hits me at once. Forcing me to see past the carefully woven facade that he has crafted together over the last decade. He's as guilty as I am for guarding his heart.

The tattoo conference where we met.

The dark-haired ink virgin who flirted with me in my chair.

The same dark-haired guy who bought me a drink at the bar, who lured me into his deceptive web after charming me with his innocence.

The wild night of sex that left me aching in the best way for several days following it.

The morning after, when I awoke in an empty bed, nothing but a torn piece of paper remaining from the night before.

A note that read, *Your crux is the moral war in your head. Rise above it, and you can conquer everything.* It was signed with a single letter—the initial M.

*Mazen is M.*

The harsh reality of my past stabs at my chest like a knife. I'm impaled by a truth so ugly, so earth-shattering that I almost wish Caddell had taken me out. A deep pain gnaws from the inside out of my already-hurt heart.

*How could I not have realized it sooner?*

Mazen has known all along. The truth has been written in his eyes. He's been living with a ghost from his past.

I feel as if my throat is closing, a tunnel collapsing inward on itself. I'm on the threshold of surrendering to the nagging voice in my mind begging me to tell him the truth. Right here, right now. To spill the beans on everything, Roman's existence included, as if he doesn't already know.

Is this why he tortured me in the beginning? Making cruel remarks, fucking all but a light socket in front of me. Was he punishing me for not remembering him? Our sordid past, a past I didn't remember we even shared.

*"Where is your son?"*

The answer about *our* son causes my body to tremble from head to toe. The swell of pain in my chest is beyond tears. It's beyond words, and only I'm to blame.

It would be easy to cast some blame on Mazen too. The devastatingly beautiful man in front of me.

He left me the morning after a wild night of unprotected sex.

He left with nothing more than a scribbled note on a hotel pad. No name. No contact information.

Anger lights like a lantern in the pit of my stomach. I will not hold the weight of all this on my shoulders. I refuse to be the scapegoat for both of us.

Mazen's not the only victim of our wretched past.

*I* went through my pregnancy alone.

*I* went through the life-altering surgery that brought our son into this world after being pushed down the steps by Caddell's goons.

*I* birthed a child prematurely, only for him to succumb to his injuries a few days later.

*I* buried our son.

*I* carry the agony, the memory of holding his body—my heart—frozen in time.

And yet, despite the hurricane of emotions threatening to leak down my cheeks once more, I know this truth will break him. It would break even the stablest person, and despite the carefully coordinated mask Mazen has constructed over the years, he's not stable. He's a shell of the boy who lost his kid sister. He's eaten alive by his own depraved grief and guilt. It's bled into his music through lyrics crafted from despair.

Over the last couple of weeks touring with the band, I've learned that Mazen is a lot of things. He's condescending. He's cocky, entitled, and so fucking sure of himself that his arrogance drips off him like water droplets.

He's also *deep.* Carrying a tune that is only fueled by heartache. A beat that can only be strummed together from firsthand emotional torment. Like most musicians, their sorrow-leaden souls guide their music. It's what connects listeners to certain songs. Lyrics resonate in our hearts. From feelings of not being alone or understood, lyrics have the power to bind us, searing our souls in a way that many different forms of art lack. Music can encourage, ignite, and soothe.

As sure as I am that the sun will rise in the morning, I'm sure my answer to his burning question—*"Where is your son?"*—would wreck Mazen, sending him tumbling into a place that not even music could pull him back from.

The thought of looking him in his slate-metal eyes, telling him that he fathered a child—a child who is no longer alive, no less—makes my stomach twist. I refuse to be the reason for his demise. Even if the truth eats away at me from the inside out. Julian Caddell might have hinted that I was keeping secrets, but to my knowledge, based on the fact that Mazen hasn't totally shunned me yet, he didn't tell him about his suspicion that he's my son's father. I intend to keep it that way.

Swallowing down my own angst, I pale at the enormity of the secret that is cemented between us. It's thick and sour. I decide right now that it's a truth I'm prepared to take to my grave as unspoken words slide down my throat.

A beat passes before he finally says, "Sophia."

"Thank you for not leaving me alone." It's the only thing I can muster. My thoughts a mess.

I dead-bolt everything else I desperately want to add deep inside, smothering the desire to do what I know is *right* and tell him. Silently begging for his trust, like he begged for me moments ago.

Mazen is mine to protect. Even if my feelings for him are confusing, frightening, and muddled. There's no paternity test to prove Mazen is indeed Roman's father, and I hope there never is because no one—and I mean, no one—deserves to lose a child. Much less mourn one they didn't even know they had lost.

Hiding the shame in my tone, I attempt to guard this secret as best as I can. "I just needed to gather my thoughts."

We've been sitting together long enough for the water to turn cold.

Nodding, Mazen accepts my answer before saying,

"Let's get you clean." He eyes the battle wounds littering my face. "It's the least I can do for allowing you to board that plane."

"It's probably cold now."

"Then, we'll sit here until it has time to warm up again. Do you want to talk about it?" His voice penetrates my ears, though I don't really register his question. "The nurse threatened to call security when I refused to leave you after visiting hours ended tonight." He sighs when he realizes my mind is elsewhere but keeps rambling. "I promised to double her salary by morning if she turned the other cheek."

My head pounds with every word he speaks. The battle waging inside consumes my every thought as the shackle I just placed on the truth begs to be unlocked and set free.

Mazen's voice becomes muffled, my thoughts ringing louder, echoing in my mind.

*Tell him.*

I can't.

*He has a right to know he fathered a child.*

He'll hate me for hiding it.

*He'll hate you anyway. For not remembering him.*

I'll never be able to forget him again.

I shrink from the cast iron of his watchful glare that cuts through my avalanche of thoughts.

What kind of woman forgets she slept with Mazen Wilde? His face is plastered everywhere from billboards— that taunted me for years, begging me to remember him—to websites and apps. His memory has prodded at my subconscious for years, only for realization to suddenly slap me in the face.

"Where'd you go there?" he whispers. His Italian accent thick, heady.

I feel his warm hands bracing themselves on my shoulders again. Gently shaking me from my stupor, trying to gain my attention once more.

Mazen's voice finally lulls me back. "Do you want me to call Ollie or Cannon?"

The question is loaded.

I'm not entirely sure how to answer him. Of course, I want him to call them both. I want us—all four of us—to ride off into the sunset shacked up in the bed of their tour bus together. That's not what he's asking, implying. He wants to know if I need them here instead of him.

That hurts my heart a little.

I steady a look at him through the darkness before I huff, lean forward, and hit the switch on the wall. A fluorescent light illuminates our bodies. We're still as close as humanly possible where we sit on the bathroom floor. I look at Mazen. Really look at him. Not with lust or amazement of his musical talent, but in awe of the possibility that he is the father of my son. Even without a DNA test, I have an inkling that he is. I feel it in my soul. We created a life together all those years ago.

Roman had a wealth of dark hair, just like Mazen. His skin was dark, tanned by their shared Italian roots. I close my eyes, thoughts drifting to Mazen praising his name in Italian when he took his first steps. A moment later, another picture comes into view. It's Mazen gifting Roman his first guitar. Nothing but pure pride is etched on his face.

My chest aches because these thoughts, hopes, will never come to pass.

The truth is on the tip of my tongue. Foolishly, I bite down, almost drawing blood, refusing to give in. I can't bring myself to say it. To voice the words begging to be unleashed into the world. Instead, I cry out, reaching for him to hold me once again. I'm desperate for his touch.

When we collide again, my arms offer a sliver of truth, an olive branch.

He holds me as I cry. Not Oliver or Cannon. It's Mazen who bribed the nurse and was awarded a night alone with me. It's Mazen who's held my fragmented heart together in his tight hold. It's Mazen Wilde who I want here with me tonight, no one else.

"I want you to call them."

A quick shudder of his body follows my request.

"Tell them that I'm okay and I'll see them tomorrow."

I sense his relief like it's my own.

He nods repeatedly before saying, "Shit."

"What?"

"I broke my phone after your plane left. I'll have to use the hospital's to call Ollie. Give me a minute. Stay here, and I'll be right back." He goes to stand.

Still high on the only truth I can muster, the word, "Wait," blurts from my mouth.

Instantly, Mazen freezes, knees still bent.

"I remember. Everything." The next sentence flies out in a rush of garbled syllables. "The convention. The bar. The night we were together. Your note. I remember it all. I don't know why I forgot or how it was even possible to block out that period of my life. I'm sorry, Mazen. I ... I remember everything."

"What?" His question is a whisper on his lips, a plea.

My outreached hands cup his face, guiding him back down so that we're eye level once more.

"I remember you. Us. Chicago."

"Finally. Thank the fucking stars." The relief in his voice threatens to shatter my resolve. "Rosella." His voice is pained, though I know it's excitement in his tone. "I've been waiting so long for you to remember. Fuck."

Warm arms blanket me faster than I was prepared for, and in a second, I'm straddling his lap, his face buried in my neck. I should blush because I'm still naked, but I don't. I've never felt more cherished or protected in my entire life than I do right now.

"You remember." His breath is warm against the hollow of my neck.

"I didn't at first. Not when we met ... again. Then—"

"What triggered your memories?"

Caddell's backhand must've been stronger than I thought. It beat Mazen's memory back into the forefront of my mind. His question hangs between us as we sit in the quiet of the bathroom, two strangers tethered together by a bigger secret I'm not ready to share. A truth that could crumble a life. *His* life. I hold back, only offering my recollection of knowing him.

I decide to offer him a semi-truth, admitting that since Caddell and I are both from Chicago the connection must've jogged my memory of Mazen, and my night spent in each other's arms eons ago.

The rest of it I conceal, including my plan to finish the tour and pay off Caddell and the fact that he let me go on nothing but a promise. One that he and I both know I'll make good on.

The lives of everyone I care about depend on it.

The truth could abruptly end my time touring with the band. Not being able to fulfill my contract and tattoo them on tour means not cashing in and possible death when Caddell shows back up to collect and I have nothing to offer but my life. This uneasy feeling that has lingered in my chest since receiving Lacey's frantic call is embedded deep. It's now doubled—no, tripled—in size.

*One earth-shattering dilemma at a time*, I tell myself.

"I'm going to kill that bastard for doing this." He cups my jaw, his finger grazing against my cheek. "I don't know why, after weeks of living with you, you now remember. I don't even fucking care. I'm so relieved."

"I didn't realize you cared so much."

"Seriously." He pauses for a breath.

I don't know if it's a statement or a question. When his sword-colored eyes meet mine again, the glare that encompasses his face says more than his words.

"You have no clue how much I care. I've loved your ghost for ten goddamn years, Rosella. It would have been excruciating, but I'd have waited ten more just to hear you say you remembered me."

*A rock star and a lying tattoo artist, reunited at last.*

# 9

## OBSESSED FAN

MAZEN

THREE DAYS AGO, the trajectory of our lives went off target like a derailed train blinded by the cusp of a sunrise. The soundtrack of my life morphs into "Would You Still Be There" by Of Mice & Men. The lyrics resonating deep in my soul.

If I hadn't allowed her to go to the airport that evening ...

I banish the thought for the umpteenth time, refocusing on the thoughts that should be consuming me. Sophia was discharged with a clean bill of health. Thankfully, her nose was not broken, just severely bruised.

*She's tougher than even her hard exterior lets on.*

The physician told us collectively that her outward bruises would fade. It's the internal ones that will take the most time. The ones the fucker Caddell left on her heart.

Lindsey shifts in my peripheral vision, the gems on her sparkling headband catching my attention.

"You think the media will buy it?" I ask, refusing to let

out the puff of smoke my lungs are holding hostage. There's never a shortage of herb when you're a rock star. One of the perks of my chosen career path.

"Do I think the media will buy a fabricated story being fed to them on a silver platter? Why, yes. Yes, I absolutely do. It's insulting that you'd think otherwise," Lindsey says, reassuring me of her persuasion in the limelight.

"Pull the trigger then. I think we all agree that we need to spin this in our favor before the masses make their own assumptions."

Oliver rubs his hands down his cheeks roughly. As the self-nominated jokester of our group, he's been anything but funny since the incident. His serious side is a version I haven't seen since we were kids.

"I agree. The last thing we need is the tabloids coming after her, exposing private details that don't concern anyone." He shifts, looking at our drummer.

Cannon nods lazily in agreement. He's been on edge. Quieter than normal. Which is odd since he wouldn't shut the hell up since he declared his unyielding adoration for Sophia.

We've all changed, if I'm being honest. I get it. Lost in our own feelings, trying to make sense of what happened to Sophia. Even more so for me because my stupid fucking traitorous heart longs to be near her now that she's voiced her recollection of our night spent together.

Try as I might, it's hard to ignore the giant red flag that waves over her head like a flashing neon sign—a reminder that she's not only mine to worry over, but my two best friends' as well. Still, I find my mind consumed by her. Fighting it is futile. Trust me, I've tried and failed miserably. I *wanted* to hate her. An even bigger part of me just simply wants her now. Even with the secrets that still loom between us.

When I saw her again in her tattoo studio, it was foolish to think that feigning any malice toward her would work in my favor. Ten years of hate has nothing on the infatuation that has built over the last couple of weeks. Sophia is the sun, and we're all just circulating around her, hoping that some of her rays find us, forcing our dark, tainted souls to glow, basking in the warmth of her wide smile.

We're all perplexed by her cavalier attitude. She seems unbothered by it all. Aloof to the fact that she was kidnapped and held for ransom—that I never even received because I'd shattered my cell on the concrete beneath my feet when I watched her plane disappear into the night sky.

The result of my stupidity is on her face. The proof is deep purple and yellow. The sight alone fuels my desire for revenge.

Hell, nothing says you've fallen into a puddle of feelings than waging a war in her honor, and that's exactly what we plan to do. Caddell will pay for hurting Sophia. We just have to lure him out, despite her begging us not to get involved. If she thinks for one second that now that we know the truth of what happened—what transpired with him and his dickhead of a nephew, Knox—that they'll live to tell the tale, she's sadly mistaken.

We might be America's heartthrobs, shoved into the limelight due to our jobs. Forced into the glitz and glamor of it all. At the end of the day, we're just a group of misfits, juveniles who bonded over booze, tits, and music in our garage with nothing to lose.

Except now, as grown men, we have everything to lose.

"We're going with *a disgruntled fan attacked her outside*

*of the concert venue.* Jealousy is a bitch," Lindsey says, tugging my thoughts back to the present.

I'd much rather let my mind wander, contemplating what we'll do once we locate her attacker.

"Works for me." I shrug, taking a long hit from my one-hitter.

"Well, it *doesn't* work for me."

All heads simultaneously turn in the direction of Sophia's voice.

Sauntering into the shared living room of our suite, she's dressed in comfortable attire. A pair of pajama pants and matching camisole. Looking beautiful beyond words despite the discoloration lingering on her face.

"No one will believe a demented, Mazen-obsessed fan could overpower me. I'm tougher than you're all giving me credit for." She offers a weak smile. Another reminder that this cool approach she's taken to her kidnapping is a front. "Not to mention, who would be that obsessed with Mazen?"

I bite back my own smile, knowing that her smart-ass retort is as good of a sign as any that she'll be just fine in time. Even if I know her jab is also a show, a facade, now that she remembers me fully.

"You'd be surprised." Lindsey shakes her head. "Your fake boyfriend over there is a hot commodity. Don't ask me why though." She rolls her shoulders. "I knew him before he hit puberty and became"—she waves me up and down—"all of that. He could have been an extra on those commercials for prescription acne creams back in the day. Trust me when I say America wouldn't have batted an eyelash at the version he was before he covered his body in ink and hit the gym."

"You both wound me." I take another draw, welcoming

a lungful of smoke like it will somehow placate the questions I'm keeping bottled inside.

After the initial shock of the event started to wear off, three of the four of us—Murphy was the only one not hounding Sophia relentlessly—pushed her for answers, ones that Lacey couldn't give us. All we got was a generic, well-thought-out version of events, curated to leave out important information. Information she continues to hide from us.

The story she gave us was that her father owes a debt to Julian Caddell, and he and his nephew, Knox, came after her for said debt. She did tell us about the brick and the frantic phone call she'd received from her little sister that started this whole trip back to Tampa. Not much more about her encounter with them and absolutely nothing more about what caused her to suddenly remember our shared past.

Sophia agreed to come back on tour with us under a couple of conditions. One, Lacey would be joining us for the remainder of the tour. She said she refused to leave her alone again. And two, we wouldn't probe for more information or hunt Caddell down and dismember him limb from limb for laying a hand on her.

Nonetheless, in addition to her demands, we as a group, decided to park the whole *Sophia had a child and never told us* bomb that was dropped—well, delivered to us ... *me*—choosing to focus on the more pressing situation: our live-in tattoo artist/cohabitee/spit swapper was kidnapped and beaten. I, of course, tried to veto the unanimous agreement.

I'm torn between wanting her to heal and fighting against the nagging feeling in the pit of my stomach that tells me that there's something she's still keeping from us. Aside from the whole *she birthed a child* thing. Why else would this Caddell guy have the birth certificate sent directly to me? Questions gnaw at my mind before my attention is drawn back to the people in the room as Ollie calls out to Sophia.

"Come over here. You should be relaxing." His attention quickly turns to me. An attempt to calm the room slides from his mouth. "Do you remember when you almost went blind?"

"Don't you fucking dare." I laugh gruffly. "What is this, the roast of Mazen Wilde?"

"It can't be worse than Justin Bieber's roast," Oliver quips. "That shit was brutal."

I watch intently as Sophia obliges his request, sinking onto the sofa between him and Cannon, a smile curving her mouth. I want to make a joke about the three of them. Turn the attention and laughter from myself, pointing out the obvious—their relationship will never work. It's the biggest joke I've ever heard. Doomed from the start. When the tour ends, so does their little tryst, and that's only if I don't end them first because I'm territorial like that. I want to whip my dick out and pee on her leg, marking her as mine.

*Even if I'm desperate to be included in the train wreck waiting to happen.*

A sudden nagging pulls at the torn and tattered strings attached to my heart because while I want to poke fun at them, divert the attention from myself, I want to be a part of their little trio even more. I want Sophia to look at me with the same respect and yearning in her eyes that she does them.

I'm a paradox of fucking feelings.

Which is why I once again light up the object in my hand and take a puff, swallowing down a lungful of smoke and my raging jealousy.

On inhale, I spy Cannon's broad shoulders relaxing as

Sophia settles in between them. They visibly drop an inch or two at her close proximity. Another gust of jealousy climbs up my throat. I'm ready to spew something stupid that will undoubtedly make Sophia loathe my very existence when Oliver continues his story in spite of my request.

"Like I was saying, I think we were—what?—thirteen or something? I showed up at Maz's house, and he was crying. Dude was a mess. White dots covered his face like he had leprosy. He had heard from someone at school that toothpaste helped cure acne so he covered his face and then went to sleep. Not thinking that it would be rubbed into his eyes as he slept. When he woke up, he claimed he couldn't see. I remember when he opened the door. His eyes were bloodshot and glossy." My malicious best friend turns to face me. "Much like they are right now but for a very different reason."

"I think if I remember correctly, you proceeded to pee your pants in the foyer of my house from laughing so hard."

"We were both idiots." Ollie slides his arm behind Sophia's neck and shoulders. Extending his hand, he rubs Cannon's broad shoulder. "Not this one though. He was the keeper of the chaos."

Cannon refuses Ollie's bait. His jaw is fused shut. His attention is anywhere but trotting with us down memory lane.

Before Ollie can taunt our drummer again, Lindsey clears her throat. "Since everyone's here"—her framed eyes dart between the three Kings of Jupiter band members in the room—"mostly everyone—we need to discuss getting back on tour. I'll catch Murphy and his bride up later. We've added Prague back to the schedule. We'll circle back there first, then resume the final leg of the tour. Once the story goes viral, you'll earn enough sympathy that the fans will understand the delay in their concert. We're banking on it."

"You guys shouldn't have left to come after me." Sophia's usually strong timbre is meek. "Think of all the fans who spent their hard-earned money on those tickets or took off work to travel to see you. I'm sorry, Lindsey. I'm sure the label was thrilled that these morons took off, abandoning their fans."

"I won't lie. You're high up on their shit list. They'll get over it though. They don't have another option. That's why we rescheduled and promised that the Kings will perform their new song, 'You Stung Me.' They seemed to love it in Portugal. Matter of fact, it's been streamed more times than 'Heart on Fire,'" Lindsey proclaims like a proud mother, comparing the song I wrote after Sophia tattooed the jellyfish on my hand to our number one hit.

"Leave it to me to iron out the kinks. We'll make it up to your Czech fans, and all will be right in the world," says Lindsey.

Most of the songs we perform are about Sophia in some way. I sing into a packed arena night after night, pouring my soul into every syllable I expel, making women wanton with need. When I only want to look into Sophia's hauntingly dark green eyes, performing for her, my muse.

"Except for the fact that Caddell has Sophia under his thumb." Cannon's hefty statement hangs in the air.

*The brooding drummer returns.* Now, all is right in the world.

Blissfully oblivious of her hold on us, Sophia says, "This ordeal with Caddell has nothing to do with any of you. I appreciate the fact that we've all become close ... friends."

*Ouch.* I wonder if that stung Oliver and Cannon as much as it did me.

"I don't need your label to punish you, and I don't want your fans to suffer because you guys want to play my knights in shining armor. Caddell was an issue long before we met; he will be an issue long after. He's my issue though. Not yours. This isn't your battle to fight."

Oliver tightens his grasp on her shoulders, pulling her dainty body snug against his side. "You were kidnapped."

Sophia rolls her eyes, seemingly unaware of her effect on us. We already met without her and agreed that we'll hunt Caddell down and make him pay for hurting her.

"That's the least damage that Caddell and his minions have caused." Her lips tighten, almost as if her brain is catching up, and she knows she's shared too much.

"We're going to circle back to that in a minute." There's a placating tone in Oliver's voice that is unmistakable. "Let us just enjoy this sliver of peace, knowing that you're alive. You're safe. You're back with us where you belong. We can chat about business, revenge, all of that later on. Right now, I just want to sit here with you."

*What a smooth bastard.* Maybe he should start writing our songs.

Cannon jeers, eyes locking with mine across the room, "You know what I want to *chat* about? How it was his idea to let you board a plane by yourself in the middle of the night."

There it is, folks. A warning before shit hits the fan.

*Fuck.*

I steel my shoulders, preparing for the fight that is about to ensue. I'd have to be blind not to admit Cannon is a brawny fucker. While he's not much taller, he has plenty of mass on me—about thirty or so pounds. We've all brawled on more occasions than I can count on both hands. Being friends with a group of guys for more than two decades is ample time for us to have spoken with our fists instead of words, and it seems like Cannon has a lot to say right now.

I lift myself from the couch.

Cannon does the same.

Faintly, I hear Lindsey murmur under her breath, "*Children.*"

In a quick stride, Cannon positions himself in front of me. His hard chest pressed up against mine. There's no doubt that I can hold my own. I just wish Sophia weren't here to witness us scrapping like a pack of wild dogs—or what Lindsey said, children.

A petite leg slides in front of me like a human wedge between me and our drummer. We both glance down at the same time, seeing Sophia placing herself between us.

"I asked him—begged him—to bring me to the airport. If you need to be mad at someone, be mad at me. I brought this drama to your front door. Mazen was only helping. The last thing I need is to be worrying about tearing apart your band. I'm not worth it. Trust me."

Words freeze on all our tongues.

She genuinely doesn't get it.

She's our common ground. The tether holding us together.

*Our muse.*

# 10

# DON'T BE SHY

SOPHIA

I'M WEDGED between Oliver and Cannon when I wake, throat dry as a priest's sense of humor. I'm half tempted to nudge one or both awake to help take my mind off ... everything. Sex would surely be an escape from the reality that has literally barreled into me, captured my every waking thought, and left me feeling dirty and grimy.

Thanks to the endless questions about Caddell from the band—even after I asked them to let it go—and the incessant pings from my phone, alerting me that I've been tagged in another article about Mazen's crazed stalker who attacked me. I can't stop thinking about Lindsey's fabrication, the lie she perfected to cover up the truth, which just so happens to be masking another lie. Another female wanted to axe me because of my relationship with Mazen, and the best the universe could do was throw in the third-string quarterback. I'd feel like the laughingstock of the year if it wasn't for the hundreds—no, thousands—of Kings fans who keep the persistent comments rolling in with heart-eye emojis and well wishes.

*OMG, so glad you're safe. Luv you and Mazen 2gether.*

*Did Mazen attack the bitch and white-knight you?*

*Plz air his proposal online. I'll die (skull emoji) if I don't see it.*

A perfect distraction. It's what I *need* to keep my mind off the rumors, speculations, and lies Lindsey has blasted into the big web that caused this frenzy.

The warmth pooling between my legs from being sandwiched between these two mouthwateringly handsome men is enough to send me into a fury of wanton need. I'm appreciative for it all, of course. Thankful that the truth isn't being blasted for the world to see.

*Felon father left daughters to fend off mobster for money he laundered before he was framed for murder.*

Cannon shifts in his sleep. The dim light from the open bathroom door clings to his long torso, highlighting every mound of his perfectly sculpted stomach. My mind quickly pushes away any thought of the kidnapping and the media and is solely focused on the blond-haired bombshell of a man lying in front of me. Ripe for the taking.

His whole *bad-boy drummer* persona, tussled two-day-old waves, leave me wanting to mount him like he's Jax Teller's motorcycle. I'm ready to rev his engine. I could easily slide off my T-shirt, sleep pants, climb on top of him, and lower myself onto the large bulge in his sleep pants. In one swift motion that wouldn't warrant any prep on my behalf, I'd be fully sated.

My preoccupied mind is finally torn from the constant reel of bullshit it's been littered with. Resenting myself for the cloud of filthy images infiltrating my mind, I shake the thought of using Cannon.

*He's more than a dick for you to ride.*

It wouldn't be fair of me to use him. Even though the thought of him—both of them—being *more* is scarier than Knox's iron fist.

If the alleged news of Mazen being my son's father has taught me anything, it's that I need to stop thinking about sex so casually. Which is my singular thought as I chastise myself, peel my wedged body away from them, and beeline for the door. They've morphed into something far more than I'm willing to admit, even to myself. The two of them —three of them, if I'm being honest—haven't left my side in the days following the incident, as we're referring to it. I don't take their devotion to helping me heal or their constant concern or attention lightly, and because of that, I can't use them in the way that my body wants me to.

Even though I'm sure they'd both be willing to let my broken heart mend by allowing me to use their bodies for unadulterated pleasure. I clench my thighs again as I turn the bedroom door handle, sliding into the large, dark hallway of the suite we're in and make my way toward the kitchen.

Lacey is sound asleep on the living room sofa when I turn the corner. Everyone agreed that she is safer with us than staying at our apartment alone. Though I offered her my room and said I'd bunk with Oliver, she refused. Even at our apartment, where she had her own bedroom, I'd always find her asleep on the couch.

She'll be tagging along with me for the rest of the tour, and when this is all over, I'll collect my check and sever my connection to the band. I know their tour manager is counting down the days. Putting distance between us at the end of this is the only way to ensure their safety from Caddell hurting one or all of them just to spite me.

I spot a golden-rimmed bar cart adjacent to the kitchen as I plod forward. Discarding my thirst for water, I step toward the cart and pour a mouthful of honey-colored liquid into my mouth, straight from the decanter. This is exactly what I need to numb my mind enough to fall back asleep. The first shot of amber goes down like a gulp of thumbtacks. The second is smoother. By the third mouthful, I'm a renowned bourbon connoisseur.

Leaning back against the wall, I take in my surroundings. It's still bewildering that this is my life. I'm the personal tattoo artist for a famous rock band, and I'm sleeping with two of its members. Heat warms my cheeks, and it's not from the bourbon.

I stand like a creep, watching my sister sleep on the couch, pink-dyed locks hanging over the side. She looks so peaceful, safe. Not a bruise on her body. I intend to keep it that way. Which is why I've always tackled things on my own. Maybe it's foolish of me to want to protect her. She's no longer a child that I've been forced to raise. She's an adult, an equal. There's still a part of me that wants to protect her, an even bigger part that wants to spare her from Caddell's wrath by any means necessary.

If the tables were reversed and he got to her before me … I choke down another gulp in an attempt to rid the image from my mind when a deep voice startles me, cutting through the silence.

"You know the hotel supplies these things called glasses. I could get you one if you'd like. Unless, of course, you prefer the bottle."

The sultry sound of Mazen's melodic, gravelly voice ignites a wild flutter, as if a butterfly conservatory door was left open, and they all flew out to seek refuge in my chest. My pulse leaps with excitement, if only because he's the unreserved member of the band. The wild card. For whatever reason, after my confession about remembering our past while I was in the hospital, he's kept his space.

Keeping his distance is one thing. He needs time to process my recollection of him as much as I need it to filter through how remembering him makes me feel. It's his actions that have spoken the loudest in the days following our heart-to-heart on the hospital bathroom floor. I haven't once caught Mazen screwing anyone. It seems that he's turned a celibate leaf, as odd as that is to consider.

That ends tonight. I have no qualms about using *him* for his body. After all, he is my *boyfriend*.

"Drink?" I hold the decanter out toward him. Not that I think he needs to be sloshed to bed me. It's not fun to drink your misery away alone.

"Not really my thing," he declines quickly, shaking his head. A wealth of dark hair moves when he adds, "I have something stronger. If you're interested."

I take another swig before glancing at Lacey, who is sleeping, unaware of the scene unfolding in front of her. "Drugs are illegal." My voice is now a purr.

In less than a second, he retorts, "So is littering. Hello, global warming. Come on."

He grabs the bottle, sets it in its rightful place on the cart, and gently tugs me forward by my hand. I follow behind his large frame through the suite and toward the patio.

Moonlight shines in the reflection of the large pool. I stop to dip my foot as we walk by, only to find that it's heated. A night swim might be in my future.

*I've never had sex in a pool.*

Mazen sits on a lounger, bare feet resting on either side of the chair he straddles casually. Everything about him is casual. From the way he leads his band as their unspoken leader to the way he beckons me to sit with him.

"Don't be shy." He does that head nod thing that men have perfected that silently means *come closer*.

Like a clone of Jupiter, I submit. Listening to my master, tail wagging and all, I saunter toward him. When I settle onto the lounger in front of him, our knees hit, and our legs form a diamond, our bodies parallel. The remaining gap of space between us feels like an ocean, uncharted territory.

"Have you ever been high before?" he probes, curiosity in his voice. A thin sliver of paper, baggie, and lighter magically appear in his lap.

I contemplate giving him a simple answer, a quick nod. Instead, I flatten my palms on my exposed thighs and lazily swing my head up and down as a rush of words spill from my lips. "After my mom died, I did a lot with Knox."

His name tastes gross on my tongue. Like warmed-up frozen pizza that was a smidgen too freezer burned, but you ignored the thick layer of ice because you were starving and heated it anyway. I regret trusting him just as much as my judgment in frozen food choices.

"He used to smoke a lot. It started with him, I guess. The experimenting. I feel so stupid now. He was my mentor at first. Then my friend." I divulge this information willingly for some inexplicable reason. "Then more. Foolishly, I trusted him." I'm fully clothed in my pajamas, but I feel more exposed than if I were sitting here in the nude. "First, it was smoking, then sex. I wanted to feel numb all the time. But I stopped when I found out—" The words *I was pregnant* dangle on the edge of my tongue like a parachutist about to free-fall from a plane suspended in the clouds. "Lacey had asthma. I didn't want any smoke on my clothes.

The smell would throw her into a coughing fit." *Suave recovery*, I think to myself.

Leisurely, Mazen nods. A faint, "Noted," dances from his mouth in the inky air around us.

I watch in amazement as he rolls a joint. It's not an award-winning task, though like everything else he does, each casual movement, led by years of muscle memory, is seamless. Hello, there are laws against this in some states. Though I think even the stigma around marijuana is waning. What has me staring at him—aside from his sinful allure—is that I can tell that he's done this a million times. It's as natural as his presence onstage, from what I've stalked online—in the privacy of my own bunk, sound on silent.

"Smoking Section" by Jelly Roll becomes our announced anthem.

Mazen's thick, dark eyebrows furrow just a tad as his thumbs and pointer fingers work on the stuffed paper in front of me in an art form that reminds me of a burrito being rolled to perfection. Under the moonlight, his lips glisten as he wets them once, then twice, his tongue moving ever so slightly as it peeks out of his mouth, licking the paper in his hand in wistful horizontal strokes before he folds it over, sealing it shut.

Glancing up, Mazen quirks an eyebrow at me questioningly when he realizes how attuned to his subtle movements I've become. The perfectly shaped arches gracing his face indicate a laugh is coming. I see his mouth part seconds before the hushed sound escapes.

"What?" Girlish charm hits level ten, followed by a lingering giggle. *Here goes nothing,* I think before I go all in, committing to the idea of being thoroughly screwed by

Mazen Wilde. The ultimate reprieve from reality just out of reach.

He made me forget once before. I need that from him again. I need him to help flip my switch off, to drown out the noise. The bullshit brewing, a constant clattering of what-ifs in my mind. He's the perfect escape. Laden in darkness—from the strands of inky-black hair, to the thick eyebrows that scream his foreign ancestry, to the etching of ink across his knuckles that reads *Wild*. My thighs clench at the thought of that very hand, of those tattooed knuckles sliding past the edge of my panties, sinking into me far enough that the ink disappears completely. He's come so far from the boyish version I first met years ago. I want a taste of the man he turned into. The man who sings for a living, the man who uses his sex appeal onstage to make his female fanbase wanton.

Wrap me in a *Wet for Wilde* T-shirt because I'm here to stake claim as his number one groupie.

The lead singer of Kings of Jupiter is the perfect escape. It's an added benefit that he is my temporary fake boyfriend. Our bodies, like old friends, have already met in a previous era of time. It will be like two high school friends meeting for a cup of coffee to chat after college graduation. Except, instead of our hands holding mugs, our mouths sipping on caffeine, they'll roam one another's skin. An exploration of roads already traveled.

I'd be lying if I said I don't care about Mazen. He's impossible not to like. The bad boy every woman wants to tame. Though my feelings for him are different from the ones I have budding in my chest for his friends. Oliver and Cannon have staked their claim on me. I know where I stand with them. We've blurred the line between business and pleasure, and even though I know this tour has an end date, I have a sinking suspicion that neither of them will respect the terms of our initial agreement. I'd also be lying if I said I didn't want the same thing … them … both of them … maybe all three of them. It's a possibility that's just out of reach. I squash it before I can feed too much into it, only to get my hope diminished.

Since I admitted to remembering our one-night stand, he hasn't so much as tried anything with me or shown that he reciprocates any feelings whatsoever toward me. Just when I think I've figured him out, he somehow keeps me guessing.

"You made that look sexy. That's all."

Suddenly, his jaw is clamped tight, set in a grim line. That's the first clue that the brick wall he's standing behind is starting to crack. I get it. He's mastered guarding his heart, a heart that I forgot. A heart that my ignorance of the night we shared together broke.

I grin, refusing to cower, to accept defeat. I offer him an air of pleasure, before saying, "Does that embarrass you or something, Wilde?"

"Do I look like a guy who embarrasses easily?"

"No, but you also don't look like one who gets pissed off when a woman tells you she finds it sexy, watching you—"

A stunned expression descends over his facial features. Another crack in the hard exterior of his fortress. "I'm not pissed."

"You're also not as smart as I pegged you to be." I nonchalantly scoot forward on the lounger, our kneecaps brushing. My outer thighs are now encased by his inner thighs. "When a woman's had a couple of drinks, agrees to smoke with you, then peppers you with compliments calling you sexy, you shouldn't tense up like you just walked in on your parents boning."

That earns a tight crease on his forehead.

Lightening the mood, I motion to the rolled-up paper in his hand. "Are you going to light that up? Then ask me if I want to S and S?"

The corner of his mouth twists. "Enlighten me. What is S and S exactly?"

"Smoke and swim." I shrug casually.

"Here I thought, *we* were corrupting you." Lighting the end of the joint, he takes a deep pull, inhaling. Its red cherry end burns bright, like my attraction to him.

The moonlight lingers above us, casting us in a glow, and a comfortable silence forms between us. Mazen hands me the rolled paper after another drag. I take it, allowing its smoke to fill my lungs as I take a couple of small hits before passing it back to him.

Even in the dead of night, it's hard to miss the gray in his eyes as they survey the thick space between us. There's a lethal calm in his glare that has me questioning the intense electricity flowing between us. Maybe it's because we're sitting so close, sharing a joint, or maybe it's because we're both tired of pretending that something didn't blossom between us all those years ago. Something that even time couldn't extinguish. Something that I hope Mazen's done fighting against.

I dive headfirst into the unknown, praying that he'll catch me. "They're treating me like glass." A small pout forms on my mouth. "They haven't touched me once. I feel like I'm going to explode."

"That's because when you came back to us, you were broken. Even if you claim otherwise. They're scared to push you. Break you more. Can't fault them for caring about you."

"I was already broken before you guys strolled into my

studio." I'm walking a fine line. "I don't need to be coddled. I need to be fucked. I need them to take off their kid gloves, remind me that I'm strong enough to take them ... both. Caddell can't collect all the broken pieces of me that he shattered. Ollie and Cannon shouldn't try either." Smoke fills my lungs, along with my newfound courage. "I need to be reminded that they want me. Their tattooist. That I'm still worthy in their eyes."

Eyes full of half-promises sparkle with satisfaction when Mazen says, "Then, I won't feel guilty when I do this."

11

# SHATTER ME

SOPHIA

A HEARTBEAT LATER, Mazen's leaning in, then pressing his mouth against mine, tilting my world off its axis.

I half expected our first kiss since I told him I remembered him to be hard, punishing, and angry. Surprisingly, when my mouth opens, inviting him in, his tongue is slow, tentative, like he's unsure of the next step in the dance our mouths are choreographing. His tongue traces not only my mouth, but my soul as well, as his kiss sings through my veins in a melody that I'll remember for the rest of my life.

When he pulls back, his eyes linger on mine, a silent question. He's seeking permission. I bite my bottom lip—an answer to his question—and his eyes flick down. In a rush, his mouth moves to my chin, lips searing a path down my neck, setting my body aflame with need. My mind revels in the hungered prose of each pass of his lips. Senses drugged by the touch of his lips when they continue their survey of my ivory skin. Each lap of his tongue is a stroke of beautiful torture.

"I want you," I say eagerly, climbing onto his lap, straddling his stone-hard body.

I'm baiting him; he knows it.

Recalling the passion we shared in Chicago, I whisper a fragment of what he told me back then, "Morals be damned," I say followed by the purr of his name. "Mazen. Show me it's okay to be broken. Then piece me back together. Let this new memory of us be the glue holding me together."

As gentle as the touch of a feather, Mazen takes my jaw in his hand, planting kisses on each bruise that lingers on my face. I swallow hard, savoring the tenderness of his expert touch. I recall being held in his arms, feeling both safe and sought after. As young as we were back then, our souls called to one another just like they are once again.

He's intruded in my life like a hot tide that I want to drown in. I want to bask under the moonlight with Mazen filling me, claiming me again. Reminding me that I'm not glass.

Rekindling old, forgotten feelings, I press forward, my core rubbing against the swell in his sweatpants. A deep bellow booms from his parted mouth as he leans forward and licks from my collarbone then up my neck in a solid stroke.

I grow impatient, achy, and exhausted. Letting out a faint sigh, feeling drained and unsatisfied, I realize that he's not going to drive me into oblivion like I so desperately need. While my body grinds against his, legs wide, open for entry, Mazen doesn't advance.

*What kind of ethical rock star is he?*

"Aren't your arms tired from holding a grudge against me?" I watch for his reaction as the question leaves my mouth, hesitating only momentarily before I depict an ease

I don't entirely feel. Choosing my words carefully, I offer him something he hasn't asked for, yet I know he needs. "I'm sorry I didn't remember you when I first saw you again. I know how deeply that hurt you."

His usually stone-cold eyes sparkle with reserve.

"It would have killed me, ya know. I just don't understand why you didn't say anything before. Why'd you let me share a bed with Ollie and then Cannon and never say anything?"

His silence speaks volumes.

I shrink from the cold of his gray eyes, feeling suddenly ill-equipped for this conversation.

"I chose my love for music over the chance to get to know you." He frowns, though the rest of his mask is expressionless. It's unnerving. "Ollie said he banged you that night in your tattoo studio, and then he told me your name. For a split second, I felt like I could breathe. For a moment of suspended time, my muse was within reach. Then, I could see it in your eyes—your aversion. You really didn't recognize me, and then you slapped me."

With an apologetic smile, I say, "I'm sorry, but you did basically call me a whore."

"I was jealous. I'm sorry too. I wanted you to remember. More than anything though, I wanted to hurt you as badly as you hurt me." The captivating picture he paints is etched with so much more pain than I've ever seen on his usually casual character.

Placing my hands on his shoulders, I stroke them. I glide up his neck and then settle with my hold on either side of his strong jaw. "I don't think I could force myself to forget you now if I tried."

"Promise?"

One firm word, spoken into the night air, holds as much power as a lightning bolt before an earth-shattering storm.

"I promise"—I kiss the side of his mouth—"to never forget you again." Another kiss is planted on the tip of his perfect nose. "To make you feel as good as you make me feel." I hover over his mouth, ready to offer him the biggest promise of all. My palms sweat, and my stomach bottoms out, but I find the words that I know he needs to hear. My take on lyrics pours from my parted mouth. "I promise to let you in, as long as you let me."

A soft brushing of his fingers against my cheek has me settling onto his lap fully. "Now that I have you in my arms, nothing will be able to tear you from me. Leaving you behind that morning was a mistake."

The air in my lungs feels like it's getting vacuumed out.

"I will never ever make that same mistake again. If you want me, I'm yours. Wholly. Just know that I don't half-ass anything, *Rosella*. If I claim you, like my friends have, it's only you."

My body tenses briefly. I hope he doesn't notice.

It's wishful thinking because he says, "I know you're with them too. I'll learn to accept it, understand it. But this" —he takes my hand, placing it over his heart, on top of a Kings of Jupiter logo on his chest—"beats for you and only you."

The tenderness in his expression stuns me as his eyes drink me up, undressing me under the moonlight hovering above us.

"Mazen ..." I cast my eyes downward. Ashamed of the one lie I'm still keeping. It's as big as a vast ocean between us. I know it will be our demise. I can feel it in my bones. Though I can't stomach telling him the truth. Forcefully swallowing it down, I pause to catch my breath, feeling like I just finished a sprint though my legs haven't moved. Fears of him finding out about Roman increase by the second. The sudden nagging in the back of my mind refuses to dissipate.

My gaze lowers once more, like his voice.

"I'm going to kiss you—again. I've been so damn envious of Ollie and Cannon. I've never wanted to hurt them before. Genuinely hurt my best friends for having something I was denied. Don't deny me anymore. I have time to make up for. Years of it."

"You denied me. That night in the hot tub, you walked away."

We're interrupted by the sound of the glass door sliding open. Our mirrored gazes dart to the patio door as Oliver folds his arms across his bare chest in a swift movement. He leans against the wall before he crosses his feet.

With a quick shake of his head, I can feel the words he's biting back—*Took him long enough.*

"No one invited me to this wake and bake. I'm not intruding on something, am I?" A friendly, bantering smile forms when he pushes off the wall, then carelessly strolls toward us.

There's always something warm and comforting about Oliver's presence. Even now, as I'm caught straddling his best friend's lap, there's nothing but teasing amusement rippling through the air.

I feel the weight of him as he sits down on the lounger behind me, his knees now budded up against Mazen's. Suddenly, being trapped between the two of them is the only place in the world I want to be.

Mazen's mouth opens, then closes, like he's trying to decide what card to play. It's not like him to bite his tongue. I've only ever seen the irrational side of him that says what he wants, when he wants. He seems to be weighing his options now, choosing the right words.

Then, as he regains his natural composure, he speaks in the standard jesting tone I've come to like, which causes my legs to tighten around his waist. "Yes, you fucking are, and you know it. Unless you have a little cunt as sweet as Sophia's in those sweats, then you should just hightail it back inside."

"I have something that tastes just as good, don't I, Fireball?" Oliver nudges my hair with his nose, breathing in deeply from behind me.

My head bows. I'm frozen. Scared to move and pop the bubble of lust I'm sandwiched between. Having Ollie and Cannon is one thing. This—being the tether between Ollie and Mazen—feels forbidden, taboo even. To my understanding, there isn't a bisexual bone in Mazen's body. I wonder if he could be swayed to share me with Oliver. To ignore what society deems as right and wrong and just follow what our bodies need, what they long for.

I long to be filled by both of these men at the same time. My core wants to be the space where they connect.

"That's debatable," a deep timbre booms, grasping our attention, and beckons it toward the glass door once more.

We watch as Cannon shuts it behind him.

In all his glory, under the midnight moon, he stalks toward us, as naked as on the day he entered this world.

"For fuck's sake," Mazen whines. "Cover that anaconda up. How the hell do you walk after taking that, Ollie?"

I feel Oliver's head as it shakes with laughter. When I glance over my shoulder, my eyes meet Oliver's before I shrug in mock annoyance at our coy little friend Mazen. It's funny that he thinks Cannon tops. Based on appearance alone, I totally get it. I don't fault him for automatically assuming that the beefy, broody drummer is the one swinging dick and laying it down.

Mazen's assessment is as far from the truth as aliens *not* being real.

"Get the hell out of here." Ollie smiles easily. "You think I'm the bottom?"

If it wasn't for the awkward silence dangling long and hard between us, like Cannon's thick third leg as he nears, I wouldn't be clamping my own jaw near as tightly as I am.

"Shit. You think Ollie's man enough to take this?" Cannon slides his palm up and down his rock-hard girth, like he's holding a sub crafted by sandwich artisan, Jimmy John, himself.

I glance back over my shoulder at Ollie, who is now arching an eyebrow, nodding at the taunt in his lover's masculine voice. My eyes pivot back to Mazen, and hand on the Bible, I see him swallow, his Adam's apple bobbing at the slowest pace I've ever seen. His eyes are glued on his drummer's junk, and holy-freaking-Christmas-morning, have I hit the trifecta of foursomes?

Oliver's voice booms over my shoulder when he says, "Is that a dare?"

Cannon's barely visible blond eyebrow is rounded when he mocks, "Is that an acceptance?"

"Get the fuck out of here. You know damn well I don't back down from any bet. I own that tight little hole of yours. You'd feel empty without me balls deep in it," Oliver says with a slow, seductive smile that is meant to remind Cannon that Oliver's the alpha in their pack. "As much as you've grown to like being in charge, I am and will always be the one forcing your giant body to surrender to mine."

"This is fucking strange." Mazen shakes his head, seemingly breaking the spell Cannon's junk had him under.

He didn't even try to hide his blunt assessment. Maybe he's more on board with things than he even realizes.

Smiling leisurely, I utter, "It's really not strange if you open your mind up to it. We were made to enjoy our bodies. Who's to say that enjoyment has to solely come from someone of the opposite sex?"

"She's high," Mazen clarifies, brushing my comment off at the same time Cannon sits down behind Oliver.

We're a train of bodies, uncertainty, and lust.

"Night Moves" by Bob Seger & The Silver Bullet Band fills the night air around us from the speaker Cannon is controlling from his phone.

"Fitting tune," I chime. "Anyone down for a swim?"

We all slide into the pool a couple of minutes later. We're splashing, laughing, and cutting the breeze.

Only the man in the moon and the four of us are privy to the palpable charge between our exposed flesh and souls when the sound of our collective laughter fades and is replaced with harsh breathing.

It dawns on me then, as I'm submerged neck deep, that the ache in my core that woke me up is still there, nagging for release. It doesn't help that three of the hottest men on earth are watching me with predatory stares, no doubt sensing the change in mood as well.

"Like something you see, boys?"

Leave it to Oliver to fill the silence. "I think it's safe to say," he starts as his head swivels to meet his friends' eyes, all glossed with need and honed in on me. "We're far past seeing something we like."

"We're entering uncharted territory here," Mazen states the obvious.

"Are we though? If memory serves, the only time we don't ignore this pull to each other is when we're wet." The drummer says before he swims closer to my body and pins me to the side of the pool's wall. "What is it about water activities that draw us to you, Sophia?"

*The hot tub incident.*

My thighs unconsciously rub together with the recollection of one of the hottest nights of my entire life.

Oliver, with his naturally tanned skin, swims toward the edge of the pool cutting through the water with ease like the jellyfish tattooed on his penis, effectively cutting my thought short. "Ten dollars says the reason our girl is dripping wet has nothing to do with our midnight swimming excursion."

I swallow hard.

*Our girl.*

Our girl. What is it about that simple statement that has my body lighting up from the inside like a match has been struck?

My eyes meet Cannon's, then Oliver's, before I straighten my head and meet Mazen's heated glare. Playing coy, I ask him from a few feet away, "Am I your girl too?"

Water sloshes around his chiseled frame as he plunges under the water's line. I'm encased by my men, one on each side of me as Mazen glides through the water, only to break the surface directly in front of my face a heartbeat later.

Beads of water cascade down his beautiful face. When his thick eyelashes open, dark eyes land on me. I'm held captive by his intense stare, so much so, that I barely register his movement when his large palms reach forward and grip the back of my head. He pulls his body tight against my own using my head as leverage. Neither Cannon nor Oliver budges an inch. We're all pressed so tightly together that even our breathing seems to be in unison.

As if a rubber band has snapped, Mazen's mouth

roughly lands on my own. He kisses me...no...he *devours* me, searing the answer to my question into the depths of my soul without words. With each lap of his tongue, my body grinds against him. I don't even have to worry about treading water because I know that the three of them will keep me suspended above the water.

*I'm safe*, I think to myself.

Our lips don't break for what feels like an hour. When they finally do, Mazen and I are still pressed up against one another. He whispers, "You're everything," and suddenly his acknowledgement of my question surges me closer to him. I wrap my legs around his torso, begging for friction.

"I need you," I admit before turning my head and giving attention to Cannon and Oliver. "I need one of you... all of you. Please."

"Lift her up," Cannon addresses Mazen, who picks me up and out of the water as if I weigh less than a pillow.

I'm sitting on the edge of the pool when Oliver jumps out and rushes to a small storage bin. He comes back with two towels in hand. He lays out one on the concrete then gestures for me to lay back on it, the other he rolls underneath my head like a makeshift cushion.

"You're going to need to work up to taking all of us at the same time, Soph." Cannon's husky voice bellows through the night, yet is still low enough that I'm not afraid of Lacey hearing from the other side of the glass door. "Until you're ready for that, I know that I, personally, cannot wait another second before tasting that sweet pussy on my tongue again."

I don't even have a moment to swallow Cannon's words and take a breath before his fingers pull my panties down my legs, and his tongue slides through my now exposed slit. The warmth of his touch explodes on every nerve ending in my body. I fall back into the feeling of being worshiped, not giving two shits that I'm at their mercy.

At their mercy is the only place I want to be right now.

"Cannon," I moan, lips parted in ecstasy, eyes closing.

When I open them, Mazen is hovering above me. His dark-steel eyes dart between my parted mouth and down to where Cannon's head is pressed against my core. The faint sound of him lapping my folds and sucking on my swollen clit create the most seductive melody I've ever heard.

Oliver's voice cuts through the darkness, always the light in my life. "He was never good at sharing." He lowers himself so that I'm now looking down at his head and, without missing a beat, his mouth is nestled close to Cannon's as both of their mouths glide over me in a smoldering dance of their tongues.

The sight alone has the muscles in my lower belly growing taut.

"Look at me," Mazen cups my cheek. "I want to see the moment you come apart. Don't move your head." He leans forward and kisses me chastely before pulling back an inch and watching me explode.

Tingles stir in my core seconds before the feeling of someone's mouth—either Cannon or Oliver, I honestly have no idea who—pulls at my clit with their teeth. I explode. My legs press together as quake after quake becomes of my lower body. Fireworks ignite through me with one of the most earth-shattering orgasms of my life.

I'm still reeling on the wave of euphoria when Mazen lowers himself down the length of my exposed body. My pussy is still pulsating when I feel his warm tongue lapping up my cum. "I'm always cleaning up after these two," he says nonchalantly, like his friends didn't just turn my world upside down poolside.

My eyes close then reopen to now find Oliver and Cannon watching me intently.

"Will you be able to sleep now, Fireball?" Oliver smiles and then adds, "Should we come up with a rotation schedule or something?" His attempt to be funny breaks the contentment we've finally found.

"Don't be an asshole," Cannon says, pulling himself from the pool. "I'm going to bed." Before he makes it to the sliding glass door to head inside, he turns. "I call Mondays and Fridays."

# 12

# LITTLE LOZIER

MAZEN

I STUMBLE through the kitchen like a newborn fawn, remnants of egg wash clinging to the apron that is tied around my waist. I'm no fucking good at being docile or domesticated.

"Shit," I call out, cracking yet another yolk. Its golden center no longer a globe. "Fuck, how do people make this look so easy?"

About the same time the yolk cracks, the toaster sends a piece of blackened bread into the air, like it's a flying squirrel preparing to glide toward a tree. I'm caught so off guard that I don't have time to catch it before the burned square and crumbs tumble to the ground.

As if it were a rare steak, Jupiter leaps off the love seat, abandoning his morning-sun basking spot, and makes it to my side in a nanosecond. Hell, that's quicker than I've ever seen him move. Much to my dismay, I watch as our husky eyes the blackened bread. His snout scrunches in horror at the monstrosity, and he tilts his head to the side as he glances up at me with almost as much disgust as he eyed the bread.

"I wouldn't eat it either, buddy. Cut me some slack though. You know I'm no chef."

His bark is all the confirmation I need to know that I would die on day one of *Naked and Afraid*. We're holed up in this five-star hotel, all the amenities you could want, and here I am, unable to toast a fucking piece of sliced bread to perfection.

My goal was to get up before everyone and prepare breakfast—another peace offering, if you will—to enjoy our last couple of hours of normalcy before we hit the road again. We're going back on tour with an additional female. Leaving without the Taser-wielding, pink-haired psycho was a deal-breaker for Sophia, which means I'll be sleeping with one fucking eye open for the next couple of weeks.

"I've heard happier servers slinging plates at Waffle House," says the Taser-wielding psycho, Lacey, as she sits up from her claim on the couch, a mound of neon hair on her head.

"A delicacy during our adolescence," a sultry voice booms from the hallway, joining in on the mockery before she's even rounded the corner.

I smell *her* before I see her. My senses are already that in tune with her essence.

"Morning, Lace."

Sophia stretches as she nears the couch. A thin line of skin on showcase makes me weak in the knees. I lean against the cool edge of the countertop, hoping that the large island is enough to hide my monster cock as it pants a hard throb in my sweats, begging to say good morning to Rosella.

A smile tips the corners of my mouth up, and I watch

her sink onto the makeshift bed, a yawn leaving her luscious lips.

Morning Sophia is a sight for sore eyes.

In the weeks she has been on tour with us, I'm usually not around this early. I'm either still passed out from getting blitzed out of my damn mind after our show and post-show tattoo session or at the gym. There's no in-between in my schedule.

If we're being honest, I've been doing pretty much anything to keep myself occupied and away from the red-haired beauty in front of me. Smoking so much reefer that I could float away usually does the trick at keeping my thoughts of her delicate mouth at bay. I'm kicking myself in the ass for it now. If I hadn't been so caught up in pushing her away, punishing her for not remembering me or the night we shared, I could have had her in my arms sooner.

Apparently, I'm a shit cook and a shit human.

Last night, things changed. Today, I woke up for the first time in a long while with an excited energy coursing through my veins.

There's something so serene about seeing someone fresh out of bed, sleep clinging to their voice, hope of what the day before them holds dancing in their irises. I want to bottle this version of her up and use it to supply aid to my spank bank for eternity.

"You hungry?" I call out from my position in the kitchen, a gold knob poking into my flesh, as I'm still holding up the island with my morning wood.

*If music doesn't pan out, I wonder if I'd hack it as a carpenter.*

"Not really. I'll take some coffee though."

Filling up a steaming mug, I add a splash of creamer, uncertain how Sophia likes her coffee. I decide to add another pour of creamer, remembering Lindsey delivering sugar in a cup with a splash of actual coffee once before, and then I walk into the living room. I offer her the now-milky-white cup of coffee, and our hands brush innocently as the mug slips from my grasp to hers. Though I know this, it doesn't stop the jolt of fucking electricity, strong enough to power all of the Vegas Strip, in this one embrace. My skin burns in a delicious ache as my hand falls back to my side.

"You're a cup short, Wilde," Lacey teases, eyes slanting with a gleam as wild as her personality. "Lucky for you and your unchivalrous ways, I already have plans this morning."

As if she summoned him with her words, the door to our suite opens, welcoming Ashton, our band's head of security. Jupiter is hot on his heels when he darts forward, as if sensing that he, too, has plans with a new friend.

"Morning, handsome," the demented one says, extending her hand and rubbing Jupiter's thick mane when he jumps onto the couch, nuzzling his way between the two Lozier sisters.

*And they say dogs are loyal.*

With a click of the clasp on his leash, Jupiter jumps back off the couch and bounds back toward Ashton. I debate getting them *Traitor Crew* T-shirts made.

"Lacey, you still want to come on our morning walk?"

Jupiter wags his bushy tail.

Sophia awes.

Ashton fucking blushes, and I groan internally.

"Give me five minutes, and I'm all yours." She jumps up, gives her sister a quick peck on the cheek, and then bounces down the hallway.

The three of us, including Jupiter, make our way into the kitchen and shoot the breeze, standing around the island. Yes, the very one that looks like an atomic bomb detonated on top of the marble slab by my lack of culinary finesse.

"Decided not to wait for Oliver to make breakfast, I see." Ashton rolls his eyes at the mess I've made of the kitchen. He's been around too long for his own good, which means he has zero remorse about calling me out on my bullshit and my obvious lack of domesticity.

"I don't need Oliver or anyone else to feed me."

"Clearly," he retorts with another eye roll before his gaze darts back toward the empty hallway.

We haven't even left for the tour yet, and the brawny bastard already has it bad. Maybe we should set some ground rules about fraternization on tour. Who cares if I'm the one to break them? Rules are meant to be broken.

"Says the man who appears to have gone through a carton of eggs." Sophia nods to the empty container, and then her eyes track toward the empty plate resting next to said container. "With nothing to show for it." Peering at the stack of plates and then straight into my soul, she nods to herself, sending a string of embarrassment down my spine.

What feels like a century later but is only a couple of minutes, Lacey reappears, sliding up to her sister. Great. She's just in time to break the tension of my epic failure. Praise the little lunatic for doing me a solid for once.

"It's a good thing he's pretty, and he can sing, huh? Otherwise, he'd be totally useless."

I take back my previous compliment.

"You a fan of our music?"

"I'm a fan of music in general. Kings of Jupiter is subpar. I'm just here so my sister doesn't lose sleep over my well-being. Don't get it twisted."

"Bet you a hundred bucks by the end of the tour, you'll be our biggest fan," I counter her diss.

Her eager response matches mine in potency. "Bet you a hundred bucks my sister falls in love with your best friends before you even have a chance to show her that you're not just another pretty-faced male who never outgrew his emo phase, allowing it to become his entire identity."

Words as sharp as a knife cut into the hard armor of my skin, slicing through muscle and tendons until they're close enough to pierce the confines of my heart.

*What the fuck?*

Her bet resonates for a few beats before the challenge in her eyes pulls me forward, beckoning me to prove her wrong.

The bitch is goading me. The faint purse of her glossed lips, which tilt upward at the same time that I take my first step toward her, confirms it.

And it's working.

Little Lozier doesn't know it yet, but I never lose, and I don't take well to intimidation. Even if it's coming from a woman covered in ink, highlighter-pink hair, and balls of fucking steel. She might be standing next to my linebacker of a security guard, but his presence doesn't stop me from leaving the space I labeled as my own behind the island and intruding into Lacey's bubble.

Our chests butt up to one another, each of us gambling with high stakes.

I lean forward until my mouth is at the shell of Lacey's ear. It's not surprising that she doesn't gasp or move an inch. Her backbone is built from the men she's broken in her short time circling this earth.

I'm a different breed, and she's going to fucking learn it the hard way, it seems. Sophia's sister or not, I will win this bet, and when I do, she's not only going to be Kings of

Jupiter's biggest fan, but she's also going to give an epic speech when I marry her sister.

This broad will eat crow for breakfast because it's the only thing I actually do know how to serve.

"You're on," I whisper through the pink locks framing her face. "Be sure to order your fan merch now though. I hear our website sells out fast."

The cunning woman in front of me turns her head to face me so quickly that I have to jerk away to nearly miss our lips brushing. Deranged is putting it mildly. She's a certified lunatic. My eyes widen as I wonder what Sophia is thinking. I can't move to take a glance because Lacey's next words steal all the air from my lungs, and I freeze in disbelief.

"You're already losing, Wilde. Don't you see? Your head has been too stuck up your own ass to notice. She's head over heels for your drummer *and* guitarist, and I don't know if you took anatomy, but she only has two holes below the belt that can be filled comfortably." Her hand, with her sharp-as-sin nails, pats me on my shoulder as she drives her warning home like a whack across my skull. "You're the odd man out. The sooner you accept that, the better you'll be."

Turning on her heel, she kisses Sophia's cheek, once again driving home the point of who is closer to her sister. In a cool, aloof manner, I stare at the crown of her head, speechless. I can't even rally up a quick enough response to protest her threat as she tells her sister she'll bring her back some food and leaves before I have a chance to trudge through the havoc her words left me in.

Words are my expertise. I'm a songwriter. A weaver of tales. In this moment, I've been reduced to nothing more than a crumpled-up piece of paper, waiting to be tossed in the garbage.

Before Ashton, Jupiter, and the worst future sister-in-law in the entire universe make it to the door, I dig deep and find my voice. The sound of the spatula I toss into the sink echoes as I call out, "Ash, will you please do me a solid and bring back enough for everyone?"

"You got it. Come on, Jupiter, Lacey." He gestures for them before shutting the door, leaving me with my hardened jaw clenched so tight.

I'm disoriented by what the fuck just happened.

"What's with the Martha Stewart impersonation?" Sophia asks as she backs away from the island, seemingly not shocked or disoriented at all from the tug-of-war that she just witnessed. She sinks onto her sister's makeshift bed on the couch, eyes still glossy with sleep, awaiting my answer.

I try to remain rational as she pulls a blanket over herself, but my thoughts are reeling as I sink onto the couch next to her, fighting the urge to pry into her indifferent attitude. I shoot her a commanding look, irritated that she's able to brush off the start of a war between her sister and me. I guess if we're being honest, the war started when she tased me. Her little declaration this morning only solidified that she'll fight to the death.

She doesn't know it yet, but I will too. I finally have Rosella back in my life, and I refuse to lose her again.

Swallowing down my insecurities, I lead with the truth. "Trying my hand at being nice."

"How's it going for you?" Her smile is infectious, as bright as the looming sun in the sky. Her pun is no doubt a dig at the tension that just wove itself around the room like a cat dragging a ball of yarn around on its paws.

Folding my arms behind my neck, I stretch out my legs.

My shins gliding under the coffee table. "Not well. I can't cook or—"

"Be cordial?"

It's as if she's trying to erect a wall between us too. I thought last night ... showing her ... *them* ... that I could be a team player, share her, meant something. At least for me, it did. I thought it was a step forward in the right direction. Partaking in their little group sexcapades was a sign of good faith that I'm here, I want in, with them. An indication that I could be what she needs me to be. *Fuck.* If I can't have her to myself, there's no one aside from my two best friends that I'd rather share her with.

It's not in my nature to share. My father instilled that notion in my head practically before I took my first steps. He ingrained in my sister and me that we were superior to everyone. He put us on a pedestal next to him in the limelight. After Bethany's death, when the world crashed around us, I broke every image he'd tried to fit me into. I shattered the perfectly sculpted family tree and burned it to the ground, along with any relationship that he sought after.

My sister died, my mom fled, and my father became nothing more than a name and a signature on a piece of paper. Oh, and my governor, but I've never cared for politics anyway.

There's no one else on the face of this miserable fucking planet that understands me like Oliver, Cannon, and Murphy do. They're the family I chose when my father tried to force his lifestyle, dreams, and ambitions on me.

Lacey's threat has a tinge of truth in it that rings loudly in my ears. I think that's what hits so close to home. The pain of that truth is like constant ringing, but it's nothing compared to the pang I feel in my chest knowing that

Rosella has already fallen for my bandmates, and I'm the fourth wheel. They chose *her* over *me*.

*Can I really blame them?*

No one chooses Mazen Matthew Wilde. Not my mom, who deserted me, leaving me to mourn Bethany's death alone. Not my father when I refused to follow in his footsteps, and now, not my friends ...

Somehow, Sophia's soft, "Mazen," clamors in my chest. Her voice is reserved yet packed with concern.

My internal monologue grows silent as she steals my attention for the seven hundred and forty-sixth time since I met her. The cushion moves when Sophia pulls herself off it and shocks the shit out of me as she climbs on top of my lap, straddling me. Her inner thighs hold firm to my outer thighs, as if she's got my entire body, heart, and soul in a vise grip.

# 13

# KISS HER SENSELESS

MAZEN

## "DO YOU WANT TO KNOW A SECRET?"

Sophia's mouth is a hairbreadth away from mine. I can smell the faint whiff of her toothpaste, mixed with the coffee I made her, when her mouth parts.

Unashamedly, I admit, "I want to know all of your secrets."

"I like the not-nice, dickhead version of you the best. It makes me feral. I already have Ollie, my fierce protector. The one who makes me laugh, promising me something he didn't have until adulthood—a happily ever after. Then, there's Cannon, my dark-knight drummer. His Dom side hurts me in the best way possible. Contrary to what Ollie led you to believe and witness last night, Cannon is full-throttle Dom toward me in the bedroom. He only submits to Oliver, and that is so freaking hot. But underneath the brooding, demanding man, he's a gentle giant. He soothes me just as much as he punishes me. And then there's you."

The very curve of her body glides over my core as she

plunges onward with a tinge of defiance tipping up her sweet smile.

"The man behind the T-shirt slogan *Wet for Wilde.* I'm placing my order for a box of those shirts because that's what you make me. Wet."

An awakening of flames ignites within me by the devious, filthy words that leave her sweet mouth.

I'm shocked by the emergence of feelings—lust, desire, possession—that stir in both my gut and in my pants, and try as I might to be the gold-standard gem of a bastard this morning, I fail miserably as my hands slide around her waist, planting her core right over my thickening bulge. I know we've reached a point of no return when I look into her deep-fields-of-luscious-green eyes, and the look of enthrallment mirrors my own in them.

Our souls sing out to one another because we're the same. Her broken pieces fit together with mine like a puzzle.

"You pushed me away for so long—with your hate for me, your snide remarks, your distance—but it only made my pussy ache that much more for you, Mazen. Feel *her.* She's dripping onto your pants."

*Holy. Fuck. Are you shitting me? Hell.* She called her pussy a *her,* like it's a living, breathing entity.

I'm momentarily taken aback by the immensity of my desire for Sophia Rose Lozier. My cock and my heart wage war on one another.

*This is not the time or place to have a mental breakdown.*

There're a hundred reasons why I should remove her from my lap, plant her petite, perfectly-sculpted-for-my-hands body back on the couch next to me, and ... I don't know ... quit my band, move to New York, and start a career as a street performer. I should do so many other things than the one thing I do. Because I'm not a saint, and I'm *not* a good fucking man.

Despite my flaws, this beautiful, cunningly smart woman grinding on my lap wants me anyway.

If only for a moment, Sophia is choosing me.

And fuck does it feel good to be chosen for once.

Scars and all. Sophia wants *me*. Not my band, not my friends. Not Mazen Wilde, the singer. Right now, she just wants me, and the magnitude of that sends me into a frenzy. It doesn't matter who hears what's about to happen. I need to mark her. Stake my claim. Reclaim what is rightfully mine.

I don't even care about the obvious fact that I'm the only one in the triad of men at her disposal that is awake, which could mean she is choosing me since the others aren't around. Fuck those thoughts. Fuck them with a giant dildo.

I bite down on my bottom lip, not for a dramatic effect, although my movement does catch her attention. It's more so to bite back a throaty moan that threatens to pass my lips at her blunt confession. Her heavy lashes, thick and black, shadow her rosy cheeks as I lean forward into her space, soft and slow, like a cat sneaking up on a mouse.

"I'm not a nice man, Rosella. Thank you for realizing that early on, and thank you for accepting it. It's going to make this so much easier."

Peeling her needy body from mine, I push her down to the floor by her shoulders with enough force that she doesn't have time to readjust or contemplate what is happening before my pants come down.

"Open," I demand.

The compliant little beauty kneeling at my altar is a very good listener, even in her shocked state. She rounds her mouth, opening it wide enough to fit my aching length into it before she slides her warm lips around my crown without further instruction. There's no hesitation. No contemplation in her eyes when her tongue circles around my opening. Sophia wants this. *She wants me.* Her eyes are begging for it, lips thinning as they stretch around my engorged shaft the further down she takes me. Sophia's mouth becomes nothing more than a house for my arousal to spill into. I pump once, then twice, hitting the back of her throat causing her to gag. It's a sound sweeter than any chorus I've ever heard. Still, she doesn't retreat.

I'm so fucking hard. I've been hard for her since the moment I saw her sitting on that fucking stool in her studio, wearing that pink bodice top and black leather pants. Even knowing they were around her ankles as my best friend fucked her silently down the hall was a different type of torment.

Last night, we all took turns licking her tight little cunt poolside, side by side, like we were performing, and she was our stage, and it was maddening. I jerked off in the shower three times back-to-back before the hard bastard finally got the hint, succumbing to the fact that he was only coming by my fist and not buried in her sweet pussy.

That's how much pull she has over me. I want to punish her honey-scented pussy for forgetting about me. More than anything in the world, even more than I need my next depraved breath, I want to drive my fucking existence into her brain matter. Which is exactly what I do as I fuck her open mouth with relentless abandon.

I can see my bleached knuckles holding tightly through the strands of her wealth of red hair, demanding her head to bob. Round emerald eyes peer up at me, tears wetting their edges as I fuck her gaping mouth.

Nothing but the sound of her gagging again, choking on

my dick, and loving every minute of it as spit leaks from the corners of her mouth fills the air around us. It's the most breathtaking sight I've ever seen. Sophia on her knees, submitting to me like I'm her *king*.

"The only thing that comes naturally to me is singing and making you come," I say, breath choppy. "The evidence of that was still on my lips this morning. I showered, fucked my fist like it was your mouth, and even then, I didn't wash my face, Sophia. I want to taste your honey-flavored pussy on my lips every day until the day I meet my maker."

She whimpers at my confession, and I watch as her parted thighs press firmly together in an attempt to get any friction between her legs.

Without warning, she pulls back, my cock nodding in the air between my core and her face. Strings of spit drip from the corners of her parted lips, and I die little more by the sight.

Fucking dead.

I'm a shell of the man I once was because the sight of this—her looking like she's been used, and she's fucking happy about it—sends me to my early grave.

As if she's taking the reins from my hand, she sits back on her heels, pushing another boundary between us, and she strokes my long shaft with one hand, places her other palm around my leg and over my ass cheek, and leans forward to suck my balls into her mouth.

The sound alone has my knees almost buckling. I place my hand on her shoulder to keep from bending like a pretzel.

Working my shaft with her expert hands, she licks up the underside of my length, then focuses again on my balls, and then ... as her tongue drags across the forbidden land of my taint, my soul leaves my body.

Euphoria like I've never known creeps up on me. It starts at the soles of my feet, tingles through my legs like fireworks going off in my veins, and before I can protest or clamp down my need to come, I explode in her fist.

IN THE SECONDS after I bust a nut in her mouth, Sophia cleans every last drop of my arousal like she's my own personal cleaning crew. She gets my star of approval, a solid five out of five.

I've never had my dick sucked so well. It wasn't even just the head. It was the full experience, and I can't—I won't be able to—go back to anything else that doesn't involve all the extras she put into that experience. The tug on my swollen nuts, the lingering trail of her tongue down my taint.

*I'm hard again.*

Wordlessly, she pulls herself off the floor and tucks my dick back in the confines of my sweats like she's the one in charge—and, damn, I won't even lie, she is. She owned me—owns me. It's evident by the smile on her swollen lips. She pushes me down to a sitting position on the couch once more. Her hair is disheveled, her lips pink and swollen, her smile jubilant. It's like nothing transpired between us when she plants her body back on top of mine and pulls me into her embrace and hugs me. Her embrace is as tight as her mouth was. It feels *just* as good.

"This okay?" Her nose nudges mine.

"What if I said no? Cuddling after coming isn't something I'm used to. I just told you I wasn't a nice man."

I also promised her something last night that I've never promised another female on the face of this earth.

My heart.

As if she's detected the condescension in my demeanor, she motions to the spot on the couch she previously abandoned. "I guess I'll go back to sitting over there. Bored and alone until Ollie or Cannon wake up. Then, I'll climb on one of their laps because they'd never push me away."

The reality of her statement should feel like a slap to my face. Having felt gutted for weeks with their open PDA, I should be ecstatic that she is choosing to be so openly affectionate with me right now, and I am. Trust me, I am. There's still just a small part of me that wants all of Sophia. After her little performance, I can't imagine her offering the same type of treatment to anyone else. I want all of her. Just like I had her ten years ago, if even just for one night.

The reality of her statement is another reminder that if I want her at all, I must play nice, conform to this little foursome situationship we're charting in. There's no other option because the alternative of not having her at all isn't on the table. I know I won't survive losing her a second time. Especially not with her under the same roof—and under my best friends. That'd be a torture worse than death for a man like me.

"I'm not pushing you away, Rosella. Not anymore." I lean forward, nuzzling my nose into her hair that hangs over her shoulder. "I'm not an affectionate person. This"—I motion to her encompassing embrace—"is new to me. No one's ever cared about cuddling after sex. I'll need time to be what you need me to be if this is what you want or expect."

Raw vulnerability. The truth is out there now.

"I don't have any expectations, Mazen. I want whatever

pieces of you you're willing to give me. We have a lot of time to make up for. Last night, we bared it all, but if you're not ready to let me in fully, I get it. I'll wait until you are."

I'm about to kiss her senseless when the sound of a headboard thrashing against the wall echoes down the hallway. It's followed by an obscene number of unholy grunts that give the phrase *morning wood* a new meaning.

"Sounds like those two are occupied."

Sophia stifles a laugh, wraps her dainty hands around my neck, and pulls our faces together. "If the kitchen is still closed, I have something else you can eat for breakfast. What'd you call it before?" She pauses, seemingly deep in thought. "Oh, that's right. Breakfast of champions."

The dig of her words cuts me deep. I was such a tool, pulling that stunt. Her dig tells me that she's not as over it as I'd hope she'd be weeks later.

"If I could only eat you for every meal for the rest of my life, I'd be sustained. Trust me. I'm sorry for all the stupid shit I did or said."

"Better late than never," she says as her teeth sink into the lobe of my ear. Pulling back, she looks into my eyes, her glare reaching the very depths of my soul. "I know why you did it though. All we can do now is move on, move forward."

A loud thud booms, rumbling down the hallway, causing another laugh to slip through her lips.

"You're really okay with them being in there ... together ... without you?"

I don't miss the slight upward motion of her hips when she replies a little more breathlessly than before, "Why wouldn't I be? Them being together is the sexiest thing I've ever watched in my life. Just knowing that they're in there, doing what they're doing"—she clears her throat—"turns me on more than anything."

*Defuse the situation.*

*Come on, brain. Think of something not sexy to respond with.*

Otherwise, I'm going to take her on this damn couch, where her sister slept last night. I don't want the first time we're together like that again to be so … meaningless. Even though I just fucked her face with no remorse, as if it were a pocket pussy. A man only has so much willpower.

"I think I knew Cannon was bisexual before he did." *Solid execution,* I think to myself as I steer the conversation in another direction.

"This story sounds promising."

I don't mean to throw Cannon under the bus. "He left his computer on one day when I was in his room. We were getting together for practice, and I had to take a shit, so I went up to his room to use his bathroom in peace. I saw his computer screen. He had taken a quiz and left the browser open. It said, *How do you know if you like the same sex?*"

"Did you ever tell him you saw that?"

"I didn't have to. A couple of weeks later, after an hour-long practice session, I realized I'd left my phone in his garage. I rode my bike back to his house, and when I opened the side door, Ollie was giving him a hand job."

"Holy crap. That must've been mortifying for them." Her quiet smile speaks volumes.

"It was mortifying for me." I match her genuine smile. "We were teenagers with raging hormones. Hell, seeing them … together … made me question my own sexuality. I remember rushing home and pulling out my dad's titty magazines, praying to God that I got a hard-on from seeing a woman's naked body."

"Well, did you?"

There she goes, rubbing her core against mine again. Except this time, my cock isn't just hard, it's steel.

"You tell me."

"So, Oliver was the one stroking Cannon?"

Leave it to Sophia for her mind to circle back to that discovery.

"Sure was. They danced the line of lust and friendship until—"

"Cannon told him he loved him, and Oliver pushed him away."

"He had a tough upbringing. Cannon took him under his wing. Not that Murphy and I didn't, but Murphy's parents were really strict when we were younger, and I ... well, I was the same asshole I am today. In hindsight, I think Cannon was there for Ollie in ways that we weren't. When you've never known love or experienced it and you get sprinkled with the attention that Cannon gave him, it did something to him. The rest is history."

14

# CUCKOLD MOMENT

SOPHIA

**LACEY IS RUMMAGING** through her luggage, tossing article after article of clothing out like the bag itself is on fire and the clothes themselves are the source, when I tiptoe into a question.

"Are you sure you want to go tonight? We could stay in, order sushi, watch a movie."

I pet Jupiter on his head, praising him for being on board with the idea of staying in with me. He licks my hand about the same time that my sister starts to open her mouth.

"Am I sure I want to go to a free concert, drink free booze, and dance the night away?" Her pink-covered head swivels to meet my gaze. "Buzzkill. Come on, Soph. It's our first night here. You might be used to all this"—she waves around dramatically—"but I'm not. Let me live, woman! I want to see what all the fuss is about. You know, if the Kings can actually play and sound good while doing it. Don't rob me of this."

A knock draws our attention to my bedroom door before Vanna peeks her head in. "It's just me. Can I come in?"

"Of course." Backup has arrived. "Help me talk my sister into staying in with us tonight."

"Oh, I'm not staying in. In This Moment is opening for Kings, and they're, like, one of my favorite bands. Their lead singer is a total badass babe. Shh, don't tell my husband though." Vanna turns her attention toward Lacey. "She's trying to convince you to stay at the hotel with her and order room service, isn't she? She never came to one show BCK—Before Caddell Kidnapping," she explains. "She was all business. In tattoo mode. Never *let's party and enjoy ourselves* mode."

I deadpan, "Fine. Whatever. You both can go and bond over the band. I'll be right here. I have my Kindle. I'll make some popcorn. Jupiter and I will cuddle. Won't we, boy?" I rub his head as his tail wags a hundred miles a second.

"Like hell. You have three men at your disposal. Do you hear me? They're literally pining after you, all vying for your attention. Before I came in here, I overheard them arguing about which one of them you're going to think is a better musician after the show. You'd rather binge popcorn and read page porn than live your best life in high-def?" My sister blazes through her spiel, expelling enough energy in her speech that she's left winded.

The word *yes* is on the tip of my tongue.

Getting lost in a book—someone else's fictional reality— is exactly what I need right now.

Huffing at my demure stance and lack of response, Lacey plants her hands on her beautifully curved hips preparing to rip into me some more.

Vanna beats her to it when she blurts, "Three sexy-as- hell men want to screw you into next week. Nope. We are not doing this on my watch. I will not take no for an answer. Get up. Put on something skanky because you won't fit in if not, and let's go grind on each other and make our men so envious of us that they forget the words to their own songs."

"Do you have a best friend?" Lacey interjects. "I suddenly have a vacancy." Her eyes dart to me, then back to Vanna. "I think you fit the bill."

Rolling my eyes, I saunter into the bathroom and turn on the shower with enough force that I think I sprain my wrist. If I'm going to be forced to attend a concert, I'm going to look the part. You can count on that.

"Don't be mad, Soph," I hear Vanna's soft voice say over the steady stream of water while I'm rinsing my hair.

"I'm not mad. I just ..." My voice trails off.

"You just don't know how to act in public with them all?" she asks, reading my mind.

"Exactly." I breathe a sigh of relief that she understands. "It'll be my first outing since ... everything happened, and then I'll have to hide my feelings for Oliver and Cannon on top of already lying to the public. I feel like I'm making *them* my dirty little secret. I hate this. I'm sure people—the road crew, driver, everyone—are already judging me."

"For what, being with them all?"

"Yes," I say, defeated.

"I know we haven't known one another for long, but we've been together almost twenty-four seven for weeks. We eat, sleep, and play together. You get to know someone, the real version of them, on a more intimate level when you're forced to be in their direct proximity like we've been. And I can see that you're not just toying around with their feelings. I know you genuinely care about them, whether you're ready to admit it to them or the world yet. I'd never judge your heart for who it cares about."

"So, you don't think I'm a big fat slut for being with the three of them?"

"Now, I didn't say that," she says, casually amused by her own quip. "Kidding. No, I don't. I think you're exactly what they need, and vice versa. Even I was getting blue balls from all the sparring you and Mazen were doing, so I'm thankful that you're coming to terms with liking all of them."

FORTY MINUTES LATER, in true VIP fashion, the three of us are packed into the back seat of a blacked-out SUV. Ashton is behind the wheel, eyes glued forward. His demeanor seems *off*. I don't know if it's my place to ask if he's okay or not. A man in his line of work probably wouldn't take it lightly if a woman asked if he was okay because he seemed stressed. Still, his bad vibes bother me for some reason.

Turning my attention to the most probable culprit, I grill Lacey instead. "Hey." I nudge her. "Did something happen between you guys during your walk? Ashton seems … distant. Night and day from this morning."

"He's not distant. That's his pouting face." A glint of indifference glides across her satin cheeks.

She chooses not to elaborate with a purse of her lips, and it has me demanding answers.

"Spill." I press into her with only the most relentless mandate that a sibling can demand. "Now."

Tossing her pink hair over her shoulder, she turns toward me, a wicked smile on her lips. "I came on to him."

My eyes widen larger than the red stoplight that looms before us, dangling from a wire.

"You shouldn't be shocked. He's sexy as sin and taken, apparently. Well, not *taken*, taken. He's not wearing a ring or anything. That Lindsey chick ... the publicist or whoever she is, and he have been swapping spit."

"Lacey," I warn, holding my hands together tightly, like my restraint. The need to lay into her for overstepping beats like Cannon's drum in my chest.

First, I was her mother figure. Our relationship only morphed into friendship as she aged. Right now, a mixture of feelings and commentary from both my roles in her life cloud my judgment. I want to throttle her.

"Haven't you seen a cuckold video? Scrawny white men who are looking to spruce up their sex lives hire Black dudes who are always packing the biggest meat in their pants to screw their wives. Shoot me for wanting to know what all the fuss is about. I simply told *Ash* that Lindsey was welcome to come watch me ride him like I was auditioning to be an extra on *Yellowstone,* and we could have our own little make-believe-cuckold moment sans the marriage part." Vanna's attention is piqued, a gleam of interest shining in her tawny eyes. "And his response was?"

Lacey's tone is clipped when she responds, "He said that I was breathtaking, and if the timing were different ... ugh ..." She groans into her hands, rubbing her face without using too much pressure. Not even her disappointment could cause her to rub away the cosmetics on her face. "He turned me down."

"So, now, you're going to flirt with Lindsey to rub it in his face?" I know my sister better than even I think she knows herself.

"Damn right, sissy. She'll be begging me to wax her ass

with my tongue, and when that happens and Ash comes begging me for the opportunity to watch us, I'm going to shut the door in his face and steal his girl."

As soon as her threat hits the air, a fly must enter Ashton's mouth because he goes into a coughing fit that lasts the duration of the drive. He doesn't stop clearing his throat until we pull up to the rear of the venue and exit the Suburban.

## VANNA WAS RIGHT.

In This Moment is dope. I was part of the Paramore era, but this is some darker shit that claws at my chest. It doesn't hurt that Maria Brink is a total bombshell.

*I want to be her when I grow up*, I think to myself as I peer around the stadium.

It's wild to think that Kings of Jupiter were all best friends in middle school, singing in Cannon's garage. Now, look at them. Selling out shows overseas. A sudden pang in my chest reminds me that I knew Mazen *before*. Before ... all of this. Cher's "If I Could Turn Back Time" chimes in my mind while the stage goes dark, signaling what appears to be a brief intermission.

The stage crew shuffles around, preparing for the Kings to take the stage. I don't know why I'm suddenly sweating.

"Are you guys hot?" I cup the nape of my neck. Small strands of hair are sticking to my neck, drenched in my sweat.

"No. Now, calm down. It's not like you're banging three-fourths of the band or anything. They won't even notice your presence," my sister lies through her pearly-white teeth, biting her lip—signaling her tell.

"I knew you told Mom I snuck out when I was thirteen," I accuse, remembering that she bit her lip just like she's doing now when I had to call my parents from a pay phone because my bike tire had gotten a flat after I met Nolan Barker at the park, where we had made out so long that my lips were chapped for days.

Lacey looked just as pleased with herself then as she does now. In hindsight, being grounded meant I couldn't hang out with my friends, and I was forced to chill with her. Being besties with your kid sister wasn't always as cool as it is once you're both adults.

"Would you be mad if you knew that I woke her up before you even called?" Lacey lowers her thick black lashes.

"You brat. I was grounded for two weeks."

"Whatever. That wasn't half as bad as the punishment you dished out on my prom night."

"Let me remind you by that time, I was your legal guardian, and I caught you pegging the gym teacher. Who was happily married and a grandfather, by the way. Come to think of it, my punishment was kind of lax. You should have been sent to an all-girls school."

"Why? I would have made it my mission to have the headmaster on her knees, begging me to ride her mouth."

With renewed humiliation that my sister is a depraved individual who has absolutely no boundaries, I look away. Needing a break from the sweltering lights and this trip down memory lane, I shake my head, then make my way across the rectangular area we're standing in that looks more like we're in time-out than a VIP section.

*I've succumbed to not even being a free-roaming human anymore.*

Ashton blocks my exit. "Need something, Fireball?"

Great, the nickname is spreading. I'll be sure to thank Ollie for that later.

"A drink. It's hotter than hell. I'm feeling a little claustrophobic by the, you know, crate we're being kept in."

"They're worried about you." Ashton's expression is tight, determination etched into the golden-brown hue of his eyes. "Don't pretend that you haven't noticed all the extra precautions they've taken lately."

I've noticed them all.

How our driver waits to open the bus door until after the band's security team does a sweep, to the extra security personnel on our floor. It's not lost on me. I'm thankful for their concern. I just don't need or want it. Caddell already knows exactly where I am. He knew before I even knew he knew. There's no need for these extra precautions. I keep that last bit to myself. I also don't tell them that I'm currently in cahoots with my captor or about my plan to finish the tour, collect my check from Near Death Records, and pay him off once and for all.

The band, my sister, and Lindsey don't need to know about any of that ... because they'll ruin it to protect *me*, and I'll do anything to keep them safe.

"I get it," I huff, half annoyed, half ... something else that extends far past just being their live-in tattoo artist. Feelings I'm not prepared for start to swarm in my stomach. "I appreciate how thoughtful they've been. This"—I motion to the cage—"is a little too much. What if we have to pee?"

"You're not a prisoner. This is the VIP box. It's for important people. You and Vanna are the most important people to them. Aside from their dog child, that is."

*Jupiter is the real king.*

"Can I order a drink then?"

Ashton collects our drink orders, repeating them into the receiver on his phone. Ten minutes later, beverages are served, and the band is introduced. Like they *need* an actual introduction. The crowd goes freaking ballistic. You'd think Santa Claus just landed on the rooftop and started passing out black Amex cards.

Murphy walks onto the dimly lit stage first. A voice that I didn't even know could be bellowed from her petite frame roars from Vanna's lungs. Pride for her husband thunders from her, along with everyone else's screams reverberating around us. I watch in awe as their eyes collide. Even in this packed arena, their love is palpable. The unmistakable tether binding them reaches from the stage to where she stands next to me. For a brief moment, I get lost in what it must feel like to be stupidly in love. Infatuated beyond belief with someone else.

The thought is fleeting when my attention is stolen by another member of the band. Cannon strides across the stage and takes his place on his stool behind his set, and all the air leaves my lungs. He raises a pair of wooden sticks in his clenched fist above his head. I watch in awe as his fingers spread, allowing the sticks to spread in his large hand. Lowering his hand, he begins to rotate the sticks between his fingers, twirling them over and over with an expertise that only comes from years of skill. As soon as his eyes meet mine, the biggest smile I've ever seen widens across the brooding blond's face, making both my heart and my lady bits further south heat. Even in the distance, I can see the sharpness of his penetrating glare.

He looks at me like I'm not just another scantily dressed

woman shooting heart eyes at him. Like I'm more than just his tattoo artist.

Cannon's eyes bore into my soul, and though our standoff only lasts a few seconds, the enchanted feeling that I matter to him—truly matter—floats between us. Heavy like a dense fog that I never want to sift through.

I don't have time to process what that means because the crowd once again erupts. Chants and chaos unite in a rumble of yells and whistles. Ollie casually strolls onto the stage, looking every bit as relaxed as the seasoned performer he is. A smile tips the edge of my mouth when I notice him offering a wink toward the booming crowd. Then, he stops in his designated spot on the stage, takes the guitar he's handed by its neck, and suavely, in an almost-seductive manner, slides the strap over his head, placing the edge of it in his mouth. He bites it like it's a bridle, his white teeth tugging against the cloth. I can almost smell the arousal of the women surrounding us.

Oliver Collins, in all his charismatic glory, owns the stage and *me*.

The fans eat his act up. They devour every morsel of wanton lust he throws their way.

The crowd's volume increases, as if turned up a notch, and my chest reverberates with the vibrations echoing around us. I glance toward my sister. Her face is glowing; she's enraptured. It feels as if my body has been placed inside of a speaker. Everything is muffled.

And then the stage goes black.

The distinctive sound of a woman's voice pierces through the madness. "Wet for Wilde."

"You and me both!" Lacey yells back, earning a shriek from my mouth.

Disbelief burrows in my perfectly arched brows as a,

"Get your own band," rolls off my tongue. I wink at her, tossing a playful smile in her direction.

Kings of Jupiter hasn't even started to play their first song, and the atmosphere is electric. Charged to the max. The hair on my arms stands straight up, as if I put my finger in a light socket. Sadly, I fear that Lacey will be the one losing her bet to Mazen. How can she not be impressed by the energy that is this band? Even Marilyn Manson himself would be offering a slow clap for these guys ... *my* guys.

When the lights turn back on, my eyes track the movement of a spotlight.

Jupiter is sitting on a skateboard, one paw dangling off the side, helping him propel himself forward as he walks beside Mazen. I'm torn between watching the husky in complete and utter amazement and taking in the lead singer.

The sight before me is mind-boggling. Their dog ... an actual animal ... is riding a freaking skateboard. Remind me why I never came to one of their shows before now?

I force my stare away from Jupiter, turning my attention to Mazen.

He looks like he was skateboarding behind the stage, carefree and in his element. Wearing tight black jeans with a few fashionably ripped holes, an all-black T-shirt with the sleeves cut off—showcasing the ink adorning his arms—and a pair of checkered Vans, Mazen Wilde looks like the epitome of punk rock.

He's a walking billboard, and at this moment, I'm his biggest fan.

# 15

# FAILS IN COMPARISON

MAZEN

MY EYES LAND on her velvety-green orbs when I make my way to the center stage, where my microphone is waiting for me. From my stance on the stage and the distance to the VIP section we keep reserved for close family members and friends, I can feel her stare radiating into my bones, as if we're only centimeters apart rather than separated by hordes of boisterous fans and security guards.

Since I've accepted the fact that Sophia's here, on tour with us, working for us, I have abandoned my plan for revenge and come to terms with accepting her presence for what it is. *A blessing.* One I refuse to fuck up again. I've done the distancing thing with her. My heart and brain both longing for the woman while simultaneously loathing her very existence.

I won't lie and tell you that my palms aren't a little bit sweaty when I grab my mic, holding on to it with a death grip, using it to tether me to reality. The anxiety coursing through my veins isn't from the large crowd we pulled in or even the fact that this is our makeup concert, and we owe it to our fans to put on one hell of a show. I'm jittery because *she's* here.

Sophia's in my territory, my element.

After our shows, when she gets a chance to showcase her art—her purpose for being on tour with us—she lays out her expansive tattoo supplies with nothing but pride on her features. I've watched her do her thing for weeks. Creating something from nothing. Art that is permanently carved into our skin. This is different. Though I know she's listened to our music—after she finally admitted to it—us performing for a crowd that is oblivious that her essence is behind every goddamn lyric that bleeds from my heart is indescribable.

My muse tilts her head, as if to say, *What are you waiting on, Wilde?*

It's all the reassurance I need to slide back into character—the one the crowd has paid to see, not the one that only the beautiful, red-haired tattooist owns.

I open my mouth, ready to scream my usual intro into the mic. "Are you ready to rock?"

The crowd chanting is my answer.

Before I know it, time has flown by, and we've played almost the entire show, jamming right along with our fans. The song comes to an end, and the lights dim around us. The only sound remaining is that of Ollie strumming his electric guitar. Riff after riff, he enchants the crowd, distracting them long enough for our stage crew to bring out a black stool and place it front and center.

Knowing that Sophia was going to attend our show tonight—I need to remember to send Vanna a thank you basket for her part in making that happen—we collectively decided to end our show on a different note. Before we went onstage, I called a meeting and admitted to meeting Sophia before that night in her studio. Oliver said his Spidey-sense was never wrong, that he had a suspicion. Cannon seemed indifferent. I shook it off as him being shocked by the news.

*Get in line, bud.*

Murphy gave me a side-eye that promised he'd be drilling me for more details after our show.

In less than a few heartbeats, my shoulders felt lighter.

Coming clean to my band was task one. Task two is capitalizing on Sophia's presence here tonight.

This show might very well be the only one Sophia attends. By changing our show's end routine, it helps make my public relationship with her as cut and dry as it can be for those in attendance. Everyone is recording on their phones, which means their videos will most likely be loaded onto different forms of social media before our set is even over.

Lindsey's words echo in my head as I take my place on the stool. *"Show the world that Soph is yours, and dare anyone to fuck with her again."*

Sending a message to the fans and media about her attack by my crazed stalker is one thing. What we—Ollie, Cannon, and I—plan to do is communicate directly to Julian Caddell. Letting him know that he won't ever get close enough to Sophia to hurt her again. We'll make sure of it.

"Ten years ago"—I pause, my eyes drifting over the horde of people before I hone in on Sophia— "I was an average guy."

Cannon hits his cymbal with his stick, creating a clang pitch behind me.

"I had fewer tattoos then too—I can tell you that for sure. Anyway, I met a woman who had never even heard me sing before. We talked; we bonded."

When I wiggle my eyebrows, the row of women in front of me catch my meaning of *bonded*, and I swear I can visibly see them pant, jealousy over this woman—my *Rosella*— I'm speaking about written on their faces.

"Music has always been my solace. For as long as I can remember, it set me free, gave me an outlet, and more than once, I thought I'd die if I wasn't able to create anymore. The morning after I met this woman, I left her sleeping in her hotel room. I met up with these fuckers." I motion behind and beside me with the wave of my hand. "And we left to go on our first tour. We were opening for Sum 41 and on cloud fucking nine. The thing is, I knowingly walked away from the only person in the world who saw me for me, and I'll never do it again."

Fear of admitting this truth—my truth—to not only Sophia, but the thousands of people watching me with curious glints in their eyes has my throat threatening to close. Knowing that I'm not only speaking for myself, but also for Oliver and Cannon, who sadly can't publicly voice their adoration for Sophia like I can, gives me the courage to continue.

With my heart on the line, I say, "Music fails in comparison to you, Sophia Lozier. Everything does. I'll happily lay down my microphone at your feet if you ever doubt what you mean to me." *To all of us.*

Not missing a beat, we slide right back into our next song. I open my mouth to sing, this time when my eyes dance over the crowd and collide with Sophia's, I see her wipe at the corner of her eye right before her sister hugs her close to her side.

I hope she can read between the lines when I offer her one last glance in her direction, begging her to believe my confession—*I meant every word. Even if the spectacle was built on antagonizing Caddell. We all meant it*—before I start to sing.

*I'm going clinically insane*
*Screaming out your name*
*Ripping at my hair*
*Clawing out my brain*
*Your memory haunts me with every mention of*
*our fame*

The song comes to an end as the band and I bask in our collective admiration and infatuation toward Sophia. If Caddell is watching from afar, we aim to cut him at his knees. My admission to Sophia was as genuine as one can get. It served two purposes though, and I hope the bastard knows that we're not playing when it comes to keeping *our* girl safe.

This entire stadium, filled to the brink with thousands of spectators, now knows it too.

Love isn't a weakness. It's the purest form of strength. I've never once not had Murphy's, Cannon's, or Oliver's back, and starting right now, the same goes for Sophia.

"You fuckers ate this up at our last show. There's no way we could end tonight without it. Make some fucking noise if you want it," Ollie yells into his mic, demanding the crowd's attention and earning several whistles.

"This song was inspired by this little guy." I hold up my tattooed hand, showcasing the jellyfish that Sophia did weeks ago. "My girl tattooed it for me. I don't think she knew at the time that she stung me like a jellyfish or the impact she'd have on me." Pausing, I slide off my shirt, wipe the sweat off my face and neck, and toss it to the side of the stage.

Baring myself in more ways than one, I address the crowd one last time before diving into our final song of the night. "It's been rad to jam with you tonight. Thank you for your understanding in postponing our previous show. We're so fucking blessed to have fans like you who understand that nothing matters but family. You guys earned this one, and you can thank Sophia for inspiring it. This is for you, Rosella. It's all for you, baby."

You stung me like a jellyfish ohh ohh
Your hands are toxic tentacles ohh ohh
I welcome their sting
I welcome their burn
I welcome the way your touch makes me yearn
Out of all of the monsters in the big bad sea,
I'm begging you, baby, to keep stinging me

# 16

# DICK MASTER

## SOPHIA

IF MY DOPEY expression isn't a dead giveaway that I'm still reeling even though the show ended over an hour ago, I don't know what is.

Specifically the band's lyrics and Mazen's heartfelt performance have me floating on a cloud, I don't ever want to get down from.

*What does this mean for us—the four of us—moving forward?*

Uncertainty stirs in my stomach. It sloshes around with the concoction of mixed drinks that seemed to be never-ending. I'm thankful that the guys were forced to ride with Nick in their own vehicle when I let out a burp that would have had them checking my chest for hair. That's the beauty of being around other women. No one even bats an eye or snickers.

*Women are so mature.* I stifle a laugh at my own commentary.

"Earth to Soph. What's so funny?" Lacey snaps in my

face. "Hello?" She knocks on my skull. "Is anyone home?" When I tilt my head in her direction, she feigns shock. "Alert and oriented. Good."

"What, are you giving up piercings for nursing now?" I ask, crinkling my nose.

Sidenote: no offense to those in health care. They're the real heroes of our nation. It's just a profession I cannot see my sister fitting into. Hello, pink hair, cleavage that simply cannot fit into those adorable little scrub tops, and top-notch vulgarity that would leave human resources busy for days.

Lacey's still sweaty with a post-concert glow, and her forehead glistens in the light from the streetlamps we pass as we drive down the road. "Are you giving up monogamy for polyamory?"

Her retort is a solid question. One I pondered more than once during their concert. My eyes drifted from one musician to the next, capturing them in their own elements. Appreciating them in different ways. While I was enamored by their raw talent, I'm more intrigued by the people they are when they're not onstage. The men I've gotten to know on a personal level are just as deep as the rock stars pouring themselves into their music for their fans.

Vanna's gentle voice coaxes me back to reality. "If Sophia were a witch, would she say she's leaning toward group hex?"

"I can't with you." My stomach hurts from laughing so hard. "You give off these sweet and innocent vibes when, really, you're just as bad as Lace is."

We exchange a smile that immediately reiterates my first judgment of her. She's good people.

"Group hex is a good one," the pink-haired diva I no longer claim as my sister chimes in, nodding her head with pride.

She, on the other hand, is not good people. She's a skank. Who I love dearly.

"I'm supposed to be the joke master." My smile is wiped away in exasperation. "What did the triangle say to the circle?" I wait a whole five seconds before blurting the answer, "You're pointless."

Tossing her head back, Lacey mocks, "Maybe dick master is a better title now. I'd rather you claim that than continue to ruin your badass tattooist reputation with the dad jokes you somehow keep at the ready."

When the vehicle comes to a halt outside of the back of our hotel, I'm relieved. As much as I love touring on the bus, sleeping in a bed suited for a grown adult is so much better than the small bunks nestled on our home away from home on wheels.

Jupiter swings his head around, eager to get out of the car to see his owners and praise them for their epic performance.

"I'm happy too, buddy," I mutter, excitement coursing through my frame, eager to lick them in admiration.

I'm a dog—a dirty, dirty dog—and I don't give a single fuck when it comes to worshipping *my* three rock stars for a show well done. The fact that I don't bat an eye at the *my* thought speaks volumes.

With Jupiter in tow, Vanna, Lacey, and I make our way upstairs, following Ashton's lead. As soon as we hit the suite, we pile into my room.

"So, what'd ya think?" I ask my sister. I don't want to put her on blast, but she was jamming. "Mazen won, didn't he?"

Lacey unzips her faux leather shorts, slides them off, then faces me with hesitation on her face. "They're mediocre."

"My ass! You had stars in your eyes. I contemplated smacking you when I noticed a little drool dripping from the corner of your mouth as you openly gawked at my men."

Seeing the teasing laughter in my eyes, Lacey giggles. She knows I'd never smack her with ill intent.

I won't lie and say that the open eye-fucking every female in the arena did with Mazen, Ollie, and Cannon didn't irk me though. How could it not? I guess it's something I'm going to have to get used to if we continue to mix business with pleasure—and I plan on mixing a lot of pleasure with those three later.

"One's mine," Vanna shouts over the stream of water from the bathroom she's standing in, washing her makeup off.

As soon as we're all changed into comfortable clothes, faces wiped clean of makeup, we lay on my bed. My stomach growls, sounding like it's hosting a rooster fight.

"Is anyone else starving?"

"Not for food," my sister coos from the left of me.

I turn my head on the fluffy pillow holding it up to glance at her flawless oval face, cheeks painted a blushing pink from pent-up desire. "You're insatiable. It's only been a couple of days since you left Devon. If you start humping the edge of the couch, you'll be on the next flight back to Tampa."

The capped mass of striking pink hair does nothing to soften the edge in her voice. "You're choosing to patronize me while you have a harem of sexy rock stars at your disposal?"

Vanna's beautifully compact build jolts upright on the bed, the mattress dipping just a tad by her sudden movement. "Ladies," she says with a horrible attempt to sound stern. Silky black hair follows her jawline when she tilts her head to the side. "There's plenty of man ham to go around."

Mimicking Vanna's stance, Lacey sits up and folds her arms over her T-shirt in a defensive gesture. "Says the woman who's holding the fourth member of the band hostage by the new wedding band on his finger. You know what? I'm going out. We passed a bar down the street."

"Lace!" I dart off the bed. "Do you really think that's safe with Caddell out there?"

"Do you think any human—or corner of furniture in this suite, as you so bluntly put it—is safe around me right now?"

She would never cross the line she's implying. I don't doubt that for a second. I do, however, doubt that she's going to make it the rest of the tour without getting her rocks off.

"I need to find someone who isn't tied down, like the entire fucking band and their security team, to blow off some steam with me. No one will screw with me. I brought this." She shrugs her shoulders and rummages through her suitcase.

"You didn't?" I ask, already knowing she damn well did.

"Sure did, sissy." A black Taser waves through the air. "Now, I'm going to get dolled up—again—and go hunting."

"This is the most fun I've ever had on tour. Your sister is my idol." The newlywed next to me smiles wide in admiration at my sister's brashness.

Thirty minutes later, much to my dismay, Lacey leaves the safety of our suite in search of a man to dominate. Yep, you read that right.

Vanna flees to her own suite, claiming all this talk of sex has gotten her own juices flowing, and Jupiter and I are left to count down the time until our three owners arrive. Yep, you also read that right. Mazen, Oliver, and Cannon own me.

If there was ever a doubt where feelings were concerned, their show laid them to rest. I still can't believe Mazen made such a public declaration about our relationship. A hum of hope thrums in my veins at the prospect of his words being real and not just fabricated, another act for the media's benefit. It couldn't have been just another speech Lindsey had him repeating to help sell our fake-dating story. I refuse to believe it was only a ploy for the crowd.

Jupiter's body, pressed tightly against my side, offers a sense of security, luring me to sleep.

MY EYELIDS SPRING open only to find darkness. The time on my phone reads one in the morning. I glance around the room to find that it's empty and then check my phone once more only to confirm that there's no text messages from my sister.

Swallowing down my anxiety about her whereabouts, a new wave of unease washes over me when my eyes skim a text message I must've gotten while I slept.

Mazen: I told them about Chicago.

His message is short, and yet, I know immediately that he's referring to the fact that he and I met for the first time ten years ago. I wish he would have given me a little bit more than an, *oh by the way* text.

*It is what it is,* I think to myself when I notice the large vacancy that Jupiter's furry body left beside me on the empty bed. In his place is a note that steals all thoughts about both my sister and the bomb Mazen dropped.

*Come eat when you wake up.*

Starvation lures my body off the bed and out the bedroom door faster than a teenage boy stashing a nude magazine when a parent flings open his door. I stop at the edge of the hallway, inhaling a deep breath as I take in Oliver's ink-covered tan body. I openly study him, smothering a groan, and walk slowly into the kitchen.

There's something incredibly erotic about a man in a pair of low-slung sweatpants, midsection taut with glorious mounds of muscle, parading around, oblivious to his charm. I find myself staring again. My attention is now directed at the apex of hair nestled an inch above his waistband. The small, manly characteristic is like a giant flashing arrow pointing downward, a map to the promise land. Pair that mouthwatering view with a pair of bare tan feet gliding across the kitchen floor in an effortless dance, smooth, graceful and downright suggestive.

I'm salivating like a woman in heat, a string of excess energy from the concert now pounding in my chest like Cannon's snare. Oddly, my sudden hunger has nothing at all to do with the delicious aroma wafting through the air and everything to do with Oliver Collins owning the kitchen, owning me.

"Come here," he instructs, his sinful voice pulling me from my stupor. I'm caught red-handed. "Do you want a taste?"

*Oh boy, do I ever.*

The minute the wooden spoon slides out from my parted lips, I groan. "Wow. That's delicious."

"Greek lemon chicken soup."

"How long have you known I was watching you?"

Detecting a flicker of heat in his intense orbs, I have my answer before he even says the words.

"Long enough for that little spaghetti strap nightie to give me a semi." He gestures to the thickening bulge in his sweatpants.

"I found something else I want a taste of," I say, standing close enough to him to feel the heat emanating from his body.

Wanting to be desired and hearing that Ollie is undeniably attracted to me have my heartbeat throbbing in my ears.

We're in a standoff, chest to chest. From the moment we met in my tattoo studio, we've been like a live wire of frantic energy. Glimpses of the times he's bedded me—me panting his name begging for release, has me involuntarily breaking our eye contact in an attempt to reel my wayward thoughts back in.

His gorgeousness knows no bounds. There's no use in pretending that he doesn't affect me. If the pulse in my neck is any indication, Oliver knows exactly why I broke his intense eye contact.

Our proximity is a kindling, a purely carnal gas for fire.

"Learn some patience, Fireball," Ollie coos, using the nickname he dubbed me the first night we met. "Good things come to those who wait," he adds with a wink before turning his back to me, tending to his soup like he is blind to the ache he left me with.

*Patience.* I've been as patient as an ant traveling from

Ohio to California. I want the soup. I want Oliver. It's debatable as to which one I want first at this point.

The hot ache that Ollie left me with stirs in my core as I stand at his back, watching him closely. His muscled forearm flexes with each stir of the wooden spoon he's holding. It's hard to remain quiet, to not pry into why he loves to cook.

Repressing my admiration for his talent both onstage and in the kitchen is interrupted by the intoxicating musk of another man approaching me from behind.

With each heavy thud against the floor, I know it's Cannon. My body knows when his is nearby. A tingle starts at the soles of my feet and moves upward, almost like our bodies are beckoning one another. His large, callous hands land on my exposed shoulders, sending an involuntary chill throughout my entire body. His touch does nothing to remedy the heat that Oliver started. If anything, Cannon's nearness only intensifies the ache between my thighs.

"Smells good in here." Cannon's lips part. "Greek lemon?"

"Is this a staple dish, Ollie?" I ask, confused that their drummer automatically knew the dish by scent alone. "Do you have a food kink I don't know about?"

For a beat, I think my questions will go ignored. I glance over at Cannon, who is now leaning against the refrigerator, eyes locked on mine. He must sense the movement next to him because a slow smirk graces his full mouth. A split second later, Oliver is standing directly in front of me again. His sculpted body is poised between my legs, and his eyes … look as hungry as mine.

His warm hand cups my cheek tenderly as he bends down so that we're eye level, and he says, "I have an aversion to starving."

The truth behind that statement resonates and turns my stomach.

Just the thought of Oliver as a child—hungry, afraid, alone—makes me physically ill. It still amazes me that he lived through so much adversity before he turned eighteen. It makes me that much more thankful for the other members of Kings of Jupiter. Mazen, Cannon, and Murphy became his family in all the ways that actually matter. Maybe it wasn't them per se that saved Oliver from a life that could have been vastly different than cooking in this plush pad. They were all young adults themselves. Though it's clear they advocated for Oliver, and in the end, their families accepted him into their lives.

This realization makes the fame that the band has experienced mean so much more. Lindsey should really be leaking stories about this if she wants to earn brownie points with the media. We've all heard the whole rags-to-riches success stories more times than we can collectively count, but seeing it is something else entirely.

My heart hurts for Ollie as a child.

Rearranging the hardening bulge in his pants, Oliver steps back, handing me a bowl. "It's getting late. Let's eat."

I nod, accepting the bowl, and fill it to the brim before sitting at a stool at the island. "Where's Mazen?" I ask, blowing on my spoon.

"Had some business to take care of," Cannon answers vaguely, as if he was banking on me inquiring about the singer's whereabouts.

I'm half tempted to press for details, until my thoughts are overtaken by the goodness that fills my mouth as I take a bite of Ollie's delicacy. We eat in mostly silence, sitting side by side, enjoying one another's company. I imagine that this is what being content is. It's a fleeting feeling that I haven't been acquainted with in many, many years.

My mom was the rock of our family. When cancer stole her from us, we were left broken and shattered. Uncertain how to move on without her, Lacey and I attempted to build a new life, one in which we forged a bond that went deeper than the word *family*. She has been my *person*. My reason. The tether to humanity that kept me grounded when life stole another person from me. My son.

Until now ... my heart has only thudded in my chest with a fierce loyalty to her and only her. The reality that it beats wildly and stretches to make room for Oliver, Cannon, Mazen, Jupiter, Murphy, Vanna, Lindsey, and even Ashton has me forcefully fighting back a sob of acknowledgement.

The silence surrounding us is calming. It feels normal. Right. I debate on bringing up Mazen's text. I'm not sure what he told them about our night in Chicago. The fact that Oliver and Cannon haven't brought it up leaves my stomach queasy, soup sloshing in it.

By the time I finish my bowl and rinse it in the sink, I turn my attention back to the two men before me. Ready to face them head-on, I say, "Mazen told me he told you guys about us meeting in Chicago years ago."

Cannon nods wordlessly.

Oliver finishes his last bite and leans back against the stool's backrest. With one arm draped over the back of the empty chair next to him, he says, "He did."

That's it? I don't know what I expected him to reply with, but it was more than that.

"I didn't know when we first met, I swear," I add, feeling a mixture of emotions. Guilt being the main one. "When you admitted you weren't Scotty Girth, I mean. I didn't know he was part of your band then." I laugh at the memory. "I only just remembered him after the incident with Caddell. I had suppressed memories or something. At least, that's what the psychologist I spoke to on a telehealth visit said."

"Psychologist?" Cannon asks on a deep huff.

"When I was discharged from the doctor, they mentioned speaking to someone, a counselor or therapist, about the attack." I flinch at the last word. "Lindsey set it up since the whole situation was all hush-hush. When I mentioned I remembered something from a long time ago, my therapist had her colleague reach out. I guess I had repressed his memory, she explained. It doesn't normally happen unless a trauma occurs, but she said it's not an anomaly. Then, she suggested that the trauma of being kidnapped unlocked that hidden memory."

"That's why he was a dick for weeks. He remembered you, but you didn't remember him," Cannon states bluntly, almost as if he's just pieced the puzzle together himself.

"Yep," my reply is short. It's all I can muster without tearing up or feeling like a complete monster.

"He had you first?" There's a tinge of remorse in Cannon's tone. He knows the answer before I answer.

"My body, yes. Not my heart. That trophy belongs to you and Ollie."

Oliver runs a hand over his spiky blond hair. "I can live with that."

When Cannon doesn't agree, my palms begin to sweat. I need to know that this hasn't ruined what's been budding between us. Everything has happened so fast since we got back on tour. There hasn't been any time to confront them.

That's a cop-out.

Mazen found time to tell them. Then hung me out to dry and deal with the aftermath of that confession alone.

From my brief research on polyamorous relationships online, I learned trust is the foundation. That's the same for any healthy relationship, though I've never really had one of those to compare this to. I inhale, prepared for the reality that Cannon won't be able to accept my past.

I shake away the thought and ask, "Can you live with that too, Cannon? Knowing that I met Mazen years ago at a tattoo convention and slept with him."

"He wasn't memorable enough," his reply is curt, short, and to the point. "Ollie and I won't make that same mistake. You'll know we've been in you with every step you take for the next week."

My chest constricts, along with my core.

He called Oliver Ollie. That simple fact tells me that all will be okay. Along with the thick fog of desire hanging in the air between us. We haven't been together, the three of us, since the day on the tour bus when Oliver caught me blowing Cannon.

I have a feeling that's about to change.

# 17

# RAGING BONER

CANNON

BREATHING LIGHTLY BETWEEN PARTED LIPS, I step off the stool that feels like a jail cell encasing my large frame.

As if my senses have been short-circuited, a deep need to instill my memory...our memory, in Sophia's mind urges my every movement forward. I stand next to Oliver, whose body has gone still on the stool he's sitting on. For a man who screams dominance, he's awfully silent when my shoulder bumps into his. Using his compliance as a distraction, I move my hand gently down the back of his neck. The stoic expression he's wearing is seriously startling. He's a vault. Oblivious to the sensation that has overtaken my entire fucking body. I curve my fingers around the back of his neck, turning my wrist slightly, compelling him to look me in the eye.

It's when our eyes lock that his resolve seems to ebb.

*Finally*, I think to myself.

His emotions have always been hard to read. It's what

got us into this ten-year battle in the first place. Mine are worn on my sleeve, his are bundled up tightly beneath the mask he wears like armor.

I fight back, restraining myself from fondling his marble-hard nipples that stand erect by my powerful touch. They're a sight for sore eyes, a sign of his body reacting to my touch.

If I know Sophia like I think I do, seeing me and him together turns her on. I'd cast a vote, claiming she enjoys it almost as much as she enjoys our undivided attention on her. It's why he's the focus of my attention. Oliver Collins exemplifies composure. Sure, he's a hoot to be around. The life of the party. Always the first one of us to accept a dare and follow through with it. In the bedroom, behind closed doors, he's forceful, unrestrained. Free to give up the contempt that our everyday life brings. He seeks to own his lovers. Demanding whatever it is that brings him pleasure while giving it back tenfold.

My best friend has possessed my body from the very first time I sprang an erection. He's held power over me for years. Power that I, too, crave. Power that I would chase into the night. Power that I aim to take a sliver of back. The man that I am today is a far cry from the confused boy I was when Oliver strolled into my life. He awakened desires that I never knew resided in me, though his attraction to the same sex seemed to go dormant during our rumbling-in-the-sheets hiatus. I didn't lie when I told him I didn't let another man fuck me. It's the truth. Oliver is the only man who has possessed me in that way.

Me screwing men? Now, that's a topic that warrants attention. While I love Oliver to take control, I developed a taste for it myself. I've been the top, caging men in, devouring them in Oliver's absence. He has a thing or two to learn about the man I grew into, including my desires, because as much as I love having him back where he belongs, buried in my heart and hole, I long to sink into his just as much.

High on post-show endorphins with a full stomach and a raging boner, I slide my unoccupied hand down Oliver's taut stomach. It hovers over the hardness at his core for a fleeting second, then settles on his inner thigh. My hand is firm as I apply a small amount of pressure, cupping his leg. I lean down, my mouth hovering over the shell of his ear.

"You cooked. We clean." I tilt my head, motioning to a shell-shocked Sophia. "I hope you're not tired because we're going to suck you off until your legs give out as a thank-you for preparing us this delicious, nutritious soup. Then, I'm going to fill your mouth with my nutritious seed." The pad of my thumb finds the middle of his bottom lip. I drag it down a little, exposing his teeth. "I've been dreaming about this mouth sucking my cock for days."

Acceptance radiates on his face as Oliver beams in approval at my plan. Both of our glances rake back toward Sophia. At the end of the day, this only works if she's comfortable. She's our number one, our center in the storm of sexual tension in our lives. Something intense flares through the kitchen, an electricity as vigorous and eager as a summer storm.

"Let's get these dishes washed so we can drown our boy in our cum."

"Keep up the dirty talk, and you'll have to mop the floor, Cannon. I swear I'm about five seconds from doing unheard of things with this fancy water sprayer." Sophia's body aches to be touched. I can see it in the precarious flame burning in her eyes and hear it in the strained tone of desire in her voice.

"Don't spark an idea you're not going to see through, Fireball. Get to cleaning, you two. Looks like we're going to make twice the mess afterward." The sense of Oliver's excitement drives us both into the kitchen.

We don't load the dishwasher. There isn't a reason why, and we don't discuss it beforehand. Sophia washes the dishes, then hands them to me to dry. It's not as if we're stalling, trying to prolong our chores, because we know the prize waiting for us at the end. We can feel him seductively peering at us with longing in each glare. Without saying it, I think we want Oliver to suffer a little bit.

As he watches us intently, assessing us as we move in tandem around the kitchen, it's evident that he's burning to take control. The fight that he's waging to remain seated, separated from us behind the island, flares across his face as Sophia and I take our time, drifting through the kitchen on a cloud, knowing that we're finally in charge. Oliver is at our mercy.

The torture continues as Sophia slides past my front, in search of the drawer housing the hand towels. Her ass rubs against my throbbing cock. It takes every ounce of willpower I can muster not to rip her clothes off and impale her with my rod right here in the kitchen, where anyone can walk in and see.

*Music.* We need music as a diversion. *Jesus Christ.* I don't think music can even defuse my need to be buried in them.

I thought music was my soulmate for so long. Then, I met Sophia, and Oliver came to his senses. The thought of adding music, my aphrodisiac, to this moment might have me nutting in my pants before I even have one of them naked.

Ignoring my throbbing cock, I unlock my phone, open

my app, then hit play, all the while begging the universe that the song I chose works as a diversion. Machine Gun Kelly's "Kiss Kiss" bellows from my phone speaker. Thank fuck the mood in the atmosphere shifts from boning to jamming.

Sophia surprises me, grabbing the wooden salt shaker from the counter. She starts to sing into it, using it as her own personal microphone. Her tone is off and she stumbles over a few lyrics, but the look of happiness radiating in her eyes and the wide smile on her face are infectious. She moves, prancing along the tiles, not giving two shits that she looks like a talent-show reject. Ignoring my rock-hard shaft pulsating in my pants, I pick up a freshly washed soup ladle and its matching spatula, accepting that I, too, am going to look like a fool and follow her beat. My makeshift drumsticks pound against the edge of the countertop.

Powerless to our stupidity, Oliver pushes his stool away from the island. He gives a *what the fuck* shrug of his shoulders, then leans into his signature stance. In a blink, he joins us in the most idiotic performance of our lives.

The three of us are jamming hard-core, oblivious to anything outside of this moment, when the suite door swings wide, and Mazen stumbles in. With tense shoulders, he saunters over to us, seemingly enraged. It's not the time or place to inquire what's got him so bent out of shape. I can only guess it has something to do with the private investigator he hired to tail Caddell. As the main point of contact, he excused himself to handle business and asked us to keep Sophia occupied.

Sophia dances over to him, the wealth of red hair she had piled high on her head now cascading over her shoulders. Not missing a beat, Mazen's brows flicker a little, his stern expression softening at the sight of our girl enjoying herself. The hard line of his jaw relaxes a little when he accepts this minute of reprieve, our pocket of happiness, for what it is. An escape from the drama that has become our everyday lives. If we don't latch on to these moments when we get them, we'll go crazy.

A deep laugh floats from his lungs, its sound is rich and throaty. Then, he runs into the living room, jumps on the couch in a wide stance, and plays the meanest air guitar known to man.

This is the Mazen we grew up with. The carefree dude who wanted everyone to have a good time. He used to be a lot like Oliver. They shared a humor that edged on evil. It wasn't until after his sister's passing that he withdrew, becoming serious.

When the song comes to an end, laughter thunders from our lungs. Silence befalls a few moments later, we're brought back to reality. The one where we're three best friends who are falling head over heels for our live-in tattoo artist. The wide-eyed innocence Sophia gives off wafts around the three of us. She beckons us toward her, and we're like moths to a flame. Emerald eyes, full of magnetism, motion us closer, like the crook of her index finger, but her hand never moves.

As if a rubber band snaps, the tension in the air, along with our inhibition, flies out the window.

It's Mazen who gets to her first. Their push-and-pull is magnetic. It's almost as if they're privy to a secret that's shared only between them, and now, I know why. We sit in silence for a beat, watching as Mazen ravishes her mouth. The barrier of their hidden relationship has vanished, putting Oliver and me on an equal playing field once more.

For a split second, I almost take back my comment, feeling a smidge jealous as I watch their explosive harmony.

There's nothing feral about their exchange. It's not driven by sex. It's guided by something much, much deeper—perhaps something that can threaten us all.

What if she loves him and only likes me and Oliver for sex? Are we just a distraction?

A soft moan flows from Sophia's lips like warm honey as their lips part. I watch in awe as his jellyfish-tattooed hand moves to her jawline.

Though his voice is nothing but a whisper, I hear him loud and clear. "I'm not in the place I need to be in when I finally get to sink into you again, Rosella. This has everything to do with me, nothing to do with you. Do you understand that?"

I'm not alone in the sudden curiosity that locks my shoulders in place. My body feels as if it were being doused half in fire and the other in ice.

*Don't ruin this, Maz.*

We've only all just accepted that this could work. Inferiority or not, I'm still all in, knowing that *we* really could work, the four of us, together. We haven't discussed it as thoroughly as we need to, especially being in the public eye, but the feelings are there. I know we've all sensed this pull.

Sophia is our tether.

Cautiously, she nods her understanding before he continues, "I'm going to sit down. Right over there." Mazen motions to a chair behind him. "I'm going to watch my best friends make you come on their faces so many times that they won't need to moisturize for a week. Then, when you don't feel like you can come anymore, you three can go to your bedroom, and you'll let them fill your tight hole with their nut."

The emphasis he puts on *their* pulls me from my jealous stupor. He's telling us without having to spell it out that he knows we share her heart and body, and he's on board with it.

There's no denying the disappointment on Sophia's face, even with the prospect of him directing the scene that will end with her full of a mixture of my and Oliver's cum. It's a brief bunch of her brows that has me noticing her impatience toward him giving in and joining us fully. The other night, poolside, he shared her with us. We took turns lapping her up, our fingers brushing as we finger-fucked her until she was wetter than the pool we swam in. When she begged to be filled by our dicks, Mazen dipped then too.

I think there's more going on than he's willing to admit. At first, I thought it was the group thing he wasn't interested in. Now, I think it has more to do with their past. Oliver told me he had a sinking suspicion that Mazen is the father of the son she still refuses to tell us about. I see the way Maz looks at her. I can feel the desire he has rolling off him like steam. With the information we know now, it makes more sense. Caddell mailed the birth certificate specifically to Mazen, not to me or Oliver or, hell, even Murphy.

If I've learned anything in my time circling this globe, it's that leaving things unsaid is almost as bad as confronting them head-on. This isn't the time or place for that conversation. I store it in a box in my mind and slam the door shut.

"My sister is out. Could be back at any time. You want her to just storm in and see them with me? Anyone can walk in." Sophia defiantly crosses her arms over her chest.

Getting caught has never been an issue before. It certainly wasn't when we all lapped her up poolside.

She feels rejected.

"It's the middle of the night, Rosella. No one is walking in tonight except Lacey, and I have a hard time believing that anything could make her blush. I dare someone else to come in here and see you ... what's ours ..."

Her eyes gloss over at his statement.

"They wouldn't live to see the sunrise tomorrow. I promise you that."

"Pussy is my favorite meal of the day." Oliver leans forward, caressing her shoulders. "Couch. Now."

Her body arches toward him. "Yes, sir."

A tormented groan leaves Mazen's mouth.

"He asked for a show, Oliver." I take his hand in my own, guiding him to where Sophia now lies. "Make her cry for her release."

# 18

# SINKHOLE

SOPHIA

THERE'S something magical about being out of the country. It's like when you go on vacation, nothing back home matters. The stress of your job, the balance of your bank account, responsibilities—they all disappear into thin air. Your mind abandons the worries and stressors that real life brings you. That's how it's felt being back on tour with the band. Especially since my sister is with me this time, and I don't have to worry about her safety.

In the secluded bubble of the tour bus, I become invincible.

I'd be ignorant *not* to think about our tattoo studio. Knowing Devon is there has lessened some of that worry, thankfully. He's proven to be more than just a security guard. He's managing the shop with an expertise that has me questioning why I didn't look closer at his résumé from the beginning.

While I still get to do what I love for a living and tattoo the guys after their shows, it's been nice, being allotted this time away from Tampa and some of my obligations. Which is why, as we sail through the clouds on the band's private plane, I am not excited about our next destination.

*California.*

It's not that I have beef with the Golden State itself. My loathing for this flight in general has more to do with being back on American soil. The same soil that both Caddell and Knox walk on. They've ruined any sort of comfort I have being back in the States.

The safety I felt with an ocean between us was dismantled when I was told that the Kings of Jupiter are up for Album of the Year. I'm Mazen's plus-one. I should be elated, ecstatic even, at the opportunity to hold his arm, stake my claim for the world to see. The butterflies swarming in my stomach aren't the good kind, I'm afraid.

Here we are, flying to attend a major award show, where Mazen and I will be paraded on the red carpet like bait for Caddell. That's the real qualm, my blatant fear unleashed. A shiver of anticipation dances across my skin because I know that my date is one of the most handsome, most admired—thanks to the fake-dating PR stunt Lindsey fabricated—musicians of our time. I'm overjoyed for him and the others—I swear it. Being nominated for this award is monumental for their careers.

I'm scared that the cameras will show how enthralled I really am with my fake boyfriend. Painting a mark on Mazen for his own father or Julian Caddell to loathe him more is the last thing I need. I haven't even come clean and told the band much more than the basics about my kidnapping. Small details, here and there, to get them off my back is about the extent of how we've left things. I did cave and informed them that I'm planning on paying off Caddell with my check from their record label, and they know about my past with Knox, his equally awful nephew. That's all I've given them. Though, when I think about it, it pretty much sums up the entire situation in a nutshell.

The only morsel of truth I have left to spill, I've bitten my tongue to keep quiet. The truth about Roman. I can tell that both Cannon and Oliver are onto me. It's in the way they watch me and Mazen. It's like they're reading between the invisible lines I'm trying so desperately to shield.

Another drawback of the evening ahead of us is that I can *only* hold on to Mazen's arm. Look into his eyes when they announce the band's nomination, kiss his lips to congratulate him when they call out their band as the winner— because, duh, they're going to win. All the while, Oliver and Cannon will be seated right next to me, watching with front-row seats when I gush over their best friend, ignoring them wholly. Guilt of our predicament eats at my insides as I stare out the window, eyes dancing from one puffy white cloud to the next.

There's no room for despondency in our busy schedule. As soon as the plane lands, the men are hauled off in one vehicle, and Vanna, Lacey, Jupiter, and I are piled together, driving in the opposite direction.

We spend the next several hours being waxed—holy hell, I feel like my below-the-belt-lips are being ripped from my body—styled, and pampered. By the time we make it back to the hotel, thoughts of tripping on my gown as I walk hand-in-hand with my famous boyfriend barely crosses my mind. Thanks to the copious amounts of champagne I ingested without eating lunch.

*Here's to hoping I won't need to use my clutch as a barf bag.*

Ashton says he's going to escort my sister and Jupiter to our room for the evening while another hired guard, I think his name is Paul or Preston, maybe, brings us to meet the others.

"Thank you," I tell the stern-faced security guard as he opens the back door of another limo, gesturing for me and Vanna to get in. I feel like we're children of divorced parents, being transported from one car to the next at a shady rest stop.

With my hand flat against the door, I reach behind me, grabbing on to Vanna's while attempting to hold on to my clutch at the same time. "Safety in numbers, right?" I say over my shoulder.

"Right. We're rolling six deep tonight." She encourages me to climb inside the dark vehicle, not a shadow of tension on her beautifully painted face.

"Come the hell on. I have to piss."

*That'd be my date.*

Which means the band is in tow and Vanna and I really weren't being lured into the back of a limo by a crazed stalker—and by stalker I really mean, Julian or Knox Caddell.

*What a relief*, I think.

Vanna follows me in, and we both fight back a grin as the band's collective whistles echo through the confined space.

"Baby girl," Murphy mumbles, voice deep, eyes roaming his wife from head to toe.

"You approve, Mr. Miller?" The Cambodian bombshell next to me shimmies, giving her husband fuck-me eyes that are hard to ignore.

I stifle a laugh, turning my attention to my guys. They're all black tuxes and business. If it wasn't for the ink adorning their hands and dancing up their necks, I might have honestly thought we stepped into the wrong limo.

"What, no catcalls for me?" My eyebrows arch mischievously as I fish for a compliment.

Oliver is the first to speak, cutting the silence, extinguishing my self-doubt. "The words I want to say are not for anyone else's ears."

We spent the day getting spoiled. Which was amazing—don't get me wrong. But I couldn't help the nagging feeling that kept sneaking up, reminding me that I'm not *this* girl. I'm not a supermodel or an actress or one of those influencers who crept into the spotlight by making silly makeup videos online. Though I'm not throwing shade at my girl from *Pucks & Mascara* blog and podcast. She's a riot, and she knows her stuff about both hockey and makeup. I envy her a little because she's the type of woman who would be better suited in this position. She's poised, beautiful, and drips class.

Though I may have been physically groomed for this evening, I'm not prepared for the myriad of feelings that are circulating in my lower belly. I'm sure as hell not in any position to afford the gown and jewelry that are on my body. I'm a small business owner. A tattooist. Just a run-of-the-mill woman trying to make her mark in this world. To say I'm feeling a tad inferior about this whole evening would be putting it mildly.

Inclining his blond head, Cannon takes a swig from his glass before his gaze settles directly on me.

I'm scorched by his intense glare. My insides turn molten.

"I second that," he says, mimicking his pal next to him.

With an adventurous toss of my head, I turn to face Mazen. The wild horse, the dark king. There's a pensive look on his face, almost like he's contemplating saying *screw who's watching* and taking me right here, right now. I almost wish that were the case. He's still being … distant, withdrawn. Hesitant is more expressive of how he's been toward me sexually. I don't want to rush him or push him into something he doesn't want to do. I'm a woman though, so I can't control my longing to know what is holding him back from sealing the deal between us. I *know* he wants me. I've felt his need thickening in his pants on numerous occasions since we entered our little ceasefire of sorts. I just don't know why he's holding back.

What's stopping him from claiming me like his friends have? Or maybe I do know and just refuse to believe that the universe could be so cruel.

There's still a secret the size of the Titanic wedged between us. One that only I'm privy to. One that is starting to corrode like a car battery in my stomach. It's probably for the best that he's abstaining from bedding me. I honestly don't think I could look him in the eyes as he sinks into me, knowing that I am hiding such a huge thing from him while enjoying getting lost in the pleasure I know he'd deliver.

I'm a liar—this we already know to be true. It's a new freaking personality trait.

There's no way in hell I'd do anything but enjoy myself while the man who wrote and dedicated an entire song to me about a tattoo I had given him slides into my sweet spot. I'd bite the inside of my cheek, sealing my mouth shut, forcing the truth to remain hidden. I'd relish every minute of pleasure that Mazen offered me. I'd lap it up like a dog on the brink of dehydration in the summer heat.

I'm *so* going to hell.

A giant sinkhole might as well open up and swallow me whole right now. I wouldn't even claw at the sides of the earth as it dragged me into its pit. I'm in the wrong, and I know the longer I keep Roman's life a secret, the worse the consequences will be.

Conjuring up a plan to come clean gets added to the top of my to-do list. I park the thought, offering my attention back to my friends.

If Mazen refuses to give me a compliment, I'll offer him one. "You look like you just won a trial. Then screwed the judge in front of the entire jury."

"And what are we"—Ollie gestures between himself and the broad blond beside him—"chopped liver?"

Knowing that Mazen is my date, the only male in the band that I'm permitted to be openly affectionate with in public, I seize the chance to plant a kiss on Oliver's mouth. He should know he never has to fish for compliments from me, even if I'm not allowed to show him how much I want him. He owns a part of me. My heart is split three ways.

Leaning forward, I hunch down, careful not to hit my head, as I inch toward him. Noting the rise of his thick eyebrow, I can see the question written on his face. Normally, no one is around, aside from the four of us who have entered into the vast unknown with one another. Having Murphy and Vanna as spectators is new, scary even. I'm forced to conceal my feelings for the drummer and Oliver in public, but I refuse to hide my attraction to them in front of our friends too.

"You're," I say before sealing my lips to his. They're warm and taste like ... Fireball. The realization causes my heart to thump wildly in my chest. When I pull back, I turn my attention to meet Cannon's robin's-egg-blue-colored eyes as I say, "Mine." Angling my body toward his large frame, I lean forward, cup his jaw, then seal my mouth to his, gifting him the same peace offering I did the guitarist next to him.

"Mazen hasn't made his mind up entirely if he's with *us* yet or not. Don't be jealous if I give him a little more attention while I try to convince him that he'd be stupid to turn his back on *us*, from all that we can offer him."

"Girl, you've almost convinced me to switch teams," Vanna squeals.

A deep huff booms from her husband's chest. I think he's going to retort, pound his chest caveman-style, but what he says shocks me to my core.

"Shit, even my morals are wavering. Team Quartet." He holds his hand up in solidarity.

We collectively eye Murphy, questioning his brutal term for our situationship.

"What? I've done my fair share of Googling."

Murphy's tight-lipped smile is enough to tell me he's joking. Though the married couple's commentary hangs thick in the air as we ride in silence the rest of the way to the venue.

Thoughts of walking the red carpet infiltrate my mind. Sweat forms in areas it should be illegal to perspire. Sensing the tension coursing through my body, Cannon's oven-mitt-sized palm finds my leg.

"I didn't walk the red carpet at our first show."

Ollie chuckles. "Shit. I remember that."

The small bit of information Cannon dangles like a steak in a lion's den piques my interest. Though we've been doing this dance for a couple of weeks now, he's still not very forthcoming in the communication department. I eat up his confession, chasing any crumbs he's willing to spare.

"The tabloids blew up, claiming there was turmoil in the band already. Lindsey had a field day, trying to repair the damage my absence caused. If I remember correctly, she chose to be spiteful. Telling the press that I came down with a horrible stomachache and was stuck in the restroom."

"She didn't!" I laugh.

Lindsey is my hero. There hasn't been a time when she isn't on her A-game. She's as professional as they come, but knowing she blasted Cannon like this paints her in a new light. I like her style even more now, knowing that in the end, that was probably the last red carpet he chose to miss.

"She sure as hell did," Oliver answers. "Remember when we won and the stage crew motioned for us to get up and go onstage. One of them was holding their stomach, bending over. It was a silent gesture, asking if you felt well enough to join us onstage to accept our award."

"I could have died from food poisoning." Cannon pats his hands on his thick thighs—a nervous tic I've come to notice.

"You should have died from embarrassment," Murphy bellows, joining in on the fun. "I got an alert that night that said someone saw our tour bus parked outside a 7-Eleven, and they were praying for you, dude."

All jokes aside, I might have to pull my own Cannon-carpet-fiasco when the limo comes to a halt outside of a building that looks like it could house the entire United States Senate. Flashing lights ping every which way, causing my stomach to gurgle in a very unladylike way.

# 19

# LAWS OF ATTRACTION

## MAZEN

**FEAR GLITTERS** in a dusting of apprehension that spreads across Sophia's polished face when we pull up to the curb outside of the venue. The faint sound of "Dancing with the Devil" by EMO travels through the speakers in the vehicle when it comes to a stop.

There's a thick unease emanating from Sophia, displayed by the heavy beat of her pulse at the nape of her neck. It might have brought me satisfaction a couple of weeks ago. Back when I wanted to hate her. When I still wanted to punish the beautiful woman in front of me for forgetting the night we'd shared, the moment of suspended time that had plagued my memory like a reel being played on repeat for years.

That first night, when I thought my depraved mind had conjured a ghost, was a rush like no drug had ever made me experience. Seeing her sitting there in her tattoo studio felt like life was being blown back into my charred soul by an industrial-sized fan. My heart had been dormant for so long. Beating solely just to keep my catatonic mind alive.

Though at times, I wish its movement had ceased. The first time I felt that way was when I left Sophia sleeping in that hotel room, closing a door on a chapter of my life I didn't realize I was going to miss, and then once more when my sister, Bethany, took her last breath.

Our band had accomplished everything we had ever dared to dream of having. The world was ours, ready for the taking. Night after night, we performed our hearts out, and the world ate it up. The fans begged for more, demanding not only our time, but our sanity too. I gave and gave and gave until there was nothing left of me. I bled for my art. We all have, through illnesses, stress, and fatigue. If I'm being honest, being a musician is not for the weak or weary. Living in the limelight often means that nothing's private. Secrets always have a way of being brought to the surface.

As a punk rock musician, I wore the whole tortured-soul demeanor like a second skin. I was in a dark place after my sister died. As long as I kept writing hits and touring, our label kept backing us. My brothers—the band we built from friendship, shared dreams—kept me sane, or at least that was what I let them believe. A sane man wouldn't have thoughts flash in his mind about ending it all, making the pain stop—I'll spare you the details. A sane man wouldn't drink and smoke anything he could get his hands on just to numb the voices and images in his head. A sane man wouldn't use sex as an escape so often that even that lost its appeal.

I was anything but sane. Insane is more accurate.

As soon as my soulless eyes met her delicate, petite body, and I saw the small rose tattoo on her exposed shoulder blade, things snapped back into place. Standing in the dimly lit hallway, admiring the woman I'd walked away from years prior, I felt as if I was finally able to catch my breath. My lungs expanded fully for the first time in ages just from the sight of her, *my* Rosella. Her presence alone was as invigorating as free-falling from a plane. I dived after that feeling headfirst, knowing I wasn't wearing a parachute to catch me.

I'd happily collide with the earth if only it meant earning one of her lighthearted smiles. I remembered her fondly, kept her image and memory alive for years before the dark erased anything good that had once offered me reprieve.

I'm standing here with another chance, scared to take it. It's an opportunity I'm afraid is too good to be true.

If only she'd just confide in us ... in me ... about her past, about Roman. The son she birthed, based on the birth certificate that was anonymously mailed to me—although the sender isn't so anonymous anymore. Julian Caddell sent that paper as a ... what? A warning?

It's the one thing that's holding me back from truly partaking, giving in, filling the missing gap that all three of them are waiting for me to fill. The only difference between Oliver, Cannon, and me is that they've seemed to accept the fact that Sophia's past is not our business. They're okay acting blissfully ignorant, living in delusion that she's not still hiding something as huge as birthing a child from us. They're both content that when she's ready to trust us with that information, she will.

It's a bunch of noble bullshit if you ask me.

I can't just move on. Where is Roman now? Why is she here on tour without him? Lacey, her sister, obviously isn't raising him because she's here with us too. Her mom is deceased, and her father is in prison.

The question I asked her before she boarded our plane haunts me. *"Where is your son?"*

There's a nagging part of me that won't let it rest. A curiosity that has festered, only getting worse with each exchange we have. I can feel myself falling hard for Sophia. How could I not? She's smart, talented beyond belief, breathtaking. The artists that have taken residence in our souls call out to one another. Maybe wanting to know about her past makes me old school, neurotic even. Call it what you will. The truth is the only thing that's going to bind us, allow me to one hundred percent commit to this strange-as-shit situationship or whatever the term Murphy deemed us as.

I'll continue this ruse a little while longer before I demand answers. Before my mind and need for them override the thundering beat of my heart.

"This is important to us, Rosella."

My stomach churns at the thought of her refusing to take my hand when we exit the vehicle. We've made headway with one another, but she can tell I'm holding back. I can't even blame her for sensing my trepidation. It's like a neon sign dangling above my head.

For someone who has been through the wringer like she has, she's mastered the art of being observant. From her begging for a compliment to slip through my lips to all but rubbing it in my face that my friends aren't afraid to show they adore her. We're both walking red flags.

*Stupid.* We're both willfully ignoring the warnings we cast like stones at one another.

Straightening her back, she glances toward me, cutting me with a look of annoyance. "You don't have to tell me. My life is riding on the line. If we fool the media, we fool

Caddell, and I get paid. I know the risks and importance of our relationship ruse, Mazen."

*And we're back to grating on one another's nerves.*

Oliver clicks his tongue before planting a kiss on Sophia's head. "Way to ruin a good night." The glare he gives me burns into me like a laser before he slides out of the limo's parted door first.

I hear a wave of chants, fans all clamoring for his attention as he turns on his charm and waves to the steady surge of flashing cameras.

Vanna squeezes Sophia's arm. "If all else fails, you can fake a stomachache, like Can Man here did."

Murphy climbs out before his wife, then bends, extending his hand to help Vanna out of the vehicle, like a gentleman. Probably the only one of us in the band.

"You know what I like most about you?" Cannon's eyes meet Sophia's. After she shakes her head, he continues, "You don't cower to anyone. Not Knox when he kidnapped you, or Caddell when your life was threatened, or this bastard over here, who continues to prove that he's the asshole everyone thinks he is."

Leave it Cannon to speak more words at this very moment than he has the entire time Sophia's been on tour with us.

I see what she sees in him though. He's as loyal as Jupiter, it seems, and when he chooses to speak, you listen because it's always from his heart. Words aren't his specialty, but they're a weapon he's mastered since being introduced to Sophia.

"You're the strongest person I've ever met, the most beautiful woman to ever walk this carpet," my drummer finishes, and damn it, he's right.

I need to pull myself together.

The shuffling of material draws our collective attention to the open door.

"I heard that," Oliver shout-whispers, leaning into the vehicle. His gaze lands on Cannon. "Nice save, throwing in the gender specification. I'm a fucking catch if you're into hard abs and a dusting of chest hair. Which. You. Are." He bites out every word, looking pissed, but I catch the hint of a smile on his mouth.

"Your hands feel like sandpaper," Cannon retorts.

"I play guitar for a living, asswipe."

Sophia's cheeks redden. "I happen to like your hands, your mouth ... and both of your co—"

I feel like an outsider once again, and my jealousy boils over like a pot of water without a wooden spoon draped over the rim. "I get it. You're all obsessed with each other." An aggravated huff leaves my mouth. "Let's get this show on the road. We have an award to collect. Then, I'm getting higher than a balloon."

One by one, we pile out of the vehicle. Sophia's the last to exit. I extend my tattooed hand toward her, a peace treaty of sorts, and she grabs it without blinking. Her flesh against mine causes a smoldering zing. A fire ignites between us that we can't seem to extinguish. There's no denying our pull. It goes far past surface level. I only passed high school chemistry because I cheated off Murphy, and even I know this is some next-level law-of-attraction shit. It's molecular.

"For what it's worth, he's right." That earns me a raised brow. "You're the most beautiful woman to ever walk this carpet, especially holding my hand. I want the world to know you're mine. Not just tonight either." I add the last thought for good measure.

"Flattery won't get you back in my good graces," she whispers, her smile doing its job to camouflage her distaste with me. "News flash: I'm not yours, Mazen. Not in all the aspects that count anyway."

It's hard to stand my ground where she's concerned. She's so stunning that my eyes physically ache. Especially as she glides beside me, looking every bit the seasoned veteran Lindsey coached her to be. If I wasn't standing right next to her to see the sparkles shimmering in the flashing lights of the cameras as we walk, I'd swear the dress was painted on her skin.

I'm instantly jealous of Vanna and Lacey. Not only did they spend the day at the spa with her, but I'm also sure their eyes were privy to the joy of watching her pull this dress on. I wonder which one zipped it up for her.

"I didn't realize I ever left your good graces. If memory serves, we called a ceasefire by way of my dick tickling your tonsils." I refuse to give light to the jab about what we share not being real. It's *real*. As fucking tangible as the crowd that's gawking at us, cameras flashing at lightning speed in front of them.

We continue our stroll down the red carpet, stopping every couple of feet to pose and smile. Sophia fits perfectly in the crook of my arm. I feel for my brothers, who are lagging a few steps behind us. Smiling into the cameras like a pair of bachelors who haven't found their *Sophia* yet. I find perverse pleasure in knowing, as I'm sure they both do as well, that the facade they're weaving for the media is a crock of shit. Not in the sense that my relationship with Sophia isn't real, more in the fact that *we're* not the only ones in it. Ollie and Cannon are the other two sides of our jaded square.

People are eating up the show we're putting on for them.

Exchanging a side-eye, we stop in front of another camera crew nearing the end of the carpet.

Sophia finds her voice when she bites out, "Indeed, we did. Yet you still won't fuck me."

I choke. Right there, standing in front of a sea of lenses.

It's not just a small cough. One that passes as you swallow a little spit that helps moisten your throat. Nope. I barrel into a full-fledged choking fit that has a worker scurrying to hand me a bottle of chilled ice water.

"Mr. Wilde, are you okay, sir?" the young man clad in all black asks, worry etched onto his face, his head adorned by a black headset.

"I'm all good. Thanks." I turn to Sophia, nuzzling my face into her neck. To the onlookers, my movement looks like nothing more than a lover's embrace. "I want to fuck you just as bad as you want to be fucked by me. Don't get my willpower confused or twisted. You forget that I've tasted that sweet little cunt of yours. I was there first. I coated your walls in my cum, and I will again." Another promise is made as the words leave my mouth.

Sophia's reply is breathy, "What's stopping you then?"

The incessant nagging in my gut is a reminder that there's more to the story she's woven about her past. It's like the time Jupiter ate a condom and had a bowel obstruction. Everyone said he was fine; he must've gotten on the counter and eaten something that upset his stomach. I knew it was more than that. I felt it. An irksome feeling that something was seriously wrong, and I was right. It cost a small fortune for his surgery. Another reason why I hate condoms to this day.

I bite back my real answer. The desire to say *the truth* is heavy on my tongue. It's not the time or place for that conversation. Rationally, I know this.

Her nearness and the tension that only continues to intensify every time our bodies meet have me amped up without an outlet in sight. Surprising even myself, I use her momentary distraction to pull her flush to my body; the heat of her skin in my arms will have to suffice. I urge the feeling of her wrapped in my arms to settle my nervous system.

If the media wants a show, a show they'll get. Without warning, I kiss her, chasing that outlet. It's not a chaste kiss either. It's meaningful, heated, and sure as hell not suited to be done in front of a throng of strangers.

*Fuck them.*

Our lips align like they've been partners in this dance for years. The world fades. The tension in my back ebbs before it disappears, until all that's left is me and her. My desire for the woman in my arms is made crystal clear. Surely, she's smart enough to catch on to my unsaid answer as I devour her mouth like I just scored a golden ticket to Wonka's factory.

She's the chocolate, the forbidden treat that my soul can't afford but desperately wants.

A hard slap on my shoulder breaks our trance, grabbing my attention.

"Save some saliva for your mouth, bro. Don't you know that's what gives people bad breath?" Ollie rolls his eyes, dismay clearly etched into them.

I take Sophia's hand once again, ushering her forward and tailing the rest of my band off the red carpet, through a narrow hallway that leads us into a large room. I feel a little lightheaded and a whole lot hard. We're guided toward a circular table that has our names written on fancy note cards. Cannon leans in, and on autopilot, he pulls out Sophia's chair.

"My bad," he says, noticing what he did before taking a

step back, remembering that hundreds of eyes are on us.

I hear a faint whisper of, "Thanks," that she directs toward my drummer.

I slide my hand around Sophia's slim waist, reminding her who her date is tonight. It's a childish move. Knowing that doesn't stop me from moving her body directly in front of mine before I cup her cheek.

"Mazen, the cameras are gone. No need for a show."

Her words are like a knife to my heart. They flay me open, affecting every single nerve ending in my entire being. Even my fingers go rigid. Time isn't my friend. It never has been. At this moment, I don't know how much longer I can keep my cool. If she doesn't willingly tell me ... us ... about her son, I'm going to have to ask. Or worse, have the private investigator we hired to dig up dirt on Caddell dig up her past too.

She'd never forgive me. None of them would.

"I'm not an actor," I say offensively.

"Sure fooled me." Her sexual frustration with me has now morphed into anger. "I know this isn't real. I've known it since our first date at the boardwalk. I know it in my bones every time you turn me down. A girl can take a hint. Even if she doesn't want to accept defeat."

The hot and cold that has become our relationship has somehow misled her understanding of how I feel about her. Sure, I haven't screwed her, as she so eloquently put it, but that doesn't mean I don't want to. I thought I proved that at the pool and the morning after with my awful attempt to woo her with a homemade breakfast. Hell, I just declared in front of thousands of people how much she means to me. Just because my body hasn't shown her how maddening she makes me feel doesn't mean my heart isn't pounding in my chest, beating only for her. Even with her secret hanging between us, there's no denying how I feel about Sophia.

*Why the fuck can't she realize that she's it for me?*

I've done a shit job of showing her, apparently. This is why I've never dated before. I can't keep myself happy, let alone having the responsibility of keeping someone else happy too. Goddamn it though, I want it with her. I want the titles, the dates, and the *where are you* text messages.

I want it all with Sophia. She's the only future I've ever wanted. If I could just accept her act of omission like the rest of my band, we'd have smooth sailing. Paradise upon the horizon. She'd be fucked seven ways to Sunday already.

*Reality can choke on a dick.*

Glancing around, I watch Murphy pull out a chair for Vanna, and then Oliver and Cannon sit down. A couple of spectators at neighboring tables are still eyeing us with morbid curiosity. If Sophia feels like this is all still a gimmick, they undoubtedly could too.

*We get it.* I've never shown up to any awards show with a plus-one. This is different. I'm different since she walked back into my life like a damn hurricane, wreaking havoc and taking names.

Running my knuckle down her jaw, under her neckline, my hand stops at her chest, where I open my palm and lay it over her heart. I can feel her breath catching, her lungs holding the air hostage. I don't give a flying fuck that people are watching or that we're on a time crunch, and we need to take our seats and get situated before the host takes the stage.

None of that matters right now. *Nothing* matters, except making Sophia understand that this fake-dating ploy she continues to hint at ended for me a long time ago.

Secrets or not, I can't feign indifference, and I sure as

hell can't let the most beautiful woman in this entire venue think that she's not good enough for a second longer.

Using my other hand to grab the one dangling at her side, I slowly glide it toward the center of my dress pants where the thin fabric is rising.

"What part of this feels fake?" I ask a little breathier than I expected to sound. "My cock is getting hard in a room full of people clamoring for my attention. My eyes haven't wavered from you once. The only person I see is you, and the only thing that is fake between us is the image that you're only mine. You're not. You're theirs too." I nod toward where Oliver and Cannon are sitting. Like the rest of the room, they're honed in on the spectacle I'm causing. "I'll share every bit of you with them. Please just wait until I'm ready and understand that you aren't the issue. It's my insecurities."

It's a half-truth, which is more than what she's offering.

# 20

## POPPIN' BOTTLES

### CANNON

**KINGS OF JUPITER** has been nominated for a Grammy. It's the highest honor in music, being it's the only peer-recognized award there is in the industry.

I'll appreciate winning a little more knowing that fact, though I don't get off on the prestigious novelty of being called onto the stage like Oliver does. He eats it up every single time.

Give him a morsel of attention, and he'll come back for more.

Tonight is different. The vibe is heavier. I'd like to say it's because Sophia's presence has an added layer of pressure, weighing down our shoulders. There's no doubt that we want her to see us win. For her eyes to widen when the host calls out our name on the microphone and she realizes that the camera isn't even panning on us, but her because she's stolen the show by her raw beauty and eloquent class.

My head is usually in a cloud at these events. Daydreaming about anything else other than the reality of sitting in a penguin suit in a sea of people. It's my worst fucking nightmare. I loathe these events. No, that's not true. I loathe being around people and public places.

Give me a good book, an island, and my dog, and I'd be golden. *Shit.* That's not true. I need my drum set, Oliver, and Sophia too. Then I'll be as content as a man can be.

It's just not my style. I'm the background guy. The fourth wheel.

I don't make music for *them.* Not any of them. So, why should I accept any praise from a faceless crowd applauding us with nothing but jealousy in their irises? My relationship with music is all mine. I play for me. Every single time I pick up my sticks is like a Band-Aid to my soul.

Except tonight, when they call our band's name through the tense, hushed silence, and a fucking tear rolls down Sophia's ivory cheek. I've never been more excited to win anything in my entire life. The pride that dances between us, Murphy included, is abundant. It feels like she is hugging us all, though all she can offer everyone—except her date, Mazen—is a polite nod of her head and a friendly smile.

Tonight's victory is sweet.

Which is why our group demands we go out and celebrate our accomplishment, our win. Thankfully, it's decided we hit up a club a couple of blocks from our hotel and forgo the usual gaudy parties that follow award shows we've attended in the past. Another small win, even though the idea has me grinding my teeth. If I could stay in our suite, preferably between Oliver's and Sophia's legs, I would be satisfied.

"We good?" Mazen asks into the cell phone he's holding to his ear. He nods, then hangs up. "We have the whole VIP section tonight."

Vanna and the girls let out a string of collective squeals. Oliver pops the top off a bottle of chilled champagne enthusiastically. Murphy leans back, planting both arms across the back of the leather bench seat and takes it all in, in true Murphy Miller fashion. Always the observer.

"We're poppin' bottles tonight!"

I can't even hide the upward curl of my lips if I wanted to as Oliver starts to spray everyone with foaming alcohol like the child he is. Undiluted laughter fills the limo. All feels right in the world.

Entering through the club's back entrance, we follow Ashton and a couple of other members of our security team through a dimly lit hallway. We're still sporting our tuxes, and the girls are still wearing their dresses. Lacey didn't attend the awards with us, so she's dressed a bit more casually in a form fitting jumper that cuts in the front to her navel. I bet we look like we just left an adult prom.

"I needed this." Lacey grabs her sister and kisses her on the cheek before turning her attention to Ashton.

Something is flourishing there even if the brute won't admit it.

"Let's dance," Vanna suggests, locking hands with Sophia and her sister. "I know the rules. Stay where we can be seen at all times, and don't take drinks from anyone not employed by the label."

Damn, she's good. It makes sense why Murphy was quick to tie her down.

The next hour is spent watching the three of them grind on one another like they're auditioning for a music video. Definitely not one of ours. We might need to change our genre if it means getting to watch Sophia hike up her dress, shaking her ass like the provocative little vixen I know she is. My dick throbs in my pants from just the sight of her letting loose, enjoying herself. She deserves it.

"I don't know how much more I can take of her being out there. Doing that." I adjust my junk, eyes trained on my woman.

Over the brim of his half-empty glass, Oliver says flatly, "Who knew she could let loose like this?" as more of an observation than a question. "I could get used to this version of her."

Mazen's dark brows bunch together like he's deep in thought before he chimes in by adding, "It's her sister. Lacey being here makes her comfortable. She can be herself."

The three of us nod in understanding, not speaking.

The truth is, Sophia has been different, more relaxed since Lacey joined us on tour. I get why. She was scared to death of Caddell hurting her sister, so she was in constant fight or flight mode. I just wish she had been open with us from the start. Been honest when she accepted Oliver's proposition to come on tour with us. There's not an ounce of doubt in me that she could have batted her eyes at him, and he would have accepted Lacey's presence as part of the deal.

Utilizing our time wisely, I break into a more serious topic. My voice grates harshly as I push out the question that's been haunting me. "What'd you get from the PI?"

After a long sigh, Mazen answers, "Mostly summed up everything we already know. Now that you guys know about her and me meeting before this tour, everything seems less like a coincidence. We're missing something vital. I can feel it. Don't you think?" Mazen's eyes are glossy. A mixed effect from the blunt he smoked before we walked in and the lingering questions he doesn't want to give light to.

I muse over his reply as his face pulls together in a somber expression. There's so much weight on his shoulders. Weight he thinks he must bear for everyone. Ever since Bethany's death, Mazen has developed a savior complex. Don't get me wrong, I understand why. He couldn't control the wreck, so he tries to have a hand in everything else. It's a fine line he's dancing since he used to be the reckless one of the four of us. I've never known a drug or thrill he would turn down.

As we stare through the horde of people dancing, rubbing up on one another, the evidence of his stress settles under the pockets of his eyes. His shoulders are set in a straight line, his spine rigid. Even with a drink in his hand lulling him into relaxation, his eyes stay glued on Sophia, tracking her every movement. He can't fight the need to be the protector, and truthfully, I don't think it's a battle he even realizes he's been waging.

Wary of the argument this might cause, I probe anyway. "You're going to dig into the secret she's still keeping, aren't you?" I ask, referring to the whereabouts of her son.

I'm amazed he hasn't flat out asked her again. Keeping true to his word, he's allowed her time to confide in us. There's no denying the attempt he's made *not* to push Sophia, even with multiple resources at his disposal.

He's already made his mind up. Time has run out.

My body stiffens. Exhaustion, caused by his need to know every detail she refuses to offer us, takes over. I want to refute. To scream in his face and tell him he's going to ruin this ... with her ... for more than just himself.

Blood roars in my ears. I'm trapped between telling him to leave it be and encouraging him to find the answer he so desperately needs to finally accept this thing that has blossomed between us.

I feel him staring at me, his look as sharp as a laser. There's a change to his face, a *how the hell do you know me so well* look in the form of a glower bunching at his brows. Our gazes hold for a beat before he dips his chin, offering me the answer I already knew to be true. It's a small movement, but it's there, and I accept it for what it is, knowing that he can't get past that detail of her history. I know that's what's holding him back from going all in with us. As much as I want to know the answer to that burning question myself, her withholding it won't keep me out of her pants. I'm afraid nothing will at this point.

At first, I contemplated why Mazen was so hesitant and thought it was due to his nerves that Oliver or I would make a move on him. Hell, I get it. Oliver repressed his desires for years, and I hid the details of my sex life from everyone.

The gloves are off now. We're open about our affection in front of our friends, most people on tour with us. I know Mazen though. I've watched him when Oliver's leaned in to claim my mouth on the tour bus. He's not fazed. Which is a relief and a burden because that can only mean one thing, and I know he won't stop until he knows where Roman Lozier is.

I don't fault her for keeping her past a secret. I don't even fault him for wanting to know. What I do fault him for is potentially ruining a good thing between the four of us by forcing her to tell us before she's ready. For dredging up her past while she's still dealing with the emotional turmoil from being kidnapped. I'm half-tempted to phone her psychologist as a precaution.

The look in Mazen's pewter eyes says he's determined and won't cease until he's uncovered everything there is to know about his father, Caddell, and the child the woman who stole all of our hearts birthed.

"Do us a favor." I swallow, knowing he's going to take offense to my warning.

"Don't mess this up."

Leave it to Oliver to call him out by blurting the sentence ringing loudly in my head. I didn't even realize he was paying us any attention.

"Me, fuck it up? You must be kidding." Mazen's laugh is anything but amusing, it's throaty, rough, offended. "I was buried in her before you ever even knew she existed." Heat flares from Mazen's nose like he's about to erupt in flames.

The sound of Oliver's empty glass clinks against the table. I can hear it over the blaring music. "Whose fault is that? You chose to keep her to yourself. You climbed on that bus with a shit-eating grin on your face and never spoke a word about her."

"You need to respect her boundaries, man. Before you push her too far, and she decides her privacy is more impor-tant than finishing this tour with us. This shit isn't cool. If she finds out you've been snooping, she's going to be pissed. It's not just you who's invested here. My heart is on the line. Ask yourself this: can you live with her leaving for good? I sure as hell can't." Oliver says without taking a breath.

Murphy and I sit, our eyes bouncing between our two friends. Neither of them seems willing to offer a ceasefire. This moment of reckoning is hanging on by a thread.

"We hashed this out before. No?" Murphy questions, stating the dreadful truth, reminding them both that we had a plan.

Mazen is bluntly choosing not to follow it. Threatening to shatter everything.

*So much for him being patient.*

"We were going to lay our curiosity to rest unless she decided that she felt comfortable enough to tell us about her son," Murphy repeats our plan as if he can will the idea to stay the course into Mazen's thick skull.

Mazen cups the back of his neck. His tension is palpable, his voice hoarse when he confesses, "I can't tell you guys why I need to know. I just do." His hand palms his chest. "It's ... I just feel like—shit. What if I'm—" His words falter.

"What if the baby is yours?" Murphy interrupts, seemingly watering a seed that already took root in Mazen's chest long before this evening.

The question seems to come as no surprise to any of us. It makes perfect sense why Caddell mailed the birth certificate to Mazen specifically.

A cynical inner voice pulls at my thoughts, arranging them into order, forcing myself to consider the very real possibility that Roman's paternity could point back to him. My best friend could be a father.

I'm thinking, *Where is your son then?*

Mazen interrupts my train of thought. Several questions come out at once.

"What if he is? The birth certificate aligns with our one night ... when we were together. Why else would someone send it addressed to me? Someone, most likely Caddell, was sending me a message, but why? I have a bad feeling I can't shake. I've tried. Fuck, I've tried. What if Roman is my son? Who the hell has him if Sophia is here with us?"

I try to ignore the pain in his voice, but it's unmistakably there, noticeable. Once the questions are out of his mouth, there's no taking them back. We sit, pondering on the answers.

The depth of his desire to learn the truth is as thick as

the steady stream of patrons at the bar across from us. There's a stillness that seems to overtake the air surrounding the four of us. My heartbeat increases at the possibility of this situation blowing up in our faces, changing our lives, more so than Sophia's presence already has. Reality, logic, and reason claw at my insides.

"Holy shit." My lip trembles as the excitement of our night dulls. "I get why you need to know. I support you fully." I offer one of my best friends my understanding, knowing all the while if this turns south, my heart will be broken in the process.

"Call the PI. Tell him to look into Roman's whereabouts." The gruffness of Oliver's voice slices through the air. "We've got your back, man."

It's a declaration, an understanding, an acceptance that finding out the truth might change things for us all.

Our songwriter is at a loss for words. As Mazen bows his head, frozen in stillness for a long while, my thoughts race. I know if I feel like my world is crumbling, then he must be feeling ten times worse.

It isn't until the girls saunter back toward our secluded VIP section that he finally tilts his chin up.

# 21

# HONEYBEAR CAFÉ

MAZEN

IF THERE WAS a limit on heartbreak per lifetime, I'd be nearing it.

I know the moment Sophia's petite frame stops in front of me that I'm a glutton for punishment. Hair sticks to the sides of her perfectly carved cheekbones with sweat. Her chest is glistening. And her smile is so pure that it nearly wrecks me. Searching for answers that I shouldn't have any business needing, but desperately do, my lungs begin to clench. It feels like all the air has been vacuum-sucked out of the large room.

"Shame on Me" by Catch Your Breath infiltrates my mind at the same time a burst of adrenaline courses through my veins. Thoughts muddle. The apprehension I have about outright asking her sloshes around in my empty stomach, alongside the alcohol I've swallowed by the pint this evening.

"My legs are going to feel like jelly in the morning." She

falls onto the thick leather cushion next to me. "I haven't danced like that in years."

Sitting forward, I look at her intently, silently trying to drag the truth from her beautifully carved lips. *Did we create a baby together in Chicago, Rosella?*

It's on the tip of my tongue when Oliver sits back down, having returned from the restroom, wedging himself between us. "What flavor would you be?" he asks, masterly pulling me from my thoughts. Breaking the tension with his wit. It's what he's known for. Good at even. He's the one who keeps us all smiling, on our toes.

"What?" Sophia asks.

"Of jelly," he states matter-of-factly. "I'm a strawberry guy. Grape is too tart for my liking."

"You're a mess, is what you are." She laughs, her infectious smile lingering.

"I'd be honey. Thick and sticky." I chime in.

The amber liquid I've been steadily sipping has me relaxing into their conversation. It's a lot less accusatory than the one I want to have with her.

"I'm plain butter." Cannon shrugs before taking a sip of his drink. "Nothing special."

I watch as her forest-green eyes flicker with hurt.

"Believe it or not, butter is how I prefer my biscuits." Her eyes sweep down as she drinks Cannon in before they move upward to his broad chest.

The buttons of his white shirt are undone at the top, showing just enough skin to entice Sophia.

Lust lingers in her polished jade eyes as they turn from Cannon to me and then land on Ollie. The invisible web of attraction that connects us builds at a rapid beat. The music pulsating through the air mimics the pulse throbbing in her carved neck. I stare a little too long, my lips wanting to sear a path down her neck, urgent and exploratory.

"Why don't we move this party to the diner down the street before you all eat one another in front of us?" Murphy asks sternly, sensing the hunger forming between us.

"Yes, please," Lacey begs. "I'd rather not be present when my sister gets plowed by these three."

THE DINER IS NEARLY empty when we arrive. Ashton slides the label's black credit card across the counter. The owner takes it greedily before unplugging the *Open* sign in the window. Another perk of our line of work.

We order and eat in silence. The greasy food soaking up the liquor in our stomachs.

The sound of my phone dinging causes my heart to pick up a steady hammering motion in my chest. I texted my PI before we left the club. One simple request, a sentence: *Find out where Roman Lozier is.*

"So, a Grammy." It's the pink-haired Lozier who forces my attention back to the table. She can't leave well enough alone. "That's gnarly."

Giving the table my attention, I decide to finish eating before I slide my phone out of my pocket. It might not even be him. It's most likely not. He couldn't have tracked down Roman's whereabouts that quickly.

"Are you conceding?" I ask, reminding Lacey of the little wager we shook on.

Of course it'd take our band winning a Grammy for her

to see we're real musicians, and we're kind of good at what we do. I think the Grammy indicates we're the best actually.

"Are you?" she presses, lips pursed, daring me to answer.

Sophia interjects, drawing my attention from the plate in front of me, "This place reminds me of Honeybear Café. Don't you think, Lace?"

"Yeah. A little. Rogers Park was always so crowded though. This gem seems like a hidden treasure, and these biscuits are mouthwatering. I think I'm going to ask for a sack to-go for breakfast."

With a mouthful of hash browns, Ollie asks, "Where's Honeybear Café? Cute name."

"It's a little café in Chicago." Lacey's tone holds an edge that she usually only reserves for me. The word *Chicago* cold on her tongue.

There's no amount of willpower in my six-foot-two frame that stands a chance against the incessant nagging in the pit of my stomach. It's as if fate backhands me across the face. With my cheek still stinging, her remark echoes through the drunken wavelengths in my brain. A simple reminder that there are important questions that need answering. Much more important than where a fucking café is located.

"Have you been back to the tattoo convention in *Chicago* since we met, Sophia?" I ask, shifting a guard around my heart just in case her plate of pancakes hasn't absorbed all the alcohol in her system, and she falters at my question.

Wide-eyed and stunned, she chokes on her orange juice. She pounds on her chest, and those green eyes of hers are quick to douse me in scrutiny. Her silent question—*Why are you asking?*—is replaced by a quick, awkward clearing of her throat.

Ignorant to the palpable shift in the diner, Lacey carelessly clicks her tongue, opening a door that teeters off its hinges. "We used to visit home every year on the anniversary of his dea—"

Regaining her composure, Sophia cuts in. Her answer is chaste, to the point. "No, I haven't." The usually enchanting emerald of her eyes fades into a hazy mist. "Is everyone done? It's late. I'm getting pretty tired. I hope no one wants celebratory tattoos."

There's no going back now.

"Whose death?" I demand an answer, nostrils flaring.

Lacey must sense my resolve crumbling, or she drank more than I thought because she answers immediately, without pause, like I've summoned a fact she can't swallow down.

"Roman's." Her voice is nearly a whisper, yet his name pounds against my eardrums with a force that is hard enough to knock the breath from my lungs.

My eyes dart to Sophia's at the mention of her son's ... *our* son's name. I don't need a DNA test to confirm my suspicions. My gut hasn't led me astray thus far. I don't even need to pull my cell phone from my pocket to confirm the worst possible news I've ever heard. I do it anyway. Just in case Lacey's just sloshed out of her mind, telling tales.

I skim the text message from my PI, and my heart sinks when I read, *Roman Forest Lozier. Date of birth: July 13, 2013. Date of death: July 15, 2013.*

*No.* There must be some mistake.

Seemingly lost in her own musing, Sophia painfully slowly pans her glossy eyes upward until they meet mine across the dingy linoleum table. The answer I've been searching for is reflected both on my screen and in her ashen face. There are no more diversions for Sophia to hide behind. His name ignites a spark of grief, despair. Like she hasn't allowed herself the pleasure of speaking his name out loud for some time.

The seconds pass by as the fearful clarity of the moment solidifies. A veil of reality hovers over the seven of us, a rainstorm on the horizon. A deep thunder on the verge of a rousing storm.

I am the hail. The wind. A disaster about to wreak havoc.

"Who was Roman's father, Sophia? Surely he visited his son on the anniversary of his death too, right? Do you still speak to him? After all this time, I mean, I'm sure you've remained friends, haven't you?" I goad her.

She stirs uneasily in the booth, and the silence growing between us becomes more uncomfortable. If I had expected her to answer me directly with a yes or no, I would have been indisputably mistaken. Dread swells in my heart with the pregnant pause that hangs from Sophia's parted lips.

My fist slams down on the table. Plates and cups rattle as the first round of the brewing storm inside me flares. The contents of juice, water, and milk slosh over the rims of our half-full glasses.

Like my heart, they overflow, puddling into nothing.

"That's enough," Cannon huffs, sensing the escalation of the situation in the air. "Do not do this right now." The anger illuminating in his blue eyes cautions me not to push his resolve.

There's not a soul in this restaurant who thinks I'm the person he's protecting right now. Even as my heart slowly stops beating, falling stagnant, it's Sophia's heart that my drummer is guarding.

Murphy stands at the edge of the table before he briskly walks up behind me. His callous hands grip each of my shoulders, grounding me in place. "We don't want to cause a scene. Let's go back to the hotel. Take a beat, and get some rest. We'll come back to this conversation tomorrow, when we're all not so on edge and drunk."

"Take a beat," I scoff, my body flinching at the audacity that *I* need to chill.

Anger is a tangible being in my chest, flicking a lighter with the promise of destruction on his face.

"I can't even fucking breathe right now, and you want me to take a beat." My fingers find the long black strands of hair on top of my throbbing head, and I pull so hard that I wince. The pain is a welcome distraction. I call out to it. Allowing it to tether me, an attempt to rein myself in from the madness darkening my vision.

With the snap of a finger, I lose all sense of reality. Misery takes up all rational thoughts. The raw, primitive sorrow that marred my heart at the mention of Roman's death leaves me feeling grief-stricken, tormented by the fucking truth she still won't give me.

I deserve the truth.

I have the right to know I *was* a father.

I deserve to hear it from her goddamn mouth.

Clinging to the wretchedness that has filled my entire body from head to toe, I grip the edge of the table before tossing it to the side as if it weighs nothing. The dishes that were atop it shatter as they hit the floor. Chaos erupts, but my eyes never leave Sophia's.

With the barrier of the table now out of my way, I take a step forward, sinking to my knees in front of her. With my arms outstretched, I hold on to the top of the bench behind her, caging her in on either side. She presses a hand over her mouth compulsively, like seeing me reduced to the shaking, blubbering man in front of her physically pains her.

It should pain her. I want her soul to be split in half like mine is. I want her throat to feel like it's closing, restricting the very breath she needs to survive like mine is doing.

A glazed look of torment spreads over her face as I lean forward, crowding her, demanding her attention.

"Who was Roman's father?" My voice is raw, devoid of all emotion, even though emotion is the only thing guiding me. "Look me in my eyes, and tell me, Rosella. There isn't a father listed on his birth certificate. But you already know that. I need to hear it from your mouth."

Unbridled anger hardens my features.

Sophia's arms fold around her sparkling red gown as I trap her in, refusing to back down now. I clench my teeth, furious, bathing in a rage that's consuming me whole.

There's a deep tremble in her body when she whispers, "I don't know."

I crack.

I bleed.

I die a little on the inside.

A tense silence cloaks the diner as recognition settles over our friends.

The sharp intake of breath from my left sounds like it comes from Vanna, and it is the only proof that we're all still alive because I feel as if my world just imploded. I don't know ... anything. I don't feel ... anything other than sorrow.

Anger is replaced by an ache in my chest so robust, I can feel it in every chamber of my heart. It's so forceful my knees weaken. Nothing registers, aside from the tightness in my chest, coiling with a frightening intensity.

A scream bellows from the depths of my soul when I stand, stalking toward the counter. It's as if I'm reliving the pain of losing my sister again. Except this time, the ache is deeper, greater, clinging on to every fiber of my being in a vise grip. It bleeds into each crevice of my shredded heart.

The torn pieces break into smaller shards over the son I didn't know I had. The child who was laid to rest without his father there to bid him goodbye.

Caddell knew all along. It's why he mailed the certificate to me.

*I'm a fucking fool.*

Rage engulfs my soul, guiding my clenched hands without thought. Paper towel holders, salt and pepper shakers, and bottles of half-used condiments fly into the air as I slide my hands down the entire length of the counter, sweeping everything off.

How did the best night of our careers, turn into the worst night of my entire fucking life?

Darkness is all I see.

Emptiness is all I feel.

Without a backward glance, I stagger toward the restaurant door, swing it open, and step out into the night with nothing but my savage heart beating wildly in my chest.

# 22

## ON A HUNCH

SOPHIA

I BLINKED, and the entire trajectory of my life changed.

*Again.*

There aren't words to explain the deep-rooted betrayal I saw in Mazen's eyes when I answered him as honestly as I could. The defining moment between despair and anguish molded together into an avalanche of betrayal.

*He hates me.* Just like I knew he would if he learned the truth.

Hell, I'm not even one hundred percent certain that he is Roman's father. I know it's a possibility—a large one.

There are so many questions *we* need the answers to. Questions that he, too, has a hand in answering.

He left, and I don't blame him for it.

That was five hours ago.

Ashton had stormed after him, phone pressed to his ear, concern etched on his face.

What should have been the best night of their lives morphed into a nightmare I don't think any of us will ever forget. Not in this lifetime at least. They'll probably hide their shiny award on the bottom of the shelf, refusing to allow the memory of this evening to spark even an ounce of happiness.

I ruined it for them. My selfishness ruined everything.

When we're ushered back to the hotel, I go through the motions in utter silence. I undress and discard my gown, wishing I could light it on fire, burn away all recollection of tonight. I brush my teeth. Pile my hair on top of my head and crawl under the blankets in my own room, refusing to see Oliver or Cannon.

It isn't that I want to punish them. I'm beyond thankful that they even still want to comfort me after learning Mazen very well could be the father of my child, a child that I never told them about.

I've already taken too much from Mazen. I refuse to take his band, his friends, too. Even when their faces pleaded with me to cave and accept their comfort, I refused. Pushing them away, despite my broken heart calling out to them, was the least I could do.

The damage is done.

In the morning, we'll wake, and Lacey and I will fly home, back to Tampa. I'll call Julian Caddell and tell him that our deal is off and prepare myself for whatever conse-quence he doles out.

That's the last coherent thought I have as sleep drags me into its depths.

I'M awoken by several loud sounds.

*Boom.*

*Clank.*

*Bang.*

My body jolts up in bed, and my red-rimmed eyes take in the sight in front of me. Fear coils down my spine as my eyes lock on to Mazen's unmerciful glare a moment before the rest of his band crowds my bedroom.

Everyone begins speaking at once.

"You need to chill."

"She's sleeping. Go shower, and give her time to get up. Where have you been anyway? A homeless shelter. You reek."

"You've lost your damn mind if you think I'll allow you to take her anywhere."

If my face could muster a smile, it would from the last voice that spoke. *Lacey.*

I'm so angry with her for her part in the truth coming to light. I'm even angrier with myself, at my choice not to mention the possibility when I confided in Mazen at the hospital. I'm to blame here, not my sister.

"Get up. We have a flight to catch." The clear-cut distrust in Mazen's stone-cold accent chills his eyes as he speaks. His voice is deep, rough. Like he screamed throughout the entire night. "Rosella," he says in warning, temper flaring behind his tone. "Get the hell out of bed. I'll pack your bags."

Another bang echoes as he continues tossing shoes and articles of clothing into my bag. He doesn't stop to ask what belongs to me and what belongs to my sister. He's not fazed in the slightest. He's on a mission to send me back home, shove my existence into a box, and chuck the key into the ocean.

"Where am I going?" I shudder at the thought of being tossed out of this hotel on my ass.

Hearing him chuck my belongings into my bag, knowing he already planned my departure before I even opened my eyes this morning is unsettling.

"We're going on a trip."

I watch his nostrils flare. When his eyes meet mine, there's a sardonic expression on his face.

"Just you and me."

Lacey steps into his space, beckoning his attention. Their chests collide, both puffed out, dominant. "I told you, you're not taking my sister anywhere. I don't trust you … like this."

She's undoubtedly referring to the manic state Mazen's in. His hair is disheveled, and he appears to still be wearing his black dress pants and shirt from last night.

Mazen steps forward, and the movement causes her to take a step backward, forced to retreat. "You don't trust me, Lacey? That's rich. Seems like trust is obsolete in this suite, doesn't it?"

I'm immediately alarmed that he's using her legal name. It's a first, and it should be a strong indication that his temper is on the verge of erupting.

"If she's going anywhere with you, I'm coming," my sister says before bending, tossing her belongings into their rightful home—her suitcase.

"I'm fine with going home. If you don't want me here, if you can't look at me anymore, I get it." I climb off the luxurious mattress, bidding sleep goodbye. "Chill out. Let me pack my own stuff, and Lace and I will book a flight. You don't have to see to it that we actually board the plane. It didn't end so well the last time that happened, did it?"

"Soph."

Hearing my name being called from the doorway, I glance over to find Oliver leaning against the doorframe. I flash him a *help me* look, only for the plea in my eyes to be shut down by the icy coldness in his.

The hurt lingering in my chest turns into white-hot anger of my own. I get why I'm being cast out. I can own that fact. What I can't own is the people who I thought had my back, cared for me even, are just sitting by while Mazen screams at me.

"I overheard him on the phone. He's taking you to Chicago," Lacey says in a low, tormented voice.

I huff, "Chicago. Why?" Swiveling on my heel, I turn to find Mazen, who is still packing my bag. "What's there to see in Chicago?"

"You're going to take me to my son's gravesite," he replies with enough spite to stop me in my tracks.

My next breath comes out ragged. "I ... we ... don't even know for certain."

"We will." He turns, assessing me from head to toe. "Get dressed." The insolence in his voice is like a slap to my face. "Please," he adds. "Our plane is leaving soon. We don't have time to discuss this right now. I have a right to see him."

The pain in Mazen's voice is evident. It's then that I truly listen. That pain pulls at my heartstrings, speaking louder than his anger.

Cannon's wide stance steps in front of me. His own rage quakes through his body as he guards me from one of his best friends. "Then we'll all go."

"No." I step in front of him. Casting a sympathetic glance toward Mazen, I struggle to hold his attention. It's as if it physically pains him to look directly at me. "I'll take you to see him."

That earns me a hard glare.

Out of the corner of my eye, I see Oliver start to pace alongside my bed. "This is insane. You know that, don't you?" he pointedly asks his best friend. "You're going on a hunch. A feeling. You need a DNA test to prove you're the father. Let's start there. If it's confirmed, we'll all fly to Chicago. We're a unit now. All of us. Let's face this together. Enough going rogue. Look where that got Sophia already."

I shift on my bare feet, turning toward Oliver. There's a pained expression marring his beautiful face. I've made such a mess of things.

"If we're going to run a DNA test, we'll need something of Roman's." From only a few feet away, I see Mazen's body tense as I speak his name. "We need to fly to Tampa first and I agree, we need to do this alone."

"Well, I don't agree," my sister chimes in. "Look how he's talking to you. He's tossing your shit in your bag like he's about to throw you out onto the street. You think I trust you gallivanting off to another state with him? You're delusional or still drunk from last night. This is my fault that I blurted something I shouldn't have. I'll be damned if I allow him to punish you for my mistake."

It comes as no surprise that she would try to protect me. It's what we do. What we've always done for one another. The only difference now is my heart grew, allowing others in. I can't turn my back on one of them, just like I could never turn my back on her. Even if she doesn't understand my rationale.

I'm going with him to Chicago.

I owe it to myself to find out the truth as much as I owe it to Mazen.

There'll be time to mend this rift, this disagreement in

our group later—I hope. Right now, it's Mazen who deserves my full attention.

Mazen's gunmetal eyes meet mine again. Understanding passes between us, and he offers a quick nod, abandoning his task of packing my bag. His voice sounds like gravel when he asks, "What ..." He swallows forcefully, seemingly using the extra second to compose himself. "What did you save?"

He doesn't need to elaborate. I know exactly what he means.

*What did I save of Roman's that would still carry DNA ten years later?*

"He had a head full of dark hair when he was born. The nurses were gracious enough to cut a lock of it and give it to me."

A crack in my little sister's hard resolve splinters. Her soft sob floats through the air as she remembers the day probably as vividly as I do. She was there. The only person in this entire world, other than myself, to ever meet Roman. She held me as I held my son, long after he took his final breath.

"I have a small hope chest back at my apartment. We need to go there first. Then Chicago. It's the only way to know for certain."

My thoughts fragment into a million tiny shards. I don't need the DNA test to confirm Roman's paternity.

*On a hunch*, Oliver said.

It's more like a parent's intuition.

# 23

# JUST A DREAM

MAZEN

**FLYING INTO TAMPA,** I offer Sophia some space on the plane. It's for the best, seeing how I want to simultaneously rip the truth from her lungs, then fill them with my cum as a punishment.

*Goddamn it.* I can't even think straight.

The usually crowded aircraft is empty of my other bandmates, managers, and randoms from the label. The silence from their absence is deafening, even with the incessant noise thundering in my skull. It's just the plane's captain, flight attendant, me, Sophia, and her lie—or omission, as Oliver put it—that fills the cabin today.

I glance over on reflex a couple of times, eyeing her from across the slender walkway. She's sitting in the same position she sat in a couple of hours ago when we boarded, her thin fingers tense in her lap, tapping aimlessly to a steady beat only she can hear. I can't help but wonder if it's one of our songs that fills her head. A melody that I wrote, my voice plaguing her head and thoughts, like hers is mine. I can't help but wonder a lot of fucking things right now.

*How much did my son weigh?*

*What time was he born?*

*Does he have a headstone or one of those flat plaques?*

*Why doesn't she visit him?*

*How could she* not *visit him regularly?*

The most astonishing question lingering in the forefront of my mind is the deep need to know if Sophia remembered me a lot sooner than she's letting on.

Words dangle on the tip of my tongue, each syllable primed, ready to let loose. How did she not recognize me? The father of her child. And if she did, if she knew the truth and hid it ... what was her motive?

A thousand scenarios play on a big screen in my mind. There's nothing else to do, to focus on, as we glide through the air. They're on a constant loop. I sit and stew and think and mourn until the silence is too much.

My insides twist from the battle waging internally. Though I fight like hell. One leg is planted firmly on each side of the war, pulling me in both directions. It's a battle as old as time. Love versus hate. Forgive and forget. Be the bigger person or take the low road and build a fortress so high that no other woman will ever have the strength to knock it down again. In a battle cry of epic proportions, my restraint starts to crumble.

*I hate how much control she has over me.*

I want to scoop her into my arms and breathe in her essence. Smelling the citrus scent that is only *her*. It's my favorite smell. I could bottle it up and use it as aftershave, and I'd still long to smell her. I want to take her body— petite but curvy in all the places that make my dick hard— and bend her over every surface of this aircraft. Claiming her. Marking her so deeply that she feels it in her marrow. I want her to scream my name at thirty-five thousand feet and then use her own tattoo gun on her flesh and carve my name, to scar her heart like she's done mine.

What I need is to *not* want her. My body and heart protest, each picketing on their own side. I need sleep. I need to regain some damn sanity. I'm pushing far past delirious at this point.

Sighing into the exhaustion that's whirling in my mind, I cup the back of my neck. Sleep feels like a distant memory at this point. I shift in my seat, sagging into the plush material. My index finger runs alongside my jellyfish tattoo, tracing each line. It's a distraction. One that almost works to quiet my thoughts long enough for my heavy lids to close.

Sophia's pained voice cuts through the silence, causing my lids to spring open.

"Please." Her voice is as weary as a newborn fawn finding its footing. A faint exhale, followed by a small whimper, floats through the air around us before she mumbles, "Don't."

I'm up and out of my seat. Another whimper escapes her mouth, and I'm called to her on instinct, like a beacon in the night, a moth to a flame. There's a part—a large part—of me that is seething, submerged in anger and grief, but then there's this other part. The part that has me standing motionless in the middle of the walkway, rocking back on my heels in the center of the aisle, staring at her with a mixture of concern and curiosity.

*What's she dreaming about?*

"You can't. Please. He's not yours to take!" Sophia sobs.

Her sweet whimpers morph into blatant agitation. Her lids are still closed, and I watch her intently, my eyes peeled with curiosity of what's haunting her dreams. My heart pounds when I get closer, sliding into the vacant seat beside her. There's a thin sheen of sweat on her forehead. Tiny wisps of red hair at the base of her neck are wet from whatever horror she's facing in her dream.

Suddenly, my throat feels dry. I'm on edge. *What do I do? Think, Mazen.* I'm not good under pressure. I never have been.

The temper that filled my chest dissipates when she lets out a full-blown gasp. "He's mine," she cries, eyes still closed.

I watch in stunned silence, scared to move. Scared to breathe.

*I'm such an asshole.*

I might have been robbed of meeting my son—hell, even knowing about his existence—but Sophia was there. Her cries, the guttural pleas she shouts into the air, are the evidence that he had a parent who loved him as deeply as one can. As much as I wish I were there when she was pregnant, when Roman was born and laid to rest, I don't know if I would have survived it. Losing my sister was one thing. Losing a child … I know I don't have what it takes to survive that kind of pain.

This gaping void of knowing I never got the chance to see him, hold him, kiss his sweet little forehead doesn't hold a candle to the pain radiating from Sophia as she quakes in her seat. My usual strong-as-steel woman crumbles. She's resilient, and I'm a sorry piece of shit for blowing up on her like I did. The confirmation slaps me across the face with each tear that falls.

She carried him. Then buried him. That burden, that responsibility, rested solely on her shoulders, and it's enough to clog my throat with a thousand apologies for how I acted last night and this morning.

An ache as deep as the ocean emits from her body, tears cascading freely down her cheeks. That's my breaking point.

*Fuck.*

I can't stomach watching her endure this nightmare any longer. I'll suck up my own grief. I'll swallow it down like a fistful of tacks if only I never have to see her like this again.

Raising my hand, I go to gently nudge her shoulder, to wake her from whatever hell she's living in, only to be dragged down with her as her body trembles once then twice before it thrashes in the seat. Her mind begging her to wake up.

"Wake up, Rosella." When she doesn't budge, I grip both of her shoulders, my fingers digging into them. "Sophia, wake up," I demand, my voice hard as the iron of my eyes boring a hole into her head, begging her to come to.

Her voice breaks, along with my heart. "Roman."

One word. One name. *His* name. That's all it takes for any residual anger and pain I harbored to disintegrate. Only a heavy bed of concern is left in my heaving chest.

"Please, wake up."

"Mommy loves you. I'll see you again soon. I promise." Desolation like I've never heard booms in her plea.

Oliver and Cannon never mentioned anything about her talking in her sleep.

*Shit.* Did she take an Ambien before we boarded? Or is the stress of everything the cause of her sleep talking?

The internal throttle in my chest goes haywire. I shake her. Hard, until her jade eyes spring open, wide with worry. They dart past my shoulder, back to my bunched brows, then toward the window in a quick swoop. When they land back on me, they're wet, reminding me of moss that's been weighed down by the morning dew.

There's no hesitation when I scoop her into my arms and onto my lap. My hand is large enough that it cups the back of her neck and half of her head. I hold her fiery-red hair in place as I nestle her into the crook of my neck.

"Shh. I've got you."

The words *it was just a dream* taste like acid as they form on my tongue. The hint of metal pools in my mouth when I bite the inside of my cheek, forcing them down. It wasn't just a dream. It was a memory as vivid and strong as the sun's rays that dance across the clouds we're flying over.

I clutch her to me, our ragged breaths syncing. The pain of losing our son is like a tether, a stain on our souls. Except I've only lost his memory. She lost his touch.

There's nothing stronger, more impenetrable than tattoo ink seeped into skin. That's no longer my truth. The bond we share, regardless of how we both feel about it, is forever. Even if our little foursome fades, and we go our separate ways romantically, she will never be able to fully rid herself of me. Sophia will never have to endure this kind of deep-seated pain alone again.

Through her veil of hair, I take a shaky breath. "Do you want to tell me what happened?" There's a childlike hesitancy to my voice, like I'm tiptoeing into the unknown. And I am.

Why would she feel comfortable enough to confide in me about what is most likely the worst part of her life? I made her feel like shit. Painted her out to be a liar and a fraud. I'm probably the last person she wants consoling her right now.

Oliver was made for situations like this. He's patient. Tenderhearted. A fixer. Even Cannon, who sports his unsociability like armor, is better equipped to soothe her than I am.

"He died." Her eyes close as she shakes her head. "This wasn't how you were supposed to find out about him."

"There are puzzle pieces still missing, Rosella. I'm sorry I wasn't patient enough to ask the proper way last night. I'm asking now. I want to know about him..." I choke on the thought of speaking his name out loud. "Roman. Our son. And I want to know why you didn't tell us you had a child in the first place."

"Not confirmed," she adds.

Trying not to allow her comment to rub me wrong, I take the mature road for once in my damn life. "I feel it in my chest, Rosella. I can't explain it. I'm sure I sound like I'm delusional. I just know. Please don't rob me of that instinct."

Nestling into me, she seems to find comfort in my arms, in my calm tone. A minute passes before a long exhale presses her chest into mine.

"I'm going to skip the *money-laundering father* bullshit because I know that's not the part you need to hear."

I nod, and she sits back in my lap, giving me the pleasure of staring into the depths of her eyes. I could get lost in their lush green, like fields of land, uncharted or unexplored.

"Caddell's guys were outside of my and Lacey's apartment door in Chicago when I was leaving to go to a lash appointment. I know. Stupid." She shakes her head. "When I opened the door, there were two of them in my face, shouting. One tried to grab my crossbody purse off my shoulder, and I slapped him in the face. He snapped. Pushed me against the wall, right into the corner of a fire extinguisher. Anyway, I struggled. Screamed. I tried to get the attention of anyone in our building." There's an unmistakable tinge of hopelessness in her voice when she mumbles, "No one came."

You can't tell me no one heard her. *Cowards.*

"I was able to push myself off the wall and knee one in the groin. That's when the other shoved me. Are you a swimmer, Mazen?"

"What?"

"Have you ever gone swimming in a public pool and jumped off the highest diving board they had?"

"Sophia ... my dad is the governor of Florida. I've never even seen a public pool unless it was that scene from *The Sandlot*."

"Wendy Peffercorn." She smiles.

"The one and only."

"Anyway, that's what it felt like happened. Like I had dived off a diving board, except I was free-falling backward and landed at the bottom of a flight of stairs instead of in water."

A shock wave of fury slams into my chest, wedging my next breath in my throat. She must feel my body physically recoil because she cups both sides of my head in her hands.

"This is difficult to hear," she states. It's not a question, just the honest truth. "I'm sorry."

"Don't ever apologize to me again. I'm sorry, Rosella." Swatting her small hands from my face, I grab her cheeks in my grasp. "I am so sorry that happened to you. I promise you I'll find them, and when I do—"

"I don't want you to find them." A note of pleading casts over her face like a shadow on a sunny day.

"How could you not want retribution for what they stole from you?"

"I do want that. I want those sorry bastards to suffer. I want them to hurt ten times as bad as they hurt me. They left me there, lying in a puddle of my own blood. Just walked right over me like I was debris on the sidewalk. I just don't want you to be the one to serve it."

My thumb and pointer finger clamp over her trembling chin. "You can't ask that of me. They stole the only chance I had of meeting my son. They took him from you and left you to die, like human life means nothing to them. How can you expect me not to search, to scour the fucking planet for them?"

"Because hurting them, serving the justice that your heart demands, won't bring Roman back. It will only sully his memory." As her words flow, she seems to gather her strength, pulling it from a place deep within her. "I don't know if you're much on religion, and frankly, I'm not a saint, so this objectivity might be for nothing. But I know my ... *Roman* is in heaven, waiting on me, and I won't do anything to jeopardize my chance of seeing him again. Acting reckless, indulging in doling out punishments might feel good for a moment. But what will it do in the long run?"

There's a bottomless peace that exudes from her as she lets out a long sigh of self-control. Sophia has had over ten years to come to terms with this, both her accident and his death. She's seasoned in tragedy. She's been hand-stitching her resolve, readying her heart for the day when she finally kneels on a cloud, arms stretched wide to hug him again.

I'm impressed as I look into her eyes, truly seeing *her* for the first time. The world tried its best to break her, to ruin the pure beating heart in her chest. I can tell that there are parts of her that will never ever be whole again. How could they be? Though she lost something that can never be given back, an unmistakable chunk of her heart is missing, and yet I know without a doubt that Sophia still won. I think she knows it too. The lithe body of the woman sitting on my lap isn't only a survivor. She's a fucking warrior.

Circling her in my arms, I lean forward, rubbing my nose along the tip of hers. There's something about her unwavering strength that calls out to the weakness that lives deep within me. The dark part that wants nothing more than illicit revenge is being called to like a ship in the night by the bright glow of a lighthouse that she's guarding.

Strong emotions fuel most of my songs. My pain bleeding onto paper has woven more lyrics than I can count. Now is no different. Not with my muse sitting in my lap, stirring feelings that pierce my soul.

*Your light pulls me from the dark*
*Each ray piercing the steel of my heart*
*I'm powerless on my own*
*Floating forever into the unknown*
*The abyss of my self-made despair*
*I'm an anchor, tethered beyond repair*
*Guide me into your saving light*
*Cast your net*
*Lure me in*
*Lock me in your lighthouse of sin*

I want so badly to reach into my pocket to jot down the lyrics flowing from my mind on my phone. Refusing to move her off my lap, even to type the words playing on repeat in my mind on a text thread, I divert my attention. Choosing to focus on my Rosella, my beacon of light in this gloomy fucking world, I offer her the one thing I can tell she's as desperate for as I am for her shining light.

My word.

"I won't search for them. You have my word. If we ever

cross paths though, that's a big enough sign of fate for me. Before I end them for their role in this shit, they'll take me to Caddell."

"If fate is that courteous, then you have my word that I'll watch you burn them to the ground."

# 24

# WHIMPER AND COO

## SOPHIA

IF MY FUTURE self had told me I would be straddling a rock star while flying on his band's private plane, I'd probably have assumed my sister had laced my iced coffee with something that made me trip or I was really, really overworked and drooling on my desk.

*Totally dreaming.*

Except my eyes are open, my senses on overdrive, and I'm presently sitting on Mazen Wilde's lap, enveloped in his arms as we embark on the journey to Tampa and then to our final destination, Chicago. A deep blush creeps its way across my cheeks as I revel in my current reality. It fades quickly when my thoughts align again, and I remember the reason I'm nestled on his lap, the reason we're on the plane in the first place.

Mazen listened intently as I revisited the past, weaving my memories into a story meant only for his ears. I started after the fall, telling him about the mailman who found me and called an ambulance, only to be rushed to an emergency C-section for a placenta abruption that had been caused by my fall. I didn't spare any of the gory details as I rehashed my vague remembrance of the team of doctors rushing around me after Roman was born. All I cared about was seeing my son, finding out if he was alive and healthy, waiting for his first cry to echo around the operating room.

The pain was unbearable, though it dulled in comparison to the ache in my heart as I screamed out with worry, begging for answers. Later, when I awoke in recovery, they told me I was hemorrhaging as a result of my placenta disconnecting from my uterine wall during my tumble. An emergency hysterectomy was performed.

There's a glint of something I can't quite put my finger on in Mazen's eyes when my lips begin to quiver. It's almost as if his mind has placed a shield around him, readying him for the worst part.

"Roman was taken to the NICU as soon as they put me under. I woke up without my baby in complete terror. Lacey was there. She had gotten a spray tan. Her cheeks were streaked." I smile, trying to give light to the giant black cloud that has formed over us. "From the tears. It was awful."

"I'd have liked to witness that," Mazen says, though the smile he tries to force doesn't reach his steel-colored glare.

"He was so little. I was pushing thirty-two weeks. His lungs weren't fully developed. They're the last thing to develop and ..." I pause, gathering my thoughts, arranging them into words. "He had suffered a small brain bleed from my fall. I held him every minute. I didn't lay him down once. Even when the nurses and doctors came in to check my incision and offer pain medication, I kept him in my arms."

One tear is followed by two and then three. I blink, and

there's a steady stream falling from my eyes like a summer storm.

"Roman lived for three days. They were the best days of my life. My only regret is that I refused to allow Lacey to take any pictures. I guess ... I just wanted to live in the moment. To take in every whimper and coo. My nurse cut some strands of his hair and gave me a printout of his last heartbeat. It was dark, like yours. I'm sorry I wasn't strong enough to take pictures."

Large hands cup my tear-stained cheeks, his touch meant to calm me, center me. Mazen holds me tightly, refusing to allow my head to turn. I'm glued to him as he admits, "You have nothing, absolutely nothing, to be sorry about. I'm sorry, Sophia. I'm so sorry." He chokes back a sob. "Who wants to see a rock star with virgin skin? Right. Maybe in a Christian rock band, sure. That's not who the Kings of Jupiter were or who we wanted to be. I went to that convention with one goal. Then, I met you, and every song I ever wrote about a woman ... about anything, dulled in comparison. When we met again at the bar and then spent the night together, it was like I was fighting against time. I knew what the morning would bring. I was leaving to go on tour, and nothing could stop me. Not even the most beautiful woman in the world."

Lowering his hands, he threads them through his tousled black hair and pulls roughly at the root. "Fuck. I didn't know. How could I have known you'd get pregnant?"

"It's not your fault. It's not anyone's."

"It is though. It's Julian Caddell's. He killed our son and almost killed you. He stole your chance at birthing another child."

The pilot comes overhead and tells us to buckle up as we near Tampa, our pit stop.

Mazen intertwines our hands. Squeezing mine, he beckons my attention. "Why don't you visit him?"

There's no longer a need to say his name; my heart already knows who he's referring to.

"Because he's not there. His tiny body might be but not what matters. His memory lives in here." I raise my empty hand and pat the spot over my heart. "I don't need to go see a gravesite to talk to my baby. I do it every day, no matter where in the world I am."

My words resonate as the plane starts its descent.

A moment passes before he asks, "Will you take me to see his grave when we get to Chicago? I need to see it, Sophia. I know he's not there. I get that." He nods, eyes locked forward on the seat in front of him. "I don't have any memories of him to hold on to like you do. If his grave is all I get, I want it ingrained in my mind."

THE RIDE to my apartment above Rose and Lace Ink Emporium is as silent as an empty cruise ship. There's a pit in my stomach that feels like I'm being buried alive. I'm fighting against the sand that keeps falling around me even though I know it's futile. Roman's death is a never-ending pain as plentiful as every speck of sand that is slowly filling me from the inside out. I wonder if that's how Mazen feels too.

His eyes are locked on to the headrest in front of him. Anger radiated from his pores on our flight. Has that deep rage subsided and turned into sorrow, mimicking my own?

Or will reality only set in once it's confirmed that he is Roman's father?

I'm torn between hoping that he is and praying that he isn't.

My eyes take in the familiar buildings and landmarks as I peer out the window of the town car we're being chauffeured in. My gaze as empty as his.

Home beckons like a witch crooking her wrinkly, ashen finger at me.

*Home.* I don't even know the meaning of it anymore. Your home is supposed to be your haven, your refuge.

It was that once, many moons ago. When Lacey and I fled Chicago and broke ground on the studio, renovating it to our liking, it felt like home, familiar, comforting, but I never truly felt settled. I guess that's what happens when you're running from your past. Every stop along the way is a fleeting pit stop until you're forced to pack up and move again. Abandoning each place like it was insignificant, a small blip on the scale of life.

We built a business, and in a sense, Rose and Lace and the employees-turned-friends became our home.

The thought of walking into the building, both my apartment and studio, is now tarnished by the memory of Lacey's fear when she called me. The brick Caddell threw through the window didn't just shatter the glass we had installed ourselves. It also shattered the safety that I thought we had built. Though the facade we had built was already cracked, held together by masking tape and delusion.

After I've been on the road and touring with the band for the last couple of weeks, my apartment has come to feel more like a prison cell, a tether holding me back. There's a tightness in my chest as I allow myself to think that thought. The shop has been my dream. The one accomplishment that I can truly call mine and be proud of. As soon as Lacey joined me on tour, our home, the one we're pulling into now, became nothing more than an address. My small twin bunk on wheels has become more than a home; it's my sanctuary. Or maybe it's just the people inhabiting it that feel like my home.

"I'll give you some time." Mazen nods toward my apartment before finishing his thought. "To go through his things and get whatever you think we'll need."

There's not an ounce of malice in his tone. His offer is sincere. It makes me appreciate him more than ever in this moment.

"I ... I don't want to go up alone." Nerves twist like vines up a tree in my stomach. "I'm normally an independent person."

"I know," he interrupts. "Come on. We don't have much time before we're due back at the airport."

Sliding my key into the lock, I swing the door wide before gesturing for Mazen and the security guard, Preston, to come inside. It's strange not having Ashton around. He and Mazen are usually glued at the hip. Preston is Ashton's right hand, so it only makes sense that he is here in Ashton's absence. I allow my mind to briefly drift over the idea of why he's not here himself. *Lacey.* Maybe there is something blooming there after all, and he couldn't stomach leaving her.

The broad-shouldered man I now know as Preston interrupts my matchmaker theory when he slides in front of me and proceeds to do a quick sweep of my apartment.

Room after room, he calls out, "Clear," before finally declaring my apartment safe enough for America's favorite rock star to enter.

Preston has his cell phone speaker to his mouth as he

relays the message to the rest of his team downstairs. My shoulders relax instantly. Since the incident with Caddell, I feel like I've been holding my breath. That's why finishing this tour and getting paid is so important. Freedom dangles like a pendulum just out of my reach.

The guard leans against the front door frame, shifting his focus back to his cell phone, and begins to scroll aimlessly, offering a moment of privacy.

"It's in my room." I turn, hoping that Mazen follows.

I don't waste time when I open my bedroom door and sit on my knees in front of my bed. Reaching underneath, I pull out a small wooden box. My hands shake as I snake it out from the dark depths and bring it toward my chest. It's my most prized possession. My heart literally in a box.

"I have my ultrasound pictures and the little hat he was wearing in the NICU in here. A dried flower from his funeral." My hands tremble, along with my wobbling lips. "The reason we came though is for his hair. His DNA. That's what we need, right?"

Mazen opens his mouth to speak. I watch as his lips part and then close. Once. Twice. Three times before he musters up the courage to speak. When he does, his voice is tender; it's so low that it's almost a whisper. "I shouldn't have brought you here." Our knees brush when he bends to sit in front of me. "We don't have to do this. It's not important anymore. I'm going to tell the pilot that we're not going to Chicago."

Confusion throttles into me with such force that the wind is knocked out of me, causing my tone to hold a degree of meanness. "What do you mean, it's not important? It's important. It's fucking important to me. I need answers just as much as you do."

We both make it to our feet, realizing a conversation of this caliber should be done while standing.

"You dragged me out of bed, made me feel this big"—I hold my hand in front of his face, my thumb and my pointer finger only an inch apart—"put me on your goddamn private plane and flew me home, only to what? Chicken out? I went through everything alone, Mazen. I refuse to do this alone too. So, we're going to Chicago. We're going to find out the truth, and then we're going to visit his grave." Ice dangles off my hardened words. "Together. Because you don't get to dredge up his memory and force me to relive the worst time of my life to just … claim it's no longer important to you."

Mazen looks down at me. His face pales, and his thick, dark eyebrows crease with … worry. I don't even see his hands move. His fingers tenderly take the box from my arms before he places it on my bedding as gently as humanly possible.

His captivating coin-colored eyes turn dark. A formidable, restless energy engulfs me, along with his strong palms as he cups my cheeks. I don't know what I expect when my eyes meet his again.

"Roman's paternity isn't important anymore. I say that lightly, very lightly. Do you know why?" he questions, though I don't dare move to answer him. My lips are suddenly sewn shut. "Because it comes at a cost I didn't know I couldn't afford, and I'm a fucking billionaire, Rosella. The desire to know with certainty that I … we … made a child together isn't as big as the desire I feel to never ever make you crumble like you are right now. I see it in the fields of green of your eyes. They're dulling by the minute. I can feel it."

He snakes his hands down my neck, fingers settling onto

my shoulders. He moves them up and down, stroking my arms tenderly. "In your tense muscles. I can hear your pain in the steady beat of your heart. It's a gut-wrenching tune that's going to be ingrained in my mind until I take my last breath."

"Maz—"

He holds up a hand to silence me.

"You had your time to talk, to tell me like it is. To remind me what an asshole I've been. It's your turn to listen. I really want you to hear what I'm saying." He thrusts his calloused hand through my hair, forcing my neck to bend upward, our noses almost brushing by the sudden movement. "I will live in the unknown if it means your heart doesn't break again."

Leaning forward, he rests his forehead against mine. The declaration in his words hits a chord. I know with certainty that he means them. He'd fly us right back to our friends and never look back. He'd ignore the gaping hole in his chest at the expense of protecting my heart. He'd plaster on a fake smile, and things would return to normal.

Except normal is a fairy tale.

It's an optical illusion.

Mazen and I have never been normal. Not when we first met and became a mess of wild limbs or when he left the next morning without a goodbye. Nor when he taunted me, screwing women in public places, where he knew I'd catch him. Or the most obvious fact that I am *with* his two best friends. That I want us to *all* be together, that we want him to be with *us* too. That is definitely not normal, and oddly enough, I'm okay with it.

This, whatever is happening between us right now, will solidify if we're meant to have a fairy-tale ending.

# 25

# FILTHY MAN

OLIVER

"DO you know what would help me release some of this pent-up stress?" My eyes rake over Cannon's shoulders, wide, thick, and deliciously broad.

As fucked up as everything is right now, I know there's zero chance that Mazen would ever lay a finger on a woman, in a nonsexual or consensual way. As irate as he was, smoke blowing from his ears, he'd never ever hurt Sophia. I don't doubt him one bit. Forcing the situation with Mazen and Sophia to the side, I stuff it in a metaphorical box in my mind and close the lid, then give my other best friend my undivided attention.

Cannon's leaning against the back of the couch we're sitting on, side by side, his naked chest on full display, looking every bit a combination between a Viking and professional athlete. If it wasn't for the way his hands were constantly moving, creating a beat on every single surface he touched, you'd never guess he was a musician.

He's the perfect mixture of boyish charm, innocence,

and thick masculinity. He smiles widely, and his impeccably straight white teeth—thanks to his two parents who gave a shit about his oral hygiene—are striking, a dazzling display, just adding to his overall appeal.

His maroon sweatpants dip far enough that I can see the top of the V that sweeps low below his pants. Our drummer's body is immaculate. There's not an ounce of fat on his large frame. Just thick thighs from the hundreds of squats he does, a nearly flawless bubble for an ass. I say *nearly perfect* because I'm not currently balls deep in it. Which makes the whole *openly undressing him with my eyes* a task I'm here to master.

He oozes sex appeal both on and off the stage. His body is as mouth watering as a rare steak. Suddenly, I'm feeling famished. Nothing in the kitchen will sate this feeling though. The chorus of Drake's "Best I Ever Had" booms in my head as I think about wanting what's in his sweatpants.

I've never really had to work to get laid. In the music industry, screwing around is as common as strumming your guitar. Cannon Rhodes is the exception. He makes me work for it. Clock me in for overtime because Sophia and I both hit the jackpot where he's concerned. Only a select few are privy to his kinks. It shouldn't excite me as much as it does, or maybe I'm bored or a little too wound up, stressing over the two members of our situationship who've gone rogue.

"A bath?" Cannon asks in his usual deep timbre.

His quick quip is enough to set my body in motion.

I settle on his lap. The position is new for me. I'm easily the smaller man—in height and weight—between the two of us. The slight tilt of Cannon's head, covered in his signature shoulder-length blond hair, has me feeling frisky. My movement shocks both myself and him. I use it to my advantage.

"Are you offering to take one with me?" I ask, looking into his ocean-blue eyes.

"If it'll help you chill out, sure."

"I'm as cool as a cucumber." My core grinds against his.

"Maybe as hard as one."

The thing about Cannon Rhodes that I both love and loathe is that his confidence only shows when he's one hundred percent comfortable. Even with his arm draped over the back of the couch, teeming with sexual prowess, his shoulders are tense. He keeps his eyes trained on mine, not once dipping lower to see the bulge already forming a tent in my pants. He feels it though; his commentary makes that crystal clear.

"Anyone here?" He confirms my suspicions as I grind once more, this time applying a little more pressure between us.

"I thought you liked an audience." My palms land on his washboard stomach. They roam upward on instinct.

Our bodies are so in tune. Even after the years of denying ourselves, we fit together more perfectly than a newly unboxed puzzle. We're like a glove and a surgeon's hand, a bubbling glass of champagne and a toast at a wedding, a bag of buttery popcorn and the cinemas.

"Only if her name is Sophia. Mazen fucking stole her."

"Such a filthy word for a filthy man." I can't help but notice the tingle of excitement that stirs in the front of his sweats, mirroring my own.

A nagging tinge of curiosity gets the better of me. My mouth speaks without any prompting from my brain. "Speaking of Mazen, do you ever think about what will happen when he caves and wants to *really* share her with us?"

Cannon's strong, rigid profile is a contrast to the wavy

light-blond hair and crimson that begins to dance over his cheekbones. Is he embarrassed? Does the idea of the four of us all filling our girl at once turn him on? Or is it something else entirely?

"Do you?"

The question he shoots back at me hangs in the air, thick and firm, like his tree-trunk thighs. My mouth curves as if I know he's already asked himself this question a time or two. If we're being honest, I know I have. It's something I refuse to admit first though. Instead, I tilt my head forward and place a lingering kiss on his muscular chest.

On a shrug, I say, "It's all I've thought about."

My mouth now hovers over his ear. A beat passes when I realize he's not going to respond, and I take his lobe into my mouth and suck hard. His chest stills, holding in a breath.

"There're a lot of things I think about that I probably shouldn't. Things that have the power to implode our lives if it all goes south." My voice is low even though I know that we are indeed alone in the suite. Lacey is out with Vanna, and Jupiter is with Murphy in his suite, most likely taking a nap.

That gets his attention.

A primal sound burning with desire leaves his lips. "Talk."

One simple command has me all but dry-humping his leg. Fuck, our damn dog doesn't even do this juvenile shit, and it's quite literally in his nature. All it took was Cannon's husky voice drawing obedience, demanding me like I'm his to do with what he pleases, ready to kneel at his feet.

Kiss his feet. *Foot fetish is my middle name.*

Crawl to him like he's my master. *Hold my knee pads; they're not even required.*

Suck his cock. *Call me Dyson, baby.*

Lick his puckered hole. *Tossing salad is my favorite pastime.*

As someone who clings to control like a second skin, I won't lie; the thought of handing the reins over to him right now is more appealing than arriving at a hotel after a week crammed on our tour bus, a home-cooked meal after days of eating out, turning the light off after hours of recording in the studio. If he asked me for anything right now, I'd give it to him. I'd wrangle the moon, cowboy-style, dressed like a damn astronaut.

I'm in that deep.

It's not even the look he offers that seems to burn through me, eyes brimmed with dominance and passion that has my body and heart going ablaze. Nor the smirk that curves up his mouth mischievously.

No, I come unglued, bones turning into putty in his hands. Cannon pushes his large, calloused palms under my T-shirt and slowly runs them in a tantalizing path up my back. His large palms cup my shoulders as he gathers me against him, holding my body in place. I give myself freely over to him in this moment, and he knows it.

"Tell me what makes your dick hard, Ollie," his mouth demands before he leans forward, pressing it against my own firmly, sealing his words with his lips. In a hard, drugging kiss, his tongue explores my mouth with punishment, like it's the first time he's been invited in, and he wants to make damn sure I don't forget him.

A heartbeat later, Cannon pulls back, breaking our kiss. "I want to know what you're so ashamed to voice, to ask for."

Unnerved, I hold my breath, thinking of how I should reply, deciding what hand I want to play. I asked for this, for him to show this side of himself. I crawled onto his lap obediently, all but put the idea into his beautiful blond head. It's one thing for me to admit that I'm interested in seeing what all the fuss about bottoming is; it's a whole other thing to confess that I've thought—longer than I'd like to admit—about seeing the man I love getting railed by our other best friend.

The notion alone leaves me more turned on than shaken. That in turn leads me to feel insanely fucked up.

"It's not like you to back down from a challenge." He scoffs.

"Is that what this is? A challenge?"

The hunger in his cobalt eyes is so electric that I fear a live wire is feeding right into them. The submission he's coaxing, pulling from the very depths of my soul, smolders behind his irises.

"Label it what you will." He moves his hands to my waistline.

"You just called me out, saying it was a challenge."

Lifting his chin, he nods unconvincingly. "Looks like you're failing it then."

My brows rise as high as my forehead will allow. The amused contempt sprawled across my face must be notice-able because Cannon's jaw clamps shut, mouth twisted with a threat. He's goading me. He wants me to lose my control before I willingly offer it over to him.

"You want to know what makes my cock thicken? What makes it throb until it's so hard that it physically hurts?" A half smile crosses my face, my stare now boring into his. *Two can play this game,* I think before answering him as honestly as I can. Rising up to his challenge, I say, "I think about you holding me down so hard with my face planted against your mattress that I have to fight for air."

Cannon's expression stills. It's his turn for all the air to leave his lungs, deflated, dazed. His smile vanishes. The immature taunts we had lingering between us a moment before are gone. There's a thickening desire to dominate one another that burns like a Roman candle between us, flickering unsteadily before sparking back up brighter and wilder than before.

I take a deep breath, adjusting my smile into one that's subtle, offering just a hint of satisfaction that he was right—I've never backed down from a challenge. Choosing this moment to finish my sentence, I continue, "I think about your rock-hard cock and that fucking piercing wrecking me in the best way possible. You feeding yourself into my hole with zero remorse for how bad it hurts. I want you to lose yourself in me. That's what I think about, Cannon. Giving you the gift of owning me. Body, mind, soul. It's yours for the taking. If you want it."

A couple of things happen all at once.

Cannon's knees lock when he stands. He's holding me against him like I'm a damn koala. His linebacker physique is nothing more than an illusion because he moves through the hotel with the grace of a gazelle, even with me perched in his arms like I weigh no more than a feather. If I wasn't high on the idea of my best friend owning me in the spiciest of ways, I might feel emasculated by how quickly he moves with me in his tight embrace.

As the door slams, a picture hanging on the wall trembles. I bite back my agreement with the shuddering artwork. *I feel ya.* I'm as giddy as a pimple-faced adolescent boy about to get a BJ for the first time from the badass flute-playing girl in my third-period music class.

The last thing to happen is what takes the cake. Both figuratively and literally.

He yanks my pants down before pushing me onto the bed on my stomach, then hovers over me. That large palm of his presses down in the center of my back, holding me hostage, giving me the desire I finally voice.

"Spread those cheeks. Show me what you've been holding out on."

Apparently, I'm more obedient than I have ever given myself credit for because before he finishes his sentence, both my hands are full of flesh, my fingertips digging into my round cheeks.

"Spit on my hole," I say, looking over my shoulder as I manage to fight through the current of desire.

The hand that Cannon has pressed into my back starts to trail down the length of my spine. I can feel each gloriously earned callous from years of holding his wooden drumsticks as his hand tenderly dances over my skin. My back muscles tense as his finger makes contact with an area that has never been breached.

"I'm going to do much more than just spit on it. That okay with you?"

At least he's considerate enough to ask.

I clutch his bedding in my palms. "Take me in whatever way you want. I'm all yours. I always have been."

# 26

## FOOLISH BOY

MAZEN

WITH A LITTLE MORE COAXING THAN I'd like, I convince Sophia that the paternity test doesn't matter anymore, that she's the only thing that matters to me. I lost sight of that ... of what we could be. Losing her by pushing her away is one thing. Losing her because I'm a coward, a broken man, is a fate I refuse to accept.

With double the effort of convincing on her end, she admits that she wants answers almost as badly as I do.

Hours later, we land in Chicago. It's almost midnight by the time we arrive at the hotel. After the plane landed, we went right to the private clinic of the physician we hired to perform the DNA test. These things usually take weeks. For us, the results have been expedited. A perk of being rich, I suppose.

"You booked two rooms?" she asks, brows knitted together as we step off the elevator.

"Assumed you wouldn't want to bunk with me." I'm too ashamed to say the words *after I flipped the table you were sitting at, then dragged you out of bed like a maniac* out loud. "Not after how I acted."

"We've been 'bunking'"—she air-quotes the last word—"for weeks. I literally hear you guys fart and burp. Oddly enough, I'm not even repulsed by boys being boys even though I definitely should be. You guys are like a pack of dirty, feral wolves. Jupiter is cleanlier than you." At that, she smiles.

Everyone loves our canine. Half the time, I think our fans prefer him to me.

"I thought we squashed all this insecurity on the plane?" Her chest brushes against my front.

"You shouldn't forgive me so easily. I was a dick. My behavior was inexcusable, and if you haven't noticed yet, we are wolves. Wild ones. If you were thinking with your head, not your heart, you'd run far away from us."

When Sophia doesn't respond, I nod perfunctorily once, then twice before turning my attention on opening the door to her suite.

"Get some rest." I gently push the small of her back, guiding her into the room before I set her duffel bag at her feet. "We'll talk in the morning when we've both had time to sleep and process everything. It's been a long day—a long couple of days." Running my hands through my hair, I exhale loudly before I attempt to shut her in her room.

I don't want space. I've never had anyone who looked at me like she does. Hell, even when we acted like we hated one another, that glimmer of attraction still shone bright in her emerald eyes. I fear space is what she needs tonight. This one act of kindness, of putting her needs before my own, speaks volumes about how sorry I really am for my rampage.

When I feel her arm brush by mine and see her palm

plant firmly on the cool door, stopping me in my pursuit to be a gentleman for once in my life, I know what she's going to say before she says it. Don't ask me how. I just do.

"You know this is the same room, right?"

"Couldn't forget it if I tried." My heart turns over as I stare into her soul, begging it to call back to mine.

No sooner do the words leave my mouth than the realization of my admission registers.

Sophia's head slants, and her eyes widen as she soaks in a truth that means more than any sorry I've mustered today. She looks every bit like Jupiter does when he's batting his lashes, wanting a treat another one of us previously denied him. She's looking at me like I both hung the moon and hand-planted every star in the universe.

An overwhelming floodtide of emotion passes between us. A reminder that this infatuation with her began in this very spot over ten years ago.

"Mazen." She remains shell-shocked as her plump lips spread, allowing my name to escape.

Sophia's gaze softens like the gentle caress of her hand when she tattoos me.

The sound of her whispered petition lights me on fire as much as an arena of thousands of fans shouting it in unison at one of our shows. One word, a demand. An invitation to claim what is rightfully mine. Her heart and her body.

"Mazen," she repeats, only this time, her voice is breathier, needier, laced with a tone of longing.

All gentleness has been trampled by wanton need, lying at her feet. The lush green of her eyes meets the steel-gray of mine. She dares me to cross the threshold into her room with nothing more than a couple blinks of her thick, full lashes.

*Yep. I'm fucked.*

A ripple of invisible warmth, as hot as the sun, almost as unbearable as the prolonged sexual magnetism we've been fighting for weeks on end, flutters wildly in my once-abandoned chest. There's a rush of pink dancing along Sophia's cheeks, throat, and chest as if she lost a fight with a tube of lipstick. Her desire is palpable.

"I want you. Bad. I need you, Mazen." The intensity of her heated glare in her fuck-me eyes shatters my resolve.

Something intense flares through my bones, along with a thunderbolt that goes straight to my hardening cock. Like a snap of a rubber band, my need for her outweighs all rational thoughts. Thoughts of what tomorrow will bring. Thoughts of how this situationship will really work between four people. Thoughts of her being so much more than just a casual lay and conquest.

Ignoring my subconscious, I take three steps into her room. Each one feels like I'm trudging through water, but I can't get to her fast enough.

The woman I love takes a calculated step backward. She's kicking off her shoes and hastily sliding her shirt over her head, dropping it onto the floor in one fluid motion. Every article of clothing caressing her skin follows until she's nude, bared for me in more ways than one. When she runs her talented hands over her delicious, perky mounds, my mouth waters.

Now, I know how Jupiter feels when we have a fresh bone for him.

Sophia's devastatingly beautiful body is my prize.

In amazement, my eyes dart across every inch of her ivory skin to the bed behind her, the one where I more than claimed her body all those years ago. The bed where I claimed a woman who turned into my muse. The bed where our child was conceived.

To tell you the truth, aside from my sister, Sophia is the only woman I've ever loved or cared about. I should be a little ashamed to admit that, but I'm not. She owns me in every way imaginable, and these feelings all started with that one night we shared. Two strangers planted a seed that bloomed over the years, flourishing into an untamable garden caged in the confinements of my heart.

The only difference now is that she's no longer a ghost. Our story is no longer past tense. This is our moment of reckoning, and that bed—the one that has haunted me for years—is about to create new memories in my mind. I'm going to fuck my love into her so hard that my name will be written on her organs. The sheets will forever be stained with our essence, and Sophia Rose Lozier will never be able to forget me again.

"Do you remember when I picked you up at your apartment the day before we went on tour?" I don't wait for her answer before I take a considerable step toward her, planting myself firmly against her. "I said, 'Be careful if you call out for the devil; he just might come.' You've called to a part of me that I'm afraid I can't ignore anymore, Rosella."

Not even a second passes before I gather her into my arms, holding her tightly, breathing in the scent of her hair. I catalog how good it feels to have her in my arms. I breathe in the vulnerability she radiates. I memorize the feeling of how her soft curves mold to the contours of my body.

Pushing away with my heel, I step backward despite her hands that reach forward, tugging at my shirt, trying to protest. "I don't want you."

Her eyes widen in shock … and hurt.

Sophia swallows hard, accepting my lie.

Before she can bend at the knees to pick up her shirt, I reach forward and grab her by the back of her neck. Strands of red hair tangle in my palm. "I don't want you. I *need* you. In more ways than I fear you need me."

I step back in front of her, bridging the gap, and any doubts she had are incinerated as my lips sear a path down her neck, across the ridges of her shoulders. Her body shudders under my mouth as it presses hard kisses along her body, demanding her to never forget me or this moment again.

"I want more than your body."

Capturing her mouth with mine, I press into her, allowing our emotions to whirl around us. A current of desire and lust and love ebbs between us like a volcano until we're both on fire, panting and animated. This time, when I pull back, she lets me.

"Whatever happens in this room, it's not just for tonight in my eyes." I kiss the side of her mouth. "It's not just while we're on the remainder of our tour." Another kiss is planted on the opposite side of her mouth. I don't want to leave any part of her body untouched by my hands or mouth. "I won't accept anything less than forever from this moment on."

"What if—"

Doubt is an ugly uncertainty.

"What if the paternity test results come back, and I'm *not* Roman's father?" I finish for her.

A melancholy frown flits across her strained face before she nods, giving breath to the uncertainty that coats her glossy, worried eyes.

"You can't make promises of forever when it doesn't exist. If you're not Roman's father, then this"—her arms widen in front of her as if she's mocking our sacred place—"will have been for nothing. This trip down memory lane. These declarations of forever and a future together. All of it will be meaningless. You can't tell me you'll still want me if you're not his father."

The green of her eyes darkens from a lush meadow to a dark forest, signaling her beaming irritation.

"I can't handle the rejection I'll feel when that reality settles in. You'll regret giving light to all of these pretty words. I know it in the pit of my stomach."

Dropping down onto the mattress, her hand falls to her face, hiding it. She's defeated, and I'm fucking livid. Enraged by her dismissal of what is between us, of what's right in front of her eyes. This isn't some crush I've been harboring. This isn't some hookup reunion. This is real life. What could be the start of our lives ... together.

I don't need a mirror to see the warning cloud that pairs with my stern-faced expression. "You want a dose of reality?"

Before I stoop down in front of her, I yank off my shirt first and then my pants. I want to bear myself to her like she did for me. When every bit of cloth is gone from my body, knees planted firmly on the carpet—my heart carved open, waiting for her to seal it back inside my chest— I say, "I couldn't breathe the morning I walked out of this very room, leaving you asleep on this very fucking bed. I was selfish. Fuck, I was a kid who didn't see what was right in front of him."

As bad as I want to reclaim her lips and show her with my body how much I need her, I know she needs more than just my touch. She needs my words even though she's trying to act immune to them.

"I made a decision that I'll regret until I die. I'm not a foolish boy like I was back then, baby. I'm all man now, and I know what I want. It's you, *Rosella*. I pinky promise you that I won't ever make that childish mistake of walking away from you again." Pressing a gentle kiss against her forehead, I continue, "I couldn't turn my back on you again if I tried. You're ingrained in here." I lift her palm to hover over my heart.

Pulling myself away from her, I stand and round the bed, stopping at one of the nightstands. "Look." I pull it out, away from the bed and wall.

There, on the side of the wooden nightstand, carved into the grain, are the letters *M* and *S*, a heart around them.

A gasp leaves Sophia's parted mouth.

"You had fallen asleep. I knew I had to leave in the morning, but I never wanted to forget how calm and cherished you made me feel. The sex was good. Better than good. It wasn't what made me feel alive that night though. That feeling came from your eyes. I'd never felt so *seen* in my entire existence."

Words are my weapon. They always have been. I pull them from my arsenal in an attempt to adequately portray the effect she had on me—still does.

"I carved our initials while you slept and wrote you a note." Changing tactics between heartbeats, I say, "Do you want to know how many times I've been back in this room? How many times I've sat on this bed, staring at our initials, begging the universe for a sign that you felt something as deeply as I did that night?"

Pushing her words past her dry throat, she asks, "How many?"

"Once a year for the last ten years and every time the tattoo convention came back to town. Or any city. I've scoured the globe in search of you. I thought you might still have a booth. But every year, my perusal came up empty. The guys didn't know. I didn't tell them about us and our night together. I didn't want it tainted by their commentary."

I gently ease us both onto the bed, not waiting for a reply. My lips explore Sophia's body, every curve of her pearl-colored skin. I use my mouth as a paintbrush, and her body becomes my canvas. She's all woman. Perfection. And tonight, she's all mine. *Mine.*

I'll face the truth of having to share her tomorrow.

My lips dance over her dusty-pink nipples. Her body instinctively arches toward me. I palm her body, exploring the lay of the land like I'm on an expedition of her soft flesh without a map. I'll die a happy, lost man in her arms, in her body. I crush into her like a tidal wave, my mouth covering hers hungrily, demanding entrance.

"Mazen."

Her body squirms, our mouths less than a breath apart. I glide my lips down her taut stomach.

"Stop." Her lip trembles. "Please."

Thrusting away from her, I stand at the side of the bed, body stiff by her sudden demand.

"I, um …" Jaw clamped, eyes sewn shut, she murmurs, "My scar."

Reality dawns on me. *The* scar. Her C-section scar. Is she ashamed of it?

Lowering myself back onto the bed, I cup her cheek, holding her gaze toward mine. "This scar?" I trail my finger across the faint white line on her abdomen. "The beautiful mark that brought life into this world is what you're ashamed of?" I spread her legs, positioning my body between them. My eyes never once glance at her sensitive area between her legs. "Don't ever be embarrassed of your body or this scar. You're perfect."

"Imperfect, you mean." It's not a question. "I don't

understand why any of you even want me. I'm short compared to the models I've seen you all pictured with. My boobs are a solid C cup and natural. Nothing like the porn-star women you've had. I have red hair, for Christ's sake. You guys can have any woman you want. Actresses. Singers. They're at your disposal. Ripe for the picking."

"And yet we want you."

"Why?" her counter is quick.

"You really don't know?"

She shakes her head, answering my question without words.

"You're everything we're not," I say matter-of-factly, resting my chin on her pelvic bone, looking up into her eyes, willing her to believe me.

The vacant look she offers back tells me she truly believes her allure is a mystery.

"You're unapologetically yourself. You're *real* in a world where fakeness drives people. You're so fucking compassionate that it physically hurts. That time you bought the homeless man at that Podunk gas station food for both him and his dog sort of solidified that you should win a Humanity Heart Award or some shit. Or the time when you stood in the rain, helping that elderly lady pump her gas. The kindness you offer the world just because your heart leads you to is rare. You're so pure. It's magical, Sophia. We ... Ollie, Cannon, and I don't see that often anymore, especially not now that we can't even go to the grocery store without a team of security. You call yourself normal, average. We call you unique."

She leans up on her elbows. "You adopted a stray dog, gave him a life of luxury. You paid for your sister's best friend's grief counseling for the last two years—don't hurt Ollie for telling me that; he was trying to prove a point that you weren't the biggest douchebag in the world a couple of weeks ago."

That earns her an earnest smile. I really painted myself poorly there for a while.

"You're so much more than the man the world sees onstage, Mazen. I see the real you, and I like him. This version. The one who speaks from his heart. That's why people resonate with your music so much. Your lyrics are words gifted from a place that's so full of compassion and wonder. You're the rarity between us, not me."

"What's rare is the fact that I haven't bent you over this bed yet. You know that, right?" I laugh, adjusting my hardening length that's digging into the mattress.

"See?" She playfully pushes my shoulder. "You have such a way with words."

Tossing our heart-to-heart and banter aside, I lick my lips, wishing I could taste her arousal. Would Sophia still think so highly of me if she knew the suggestive thoughts running through my head?

As if our bodies are tired of waiting, in a clash of skin, Sophia's warm embrace welcomes my body on top of hers.

"I want you to fuck me like the first night we met. Not like the man looking at me like he's picturing me in a damn wedding dress. I need you inside of me, Mazen. I've been waiting too long for you to come to your senses about this. It's been torture, watching you parade around with other women in front of me."

"I'm a piece of shit. I don't deserve your forgiveness, but, fuck, I'll work every day to earn it any way. This sounds so cliché, but I only screwed them because I couldn't be with you. I only want to be with you in every aspect that matters."

"You could," she interrupts. "You're the one who's been holding out for so long."

"Not anymore. Damn. Even the fucking tour bus driver wants you. It's what you do to men. Your essence, it's potent as hell. That's probably why the old bastard keeps the barrier between the driving section and ours pulled shut every day. He's probably so turned on by your incessant moaning—that Ollie and Cannon have gotten skilled at pulling from you—that his dick is driving the wheel."

"That's an awful image. Way to ruin the mood."

Her lighthearted laugh is a welcome sound. We've had nothing but in-depth conversations since we boarded the damn plane.

It's time to give our minds a break. Our bodies are ready to work.

"Lie back." I slowly slide back down her body until I slither onto the floor, my knees resting on the carpet, and then pull her down to me by her velvety skin. "I've been dying for another taste of this sweet pussy."

Sophia's cheeks match her rosy peaks as they harden, and her breath becomes shallower. She moans softly as I kiss the inside of her thigh while running my thumb deliciously over her scar, reminding her that there's nothing on her body that isn't perfect.

When my mouth journeys closer to her core, her body stills, craving the ecstasy she knows is coming.

"Taste me, Maz. Fuck me with your tongue."

The degree to which her raw, unfiltered demand bores into me leaves me too stunned to reply, so I spring into action.

Each moan of praise that passes from her parted mouth is a taunt straight to my iron rod cock. I want so badly to be buried in her, I can hardly concentrate on lapping up her center.

The delicate fragrance of Sophia's warm opening reminds me of a field of flowers. Her scent is clean like air-dried linen hanging in a summer breeze with a mix of floral goodness that just suits her. I remember licking her clean after Cannon and Oliver made her come by the pool, but the sweet scent of her had long been washed away by chlorine and my friends' mouths. Having the pleasure of enjoying her before anyone else this time is a jolt of wanton need straight to my veined shaft.

Soft hands caress the tendons in my neck, pulling my face closer toward her pulsing slit. Each lap of my tongue becomes a savage harmony, pushing her writhing frame to soar until the peak of her delight is within reach. I can tell by her sharp intake of breath. The way her body starts to tremble under my expert tongue.

Contentment roars in my veins at the sound of her lips parting, breathing my name, "Mazen. Oh. Fuck." Each word becomes breathier. "Mazen. I'm gonna...come."

My gaze moves over her body in appraisal. I'd usually be an ass and ask do I get a merit badge for that, but all I can think is she's fucking breathtaking. My obvious appraisal doesn't go unnoticed.

"That was...epic," she pants, her thighs still pressed together firmly.

"My pussy-eating skills rank up there with singing. What can I say?"

Sophia scans me temptingly, appreciation beaming in her eyes. "How are your lovemaking skills, Wilde?"

*Lovemaking.*

"I thought you wanted it hard?"

She seems to be floating on a cloud in deep thought before she responds, "I want it all."

Four words spoken with the deepest compassion I've ever felt, by the only woman I've truly ever cared for, unlock my heart and soul.

It's easy to get lost in the earnest look she casts me. "There are no more secrets. Just you and me, Mazen. We've lost too much time. Make love to me. Show me how much your body misses me."

The urge to give her what she's asked for leads to the spark of haste in my movements.. Easing on top of her, I hold myself up with one hand on the bed, the other fondles her breast, its pink nipple is marble hard. Her deep emerald eyes connect with the cool steel of mine. The words of our first number one hit play in the forefront of my mind, *Heart on Fire*. That's exactly what she... my Rosella...is slowly doing to me.

She's set not only my heart but my body on fire, and I'm fucking smoldering.

I want to take my time exploring, worshiping her beyond belief. I want to reacquaint myself with every inch of her exposed skin. That thought is short-lived and then abandoned fully as she squirms under my weight, begging me to show her without words what she means to me in the way only a man depraved for a woman can.

We're flesh against flesh, heart against heart, muse against musician.

When my shaft inches into her already wet center, it's instantly the best feeling of my entire goddamn life. Our bodies reunite in the most intense reunion of the century.

There's a moment where my physical desire overtakes all rational thought, and I inch in deeper, not caring in the slightest about how Sophia's feeling. Nothing more than a hungry yearning to reach her hilt spirals through my every movement.

Inch after inch, she stretches. Her greedy little cunt gripping my dick so tightly until the sound of a sharp intake of breath suddenly halts my movement.

"Shit. Sorry, Rosella. I got carried away."

Her touch is like a hit of ecstasy against my flesh as she palms my ass, demanding me through a long, shuddering moan. "Move and kiss me."

We move in unison, our bodies gliding against one another's, soaring together into a masterful hysteria of unbridled passion. And for a moment in time, I don't care about what tomorrow brings.

How could I when my entire being is being flooded with Sophia's soft moans and essence?

I will crave her until the day that I die.

# 27

# BLEED FOR ME

## SOPHIA

I WAKE to the sound of Mazen stirring. His cell phone, most likely lost in the pile of our discarded clothes, sounds from somewhere on the bedroom floor. In his search for each of the pleasure points on my body, our clothes, responsibilities, and inhibitions went out the window, along with all rational thoughts about the line we had dived over, giving less than two shits what the morning would bring.

Our hands, mouths, and desires guided our every move instinctively. His hands explored my back, running deliciously up and down my spine like he was counting my vertebrae. His lips nipped, licked, and traced a path over my skin as if he was memorizing each spot that drove me absolutely wild. Time, along with the reality that faced us, took a back seat as ripples of arousal, unsated need, and the desire to be flesh on flesh consumed us both.

Welcoming Mazen into my body was like breathing. It was natural. Easy. My body accepted him without thought of the hardships the future would bring. We spent hours exploring, teasing, bathing in the millions of glowing stars that shattered around us when we came in unison over and over again. I'd cry out my release, gasping in sweet agony, as Mazen tore apart my soul while simultaneously piecing it back together again. His kisses, gentle and maddening touches, and promises became the glue.

Exquisite harmony. A reunion. I was freed by Mazen's touch. His surrender. Glowing as bright as the sun from the passion and love that burned between us as hot as a blazing orb floating in space.

When I was pleasantly exhausted, it was far too late to text Lacey and the others, letting them know we'd landed and made it to the hotel. We were a little too preoccupied to care about mundane tasks like being responsible adults and charging our phones, completing my skin care routine or even brushing our teeth. The reality of neglecting what is questionably the most important task we forgot is chiming incessantly, beckoning us like an SOS.

"They probably think Caddell kidnapped us both this time." I laugh, unable to help it while keeping one hand covering my mouth—morning breath is as vile as the smell of a body piercing.

Huskiness caused by sleep lingers in his tone when he says, "Too soon."

"Is it?" I quip at his back. "Humor is my natural trauma response."

Feeling lighter than I have in years, I lean forward and press my lips against his naked shoulder, a real smile stretching wide across my face. Today will most likely be an even bigger shit show than yesterday and the day before. I don't let it deter my mood.

Wrapping Mazen in my arms from behind him like a cocoon of blissfulness, I exhale a long sigh of happiness.

"Want to have sex again before you turn your jerk meter back to level ten?"

I press my exposed chest into his back. The movement instantly makes my nipples harden. The passion that boiled over last night will soon be replaced with an edge of uncertainty. I might as well continue to chisel away at the stone-cold wall of hatred he likes to stand behind.

Running my hands through his night-black hair, I pull hard. The movement causes his neck to bend. It's not lost on me that I'm playing the role of the big spoon.

The epic catastrophe facing us can wait a little while longer. Hot breath slips past my parted mouth, my lips hovering over the rim of his lobe. "If you don't want to wake up, give me a sign."

My tongue darts out, running along the shell of his ear as Mazen attempts to lay motionless, but fails. A faint tremble dances through his body, causing his bones to stir.

"I met someone in the bar here years ago." My confession is meant to taunt him awake. "I'm sure I can find another willing suitor to—"

In a motion quicker than a blink, I'm pinned on my back. A very awake and angry rock star stares back at me.

"If you finish that goddamn sentence, I'll take you so hard that your pussy will bleed for me for days."

The tilt of my hips is like a doormat welcoming his filthy threat inside. Legs parting, I bite my bottom lip. "There he is."

His heart thuds wildly against my chest for a beat before his mouth parts. "Is that what you want, Rosella?" he asks stoically. "You want it so hard that I mark you?"

My skin catches fire under his palm as it skates up my body. The path it floats over is left in a burn so smoldering that I'm fearful his fingerprints are permanent, a tattoo—a reminder of his presence. He plants the center of his palm at the base of my throat, fingertips brushing on either side. Eyes as dark as the ocean's depth at one thousand meters rivet my body and soul in place. I'm helpless, immobile. It's a perfect place to be.

I couldn't tear my gaze away from him if I tried.

Hesitating for a moment, I get lost in his arresting face. Mazen looks a couple years younger with the hard gel that styles his hair missing. The absence of worry in the usual tight lines at his mouth is evidence that nothing has pissed him off this morning ... yet. His eyes are glossy with sleep. No, that's not right. They're hazy with need. I can feel his erection thickening on my stomach where it rests. I refrain from gasping in delight.

Mazen Wilde wants to ravage me.

Last night, our bodies were reacquainted. They appraised each other with familiar eyes. It was like the first slow dance at your senior prom. You and your date are both a little wary. Anxious about stepping on one another's toes so you fumble a step or two. By the third dance, you're so in tune with one another that you get lost in the music and the touch of your partner. The music fades so thin into the air that you don't even hear it over your pounding heartbeats.

This morning is like our fifth dance. The nerves are gone. The music is blaring, and we're ready to have a little fun.

When he doesn't continue, I purse my lips before deciding that open communication is something we severely lacked before. Choosing to rectify our wrongs, I toss off my proverbial corsage, unzip my prom dress, and kiss the prom king like my lips have been carved by the hands of sin.

"I want to bleed for you."

His eyebrows rise just a tad at my revelation.

It's usually Cannon who brings out this side of me. The woman who isn't faulted by her dark desires at enjoying a little pain before her pleasure. If we're doing this, there's no going back. Mazen's going to meet every version of myself that exists. I woke up wanting to block out everything that is waiting for us beyond this hotel door.

Which is exactly what I do when I reach down, bypass Mazen's massive appendage that extends higher than my belly button, even with our hips aligned, and slide my hand to his taint. With a feathery brush of my index finger, he sucks in a breath and holds it.

"You're going to get some news that might change your life forever." Another brush over his sensitive scrotum. "When you do, I want your body to remember how good it felt to be with me. To really be with me and lose yourself."

"I told you, the results don't matter anymore."

"You told me a lie. They matter even more now." Cupping his balls, I pull them back an inch. "You want to know. I want to know. Just remember this"—my hand moves up his steel-hard length until my thumb circles his hole—"felt like heaven."

"Sex isn't a weapon." His narrowed eyes appraise me.

My heart beats with the pulse of his voice when I find my own. "It is when it's the only thing you're capable of wielding."

"Sophia." My name is flat on his tongue. He wants to chastise me, but he's resisting. "You're capable of giving me much more than your body." The hand holding my breath hostage skates across my jawline, settling on my cheek. "You know that, don't you?"

"What, my heart?" I scoff, the green of my eyes dulling —I'm sure of it.

A simple nod, paired with the gentlest, most tender

glint of adoration I've ever seen, flashes in Mazen's stone-colored eyes that bore into my own.

"If you can still look at me like you are right now after we get those results, we can talk about matters of the heart. Until then ..." I pause when my face heats, and moisture gathers in my core. "I need you to fuck me like you did that night we met. Like I'm just some whore you met at the bar. Mazen, I need you to hate me again. Resent me if only just for show."

"Why?" His muscles coil, tensing at my request.

I swallow tightly. "Because last night was too perfect. You made me feel too much. The results *are* going to be a match. I can feel it in my heart." Without prompt, my hand hovers over the beating organ in my chest. "You're going to resent me for not telling you about him, just like you did when you were mad that I didn't remember you."

"What's fucking you like a groupie going to prove then?"

"It won't prove anything. That's not the point. It'll help me erase the memory of you worshiping my body like I was your queen last night."

He grumbles inaudibly in a tone that tells me he definitely requires more than four hours of sleep or less truth in the morning. Still hovering over my body, his toned arms flexing, he roughly yanks my naked body and pushes me over so that I'm face down on the mattress.

"You want to be fucked like the faceless fucking women I screwed night after night trying to obliterate the memory of you from my head? City after goddamn city, I tried to burn the sound of your moans from my brain. Nothing but meaningless sex is what you want from me, Rosella?"

The, "*Yes,*" that escapes my lips is mumbled due to the bunched-up comforter shoved in my face.

There's a split second where I think Mazen cares about me so much that he won't be able to shove aside his own feelings to give me what I need. A moment of reflection passes. He's contemplating the very nature of his being by giving in once more to the dark that the light of our passion last night finally pulled him from.

"Mazen," I ground out his name.

Almost pensively, he asks, "You're sure about this?"

*Why is he still asking, still ensuring this is really what I want?*

A chivalrous rock star sounds like the punch line of a joke.

Panic and fear riot in my stomach. I'm falling in love with the father of my child.

No amount of sex is going to be able to smother the beat of my erratic heart. The savagery of this moment, of this trip, and the results, which are most likely already waiting in his inbox, are more frightening than failing to pay off Caddell.

"Stop asking, and take me already."

Like a hunter luring out its prey, I push myself up on all fours. An offering to destroy the affection he treated me with so eloquently last night.

I'm surprised when his brash words captivate me as deeply as if he were singing one of his ballads. "Spread that hole wide. I want to see you gaping."

A wide, earnest smile is on my face a second later when Mazen gives himself over completely. Finally complying to my demand, he plunges into my opening with enough force to make me see stars.

*I win.*

# 28

# ORANGE JUICE WITH VODKA

## MAZEN

TOURING the globe with your best friends brings a certain level of chaos that never seems to wane. From the constant chatter, strumming of guitars, Jupiter barking, and crowds screaming our names when we attempt to do mundane things, like stocking up on energy drinks at gas stations, I've come to recognize that the commotion is never-ending.

A record on repeat.

The fame wavers between a blessing and a curse, and the noise can be a bit too much at times.

As I sit across from Sophia, who is moving around the yolk of her egg with the metal edge of her fork, a blank expression on her face, the silence I normally long for is overwhelming.

After I took her rougher than I ever have any other woman, we showered together in—you guessed it— complete silence. Then, I watched as she brushed her teeth, washing away the toothpaste that dropped off into the basin, knowing that we were in a hotel and the housekeepers would wipe it clean regardless. She dressed in silence. Blow-dried her long red hair—the sound of the blow-dryer a bigger buffer than I'd have liked—and then finally, finally, she spoke.

"Brunch?"

The one word she offered hit harder than a boulder rolling off a mountain straight into the cavity that houses my heart.

That was thirty minutes ago.

We're sitting, eating brunch in deafening silence at the small table in our suite like I didn't rearrange her guts for a solid hour and then get the cold shoulder. Just when I think I can't take it a second longer, my phone rings.

Sophia's eyes dart to the lit-up screen. "Are you going to answer that?"

"Are you ready for me to answer it?"

"No." The truth that bellows from her mouth speaks volumes. "I thought they'd just email you the results or something. Don't you want to see it in writing?"

"Apparently, this warrants a phone call."

Brows that she ignored the duty of penciling in this morning are a shade lighter than normal. I watch as they pull into a sharp frown. When she finally moves her gaze from my now-silent cell phone, her mouth pulls into a thin-lipped smile, which is nearly a spectacle in itself because her lips would make even Angelina Jolie envious.

I watch emotions dance across her ivory cheeks. I wish I could read her mind and ease her fears. It's my fault for acting like a grade-A asshole after the award show. I made her feel this way by painting her out to be a deceptive liar. Stomaching that truth is enough to make the contents in my abdomen swirl.

I gulp down my regret and orange juice with vodka—

thank you, minibar—and little by little, my own nerves start to disappear. "I was telling the truth when I said it didn't matter anymore. You, Sophia, you matter."

"I don't think you'll feel that way when you call back, and they tell you that the DNA matches. It's still wild that they could do that overnight when it supposedly takes weeks or months."

"Rock star, remember?" My joke falls flat.

She runs her hand through her hair, her eyes pinned on me. "For what it's worth, I truly didn't remember our night together. I never once considered you—not this version, of course, but the guy I'd met at the convention—could be Roman's father. Trust me, I know how that makes me sound."

Her fork clangs against her plate as she readies her breath to say, "You held on to my memory for ten damn years, and I forgot yours like ... like that night was as insignificant as this egg. I'm sorry."

"I feel a *no more I'm sorry pact* brewing." I fold my leg over my opposite knee, then lean back in my chair. "Listen, I was pissed when I realized you didn't remember me. I was also pissed at Murphy for getting engaged and buying his own tour bus. We all were, and we still care about him. Let's let bygones be bygones from this point forward. No more of that slut-shaming either. You're a woman who handled a tough situation all alone and came out stronger on the other side. Plus, sluts are hot," I add with a wink.

"Don't do that." She waves her hand between us. It's a dismissive gesture. "Don't paint me out to be some saint. I was a stupidly naive girl who slept with too many men to fill the void my mother's death left in me. Look where that got me—sitting across the table with a man who could be my child's father."

I reach forward, collecting her hand in mine. "If I am Roman's father, it won't change anything. Bygones, remember? We just established that."

"You're lying again. It'll change everything." Her small voice grows louder. "You could have been there when he was born. Held him before he was stolen from this earth. Looked into his beautiful little eyes." The pain in her tone is palpable. It's written on her face, carved into the depths of her soul.

Losing someone you love is a pain that never diminishes. If anything, it only intensifies. Time dulls the constant reminder that they're not here, but the grief never wanes. It gets worse with each holiday or birthday that passes. A reminder that they're forever gone.

I would know. Losing my sister was painful. It numbed me, made my heart turn to stone. Sophia made it beat again. I hope my words help mend her heart as well.

"You don't get to blame yourself for this, Sophia." I've had enough. None of this is her fault. I'm a dick for making her feel like shit about something she had no control over. "I left you in this very room without a name, number, any way to contact me again. Even if you'd assumed it was me, that I could be his father, you couldn't have reached me. Roman died, but his death isn't in vain. If I am his father"—it takes every ounce of willpower in my body to bite back the emotion threatening to spill out—"then it's a miracle we found each other again. Do you know how rare it is to be given a second chance? This is ours."

My phone rings loudly again, echoing in the room, jarring us from our moment of suspended time.

"Answer it," she whispers, then gets up and walks to the window, offering me a sliver of privacy.

I hold the phone to my ear. "Hello?"

"It's Peter Lanham from the lab. I assume this is Mr. Wilde?" The deep baritone of the man's voice registers, pulling me back from the tornado of thoughts whirling in my head. "I called earlier. As soon as the results were confirmed."

I cup the back of my neck on instinct. "Yeah. Sorry about that. I was, um … preoccupied. What's the verdict?" I ask, cutting to the point.

"There's no easy way to put this given the circumstances." There's a heavy pause. "The combined paternity index indicates that you are Roman Lozier's biological father."

My thoughts falter. All the breath in my lungs leaves in a heave that has me hunching over.

"We process every sample twice. Each test performed by a separate team of technicians. This helps eliminate the possibility of human error. You are without a doubt the father."

My phone drops, hitting the floor with a thud. "Let it Bleed" by The Used comes to mind at the exact time a stampede of emotions blur my vision. Wetness flows like a river down my cheeks. I don't think I even shed a tear at my own sister's funeral. I was too numb to feel anything. I wish like hell that were the case now because I feel it all. Relief in having the answer, the truth of his paternity. Sorrow for the time I missed seeing Sophia pregnant and the chance to hold my son.

Indescribable pain wrecks through every fiber, tendon, muscle, and vein in my body until I'm sliding off the chair and onto my knees on the floor. A violent sob bellows from my chest.

"I never got to see him," I say out loud to no one in particular. The words just need a release. Grief so thick that it causes a roadblock is lodged in my throat, preventing air from entering or leaving. "Smell him. Hold him." I grit my teeth until my molars hurt.

"I'm sorry. I'm so sorry, Mazen." Sophia sinks to her knees on the floor in front of me. My muscles tense when she caresses my arm, then my shoulder. Curving her small hands behind my neck, she forces me to face her.

Tears streak her cheeks, too, absent of debris. She didn't apply mascara this morning, I remember unexpectedly. We both knew.

"He was so little. His hair was as dark and straight as yours. He reminded me of a little monkey."

I catch her smiling at that memory.

"I have more than his hair in my chest. I have an outfit he wore once in the NICU when they allowed me to dress him, his blanket, and my ultrasound pictures. You can see it all, take whatever you want."

Trauma bonds people every day. Surviving an active shooter at your place of employment, the lifeguard of a public pool saving someone from drowning. I wouldn't wish this feeling on my worst enemy, but there's no one I'd rather have by my side as I crumble than Sophia.

IGNORING REALITY A LITTLE LONGER, we rose from the floor, gathered our emotions in a box sealing it tight, and climbed into bed for a midday nap. We both drifted off to sleep within minutes. I dreamed of Roman as an infant, toddler, and teenager. My dreams were a reel of possibilities that will never come to fruition because his life was stolen prematurely.

If I hated Julian Caddell before, I wish him a thousand painful deaths now.

We wake hours later to the sound of an iron fist pounding on the door. A voice booming from the hallway draws unwanted attention.

"Keith. Open the fucking door," the male voice calls out from the hallway. The use of my pseudonym is in full swing.

"Ashton," Sophia mutters, eyes widening. "Why's he here? Do you think something happened to Preston?"

It's adorable that she cares about my staff. Truly cares about them. It's evident by the look of sheer panic on her dewy face.

"Let's find out."

Hopping out of our bed, I throw my T-shirt over my head. Swinging open the door, I come face-to-face with my agitated head of security. Ashton pushes by me forcefully.

"Come on in, man." I motion to the couch, "Have a seat."

"Have a seat?" The flagrant anger in his tone leaves me confused.

Did something really happen to Preston or the rest of the team I assembled that could warrant Ashton flying here himself?

"You've got about twenty minutes before Near Death Records reports your ass as a missing person."

"What the hell are you talking about?" I eye Sophia, who is now sitting up in bed, a sheet tucked under her chin. Her high cheekbones turn pink.

"You flew off on your paternity crusade and didn't check in.

That's what the hell I'm talking about. Shit's hitting the fan. Everyone's been blowing up your phone. Murphy's been on band patrol. Vanna's wrangling in Lacey, who is beside herself."

The mention of Sophia's sister, the only reason I didn't ask Ashton to accompany us on our little crusade as he called it, hits hard. I went with our second-string security team. I see the way he looks at the pink-haired she-devil. He can deny his attraction to her all he wants. Been there, done that. The signs are as noticeable as Jupiter being a husky.

*We didn't check in with our friends. Shit.*

"Preston and his team are here." I roll my eyes while running my hands through my hair. "It's not like I just borrowed the plane without anyone knowing. Why didn't you just check in with him?"

"Trust me, ole Pressy's been demoted. I'll be here from now on."

"He didn't do anything wrong," I hear from the bed. Sophia's full lips are pursed together, holding in what I can only guess is another retort.

"He failed to report for his two-hour check-in. Pair his idiocy with this one." Ashton's gaze meets mine. Apparently, I'm the second idiot in this hotel. "For not checking his phone."

I spot my phone about the same time that Sophia grabs hers from her nightstand. Loose tendrils of red hair hang over her shoulder. For a split second, I forget about Ashton's presence, the reason we came to Chicago, and the news that rocked my world this morning.. I stare at Sophia, the mother of my child, in complete awe.

She's overwhelmingly beautiful. Composed and always carrying herself confidently. It's what drew me to her specifically at the convention years ago. I wanted someone who looked the part to give me my first tattoo. I was all in, the idea of what a seasoned tattooist should look like in the fore-front of my mind. When I landed on her, the first thing I accepted was her severe lack of ink. There was nothing there but velvety blank skin. She didn't resemble any tattoo artist I'd ever seen before. The simple allure she embodied, standing out like a red rose in a sea of colorful lilies, did me in. My previous notation of what a talented artist should look like went out the window as I saw her sitting in her empty booth, looking as graceful as an artist in front of a blank canvas. Even with an empty booth, determination was scrolled across her features. If I only knew then what I know now, our lives would be much, much different.

At another glance, Sophia's jaw clenches. Holding up her phone, she says, "We screwed up."

A sinking feeling in the pit of my stomach grows larger at the number of unread alerts on my phone.

I sink down onto the love seat opposite Ashton, swiping through my messages quickly. There's a handful from Lindsey and Ashton. One from the lab, which I evidently ignored, which warranted the personal phone call from the lab tech. I land on a thread that seems to have grown like the miles between me and my band. Sophia's mimicking my movements, her fingers scrolling wildly on her cell, a smile spreading on her face, most likely from the idiotic commen-tary our friends have been partaking in.

> Ollie: Did you and the demon who stole
> you this morning land safely?

> Lacey: Is Jupiter fixed?

> Murphy: Yes.

> Lacey: Good, because he's deflowering a
> blond-haired corgi right now like he just got
> out of a ten-year stint in prison.

Vanna: Aw, take a pic. Sweet boy. We can frame it at their wedding.

HempDaddy: Left the chat.

Ollie: Leave Jup and his red rocket alone. Let my man handle his business.

Ollie: Earth to Fireball.

HempDaddy: Joined the chat.

HempDaddy: Ollie, quit fn adding me.

Ollie: Why do you think it's me?

HempDaddy: Because you're sitting right next to me, grinning like a creep.

Ollie: If you don't leave it again, I'll make it worth your while.

Murphy: Will this ever not be awkward?

Lacey: I bet Jupiter's red rocket is bigger than Ollie's.

Vanna: STFU. (crying emoji) Sophia Rose can confirm or deny. Where are you?

Ollie: They should have landed. I'm callin' them both.

Ollie: No answer.

Lacey: Soph, pick up your damn cell.

Ollie: You don't think …

HempDaddy: They're fine.

Ollie: Did you see that in your crystal ball?

HempDaddy: If you want me to hold your balls and close my eyes, I promise you'll see more than the future.

Lacey: Wow. FN smooth. No wonder my
sissy is smitten.

HempDaddy: Leaves chat.

The thread ends abruptly when Cannon removes himself. I can only imagine the shit they're getting into without us. I agree with Murphy that it's taken me a beat to get used to the sudden, open affection between the other half of our band members. It's not that them being together is strange. We're in the twenty-first fucking century. It's more the fleeting feeling of dominance maybe? There's a kindling feeling that hits in my heart—somewhere lower, too —every time I see or hear Ollie and Cannon that has become unsettling. I've never been attracted to a male, much less to any member of my band. The suggestion leaves my mind reeling. I think I feel like I'm the head of the household in this new little foursome we've founded. There's a need to protect all three of them, almost as intriguing as the conversation they've been having in these messages.

Ollie: Lindsey confirmed your plane landed
in Chicago. I swear if you don't call me by
morning, I'm flying there myself.

Murphy: Ashton's already on it. Chill.

Ollie: RU for real? Chill?? Caddell probably
has them both chained in his fn basement.

Murphy: He's calling Preston.

Lacey: You're not giving Soph enough
credit. She might be into chains.

Vanna: Hard pass, Mr. Miller. Don't get any
ideas. I'm (ice cream cone emoji).

Murphy: My ass.

Vanna: (laughing emoji)

Lacey: Crap. I can't think about her kinks right now. Not when I'm really scared something is seriously wrong.

Vanna: She's okay. They're both okay. I know it.

There are zero boundaries or lines that our group hasn't crossed at this point. Hell, I can even distinguish whose boxers belong to which friend at this point. We've all seen one another naked in one way, shape, or form. Modesty is overrated, so the fact that Murphy is calling his new bride out is hilarious. It's always the quietest ones who bring the heat and the kinks.

HempDaddy: Joins chat.

Ollie: Rhodes, where r u?

HempDaddy: Stop adding me (insert skull).

Ollie: That's not what I asked.

Lacey: Here I thought Ollie was the cinnamon roll of the band.

HempDaddy: Bus.

Ollie: You have five mins to get up here and suck my (eggplant emoji), or I'm going to the airport. I can't think straight, not knowing if Mom and Dad are okay.

Murphy: Group chat! Keep the porn on your own thread.

My lip curves upward at the next message.

Murphy: Gag. You called Soph Mom.

Ollie: Sue me. I never claimed to not have
issues. Oh, and tell your mom to shave her
bush next time. I was plucking pubic hairs
out of my teeth for a week straight after
your wedding.

Murphy: Sick fuck.

A laugh passes through my lips at the blatant fact that
Ollie is goading Murphy. It'll take a lot more than *your mom*
jokes to rile him up though. He's as laid-back as a sloth. My
eyes drift from my phone over to where Sophia is still sitting
in bed. I wonder how far she's read on our shared thread.
From the wide grin on her face, it's hard to tell.

Ollie: Three mins, Rhodes.

Vanna: What if he doesn't make it in time?

Ollie: You don't want to know.

Lacey: I do! (Sorry, sissy).

HempDaddy: Hold the hell on. There's a
damn cheer convention in the lobby.
Security is having a fit.

Murphy: I texted Todd. He's sending extra
hands down.

That answers my question about who was left in charge
since both Ashton and Preston are in Chicago with us.

HempDaddy: Thx. If I ever have a daughter,
cheer is not in her future.

Ollie: When we have kids.

Vanna: I just choked on my latte.

I read the last message twice before a pitiful apology forms on my lips. "Sorry." I hold up my hand, preventing Ashton from replying or laying into me again. "Let me call Ollie before you read me the riot act."

It only takes one ring for my guitarist to answer. "Girth's Garage."

*This fucking prick.*

"Cut the shit."

"You cut your alternator, sir? Is that what you said?"

He's mad. I get it. A dull ache pulls at my chest. If any one of them had gone AWOL, I'd be acting like an asshole too.

"We're alive."

"Sorry, the connection is a little bad over all the fucking sobbing Lacey's doing, thinking that her sister has been kidnapped again. Oh, wait. She was." There's a scolding pause before he continues, "What the hell were you thinking, Maz? We've been going mad thinking Caddell got to you both or some crap. Lacey's a basket case. Lindsey called in the doctor. I shit you not; they're about to give her a sedative."

Irritability tugs at my chest. "She was a basket case before we left," I counter.

"I'm going to go in the bathroom to call my sister," Sophia murmurs, the pitch in her voice telling me she's as emotionally spent as I am.

The door shuts behind her, signaling she needs a moment. I use this time to my advantage.

"He's mine."

There's no need to elaborate. Oliver is smart enough to read between the lines.

Roman is ... was my son.

Ashton's broad shoulders stiffen, shock carved on his usually hard exterior.

"Figured as much when you went off the grid." There's not a follow-up question. No *how are you handling this?* No filler or bullshit. That's not Oliver's style. "How'd Soph take it?"

"Harder than I did."

There's movement on the other side of the line, the sound of rustling, almost like Oliver's covering the receiver. "Mazen's a dad."

My heart pumps then breaks, squealing in anguish as Oliver's words register.

While birthing, then laying Roman to rest were the hardest days of Sophia's life, today will be mine.

"We'll be back tomorrow," I assure him.

"Why not fly back today?" There's a deep question masked in the aloof one he asked.

"There's something else I need to take care of. Ashton and Preston are here. We're fine. I'll text you throughout the day."

# 29

# INTO THE WILD

SOPHIA

FIFTEEN MINUTES after my call with my sister, I'm peeling off my panties, then turning the shower nozzle to its hottest temperature. I refuse to wash away the memory of Mazen's face when he learned that he'd fathered Roman, our child, our son. What I do need is to wash away for the second time today, is the scent of him. It lingers on my skin, a consequence of his tight embrace as he held me throughout the night.

*Protected* isn't a way I'm used to feeling.

The seed of information Caddell planted that Mazen could be Roman's father was shocking. Though it felt almost too cultivated to be a real possibility. Improbability sat on one shoulder; a nagging feeling in the deep recesses of my heart sat on the other. I should have confessed it was a possibility when I told Mazen I remembered him that night at the hospital. I should have had the guts, the courage to face uncertainty head-on. Instead, I cowered. I chose to protect my heart at the expense of breaking his.

Mazen Wilde is my son's father. It's no longer a possibility, but a fact.

A small waft of cool air alerts me that the bathroom door has been opened. Through the fogged shower glass, I watch intently as Mazen slowly undresses then pads over to the shower. With nothing separating us, including the secret I held on to in fear of Mazen loathing me, we're free. We met over ten years ago. We got lost in one other, and then we lost one another. I birthed and buried our son, and then by kismet, I was reacquainted with the man who'd aided in Roman's creation.

Stepping inside the shower, Mazen shrugs. "Saves water."

His company is enough to numb my roaming thoughts. All I can focus on is him. From his exposed, naked body to the fire burning in the steel of his gray eyes. They smolder as they freely roam across my own flesh, dipping slightly to the suds of soap covering my toes. The path his smoky eyes travel is as warm as a hand. I squeeze my own eyes shut, an attempt to shut out my desire for him. Now that I've tasted him, ridden him, been cherished by him, I feel like I'm spiraling.

Fortifying the wall between my heart and mind, I use the foamy loofah in my hand to scrub away the memory of how Mazen makes me feel. Redirecting my wayward thoughts, I say, "Musician and environmentalist."

"And father. Don't forget that title."

My spine goes rigid.

"It's the one I'm most proud of."

The water feels like needles as it slides down my flesh. His words slice into me just as hard.

"Mazen," I say painfully. Is he baiting me? Why would he choose this moment of almost intimacy to bring this up?

"I'm jealous of that loofah." He inches closer, barreling through the boundary I'm trying so desperately to place. "Can I?"

My brow quirks. "We should probably keep our distance. I can see that you're hurting. I've caused you enough pain. Tossing meaningless sex into the mix will only make matters worse."

There's an innocence in the feathery laugh that slides past his parted lips. "I'm just offering to wash your back, not bend you over and use my tongue to soak up the wetness between your thighs."

I turn to offer him my back. Satisfaction bellows from his mouth in a soft moan approving my compliance. It courses through my veins. I bottle up his mumbled praise, savoring it in case the truth we've both been doused with is too much to bear and this is the last moment of civility between us.

Probing eyes and wandering hands interrupt my musings, second to his deep voice. "There's nothing mean-ingless about fucking you. Though I won't be able to do that anymore."

A bruise to my heart the size of the moon forms. Weari-ness weighs down my shoulder blades. The tepid water raining down over us washes away the lone tear that has already formed and fallen down my cheek.

"From now on, I'm only able to make love to you. You're worth too much. You mean too much to me to simply fuck."

My thighs clench instinctively.

"I'll make it as hard and rough as you need me to, Sophia. I know your needs. Don't get it twisted again by degrading our making love to simple fucking." A soft moan, a reward for his declaration, passes through my parted mouth.

"Let me show you how it's going to feel from this day forward, and don't ever"—he pushes his large palm over my lower stomach,"say anything between us is meaningless again. You might as well tattoo your name on my dick, Rosella. It's yours now."

Arousal and water slide down my leg. I don't know which flows more.

I'm startled once again by the words that pour from his mouth. So much so that I don't realize I've been staring at him, mouth agape, for a solid minute, until he breaks the silence.

"Pass me that shampoo so I can wash your hair. We need to leave in the next thirty minutes, baby."

It's the *baby* that has me dropping to my knees in front of him.

SPOILER: we don't leave the hotel in thirty minutes. It's two hours later when Ashton is escorting us with a pissed-off Preston as his shadow to the blacked-out SUV parked behind the hotel.

I mouth, *I'm sorry*, to him as I climb into the back seat.

"Are you sure you want to do this?" I ask, my face pulled into a sober frown.

"I need to," Mazen's reply is clipped, his face pale and exhausted.

Settling into the bench seat next to him, I reach over and take his hand in my own. "We'll do it together then. It'll be the first time Roman sees his mom and dad together."

"It won't be the last time. I'll have to fly back often. I

don't want him to ever think his dad turned his back on him."

Guilt at not visiting our son's grave clamors in my chest. It was too much. The pain of leaving the hospital with empty arms. The ache in my missing womb. The knowledge of knowing I'd never be pregnant again. It was all easier to lock up tight and force my thoughts not to linger in the past.

"Is that what you think I did?" My lips tremble.

Twisting his position, Mazen reaches for my face. Gathering my cheeks in his palms, he says, "I would never think that. Your reasoning for not visiting is yours and yours alone. I can't imagine what you went through, and I'd never ask you to relive the darkest moment of your life again just because I need to do this. Is it stupid of me to want to see his grave? It's not like he's there. Not his soul anyway."

I heave a deep breath, and my heart shudders for the man in front of me. The one I forgot. The very man who spent years searching every tattoo studio across the globe for the woman he'd bedded once. The one who refused to forget my memory and hung on to it with every fiber of his being. That's the man I've fallen for. One of them at least.

As hard as it will be to visit Roman's grave, I'll do it for Mazen. I can't deny the fluttering in my chest or the pulsing knot that seems to unwind around my heart when he's near.

Taking a perilous leap, I cover his hands on my jaw with my own. "He's wherever we are because *we* made him. You and me. We created a life together. Only his body is there though. His memory is alive up here." I tap my forehead. "I wish you could see him from my eyes, but I'll visit his grave with you every day for the rest of our lives if that's what you need, Mazen. I'm not alone anymore. I don't have to be. Over the last several days, you've proven that to me. Somehow, you—" I correct my thoughts, not wanting to break our moment, but to include the other men who hold a place in my heart too. "The three of you have thawed a part of me that long succumbed to numbness."

Silence lingers between us as the vehicle travels closer to our destination. His eyes never leave mine. His hands continue to hold on to my face, as if he's talking to my soul without moving his mouth.

"I'm falling in love with you, Sophia Rose Lozier."

The wall I sought to erect between us crumbles. I choke back a cry, holding my metaphorical dustpan, using it to sweep every speckle of that wall into the garbage. I melt at his declaration. Not because of the lyrical voice he whispered it in. But because I can feel the sincerity in my bone marrow.

"I know you are," I admit, doing my best to slide my facade back in place.

For a moment, I can feel his spirit waning due to the absence of my own declaration.

*You stupid fool. You love him back.*

I love him.

*Tell him.*

Feeling as if my breath has been cut off, I refuse to hide my heart from him for another second. As much as I want Oliver and Cannon to be here for this, to tell them how I feel about them as well, I can't deny Mazen this moment —*his* moment.

The moment when I speak four life-changing words into the wild. "I love you too."

# 30

# SEX SWING

OLIVER

"I'M CALLING COUCH CHRONICLES. Everyone, come in here. Pop a squat. Hurry up!" I yell while sitting in one of the recliners on the tour bus, my hands forming a makeshift cup around my mouth.

Mazen is lying across the entire length of the couch. A shit-eating grin on his face only confirms what I know in my gut to be true. He and Soph had sex. I can almost smell the smugness, mixed with her mouth watering citrus scent, on him.

"We're on a bus, bro. No need to get all amplified."

"Says one of the reasons I'm calling this meeting in the first place."

Cannon swings open the bedroom door in the back of the bus, barreling out of it with Soph's legs snug around his waist. The sound of her sweet laughter has me itching to grab my guitar. Every sound she makes is lyrical.

He sits in the chair next to me, positioning our girl so that her back is against his front.

"What's up?" Soph asks, chin high, neck exposed.

"You screwed him." It's not meant to be an accusation but it falls from my lips like one.

Mazen answers matter-of-factly, not skipping a beat, "Several times."

"What's it mean?" I probe, looking at her inquisitively. "Was it just sex or more?"

Our lead singer doesn't let Soph answer for herself when he says, "More. A lot more than just meaningless sex. Right, baby?"

This time, her mouth parts, a half smile crossing her face. "Yep." That's all she gives. A simple, curt answer with a long *P* at the end.

"Baby?" Cannon's nose wrinkles before he offers us a seriously amused laugh. "I thought Rosella was weird. Baby, really?" We've never seen Mazen serious about a woman before. The pet name hits Cannon and me like a brick to the skull.

*Is this our new normal?*

Soph suppresses a giggle before Mazen's displeasure is shown by his quick retort. "Ollie calls her Fireball. She calls you HempDaddy or whatever that strange app thing you tried out was. It doesn't matter, man. I'll call her whatever I want," he chastises Cannon with that commanding manner he's perfected.

"What do you want to call me?" There's a trace of humor in Cannon's question. Though I've known him long enough to know that there's nothing funny about his request. The blue in his eyes turns neon at the prospect of Mazen's answer.

There's not an ounce of jealousy stirring in my gut like I thought there would be when this moment came to fruition. I find this situation more satisfying than anything. Soph's eyes widened, and her pulse sped up when I told her I got the impression that our band's singer might have a glimmer of interest in our drummer. I've always been good at reading people. When you're dealt a shit hand in childhood, like I was, sometimes, your intuition is as important as a hot meal.

Restless energy swirls between the four of us. Something strong like the thick air before a thunderstorm settles at our feet.

Nervously running her hands through her hair, Soph asks, giving Mazen an out, "Why do I get the feeling that this meeting is about more than nicknames?"

"It's about so much more than nicknames. Are we all together now? A lot changed in Chicago, apparently. I do want all the juicy deets, by the way."

Cannon rubs his hands over Soph's shoulders. He's nervous. "Why do we need a label?"

Standing up, I snatch his wrist, then lean down. My chest is now pressed tightly against Soph's. "Because you're mine, she's mine, and she's yours and his. That means our square is complete. I don't like people touching what's mine. I'm needy. Fucking sue me. I need to know that we're all in agreement that no one touches *the unit* that's not in *the unit*."

When no one moves to put their hands in front of us in a hand stack—the universal symbol of camaraderie—or yells *Go Team*, I press, "Is that good with the three of you? Are you ready to commit to this ... to the four of us doing whatever this is for however long—"

Soph interjects, cheeks red with trepidation when she asks, "The question I want to know is, are you all really ready to commit to one woman's kitten for however long we're all in?"

"Put a collar on me, Fireball. Yours is the only kitten I've petted since we met."

"I'll get your name tattooed on my dick right now, *Rosella.*"

She smiles. "Don't tempt me, Wilde."

I cough. "You won't be able to be with our girl for six weeks. Just remember that before you go tatting your dick like I did. Cannon and I will let you watch us with her though."

"What's a few weeks when I've already promised her forever?"

Cannon huffs. "You went to Chicago and came back as a lovesick puppy."

We all know he's joking. We all have it bad for our girl. It's hilarious hearing Mazen's smooth talk. We're not used to this side of him. The totally smitten side.

Hell, I've never seen him have a serious relationship since middle school, and even that was fleeting. Kari Weatherby attended school with us for three short months. Then broke his heart when she was uprooted by her parents, who were both enlisted in the Army and had gotten new orders, and she was forced to move across the country. Mazen bid his first love—I use that word as loosely as possible—goodbye, then swore off women after that, claiming that he'd never allow his heart to be stomped on again.

The memory makes me laugh. He wrote a song titled "Army Brat" in our Government class, and when Mr. Reasor caught him doodling little hearts around Kari's name, he made him stand up and sing it to the entire classroom. Mazen being Mazen didn't mind, and Mr. Reasor didn't know he'd grow up to be a Grammy-winning musician.

"I don't hear you making inked promises, little drummer

boy." It's Mazen's deep voice that tugs me back into our conversation.

"I got your little boy." Cannon's threat speaks right to the appendage in my pants, as if my cock is a microphone, and he traded in his renowned drumsticks for the spotlight.

*Simmer down.*

"There's nothing little about Cannon." Soph's eyes widen. "I'm warning you."

"You seem to take him just fine," Mazen quips.

"And you three have turned a serious conversation about our commitment to one another into foreplay. Unless we're skipping the hand stack for a genitals stack—which, I'd like to add, I am game for—let's all agree that we're committed to the unit, and anyone else outside of the unit can get their rocks off elsewhere."

"Are Murphy and Vanna unit adjacent?" Soph asks. "Like we don't want to have an orgy, but we care about them in a platonic way."

"Yeah," Cannon pauses, looking at the lot of us. "I'm *in*, but *out* of this conversation."

Couch chronicles come to an end when he kisses Soph on the lips, then announces he's going to the gym. Which is code for *I'm not good with feelings or talking, but I am good at lifting weights.*

THE VOW we entered into about exclusivity within our group is solidified as we burn blacktop toward our next destination. When our next show comes to an end, and we're racing off the stage, it's no longer to rid our adrenaline with random women or drugs.

The heated glances, seductive smiles, promises of dirty, filthy acts following our show, and lust-filled adoration make up Soph's face as she watches us perform with her sister by her side. If heart eyes were a real thing, Soph has perfected them.

She's more than our tattoo artist turned muse. She's so much more. She's our tower of strength in the madness of the lives we've built. She's the ink that has seeped into our skin, forever ingrained. Sophia Lozier is our world.

We're hot, sweaty, and a little more revved up than we usually are after a show. When we bid Lacey a farewell for the evening, a thick air of wanton need settles. We've all been on edge for days. Releasing some tension is my only goal this evening.

Ashton is taking one for the team and keeping Lacey and Jupiter occupied while we—the three of us—show Soph just how serious we are about the vow we made to cherish her.

The sound of the door opening alerts me and Cannon that the after-party is about to begin, and we jolt into a standing position. Mazen opens the door of our bus, helping to guide Soph to the steps before he closes it and latches it behind him. It's harder than it should be to guide her up the narrow path, given the fact that she's been blindfolded.

"I got you, baby," Mazen coos from behind her.

"What's with all the secrecy?" She turns her cloth-covered face to look over her shoulder.

He gives an impatient shrug that she doesn't see. "Ollie has a surprise for you."

"Not for all of us?" The need in her voice, the pout in her dissatisfaction, is palpable.

It's been one full week since we've been back on tour. One week of heated make-out sessions between sets. Gentle caresses during our tattoo sessions and savory glances that have guided us to this evening.

"For all of us," I confirm, taking her hand in mine.

The corners of Soph's mouth turn upward, and her cheeks turn an adorable pink.

"Remove the blindfold," I instruct Soph as the three of us stand before her, along with the black apparatus hanging from the ceiling of our bus.

The cloth falls from her eyes to the floor, along with her jaw. "Why do you guys have a sex swing?"

"I ... it's ... we," Cannon sputters.

"Use your words," Mazen demands in a tone that borders on a reprimand or a promise of something more that I haven't fully accepted might be brewing.

The truth is, since they've been back from Chicago, it hasn't only been Soph's eyes that have darted between Cannon and me with interest. There's a curiosity burning in the depths of Mazen Wilde's sword-tinged irises that is both unnerving and tempting. Tonight isn't just about pleasing Soph. It's about solidifying our foursome, the unit finally becoming one. In the sexual sense, that is. Tonight is our initiation, a commitment ceremony.

Mazen's authority is like the ripple of courage that Cannon needs. Standing a little taller, he says, "We want to worship you like you're our queen. I want you ... *we* want you in the swing like it's your throne. Sit on it. Command your kings to deliver the pleasure you need and deserve. Make us kneel for you every day until you finally grow tired of us."

Confidence soars through the bus and my veins. "That's something I can get behind."

"Did someone say behind?" Mazen laughs. "I call dibs on that ass. *Her* ass," he quickly clarifies, though I don't miss the second his eyes meet Cannon's in a quick appraisal.

"Fuck no, I haven't had her ass yet." I throw up my hands in disgust. "I bought the damn swing. I get to call dibs."

"Sit on your throne, and strap yourself in. We'll all get a chance to own her, just like she owns us." Cannon's voice is as clear and crisp as the desire budding in the small space between the four of us.

We strip naked so quickly it's like we've been dared to. There's no shame between my friends or our *girlfriend*. That fact solidified when I informed them of our plan to share Soph after the sex swing I purchased on Amazon was delivered this morning.

"A couple of rules," I say as Cannon finishes pulling the last strap over Soph's thigh, securing her in place. She looks like a goddess, bound before her hungry servants. "You're going to guess which one of us is fucking you. If you guess right, you get to decide which one of us fucks the other."

A moment of uncertainty I can only describe as frozen stillness settles, tethering our mounting desires and the rule I just laid out before us.

Dipping her chin slightly, Soph asks, "What's the next rule?"

"I'm glad you asked, Fireball." I chuckle wickedly, ready to toss my own wrench into our well-conceived plan.

Forcing people together isn't usually my style. Neither is lusting after the men who have been my best friends for years, yet here we are, dicks swinging and nipples taut.

"Whoever you guess is screwing you has to eat the cum you'll milk from the person to his left."

As I finish, Mazen shakes his head adamantly,

signaling his unacceptance of this rule. Though we discussed sharing her in the swing previously, I will admit that tossing this rule into the mix will certainly shake things up. Call me curious, but I want to see if my instinct on the lustful glares Mazen's been trying to hide holds any weight.

"Sorry, boys. I was all in. Don't think I can screw my future wife in a sex swing in front of you anymore. It's degrading." As he uses exhibitionism as an out, his thick eyebrows unconsciously furrow.

Bending him to my will, I remind him about our conversation this morning. "We made a pact. A *fuck Soph senseless* solidarity pact. Like hell you're backing out." It's now my own brows setting into a straight line.

Cannon's voice is gruff as he steps into Mazen's personal bubble. "*Your* future wife?"

There's not an ounce of understanding in his glare, telling me that he comprehends the real reason Mazen is stalling.

Hell, two minutes ago he was all, *"I call dibs on that ass."*

It's not hard to miss the fact that we're all naked, grown-ass men when Cannon steps close enough toward Mazen that his hardening cock brushes against his. Drummer on singer is like an X-rated MTV special of my dreams.

Roughly, Mazen thrusts himself away, only to back into the small dinette table behind him. Cannon's relentless, gaining the few steps it takes to position himself directly in front of our singer once again.

"Don't act like you haven't been watching me as hard as I've been watching you this week." Cannon's rough voice matches his exterior as Mazen stares at him in mute invitation.

"A humorous surprise, but not a shocking one. Right, Soph?" I petition.

She stifles a grin from her spot in the swing, dangling from the ceiling like a potted plant, and I can see the moment she begins to recognize her own needs. She loves to watch me and Cannon. Sometimes, she doesn't even participate. She just sits back, vibrator humming against her clit, as he ruts into me and then me into him.

Male-on-male action is her ultimate aphrodisiac.

Mazen's eyes grow as wide as saucers before they hone in on our suspended queen. "I love *you*, Sophia." There's a plea in his tone, a promise that she owns his heart even if his body craves something she can never give him.

I know what you're thinking—things are moving fast—it's only been a handful of weeks that we've been on tour. The difference in our timeline is that we've been living in close quarters, spending almost every waking minute with each other. Our relationship timeframe can easily be tripled, equating to months of dating at this point.

"I love you, too, but that doesn't mean that I don't also love them. I think you love them both, too, even if it's in your own way. Even if you're not ready to admit how much and in what ways yet. We've all waited a long time to find one another. I'm sure they'll wait until you're ready."

The undeniable fact she tosses into the air lodges itself in all our lungs, forcing us to accept her words to be true. It holds a smidge of validity that exceeds the friendly love that has kept us tethered since childhood.

Sophia has never once shied away from what she's desired. Not since the first day we met in her studio. I came harder than I had in years, then watched it drip down her leg. I knew she'd be mine then. I felt it in the organ under my sternum. I just didn't know she'd end up being ours ... or we'd all end up belonging to one another in ways we never fathomed.

The masterful persuasion she casts over everyone she meets is a talent she has perfected. Make no mistake—tonight's plan was all mine, but Soph has taken the reins. Just like I knew she would. She wouldn't have three men ready to take a knee otherwise.

"What if I told you I'd love to see Cannon's mouth on you?" Her eyes land on Mazen's long, erect cock.

There's a deliberate indifference sprawled across Mazen's face. It's almost as if he's trying desperately not to react to how good the prospect of her request makes him feel. He doesn't need to voice what the thrill she's wishing for is doing to him, it's evident by his body on full display.

*Holy shit.* This is really going to happen.

I push down the tinge of negativity that threatens to claw at my mind because of the taboo totem pole we've now chained ourselves to.

Soph continues from her spot, front and center in the suspended swing, "What if I love you, Oliver, and Cannon, and they love you back just as hard and deeply? Would you allow that?"

She doesn't offer any time for him to answer before she adds, "You pointed out the fact that I didn't have to be alone anymore. Not in my grief or the daily mundane things that will come up. The same can be said for you, Maz. Lean on them as hard as you leaned on me when we were in Chicago. I promise none of us will let you fall."

"If our girl wants you to suck my cock, little drummer boy, what are you waiting for?"

As though Mazen's words unveiled a red carpet at his feet, Cannon lowers his large form in front of Mazen in a sweetly intoxicating act of submission.

Before he opens his mouth, he glances over his shoulder to catch a glance at Soph and me. There's a silent question in his blue eyes, begging for my permission.

The simple dip of my chin sends a surge of delight throughout the tour bus, and a couple of things happen at once. Cannon buries his face in the corded muscles of Mazen's groin. My eyes dart to Soph's then back to the vivid imagery in front of us, just in time to see Mazen's hands gathering the wealth of blond hair at Cannon's nape as he impales his mouth with fervor.

My rules are forgotten, tossed aside like the thought of condoms. We've all been tested, and after tonight, we're devoted to each other forevermore.

I spin Soph around in the swing, plummet into her slippery hole, and prepare to break for the woman who has become our queen, our world.

Her wet opening accepts me greedily.

"Fuck, you're so wet, Fireball."

A giggle mixed with a moan falls from Sophia's parted mouth. "Can you blame me? That's so freaking hot."

I don't have to divert my gaze from hers to know she's referring to our drummer blowing our lead singer.

"Not one bit, baby," I reply, holding the black straps of the swing tightly in my grip. "As good as I know Cannon is at giving head, I'd much rather be buried in this sweet little cunt of yours."

"Harder," Soph begs, her need to be pushed to the brink far exceeds my words of praise.

I oblige her request using the swing's momentum to pound into her wet opening with force.

That's the thing about our girl, to the world she appears one way, but with us—in the safety of our circle—she's free to let the depraved woman that resides in her soar without judgment.

Plunge after unmerciful plunge, the heady feeling of my impending climax builds at the base of my spine moments before my thighs begin to shake.

"Fill me up, Ollie. I want all of your cum."

On a ragged breath, I empty myself into my queen.

"Holy. Fucking. Shit," I pant, chest rising and falling as I stand before her.

Cannon stands, wiping the back of his hand across his mouth. "My turn," he gravels before taking a large step away from Mazen and bridges the gap toward Sophia.

Before he can sheath himself inside of her, she holds up her hand and turns her head toward the side to face Mazen. "Did he swallow it all?"

Our singer's Adam's apple bobs harshly as he swallows. "Yeah," he answers, breathier than normal.

"Good." She winks in Mazen's direction before turning back to face our drummer. Her beautiful lips curve into a mischievous grin when she says, "Fuck me as hard as I know you want to fuck him."

The intake of breath next to me tells me more than Mazen's lack of words ever will.

We get lost in the mayhem of slick bodies, open holes, and a melody that will never be forgotten. Nothing but the beating of our quickened pulses, growls of pleasure, and the exclamation of our joined passions fill the air for a solid three hours of suspended time.

# 31

# METAPHORICAL LION'S DEN

SOPHIA

"IT'S in a barnacle's nature to be clingy. What's your excuse?" I roll my eyes, biting into the hot ham and cheese Ollie made me for lunch before everyone left for sound check as I wait for my sister's response.

Gossip should have been her middle name, not Monroe.

When Lacey doesn't pop off within a matter of two seconds—her usual retort time—I add, "We used a sex swing, one time, like, two weeks ago. Give it a rest, Barnacle Barbie. I'm not caving on the details."

"I'll wait."

*Whatever.* Less than half my sandwich is eaten when she pushes the topic.

"Do you want it to happen again?"

"You can't handle not being in the know, can you?"

Holding up her hand in a *surf's up* pose that is better suited for a *tipping drinks back* gesture, she asks,

"Is this punishment for drinking the last Orange Kiss Alani yesterday?"

"Keeping my personal life, I don't know, personal, isn't punishment. It's respectful to my—"

"Harem," she finishes my thought, though *boyfriends* is a much more acceptable term for what they are.

"We haven't put a label on things," I lie. We have put a label on things. "If you're referring to the foursome that set my soul on fire and left me needy, like a feline in heat, then, yes, I want it to happen again. Like yesterday."

Looking delighted, she says, "I knew you'd cave. Tell me more."

"Suck a dick."

"Shit. I'd love nothing more to suck a dick, sissy. I'm surrounded by claimed ones, which does not bode well for my kitten. She hasn't purred in ages."

It was a moment of blissed-out euphoria that I had a minor slip of the tongue and confided in her and Vanna about our band bonding session. Since then, she's been hounding me as relentlessly as a bill collector to give her a scrap of information.

I'll take the details of what the four of us did, shared, to my grave, along with the notion that Mazen is airing closer to bi-land than I ever could have imagined. He basically has a PO box there now.

Lacey is one depraved detail away from humping the arm of the couch.

Giving her a small treat, I chew and talk. "It was the hottest night of my life. Ten out of ten. *What wet dreams are made of* kind of experience."

"Why hasn't it happened again?"

That's the same question I've asked myself nightly for almost fourteen days straight since we allowed ourselves to get lost in a lust-filled evening.

I've been with them all separately since then, in one

way or another. Sometimes Ollie and Cannon at the same time. Much to my displeasure, we haven't been together, the four of us as a group, again. I can only assume it has to do with Mazen. He's moodier than a broken Magic 8 Ball that keeps showing the same answer.

Mostly keeping to himself, he's been preoccupied with his music, laying tracks alone to perfect them before bringing in the others. Ollie said that, sometimes, he gets like this, in his head, tuning everyone and everything out.

That's how I feel when I'm tattooing. When I'm in my zone, there's nothing but the humming sound of my machine and a blank stretch of skin. I get it to an extent. The only peace he gets is from creating or, lucky for me, the taste of my body when he finally leaves the studio and devours me like he hasn't eaten in days.

Those nights are secretly my favorite. I've always known where I stood with Oliver and Cannon about our sex life and the connection between us. Even with Cannon, who seldom speaks his feelings into the air, there was never any guesswork with how he felt. In the times he didn't know how to verbalize it, he achieved showing me in other ways. His adoration was etched into his actions—bringing me coffee in the morning, running a hot bath, ordering me a new tattoo stool when the leather started to crack on mine.

We declared our feelings toward one another when we bared our bodies. Cut open without a hint of shame, we left it all on the table. Maybe it's a silly, naive thought to think that one foursome would change things between us. I'm not sure what I expected. But this, feeling like a yarn being strewn and unraveling, is the furthest thing from forming a relationship that one can get.

The biggest change has strangely been in Mazen. He's withdrawn in ways the other two haven't. Yes, he's also made strides, shown a vulnerability that I don't think he's ever offered another human in his life. He's been sweet in his affection both before and after he consumes my body, claiming he's making up for lost time. The passion between us is next level.

Still ... can you blame a girl for thinking that our foursome was laying the groundwork for ... I don't know ... at least a weekly reenactment?

My voice drops in volume when I say, "Your guess is as good as mine."

Lacey sinks onto the barstool next to me, stealing the other half of my sandwich. I'm greeted with a huge smile as she takes a bite that is not very ladylike from it before handing it back to me.

"Brat!" I swat at her hand. "That was made for me with love."

"Hopefully not semen."

"You're vile. Really. How we're related is beyond me."

Her cheeks pull taut over her cheekbones, her eyes narrowing. There's a look of dread that overcomes her. Even Jupiter can sense something is off when he starts to bark at my feet.

"It's okay, buddy." I rub my bare foot over his fur coat to calm him down.

While I'm the queen of jokes and Jupiter, as the band's road crew has dubbed me, I find the sudden shift in mood frightening.

Lacey's face turns serious. "Since you confided in me, there's something I need to share with you too."

"So, spit it out."

"Vanna overheard Murphy and Cannon on the phone earlier."

"Unless they were conspiring to throw me a surprise

birthday party, which I would hate," I add for emphasis—Lacey knows surprises are not my jam—"what's it matter to me?"

The mood and subject shifts when Lacey drops a bomb that has me choking on my food. "They were on the phone with Caddell."

The gooey sandwich I savored threatens to reappear as my thoughts immediately dart to the text messages that I've been receiving from Knox for a solid week— keeping secrets to prevent stress from harming those I love wasn't even a decision that had to be made.

> Knox: Count your days, Red.
>
> Knox: One dick isn't enough for you, is it?
>
> Knox: You're going to regret not choosing me.
>
> Knox: Uncle Julian is growing impatient.

If it wasn't for Devon or an employee from my shop back home needing a way to reach me, I would have turned off my cell phone a long time ago.

"It didn't sound like a friendly conversation according to Vanna." Lacey bites the inside of her cheek.

"Come again?" Smoothing my hair to keep my hands busy, I lower them toward my stomach and hug myself. Nope. There's no calming myself down at this point. "Why are you just now telling me this? Where's Vanna? She didn't say anything earlier."

Lacey's face scrunches before she leans back in the chair and closes her eyes.

"Tell me everything she heard." *Why wouldn't she have told me herself?*

She rises from her chair in one fluid moment, and her answer punches me in the gut.

"She said she heard—and I quote—'I don't do well with receiving idle threats. The next one I receive, you'll find that there's been a terrible fire at your mother's nursery. I hear river birch is highly flammable.' Vanna said Caddell was threatening Cannon's family for some reason, and Murphy had to calm him down."

There is no justification of time where the heart is concerned. It beats faster than any hand on a clock. Like my feet that are moving from the barstool, out the suite door.

Preston offered no response to my demand. No questions. Just gave me a simple nod of his head when I told him I needed a ride somewhere fast and then ushered me into the blacked-out SUV parked behind the hotel. I've never moved faster in my entire life. Even now, as we're speeding down the street, it doesn't seem fast enough.

I have a one-track mind, and it's aimed at making sure my men don't do anything reckless. "Hurry. Fuck the red lights, Preston." My knee is shaking. My breathing is labored. "How close are we?"

Preston never takes his eyes off the road. The man is strictly business. Cold and calculated in both the efficiency in which he weaves through traffic and in the static tone he responds in. "Five minutes."

"I need to get there faster," I demand, hoping that they're even at the venue. There's a sinking feeling that tells me they won't be. Call it a hunch, my intuition. Whatever the hell you want. I know that something is brewing. I just hope like hell it's not my guys that are stoking the flames.

If Caddell was threatening Cannon's family, there's a reason for it. He doesn't do anything without intent or cause. Did Cannon provoke him? He could have gotten too close to outing Caddell's shitty organization or something. Maybe he threatened to out him. Whatever the reason, Caddell's warning about Mrs. Rhodes's nursery is serious. He's the man calling the shots, never the one bowing to them.

"Where are you going?" I'm tossed to the side of the back seat when we take a hard left in the opposite direction of the venue. I know because I went with Vanna yesterday to watch them do their sound check.

"They're not at the venue."

Surprise, surprise. A lady's intuition is never wrong.

"Are you certain?" A full-body tremble shakes my body. I'm far past worry. This is scared-shitless territory. If anyone knows what Julian Caddell is capable of, it's me.

"After my job was threatened in Chicago, I started tracking all their locations regularly." I assume he's referring to the band members I'm dating.

"I'm sorry about that. You did your job. We didn't even leave our room, and you still got in trouble."

Sighing, Preston takes a sharp turn. "The label doesn't mess around with their biggest assets. Way I see it, I still have a job. Thanks for that."

It feels like an hour has passed by, but the glowing clock shows it's only been fifteen minutes when Preston pulls into a concrete parking garage. "The app says they should all be here."

"I thought it was just Murphy and Cannon." I remember quickly that they're a band of brothers. They don't do anything alone. "So, where are they then?" My mind reels, considering ten possibilities all at once as we creep upward, one concrete level at a time.

Love makes us do stupid, foolish things. Like running into a fire to protect those we care about even if it means being burned in the process. I'd willingly melt for Mazen, Oliver, and Cannon. If it was between keeping them alive and safe or myself, I'd light the match without a second thought.

"My guess is, they're on the top floor. If I were into shady shit, that's where I'd meet someone." The vehicle comes to a sudden halt. "We're going to park, then walk up the last flight of stairs. There's no way I'm about to deliver you to the lion's den. They didn't want you here for a reason."

Preston's expression stills when he comes to the realization that he just drove me directly into the metaphorical lion's den himself.

"Fuck. I'm getting fired."

"Not if I have a say in it. Okay? I'll have your back if you have mine. I'm hoping Ashton equips his men with guns?" It's a loaded question—no pun intended.

The deep frown on his furrowed brow lifts. "Bet your sweet ass I'm packing."

"Good. Then, it's set. We're embarking on a shitty situation, and we have no clue what we're getting ourselves into. We have each other's back. What could go wrong?"

# 32

# MEN WITH GUNS

SOPHIA

WHAT'S THE SAYING? *Ask, and you shall receive.*

Things go very, very wrong.

I follow behind Preston, step for step up a staircase that leads to a door with a square glass window in it. From our vantage point behind the glass, we spot Mazen, Oliver, Cannon, Murphy, and Ashton. My heart rate accelerates, even as I accept that they're all okay, alive, until I turn to see my partner in crime's face. Preston's expression hardens like marble. He's now a mask of stone that has my blood pumping at an alarming rate. My eyes peer through the glass, and my stomach tightens.

In horror, I watch as Knox Caddell climbs out of the back of a blacked-out Audi. He stands and then roughly pulls out the woman who took me under her wing and became my best friend on this tour from the vehicle, Vanna. It's a futile attempt to keep the fear that rises in my throat to myself.

"No. Damn it. Why doesn't anyone leave well enough

alone? I had things covered. A plan." I turn to Preston, fuming. None of this should be happening. Yet here we are. These boyfriends of mine couldn't just let me handle my business. "My sister was just with her earlier. How in the hell did Knox get to her that quickly?"

Preston stays silent.

"She's my friend." Anguish tugs at my broken voice. "If you know something, spit it out."

"Mazen hired a PI. His guy found a connection between Lorenzo Wilde and Julian Caddell."

This isn't news to me. I know all about their years of friendship.

"The PI went missing the day before yesterday. Gone without a trace."

Caddell's threat about me being shark food resurfaces. He's evil incarnate. Did he have Mazen's PI killed? Suddenly, the timeline makes sense. Mazen's recent emotional distance. Knox's random text messages.

"Mazen called his dad, pushing for info. Told him someone had kidnapped you as a ploy to get him to talk. Ashton said he really laid into him. Lorenzo flew into town this morning, claiming that they needed to have a conversation that wasn't suited to be done over the phone. Ashton assembled a team—"

"That you clearly weren't on?"

"The band said they only trusted you with Ashton or me."

My fingers press at my temples where the stress is collecting. "Great. You got babysitting duty."

Offering a wry smile, Preston continues, "Look, I shouldn't even be telling you this. Here I am, blabbing like the roadies." He takes a breath, then admits, "When they went to the meeting spot, Lorenzo wasn't there."

Sliding out his cell phone, he motions for me to look.

"This was." He proceeds to show me a picture of the note that was waiting to be found by Mazen. Preston's face hardens as he reads the words from the screen out loud. "*More innocent lives will be taken in the crossfire if you don't back off.*"

"A warning? What did the PI find?"

Though Preston doesn't answer me, I watch as his eyes darken a shade before they move past me. Journeying to the situation behind the glass, roaming over every person in sight, detailing the predicament the men who employ us have caught themselves in. He's assessing the scene before us in a way that reminds me that Ashton, him, and the others on their teams are trained professionals. Preston keeps his features composed, a look of merciless determination on his square jawline. The uncanny awareness of the severity of the meet and greet we've stumbled upon sets in, along with the start of a full-blown anxiety attack.

Intrusive thoughts pound like fists against my skull.

*What if this is a setup?*

*Why do they care about me so much?*

*What if I lose one of them?*

"You need to rein in whatever's going on right now. I can't save them if I'm worrying about their girlfriend."

I let out a throaty laugh as if to say, *as if.* "You're sorely mistaken. I'm with Mazen. You meant *his* girlfriend." It's not a question. A simple fact. One I've recited internally for two weeks since we all laid claim to one another in the most intimate of ways.

We're not ready to tell the world about our...situationship, yet.

"Come the hell on, Sophia. I'd have to be blind not to see the chemistry you have with each of them."

"Since you're toting around a loaded gun and all, I certainly hope you're not visually impaired."

Eyes as flat and unreadable as plywood meet mine. "Let's skip the part where we have a heart-to-heart, and you confess that you love them all, and they love you back. Which they do," he adds. "They wouldn't be meeting up with your kidnapper if they didn't."

Great. Now, my eyes are misty. Is our adoration that easy for people to read and notice?

"Julian Caddell is holding Lorenzo and Vanna as hostages." His voice is gravelly. It's the only sign that his line of work, the situation we've been pulled into, is affecting him.

If you could hear a heart break, I imagine it'd sound like the sharp intake of breath that gets stuck in my lungs.

"Stay here," he instructs. "I'm gonna slide out to get closer. When I'm close enough, I'll tackle Knox from behind. This'll buy Ashton a minute to figure out a plan from there. He's quick and resourceful. It's why he's the best in the business."

For a long moment, I hold Preston's stare. A thousand things are said between us, our silence speaking volumes.

*Be careful. Tread lightly. Don't shoot anyone unless it's absolutely necessary.*

His dark eyes reply, *Stay put. Don't you dare open this door once I slip out. Run and hide if you must.*

We exchange another moment of silent pleas before he opens his mouth, giving light to a fear. "They'll kill me if something happens to you."

"I think you seriously doubt how much your rock-star employers value their freedom," I scoff. "Can you picture Mazen in an orange jumpsuit?" Humor laces my tone. It's my factory setting. When every emotion threatens to pull me under the tide, humor keeps me afloat. "He'd probably just walk around with his sausage swinging before he was caught dead in anything other than black."

"Here's to hoping we never have to see either of the pictures you just created."

The pause between us settles thick, like the smog in the city after a rainstorm.

"Don't let anything happen to her or them. Please, Preston. They're in this situation because of me. I love them."

"There's the truth. You shouldn't deny it again. It saves lives."

"So do badass, gun-carting security men. Go save theirs."

With that, Preston slips out the door, sealing me inside with nothing but my nerves.

Sliding my phone from my back pocket, I shoot off a message to my sister. I'm not sure what is about to go down, but you can bet your sweet tits that if anyone can get a SOS into the world, it's Lacey. She might fold under pressure, but she can cause a scene like no one's business. Karens out in the world should fear the Laceys of the world.

Without giving my sister too much detail—she's not very good at discretion, and keeping secrets is not her strong suit—I fill her in the best I can, asking her to contact Lindsey before ending the call.

By the looks of the budding confrontation outside this small window my face is plastered against, it's safe to say something big is about to go down. She'll be on media control when shit hits the fan.

Convincing myself I can't hear well enough, I crack open the door. Muffled voices linger in the air. I widen the door more, as cautiously as humanly possible.

"Our money isn't good enough for you? Last time I checked, paper was green." Oliver advances toward Knox, who is planted in front of the vehicle he climbed out of.

It's not lost on me that Caddell is nowhere in sight. He's the ventriloquist. The backbone of the operation. The sleazeball made that known when he not only had Knox doing his bidding, keeping tabs on me and bedding me for years, but also when he sent his muscle to threaten me years ago.

"It's not your money he wants. It's *hers*," he says through clenched teeth.

The *her* he's referring to is me.

Cannon steps up, towering over Knox by a solid four inches. It shocks me how graceful his well-muscled body moves. "Let's cut the bullshit. We have the money you want, and you have two people we need."

"You have no say in this battle, Thor." Knox comes in hot with a joke that falls flat at Cannon Rhodes's feet.

"Fucking children."

My body goes rigid at the sound of Julian Caddell's voice as he exits the back seat, looking every bit as vile and slimy as I remember and straightens his suit.

On instinct, I'm moving. I can't just stand here praying that the people I love are safe, including the only female friend outside of my family I've ever had. If falling for three rock stars has taught me anything, it's resiliency. You can't just date the most eligible bachelor in the world and not get any flak from the media and trolls on social media.

If I can survive the haters on RockTok, I can stand up to Julian and Knox Caddell one final time.

I couldn't save Roman. I *can* save Vanna.

# 33

# ENEMY TERRITORY

OLIVER

"CADDELL!"

The only voice in the world that could rock my world while simultaneously upheaving it sounds from behind the row of bodies next to me. Soph's tone holds as much revulsion in it as the smell of a rotten deer carcass.

"It's me you have beef with. Leave everyone else out of it."

"I told you to stay put." Preston, one of our hired hands nears her side, gun drawn. There's a look of remorse in his dark glare when it cuts to Ashton. Clear indication he's failed to do his one job of keeping Sophia safe and away from this shit is sprawled across his creased forehead. His eyes dart to Soph. Shaking his head and huffing dreadfully, he says, "You listen as well as a damn goldfish."

He's getting fired, and he knows it. *For real this time.*

Beckoning her into the safety of his arms, Mazen calls out, "Rosella, come here."

"No, I can't. I'm sorry, Mazen. I'm so tired of running."

Her attention turns toward the man in the suit, which looks like his dry cleaner was high. It's not pressed or anything.

*Tool.*

I watch in horror as Sophia marches up to Julian and Knox. With each step, determination plows into her. She's all anger and hatred. I shouldn't be turned on by her powerful stance ... but I am. *Fuck.* This little fireball has amazed me from day one. Her spine was crafted from tungsten.

"I'm done. If he wants his retribution and is too impatient to wait for a damn paycheck, then he can have it now. I won't allow him to hurt any more of the people I love. This ends tonight."

It doesn't take a rocket scientist to read between the lines. This guitarist understands just fine. She's not offering herself up in exchange for us. Nope. Not happening today. Not on my fucking watch. I've had enough.

Before she marches past me, fortitude clinging to her set shoulders, I grab her arm forcefully. Her body halts. "You don't need to do this. It's why we left you out of our plan. Let us handle Caddell. Please, Fireball."

Defiance mounts, then pours from her parted lips. "You left me out of the plan to protect me, right?" She doesn't give me enough time to answer. "This is me protecting you guys, my sister. His beef is with me. Not you. For Christ's sake, you had to lure Caddell out with Mazen's fancy private investigator. I had the situation handled. You guys care about me, and I appreciate that so much, but this is bigger than us. It's bigger than—"

"He has my wife." Murphy's wounded voice cuts through Soph's tangent. "She went out for a run and didn't come back." Dark brows pinch when he looks between her and the man holding Vanna's arm in a death grip. "Look, I care about my brothers, our band, you … but right now, all I can think about is pulling the hand he has on my wife completely off and then shoving it up his ass. She's our priority."

Bridging the gap between her and Knox, Soph's small frame walks directly onto the battlefield. She glances over her shoulder and says, "You're right; she is. Let me save her."

I have half a mind to yank the black pistol out of Ashton's hand. Going all in, Al Capone-style. The other half, the sane side—do people really have those?—is telling me to chill. He has Vanna and Mazen's dad held hostage. We need to think with our heads in order to all get out of this situation unscathed.

Leaning forward, we watch in horror as Soph whispers something into Caddell's ear. By his sinister smile, I know that our queen just handed him her crown.

She'll gladly surrender in order to protect us. She said it herself. I still let her walk away from me.

A look of triumph spreads across his face. He thinks he's won. That look will haunt me for years to come.

"I'm a man of my word," he says, jaw clenching before he grabs Vanna away from his nephew's embrace and pushes her directly into Murphy's arms, like she's an empty cereal box he's tossing into the garbage.

Before there's time to collect our thoughts or think of how this needs to finish playing out, Knox is wrapping his arms around Soph's stomach, pulling her into enemy territory.

The sight of seeing her defenseless is nauseating.

I capture her attention. For a second that seems like five

minutes, I hold her unrelenting glare. There's so much said between her forest-green eyes and my own.

*Promises of a future I desperately want with her.*

*Fragment memories of the laughs we've shared during our tour.*

*Memories of the night I let her tattoo a burned piece of toast on my forearm—commemorating the time Mazen tried to woo her with breakfast and failed miserably. When you have as much ink as I do, there isn't much I wouldn't get tattooed on me at this point.*

"I'm going to fucking kill you." Cannon loses his battle with restraint. He charges toward Knox.

Out of my peripheral vision, I catch Soph flinch before her long lashes close over her lids, breaking the tether our gazes clung to and my heart in the process.

*Bang.*

The sound of a gun—I'm not certain whose—fires into the vicinity Cannon was barreling into.

My world crumbles as the deafening tone hits the air and the bullet finds my best friend's shoulder.

# 34

# THAT MAN

## CANNON

"IT'S GOING to take more than a warning shot, you sorry son of a bitch." Provoking a man holding a gun, who shot the bullet piercing my left shoulder, is probably not my finest moment.

Falling head over heels for my tattoo artist comes in a close second, followed by my infatuation with my best friends. Apparently, my decision-meter is running in the opposite direction it should be.

"Cannon!" a grief-stricken bellow comes from behind me.

I don't have to turn to know it's Oliver's voice that's calling out, pleading with the universe in my honor. I have to remember to kiss him senseless later for the concern in his tone.

*I love him unmistakably.*

"Rhodes, that's enough," Ashton's deep timbre booms with caution.

The intensity in which his warning is spoken should

alert me that I'm in deep shit—we all are. Though we hold the numbers, Knox Caddell holds the only thing that matters. Our reason. The reason we're here. To pay off her debt and wash our hands of the bastard and his nephew standing before us.

I'm too far gone to rationally heed Ashton's command. My only mission, my only purpose, is to save Sophia. She's the only woman I've ever loved—will love. I take another staggered step forward. My feet feel as if my shoes are filled with sand. The pain in my shoulder is almost nonexistent.

*Thank you, adrenaline.*

"Cannon, stop. Please. Let me deal with this. It's my mess," Sophia begs. "You're injured. Please. I don't want anyone else to get hurt because of me."

I'd move mountains for this woman. Some wannabe mobster isn't shit in the grand scheme of how far I'm willing to go to protect what's mine ... ours.

Whether I'm shot or not, her mess is our mess. She's ours to protect, cherish, adore. Matters of the heart are taken seriously in my book.

Through a tear-smothered voice, she sobs, "He'll shoot again. If only to prove a point. I can't watch you die. You're being so stupid!"

"Better me than you, Soph."

Another gunshot rings loudly. Its sound is deafening due to my nearness. Though it's unmistakably not as loud as the shriek that rips from Sophia's beautiful mouth when Julian Caddell's bullet pierces through my lower stomach.

Music was my first love. I used to feel like I'd die if I couldn't create it.

Sophia is my forever love. *I'll die to protect her.*

It's the last coherent thought I have before the chaotic melody around me fades ...

# 35

# THE BOY WHO LOVED ME

OLIVER

HAVE you ever seen the devastation left in the wake of a tornado firsthand?

As a Florida native, I've seen the aftermath of storms of that magnitude with my own eyes. But that didn't prepare me for watching my world crumble in front of me.

There's no footage in the world that can capture how numbing it is to see a storm with that kind of havoc roll through. Somehow, witnessing this ... pandemonium is rawer in person.

If this is hell, the Devil was kind enough to lay out a welcome mat.

Our world has been shaken, upheaved, obliterated. Nothing but chaos and heartache are left. The debris of our manicured lives lay in a heap of devastation at our feet, and Caddell is to blame. He's the storm. A rotating wind that has demolished us with one pull of his trigger.

Several things happen at once. It's hard to know what to do or where I'm needed through the persistent shouting.

Through the commotion, my eyes dart to Sophia. In a quick assessment from her toes upward, I sigh a breath of relief, knowing that she doesn't seem to be injured. Her glossy gaze is focused on Cannon as her tears fall in streams. The battle wounds that aren't visible will haunt her for years.

"Cannon!" *Anguished* isn't strong enough of a word for the gut-wrenching way Sophia screams out his name.

In a mixture of Italian and English, Mazen's voice barrels around the chaos, wreaking its own havoc. "Fuck!"

I force myself to look at Cannon's body. He's lying flat on his back, blood pouring from his wound. His massive body looks puny, his injury ghastly. His blond hair is disheveled, several locks lying over his closed eyelids. I know enough to know that's not a good sign. Murphy is pressing, pushing down hard on his lower abdomen to stop the bleeding inflicted by the second bullet that hit him.

"We have to stop it." Murphy moves quickly to yank off his shirt.

Vanna scoops Cannon's head in her small hands, placing it in her lap. She's gently pushing damp pieces of hair off his forehead with one hand, the other is lightly smacking his cheek. "Wake up. Let me see your eyes." There's an eerie calmness to her voice that makes me think she was an army medic in a former life. Her eyes tell a different story than her composed voice and movements. Tears spill over her cheeks like a dam has broken.

Ashton and his second, Preston, barge forward as if they were Greek soldiers, ready to fight to the death. I've never been more thankful for reincarnation in my entire miserable existence. I'm not as lucky. This life has been my only one. There's no fight-or-flight instincts that kick in, urging me to do something. Fucking anything. Nope. The soles of my shoes are glued in place. I couldn't pick my feet up to move if I tried.

I'm utterly useless. Frozen in fear of losing everyone I love. Just like when I was a boy. Abandoned by those who were meant to love me and protect me unconditionally.

*It should have been me.* I'm the incompetent one. I should be the one lying there. At least then, Cannon could be useful in saving our girl.

I should've charged forward, blocking his body with my own. I should've had the courage to step in front of a loaded gun for the man I love. I should've, and I didn't fucking budge to protect the boy who had befriended me when I had nothing more than the raggedy clothes on my back. The boy whose family fed me and got me my first bicycle. The boy who loved me when I didn't even love myself. The boy I denied who never stopped loving me well into adulthood. The man who selflessly walked toward another with a loaded gun pointed at him to save the girl he loves, our girl.

Another shot rings loudly, jarring my thoughts from the pity party of one commencing in my thick skull.

Knox's body falls into a heap on the ground, and his hands move frantically, landing on his stomach. No one moves to aid him in stopping the bleeding. Not even his uncle, who looks like he's about to combust from fury as he yanks Soph into his embrace forcefully.

"It had to be done," Ashton calls out, his tone absent of remorse.

Protecting us, doing his job, just made him a murderer.

"Stay in the fucking car." Caddell's voice draws attention to the open door of the vehicle he's standing close to. "Unless you want more blood to spill."

Mazen shouts through the uproar that's playing out in front of us, his jaw trembling. "Dad?" he calls out, certain that it's his father in the back seat. We know Caddell took both him and Vanna. "Dad!"

I've never seen him appear so childlike in our entire friendship. Lorenzo used to beat the shit out of him for what seemed like sport, and Mazen never cried. He never vented to us about it or asked for help. He took every blow willingly, allowing his father's pain to have an outlet. The relief Lorenzo chased from unleashing his own pain onto his son, in an effort to eradicate his own internal demons, was a secret to society. To everyone but us. For years, Mazen accepted every hit, allowing his father's pain to seep into his own pores until, one day, Mazen's anger grew so large, something snapped, and he started to fight back.

The version of Mazen calling out to his father reminds me of the boy I met before aggression and anger plagued him.

Sure enough, Lorenzo Wilde climbs out of the back seat of the vehicle to Caddell's left. The left side of his face appears to be black and blue. There's blood on the white undershirt that covers his chest. Thick black brows furrow when he assesses the scene in front of him.

"I never wanted this." His attention lands on Julian Caddell. Wrath as tangible as the moans pouring from Knox's mouth broadens his shoulders.

"You wanted to ruin Mazen's empire. Did you not?" This question comes from Caddell.

"We both know damn well ruining something and murdering innocent people are two very different things."

Caddell is quick to respond, "Not in my world."

Black dress shoes hit the pavement, spanning the gap between Lorenzo and Caddell.

Soph is smart enough to use the split second Caddell's grasp loosens on her arm to run past me and into Mazen's awaiting arms. I turn quickly to see him sliding her petite body behind his own. I imagine him having an older brother or Cannon around to do the same for him when he was a child, running from his father. I wonder if things would have been different. If the man he grew into wouldn't have been so damaged by the monster who raised him.

"This won't end well," Caddell seethes.

Lorenzo's Italian accent is thick when his eyes flash in outrage. "This ends now. I already told you, I'll cut you a check for Ms. Lozier's debt. Take your nephew to get medical attention. He's bleeding out. We'll take Mazen's friend. No one else needs to get hurt. No one needs to die tonight."

"Want to talk about being hurt?" Caddell moves his gun like a pointer finger. It lands on Mazen and the fiery redheaded woman we love nestled behind him. "Her father betrayed me. Talk about blindsided. He's a piece-of-shit thief. She's just like him. You wanted dirt. I gave it to you on a silver platter. You fault me for being a business-man, trying to collect what I'm owed. Ask her why she stole all those years away from Mazen. He could have known the truth long before you asked for my involvement."

"This isn't about being paid back. It's about your sick and twisted way to inflict revenge for something that woman did not do," Lorenzo counters in breathless hostility. "You can't punish her for the sins of her father."

"That's rich coming from you. Do you think growing a backbone overnight is going to win you Father of the Year?" Caddell spits out condescendingly.

The scene unfolding in front of me plays out in slow motion. All the while, the man I've loved in silence is bleeding onto the concrete.

Feeling weak, vulnerable, I lash out. "Enough of this bullshit. People are dying!"

"Let them die then. You're the ones who brought this on yourselves. You wanted me here. Well, here I am, in the flesh, and I'm not leaving until that bitch pays her debt or suffers. Just like the headache she and her family have caused me and my organization. Do you know how many resources it takes to find someone who doesn't want to be found?"

"You idiot!" Sophia yells, interrupting Julian Caddell as she fights against Mazen's arms.

He's desperately trying to keep her caged in behind his back. Red hair flies in the night breeze.

"We had a deal. I get paid next week, which means you get paid. You're nothing more than a greedy piece of shit." Anger hardens her features and her voice. "Look what your impatience has caused. Your nephew is dying. Are you just going to let him lie there, bleeding out just to prove a point?"

The look Caddell offers is a mixture of exasperation, faint amusement, and something else entirely too sinister to name. "You want me to prove a point?"

The barrel of his gun turns, along with his neck. Horror plagues my vision, my thoughts. It takes the very breath out of my lungs.

Less than a second later, his point is made when he fires a round directly into the center of Lorenzo Wilde's chest.

Mazen's gravelly accent is etched deeply in the four-letter word as he shouts, "Papa!"

Lorenzo crashes to the ground, adding to the bloodshed.

In a swift movement, Ashton's black-clad figure is raising his hand, ready to end this charade, fighting fire with fire.

*Pop. Pop. Pop.*

My ears ring for a deafening moment, following the spray of bullets from his handgun.

A bullet pierces Caddell above the eyebrow with a precision I wouldn't expect from a contracted security guard, and the once-tough, sinewy man falls into a heap beside his nephew.

Everyone is still, standing motionless in silence for a few beats of utter disbelief.

I'm overcome with emotion as thick as honey in my throat. *At least my neck works*, I think as my head swivels to glance over to Murphy, who is still applying pressure to Cannon's wound. Disoriented, I turn to look at Mazen and Sophia. I'm assessing everyone I care about.

He's pushing Soph into Preston's arms, murmuring something before giving a begrudging nod. Preston is the last person who'd get my vote to ensure her safety. She wouldn't be here, witnessing this madness if it wasn't for our second-rate security guard.

I have half a mind to call up our manager and ask if they got him on discount from mall security.

With wide steps, Mazen is rushing toward his father's folded body. Raw anguish is sprawled against his dark features. It's hard to miss the unmistakable look of despair when he reaches Lorenzo. He crouches down and grabs both sides of his father's face, forcing their eyes to meet for the last time.

"Don't die, Papa. I already lost Bethany. I can't lose you too. I won't survive losing anyone else."

"You're not losing me, son. I won't be far."

Sirens sound in the distance.

*Thank God.* Cannon needs help now.

Over the noise, I hear Lorenzo's voice gurgling. Blood

oozes out the side of his parted mouth, but he musters up enough energy to say, "I love you, Mazen. I'm going to see your sister and meet my grandson."

"How ... how do you know about him?" Mazen's eyes shoot up in surprise.

On the verge of losing consciousness, he closes his eyes. His body uses every bit of energy as he answers his son, "Cad-dell ... told me ... to-day. Proud of ... you ... so—"

Mazen chokes back a sob. *Another sight that will forever be ingrained in my memory.* "Just breathe. Save your energy. The ambulances have to be close."

"No time," his father whispers.

"Papa." Mazen holds his father's cheeks, craning his neck until their noses are almost brushing. "Promise me you'll keep Roman company until I can meet him."

The last words Lorenzo Wilde speaks are a vow I know he will keep. *"Prometto."* Promise.

# 36

## AFTERNOON BLOWIE

SOPHIA

IF IT WERE legal to sue someone for barging into your life with a backpack of anarchy, Near Death Records would hire the best attorneys money could buy.

At least, that's how I feel when the rest of the Kings of Jupiter tour gets canceled because of our run-in with Caddell. This time, there's no rescheduling the last couple of shows. Which means there's no big check waiting for me from the label since the stipulations were clear, the tour had to come to full completion— meaning all shows being played. I don't need their money, especially not now since Julian Caddell's existence has been wiped off the planet.

Keeping tabs on Knox's recovery hasn't been as important as it should be. In the last month since the incident on the rooftop occurred, I've been left with haunting nightmares. Almost to a point that they're debilitating. My mind is a constant reel of intrusive thoughts. Him making a full recovery and taking over his uncle's business are a problem for another day though.

My main concern, my only concern, is coaxing Cannon Rhodes back to full health. It's the single most important task, and I woke up with it on my mind this morning.

"What the hell?" I almost topple over when my steps falter just as I slide into Cannon's bedroom.

The rail of the hospital bed that was delivered for Cannon to recover in, is lowered. I don't have time to appreciate Cannon's bare, muscular arms because my eyes dart to my other boyfriend, who is sitting in a chair next to the bed —though *sitting* isn't the right word. He's hovering over it. His jean-clad knees are bent, back arched.

Oliver is going to town, deep-throating Cannon's impressively thick shaft, like my sudden presence hasn't affected him in the slightest. There's zero modesty in the air between the three of us.

"Anyone could have walked in."

"I'm happy it was you, baby," Cannon answers a little breathlessly. "Want a turn?"

"The doctor said no sex."

I'm determined to remain immune to the deep groan that leaves Cannon's lips.

He swallows a moan before smiling innocently. "He didn't say anything about getting a blowie. Did he? Shit. I didn't read the discharge papers, baby. Too much medical jargon."

"A blowie, really?" My chest rises with laughter. "You've been hanging out with Ollie for far too long."

Oliver's retort comes out garbled, due to his mouth being occupied and all. "Ollie is right here."

"I came in here to give you your afternoon dose of pain meds and your antibiotic." A glint of humor is laced in my tone. "It looks like you're giving Oliver the peen-icillin right now. Is he sick too?"

That gains the guitarist's attention.

Pulling his mouth off the large shaft he was sucking, Oliver says, "Really? You came barging in here with jokes during this pitiful man's afternoon blowie?"

I offer a dip of my shoulder.

"Well, get in line, Fireball. Did you see the statue of Cannon's dick?"

My eyes roll into the back of my head as I refuse to laugh at his nonsense.

"I just erected it."

OLIVER and I spend the next hour taking turns slowly torturing Cannon with nothing but our mouths. Smothering him with enough pleasure that we have him ejaculating one second, then drifting into a deep sleep the next. His mind and body have been through the wringer.

Rest is what the doctor ordered.

It's easy to feel at home when we're back in Tampa in Mazen's lavish mansion. The band decided it was best for them to be under one roof. Excluding the newlyweds that used the tour ending prematurely to their advantage. They took off for Alaska a couple of days ago. I guess when you were born and raised in the Sunshine State, the solitude of a cabin in the snowy woods with your new bride does sound rather appealing.

When the plane landed, Lacey chased her own normalcy and hightailed it back to our studio and into Devon's arms—our hired security guard at the tattoo studio. Half laughing, half crying, I thought about the two of them doing sinful things in the bedroom next to mine in our small apartment, and I was more than willing to accept Mazen's offer to bunk with them for a while.

The band has more security than I can count on both my hands and toes since that night. I shouldn't have been as shocked as I was when Ashton offered to escort her to our apartment, claiming he needed some time to *recoup his spirit*—his words, not mine.

I'd hate to think that Lacey wasn't getting tag-teamed and railed every night since we got back to Florida. She's in testosterone heaven. I can't even be mad about it. Truthfully, my sister was a trooper while we were on the road. Hence why I feel so strongly about her finding happiness too. If this whirlwind of a job has taught me anything, it's to not judge anyone's kinks.

"Have you decided what organization you want to donate to?" Oliver scoots next to me on the outdoor couch I've been nestled on for the better half of thirty minutes since we agreed not to linger and watch Cannon sleep.

We're all a little obsessed with one another. Can you blame us? We've fought like hell to not only be together but for the peace and quiet Mazen's large house provides.

The best part of his luxurious pad is that the tall fence only hinders his view of the ocean from the first floor. That's why the third-floor balcony is my favorite place. I've come up here often to sit and think. Consider what tomorrow might bring since I'm no longer running from Caddell or my past.

It's where Oliver and I escaped to, undiluted laughter filled the staircase when he was doing his impression of our sleeping drummer snoring.

"I'm thinking a jellyfish organization." There's a twinkle in my eye that I hope he catches.

He palms the bulge forming in his pants at the mention of the word *jellyfish*. "Fitting. Who knew your artwork would be the beginning of something special?"

I turn to face him on the couch. "Oh, I knew. I thought to myself, *If I can just convince him to let me tattoo an epic jellyfish on his cock, I know I'll win over his heart.*"

The smile he gives is irresistibly devastating.

"Did it work?" I scoot closer toward him.

"Yeah." His expression grows hungry and lustful. "It worked."

Leaning forward, Oliver captures me in a kiss that has me forgetting about everything that still plagues my mind.

The fact that Knox is still alive. The loss of getting paid from the label, though it was promised to Caddell anyway. Back to Oliver propositioning me to be his band's live-in employee that started this whole traveling tattoo artist companionship in the first place. Though, I didn't finish out the tour working for him. I finished it as his girlfriend. As girlfriend to all of them. Which meant there was no way in hell I was accepting his check when he tried to pay me. Even if it meant my dream of opening a second studio was extinguished.

You guessed it. Oliver wouldn't take no for an answer.

So, I decided to donate the money. That was something he couldn't argue with.

In all honesty, my dreams changed as soon as I allowed my heart to thaw and accepted the love that over-whelms me from Oliver, Mazen, and Cannon on the daily.

The studio can wait. If I've learned anything from falling for my boss ... bosses, it's that creating a future with them can't.

Gathering me in his arms, Oliver breathes me in,

savoring my scent. "You have the best-smelling hair I've ever smelled."

"It's Mazen's expensive shampoo. I hope you don't go around sniffing him like you do me."

There's a glint of curiosity on Oliver's face. His features become more animated, and the bulge in his pants goes from zero to a hundred on the hardness scale.

Using the arousal high he's on to my advantage, I push a topic that's plagued me for weeks. "I've never had a four-some before the one we partook in." I tiptoe into the water. "Was it bad or something?"

"What makes you think it was bad? Did you not enjoy yourself?" He seems genuinely concerned.

"I loved what happened. I just don't know why it hasn't happened since."

Recovering from my admission, Oliver bites his bottom lip, a sorry attempt to stifle his groan. "It wigged Mazen out."

That has my beautiful, stenciled brows rising. "What do you mean by that? He was disgusted that I allowed you guys to use me like that?"

Recollections of the day Mazen called me a whore rings loudly in my mind. Is that what he thinks I am? A whore? Sue me for feeling cherished, adored enough to allow the three of them to ravish me like my body is the fuel they need to survive.

"Quite the opposite. I think he wigged out because he liked it a little too much."

Shock flies through me around the same time the balcony door slides open to reveal the man of the hour himself.

"What's up?" Mazen casually strolls from the doorway to the couch, plopping down on the other side of me.

I'm the ice cream in this sandwich, nestled between two rock stars, and I've never wanted to be eaten more in my life. My face creases into a wide, mischievous smile.

Momentarily speechless by his appearance, Oliver takes the lead. His dazzling smile mimicking my own. "Soph was telling me that she wants to have another foursome."

"Does she?" There's an unmistakable spike in the pitch of his usually reserved voice.

"She does. Would you like to be with us ... together, again?" I take a quick breath, then hold it, waiting for his reply.

Death changes a person. I know watching his father die forever transformed Mazen Wilde's view on what matters most in the world. I'd like to think the small changes he's made within himself are for the better. He's choosing happiness, and we're choosing him.

"The better question is, when can we make it a reality? I want to please you seven ways to Sunday, Rosella. You too, Ollie. If you'll let me." Mazen's tanned cheeks turn a rosy pink. It's a stark contrast to the confidence that just poured from his lips.

Silence hangs between the three of us, almost unbearably long. Long enough that our phones buzz simultaneously, alerting us that we have a new message on our group thread.

HempDaddy: Where's everyone at?

Ollie: 'Bout to suck Mazen's dick.

HempDaddy: Soph is? That's hot. Send pics.

Oliver's eyes dance with delight. He's edging Cannon in the worst way, knowing that he's downstairs, bedridden.

The three of us burst into a fit of laughter, knowing that this isn't a joke, but toying with Cannon is.

> Ollie: Sry. Can't take a pic of myself.

My phone rings.

"Hello?" I answer, too chipper for my own good.

"Is this really about to go down?"

Looking left toward Oliver, then to my right toward Mazen, I know with certainty by the wanton need furrowed in both men's brows that something sexy is brewing. "Maybe." I hedge on the truth. "I honestly don't know where things are headed. A woman can only hope it's leading to pound town."

"I do." Cannon's voice is still gravelly from sleep. "I can hope." I can tell he's talking from behind clenched teeth. "The three of you'd better be headed downstairs right now. I know you're on the third floor. Discuss the logistics of how this is playing out on your way."

The phone disconnects.

# 37

# SEX-CRAZED HAZE

## CANNON

BEING in this godforsaken bed is agony. A man of my size can only adjust so many times. I decide to go take a piss before the three of them barrel through the door in a sex-crazed haze.

My movements are slow, deliberate, as I climb off the stupid hospital bed. I begged Oliver not to order it. The label's private physician encouraged it, claiming that it helps with overall circulation, which promotes healing. The bullet in my shoulder was scarier than the one embedded in my spleen.

A spleen is removable. My shoulder, on the other hand? Well, I can't perform without use of that. Luckily, after a grueling surgery, both bullets and their shrapnel were removed. The doctor said she thinks I'll make a full recovery and get adequate range of motion with physical therapy.

I empty my bladder, flush, and wash my hands just as

my door swings open. Mazen steps in first. Steel eyes darkened with lust. Sophia is holding his outstretched hand. Oliver trails behind them, holding her other hand.

"All right, Mr. Bossy Pants," she jokes. "You wanted to see a show. Are you ready to play director?"

The mouth on this woman. Hot damn. She's a mix of brains and beauty—I'll give her that. But her mouth, along with the bullshit that comes out of it, is her hottest trait by far. She gives it just as much as Oliver. That's probably why I'm enamored with them both.

I slowly sink onto the chaise lounger, wincing only when my back hits the cushion behind it.

"You should be in bed." Mazen's chin moves toward the cell that's held me captive for far too long.

Offering him a sidelong glance, I goad, "You should have a cock in that pretty mouth of yours." My heart pounds like my snare in my chest. The thrill of dominance has sorely been missed. This injury is ruining my life.

Mazen's body stiffens in shock.

The last time we were all together, it was me giving him pleasure. I wanted to show him that feeling attracted to Oliver or me wasn't dirty. I needed to show him how good we'd make him feel. He came down my throat in juts of warm honey. The point about bringing him pleasure was well received.

Tonight, the gloves are off.

If he thinks he's man enough to stand in front of a crowd of thousands of people screaming his name, our names, then he'll learn how to perform for an audience of a much smaller scale.

"Go ahead and take Oliver's dick out. I bet it's dripping wet for you."

Mazen's eyes dart to where Oliver is standing. A silent question lingers between them. If I know Oliver like I think I know Oliver, he's screaming on the inside. Since that day he mentioned Mazen's curiosity, there's been a heat in his eyes that only grew when he watched me suck off our singer.

I didn't know when the sexual tension would mount again. I just knew it would.

Oliver's fingers fumble with his zipper. The sound of it lowering is all the answer Mazen needs.

He stalks toward him, confident with each step. As he lowers himself to his knees, I silently beckon Sophia over toward me. The cushion dips beside me, her eyes never leaving the sight before us.

We watch as Oliver captures Mazen's chin in the palm of his hand. "Are you good with this? Don't do anything that makes you uncomfortable."

With hooded eyes, Mazen breaks their exchange, glancing over his shoulder to where Sophia and I sit, frozen. We, too, are awaiting his response.

"Will this make you happy, Rosella? It turns you on to see two men together."

Capturing the trepidation in his eyes, Sophia slides off the couch, moving toward Mazen. She bends at her knees to sit beside him. "I love you, no matter what happens here tonight. You don't have to give your best friend head just to prove you're all in with us. You have me, forever. I only want you to do this because you want to do it."

His reply is quick, "I want to."

Oliver lets out a cough, adjusting himself in his half-unzipped pants. "Since, um ... when? How long have you wanted to suck me off?"

Before Mazen answers, he reaches up, placing both of his hands on Oliver's hips. Looking up at our guitarist, he tells a truth that cuts through the three of us. "Do you remember when you crashed your street bike the summer we opened up for Ho9909? It was a couple of months before we left for our own tour."

The memory crashes into Oliver at the same time it does me. "Yeah. How could I forget? I still have a scar from the road rash."

"We couldn't afford to have our own rooms in that run-down hotel, so we all just crashed together. We slept in the bed. Cannon took the couch, and Murphy came prepared with a damn sleeping bag and took the floor."

Mazen's eyes dart nervously between Oliver and me. The truth he's about to bare happened years ago. That means he's been harboring sexual cravings for a hell of a long time.

"You stripped in the living room while we were eating pizza. Didn't give two shits. Just took off your clothes, tossed them on the bed, and walked to the shower."

"You remember all that?" Oliver's eyes cast downward, landing on Mazen.

"He doesn't forget anything, trust me," Sophia adds.

"Anyway, I guess since then." He shrugs in embarrassment when he admits, "You were ... hung. I told Cannon and Murphy I was going to get a bucket of ice, but I really went down the hallway and jerked off."

My core is aching. Hearing our fearless leader—the man who's always so composed, so sure of himself—cut his wrist and pour out his deepest, darkest secrets like blood at Oliver's altar has me growing rock hard. The veins in my shaft thicken, along with my need to be buried in someone.

"Sophia"—I beckon the someone I need to ground me right now—"take out my dick, and sit on it."

Her mouth opens to protest. "The doc—"

"I will literally die if I can't bury my cock in you. Please don't make me beg. I want you to ride me while I watch those two—our two—men pleasure each other." When she doesn't move, I add, "Come on, baby. Climb up here, and spread that pretty pink little pussy for me before I come in my pants, watching Mazen take Oliver."

That gets her feet moving. The other two watch as she slides off her yoga pants—which she wears just for show because I've never once seen her do yoga or any form of exercise in the months I've known her. No prep work is needed for her greedy core. She's slick and ready as she glides down my shaft.

"Ahh. Fuck. Yes," I exhale. "Afternoon blowies don't have anything on being buried in our girl's pussy. Sorry, Oliver."

"Shit, I'm not. I love sucking you off, but I know how good she feels. Don't use all your energy though. I want you claiming me tonight, too, if Nurse Soph allows it."

Ignoring him, I direct Mazen to take out Oliver's penis. "Look how hard it is. Is that what you jerked off to? The sight of his dick turned you on so much that you had to go blow a load in a hotel hallway?"

Wordlessly, he nods.

"You don't have to be ashamed or run away from those thoughts tonight. What we—the four of us—do in our bedroom doesn't concern anyone else outside of it." I groan when I reach the hilt of Soph's warm pussy. "It took me too long to come to terms with that. No more time gets wasted."

His eyes are pools of appeal before they dart from me to the man in front of him.

A shudder of delight leaves Oliver's mouth when his best friend glides his shaft into his mouth for the first time.

"Fucking hell." Soph bounces on top of me. "Make him choke on it, Ollie. He shouldn't have denied us all this time. Teach him a lesson in denying what our bodies want. I want to taste your cum in his mouth before the night's over."

MAZEN

MUSIC HAS BEEN my refuge for most of my life. My solace during a dark time when I clung to anything that made me feel alive. Writing lyrics felt like my purpose. It gave me an outlet for the constant chatter in my head. While my new hobby didn't quiet the noise externally, it helped me hone it into a craft that I grew to cherish.

The hours my friends—turned bandmates—spent rehearsing and performing, to a point where we no longer needed sheet music because our lyrics became instinctive to us, muscle memory, an extension of our entire personalities, were some of the best times of my life. Before long, music became *my* identity and later my career.

I didn't realize it then, as an adolescent high schooler, but my pain took on a shape of its own when I began jotting down words that soon morphed into lyrics. I poured every ounce of myself into my lyrics, even before the Kings of Jupiter formed in Cannon's parents' garage. Long before

Oliver ever found our dog, Jupiter, a stray, just like him—his words, not mine.

The written word is freeing, liberating. No sooner had I recognized that than I started to hum my words out loud, and they took on a life of their own too. They became lyrics, weaved into a melody. The tune of my life. My words were freed from the confines of my mind, and in them, a new purpose was born. I became a songwriter. A lyricist.

Remaining authentic in a world that was quick to judge, bash, or label anyone and everyone as a fraud was an easy feat. Because our songs were born from grief. That's something that everyone can resonate with, connect to. After all, isn't that what music, books—hell—art as a whole are intended to do? Offer an escape.

My little outlet that took up all of my time soon became my therapy. The one constant in my life, and I took my sessions seriously. Except I wasn't trying to heal a part of my soul by writing songs. No, the healing came later, when I met a woman, subsequently lost her, and then found her again years later.

Music was no longer my safe harbor. Sophia Rose Lozier was. My *Rosella*. My purpose for not only creating but living. Truly living. Embracing every day for what it was, a new beginning. None of that happened until I accepted her fully—and Oliver and Cannon too, if I'm being honest. They offered their love without a price. There was no admission ticket or backstage pass that they dangled in front of me. They simply gave *me* entrance into their hearts.

Not Mazen Wilde, the famous rock star, either. She only wanted *me*, the man behind the music, and the other two, well, they knew me better than anyone else. They had my heart in the form of true friendship. It was easy for *more* to blossom when I already held a special place in it.

As far as our careers, I can't speak for Murphy, Oliver, or Cannon, but I imagine they feel the same about our two-decade occupation as I do. I think in hindsight, we all know we danced a little too close to the fire, even back when we were a group of misfit kids. Each with our own backgrounds and stories to tell. That's what helped forge our friendship, united us. We each brought a separate piece of the puzzle, and together, we became a full-fledged work of art. My best friends and I are cut from the same cloth. We're one another's found family. Not the ones we were born into, but the ones we chose to love and protect.

When Jupiter came along, he quickly became our glue. Our hairy-as-fuck four-legged prince. We never got it twisted though—that mutt owned us. And just like the dog that stole our hearts, Sophia reappeared like a figment of my imagination, taking her rightful place in our lives.

Our queen, the final piece of the puzzle we didn't know was missing.

It's her eyes I look for as I climb onto the stage for the last time, ten years to the day Cannon was shot.

It's an eerie coincidence.

This time around, on our final tour, Sophia's not just our tattoo artist. She's our muse, the mother of our children, and our wife.

I know what you're thinking. How did Sophia create a life again without a uterus? The answer is simple. She didn't. The first time I thanked Lacey Lozier was when she offered her womb for rent in exchange for a forever truce— giving her sister the gift of motherhood again, as she agreed to be our surrogate. The second time was when my daughter, Bethany, was born.

The three of us—Cannon, Oliver, and I—put our names in a cup, just like we had done eons ago when we chose our pseudonyms.

Thank fuck I lucked out and didn't draw Scotty Girth. That gem belongs solely to Ollie. I'll probably engrave it on his tombstone instead of his real name, then send him out with a Barry Keoghan farewell like in the movie *Saltburn*.

Sophia drew Cannon's name first, so it was Cannon's little swimmers and an anonymous donor egg that was implanted in Lacey, who birthed a son, Elliott Rhodes, nine months later. She did it again two more times, spanning the next five years. Time and time again, the Taser-wielding psycho I now legally call my sister-in-law—my name was pulled as the lucky son of a bitch who got to legally marry Sophia, though we all proposed and had a joint ceremony— graciously offered us a blessing in the form of a bundle of joy for each of us to call our own. We're collectively raising our crew of groupies, as we like to refer to them.

Oliver's name was chosen last. I thought it was only fitting since he thought he was first at winning Sophia's affection that day many moons ago in her tattoo studio. Little Juno came barreling into the world, a spitfire, just like his rowdy father.

Sophia let us give the first names to each of our children like the true rock star that she is.

When we asked how Ollie landed on Juno as a first name for his son, he got teary-eyed and said, "My pal Jupiter is fading fast. This way, his memory lives on forever with my boy." Referring to the similarity of their names.

Jupiter ended up passing away the very night we brought Juno home from the hospital. He lived a great life, fit for the husky king that he was. We found him lying on top of Sophia's feet in Juno's nursery—always the protector of his queen—in his last and final slumber. It's been six months since we've heard him bark or tossed a ball with him on the beach.

Sophia tattooed Jupiter's name with a small paw print on each of our wrists not long after his passing. Photos of our fans posting pictures with the same exact tattoo and placement ended up going viral in the weeks after we publicly announced his trip over the Rainbow Bridge. It's heartwarming knowing Jupiter's memory and legacy lives on.

We wavered about what to do with his ashes. It only seems fitting that today, on the last day of our last performance ever as a band, we offer his ashes to the music, and those in attendance today who loved him as loyally as we did.

"It's been a long time coming." Sweat trickles down the back of my shirt, though it's the start of fall in Chicago as I hold my mic in my jellyfish-tattooed hand.

Chicago was the perfect location for our band's last show, and boy, did they show up. The atmosphere is electric. I harden my gaze on my wife, finding her like a beacon of light in the dark. I allow her to do what she does best—center me in the madness of my mind.

"We brought our friend tonight to help celebrate and bid farewell to the best fans in the world."

The screen behind us illuminates with pictures of Jupiter from his wild, zooming puppy stage to the last picture we took of him, meeting his brother Juno.

The crowd goes solemnly quiet.

It's been a fucking journey to get here. Despite the challenges and setbacks, some caused by yours truly—I never claimed to have my shit in order—we made it to the other side, together. The media had a field day when we walked together, the four of us, hand-in-hand, to the Grammys a year after Cannon was shot. Lindsey's phone was buzzing non-stop for a week or longer, magazines all vying for a quote from us. We denied them all, letting the pictures floating around of the four of us do the talking. In today's world, it doesn't take a scientist to see that we're all together.

The last thing I thought my dad did for me was make a promise. I was wrong. Unbeknownst to me, he turned over a file to the police, showcasing the illegal endeavors that Julian and Knox Caddell were a part of. The day Knox was released from the hospital, he was ushered into the back of a police cruiser. It's a core memory for us and Sophia. She'll never again have to look over her shoulder in fear.

Unless it's from Cannon chasing her with the monster he usually keeps fastened in his jeans. That dude is all show, no talk. I can assure you of that little fact.

I palm the small urn in my own jeans pocket, and my thoughts refocus. "We felt like it was only fitting that Jupiter be here in spirit for our last show." I slide out the small pocket-sized urn that holds our beloved husky's ashes. "I hope there are no qualms about scattering ashes. If there is, hold your fucking breath." I don't give the crowd the option to protest before I open the lid and shake out the contents. We're in the Windy City after all.

Oliver slides against my side. His blond hair has been replaced with hot pink—Lacey's talons run deep. "You good, Maz?"

Microphone in hand, I nod. Then, the bastard leans closer, planting a kiss on my cheek. The crowd goes bananas.

"I'll get my revenge for that later. You know that, right?" I whisper away from the mic.

He winks before sliding the strap of his guitar over his chest. "Oh, I'm counting on it."

"Don't I get a kiss? I did get shot twice, ten years ago today," Cannon calls out from his seat behind his drum set, putting emphasis on the word *today*. "I think that deserves something."

He doesn't need to remind us. We're more than lucky that he survived.

Ollie turns toward him. "Feeling neglected, HempDaddy?" he asks smoothly, no expression on his face.

Frowning in exasperation, our drummer pounds on his snare. Words have never been Cannon's strong suit.

Just as Ollie is about to abandon his spot on the stage, Murphy pulls our attention. "Can you save this marital spat or weird-ass foreplay for a more appropriate time?"

I nod, placing the mask I've worn like armor into place for the last time before addressing the crowd in a scream. "Are you ready to rock?"

As their chants echo, and Cannon's drums start the

tempo, I turn to face my bride, offering her Taylor Swift heart hands—our daughter will be so proud. Our fans, not so much. Honestly, I don't give a single fuck. "Sophia Wilde ... you stung me like a jellyfish."

The crowd erupts, and we soak it all in for the last time.

The End

Click **here** for a bonus scene: Life After Jupiter (**A glance through Lacey's eyes**).

They say it takes a village to raise a child, and while I certainly agree with that statement, the same can be applied to publishing a novel.

The conclusion to this duet would not have been possible without the most badass alpha/beta readers in all of Romancelandia: Kerri Elizabeth, Courtney DeLollis, Elle King, Sarah Larson, Nikki Grant, Lauren Sweeney, Kristi Hernandez, Megan Vrooman, Jacklyn Banyas, and Rebecca Pierce. I simply cannot convey how thankful I am for all of these ladies. From their time spent reading and rereading *Queen of Jupiter* to the constant messaging/emailing and the overall support of this fictional world/band I've created, I am truly so appreciative of each of you.

To Emily Wittig for designing the epic covers for this duet and to the talented graphic designers, Tina Reber and Devin McCain, for aiding me in the book teaser department —Your creative vision and talent are very much appreciated!

To my agent, neighbor, and more importantly one of my best friends, Savannah Greenwell of Two Daisy Media— Your presence in my life and friendship are invaluable. Thank you for believing in me not only as an author, but in life in general as well. If hugs were our thing, I'd squeeze the shit out of you. But since they're not, I hope this thank-you suffices.

A special thank-you is more than deserved by the

amazing Jovana Shirley from Unforeseen Editing. My relationship with Jovana is a lot like a traveling companion. Rather than seeing me at my worst with last night's makeup and wild hair, she's seen my manuscript at its worst, and yet you'd never know by looking at it today. Her attention to detail and patience with my lack of grammatical skills are to be admired.

If it weren't for Brittany Uller and Jen Bernacki from The Author Experience's keen eyes for detail, this book would be on its way to Hot-Mess-Express-Landia (no thanks to the many efforts of the before mentioned badasses). Thank you both for your hard work in helping me craft this work of art into a masterpiece (error free, of course)!

Thank you to the folks in my everyday life—from my best friends, Andrea Buisson, Kari Glass, and the above-mentioned Savannah Greenwell, to my health-care colleagues who hear me talk nonstop about the book world. I appreciate your constant support more than you'll ever know.

A huge thank-you to the ladies at The Author Agency for being the most kick-ass PR duo in the business.

Finally, to YOU, the readers. Thank you for falling head over heels in love with my female heroine, Sophia, and the members of the band Kings of Jupiter. Thank you for giving me grace when I left you with the epic cliff-hanger at the end of the first book, which might have had you cussing my name out loud. Though I would like to add, I didn't make you suffer and wait for *Queen of Jupiter* too long, did I? Four months between publications is no joke, y'all. Your girl is tired. In all seriousness, thank you for spending your hard-earned money on my art. There's not a single day that I take a sale or page read in KU lightly. I am honored to have the opportunity to create a fictional world in which you, my dear book bestie, are offered a reprieve from the real world.

Last and certainly not least, thank you to my real-life book boyfriend—aka Mr. Stayton. You might not be a billionaire, rock star, or a member of a harem ... but you're my world.

Thank you from the bottom of my heart for being my village.

Nacole Stayton is thirty-something years young and resides in the Bourbon Capital of the World with her husband and son. Her debut novel, The Upside of Letting Go is an Amazon top 100 bestseller. She spends her days working in healthcare as a practice administrator and her evenings pinning away on her next novel. She can usually be found playing with monster trucks and dodging Nerf gun darts or enjoying an iced coffee poolside.